Brenda Hall has degrees in philoso
has two daughters, two grandcl
Hawkesbury River with a Maltese
companion. Thalassa is her first nov

Thalassa

Brenda Hall

First published by Karingal Books in 2017
This edition published in 2017 by Karingal Books

Copyright © Brenda Hall 2017

http://brenda-hall.com/

The moral right of the author has been asserted.

All rights reserved. This publication (or any part of it) may not be reproduced or transmitted, copied, stored, distributed or otherwise made available by any person or entity (including Google, Amazon or similar organisations), in any form (electronic, digital, optical, mechanical) or by any means (photocopying, recording, scanning or otherwise) without prior written permission from the publisher.

Thalassa

EPUB format: 9781925579505
Print on Demand format: 9781925579512

Cover design by Red Tally Studios

Publishing services provided by Critical Mass
www.critmassconsulting.com

*For my grandmother
and my mother
and my daughters
in trust and hope.*

Kostis Family Tree

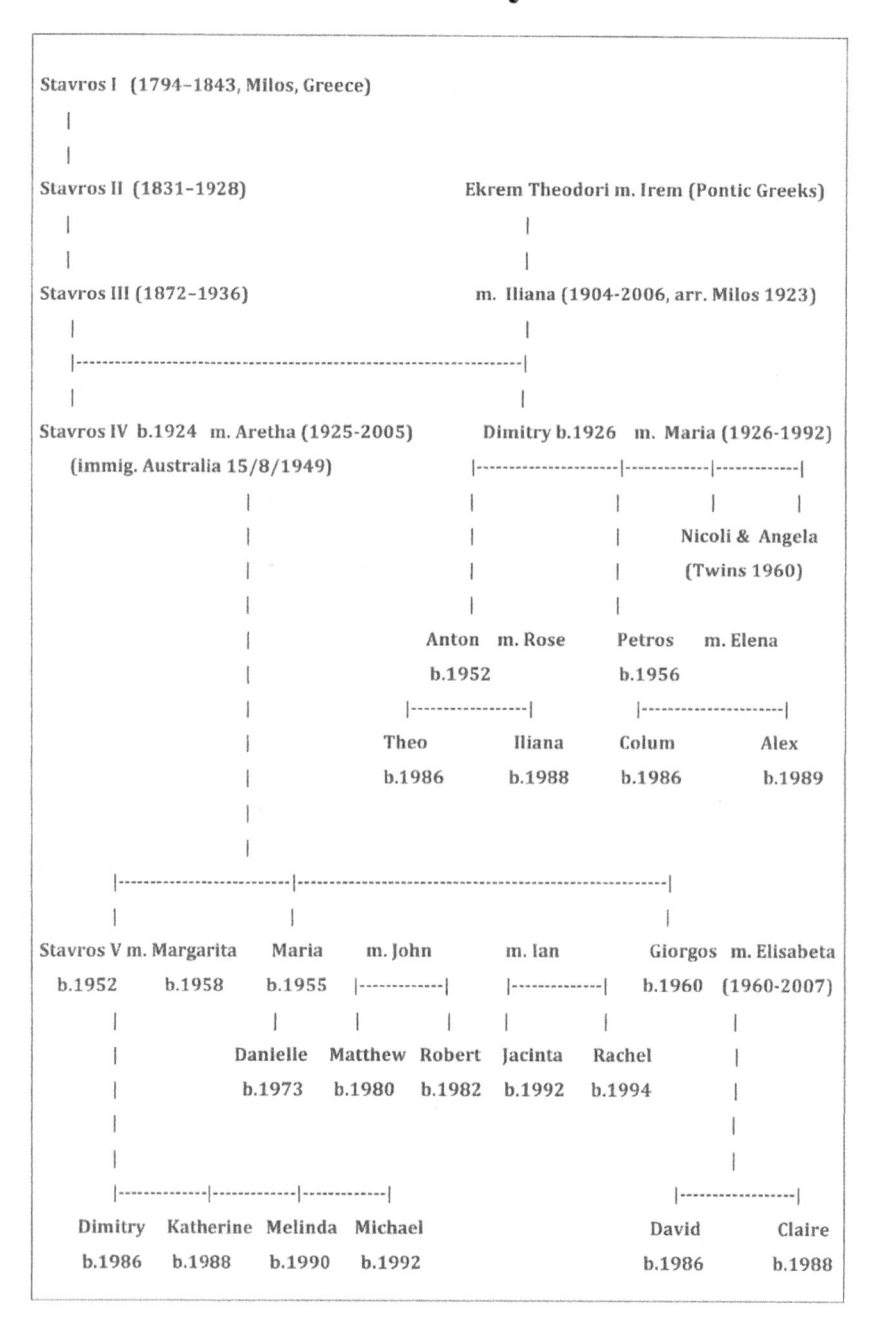

```
Stavros I  (1794-1843, Milos, Greece)
  |
  |
Stavros II (1831-1928)                    Ekrem Theodori m. Irem (Pontic Greeks)
  |                                             |
  |                                             |
Stavros III (1872-1936)                   m. Iliana (1904-2006, arr. Milos 1923)
  |                                             |
  |------------------------------------------------|
  |                                             |
Stavros IV b.1924  m. Aretha (1925-2005)   Dimitry b.1926  m. Maria (1926-1992)
    (immig. Australia 15/8/1949)           |-------------------|------------|------------|
               |                           |                   |            |            |
               |                           |                   |            Nicoli & Angela
               |                           |                   |            (Twins 1960)
               |                           |                   |
               |                        Anton m. Rose      Petros  m. Elena
               |                        b.1952             b.1956
               |                        |--------------|   |-------------------|
               |                        Theo      Iliana   Colum           Alex
               |                        b.1986    b.1988   b.1986          b.1989
               |
               |
  |-----------------------|-----------------------------------------------|
  |                       |                                               |
Stavros V m. Margarita  Maria    m. John        m. Ian       Giorgos  m. Elisabeta
b.1952    b.1958        b.1955   |-----------|  |-----------| b.1960   (1960-2007)
  |                        |           |         |        |              |
  |                     Danielle   Matthew   Robert   Jacinta  Rachel    |
  |                     b.1973     b.1980    b.1982   b.1992   b.1994    |
  |                                                                      |
  |                                                                      |
  |------------|------------|------------|                      |-----------------|
  Dimitry  Katherine  Melinda   Michael                         David         Claire
  b.1986   b.1988    b.1990    b.1992                           b.1986        b.1988
```

Baxter Family Tree

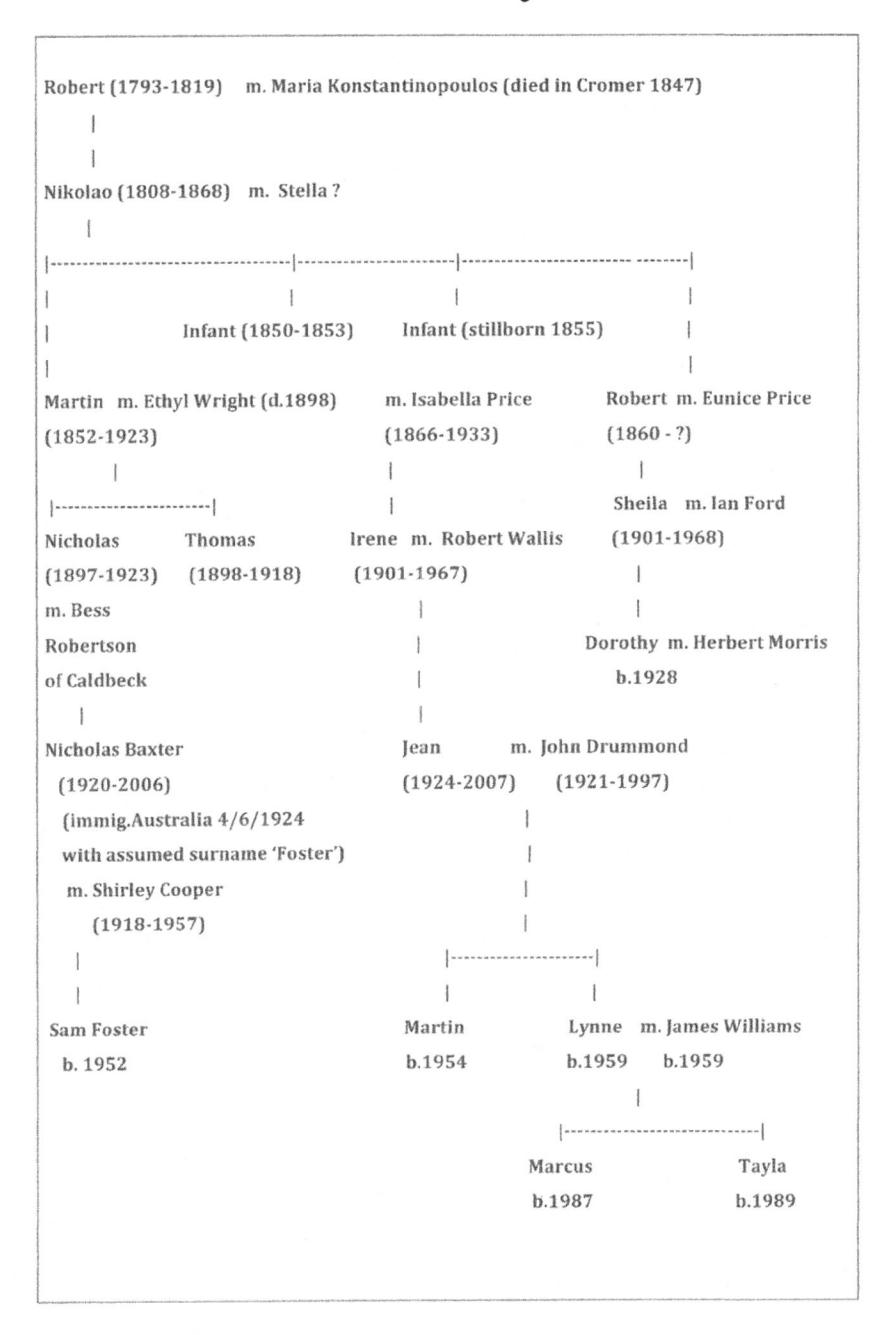

```
Robert (1793-1819)  m. Maria Konstantinopoulos (died in Cromer 1847)
    |
    |
Nikolao (1808-1868)  m. Stella ?
    |
    |--------------------|---------------------|---------------------------|
    |                    |                     |                           |
    |         Infant (1850-1853)    Infant (stillborn 1855)                |
    |                                                                      |
Martin  m. Ethyl Wright (d.1898)    m. Isabella Price    Robert  m. Eunice Price
(1852-1923)                          (1866-1933)         (1860 - ?)
    |                                    |                   |
    |                                    |               Sheila   m. Ian Ford
|----------------------|                 |               (1901-1968)
Nicholas        Thomas          Irene  m. Robert Wallis      |
(1897-1923)    (1898-1918)      (1901-1967)                  |
m. Bess                              |               Dorothy  m. Herbert Morris
Robertson                            |                   b.1928
of Caldbeck                          |
    |                                |
Nicholas Baxter                    Jean        m. John Drummond
(1920-2006)                      (1924-2007)     (1921-1997)
 (immig.Australia 4/6/1924                |
 with assumed surname 'Foster')           |
 m. Shirley Cooper                        |
   (1918-1957)                            |
    |                                     |
    |                            |---------------------|
    |                            |                     |
Sam Foster                     Martin              Lynne   m. James Williams
b. 1952                        b.1954              b.1959       b.1959
                                                                  |
                                                       |-----------------------|
                                                     Marcus                  Tayla
                                                     b.1987                  b.1989
```

Coincidence is God's way of remaining anonymous.
Albert Einstein.

Prologue

The Shipwreck Story

March 1808: The Aegean Sea off the coast of Milos

The curling tower of seawater slammed into the fishing cäique. It carved the transom away from the boat and then punched what was left of the stern forward, high on its rounded shoulder. Stavros Kostis stared in horror as foaming water fled down the slick precipice of decking into the darkness of Thalassa's mighty jowls. His bare feet clawed at empty air, and the cäique's thrashing tiller threw his full weight ferociously left then right.

As the bowsprit plunged into the salivating trough the monster wave rolled under the centre of the hull and the bow reared up again. Stavros glimpsed relief when the bowsprit and the jib came up intact before he was flung back into the tiller and felt his ribs crush. The breath sprang from his lungs in an outburst of pain, whipped away by the merciless wind.

The cäique corkscrewed wildly and was caught broadside by the next thumping wave. The gunwale disappeared below the water line, and miraculously returned, a waterfall shedding off the port side through a bright yellow fishing net that was tied to the deck.

Petros was still clinging precariously to the main mast, arms and legs tightly wrapped, knife clenched in his teeth. In the momentary respite of the trough he spared an arm in a wild circular motion. Stavros saw his lips moving, but Thalassa drowned the words in her roar of bloodlust.

Stavros knew the signal meant he must turn head to the wind so that Petros, having re-rigged the halyard, could raise the mainsail. The foresail alone could not keep the boat stable as the huge waves ploughed into the stern. They had been running for the port when the throat halyard had broken, slowed down by a full day's catch, buffeted by freakish waves and wind. They were all too close now, the repair had taken too long and the jagged contours of Firopotamos were clearer with each cresting wave.

I will breathe again. Stavros promised himself. *Thalassa, spare us now.* He clung to the tiller as another mighty wave tossed the stern and stormed away under the boat. He heaved on the tiller to turn into the wind only to have the rudder rear up at him in a thick splinter of broken wood from the shattered remains of the transom.

The next wave was upon them. It rammed the caïque broadside, rolled and pitched it, spearing the mast towards the chest of the deep green menace below.

Stavros watched the water engulf the bowsprit and the jib. The fishing net slumped into the sea's ugly mouth, and the mast cracked against the foaming waves. Arms and legs thrashed for impossibly stretched seconds in the tangled yellow turbulence, and then Petros and the net were gone.

Saint Nikolaos, protector of all seamen, save him, save my brother, save me. Stavros screamed into the wind with his returning breath.

Stavros fixed his eyes on the top of the black cliff that had suddenly solidified through the lather of sea-spray, and desperately conjured up the white-robed figure of the saint, watching him from above. With all the power he had in his lungs he flung out the oath that immediately trapped within its weave the destinies of those with whom my story is most concerned.

Saint Nikolaos, I will build you a church on these rocks, and all the generations of Kostis will look after the church in your name. On our lives I swear it Saint Nikolaos!

Thalassa, the spirit of the sea, picked up the boat under the next wave of her arm, and flung it angrily against the rocks.

I

At the moment of my death, as the truck reached me fast and loud and broadside in the midst of a hail of shattered vegetation, rock and mud, I was thinking two things: that I should have hit the accelerator instead of the brake, and that this was going to hurt.

I don't revisit the hurt. Maybe because it is too much for my consciousness to bear so I can't go there. Maybe because it is of the physical world and I have no agency there now. Iliana, who let me know how I could tune my consciousness in to the people I love, said I should not visit myself at all. She's of the school that thinks everything is predestined and we cannot do anything to change the course of fate. She said there was absolutely no point in trying to find out what I could have done differently. To her, it was God's Will, not mine.

But I don't agree. I made a judgment call more by instinct than reason in that split second. I got it wrong. I have this idea that in another reality I hit the accelerator and the truck goes behind me while I drive on, into the future I had been expecting. Back home, into George's arms for a kiss, into Claire's study where I tell her how the game went, onto David's sofa where I turn off Foxtel and try to start a conversation.

It is only *just* beyond the veil, this other reality, and I have tried so hard to go there, to see that course of events happen instead of this story.

Iliana and Aretha Kostis did not have much in common in life. I know now that they were pitched against each other in much the same way and for the same possessive reason that Aretha and I were against each other, but they are in agreement about predestination and the power of prayer. My wish to see that other reality is a form of prayer, Aretha claims, and she is still unkind enough to add that it's too late for me to pray now.

Jean Drummond, who is here with we three Kostis mothers for reasons that will become clear, is an agnostic. There might be predestination, and there might not. There might be a God with a Will, and there might not. If we knew the answer what hopes could motivate us? When Iliana offers as evidence the future we already know, Jean responds with a question that gives me hope. *Do* we know? What if history is an infinite train set bolted together by a myriad of human decisions. Where will our train of thought lead if some of those tiny decision switches happen to be thrown in the other direction? Is God's Will generous enough to grant us the freedom of an infinite number of predestined tracks?

In life I branded agnostics 'weak'. People who weren't brave enough to call themselves 'atheists'. Jean proves me wrong. She asks mischievous, intelligent, unanswerable questions that undermine any certainty of belief. Jean is what my own mother would have called a 'Devil's advocate'. On the other hand ... when she responds to my debate-winning assertions with 'Why?' ... I think of her more as an insufferable toddler.

II

October 2007: Hickling, Norfolk Broads, England

Lynne opened the front door to the smell of her mother, immediately identifiable but stale after two weeks of closure. She had expected the heaviness of familiar things, but not the weightless sting of a life-long perfume. She fought unwelcome tears with irresolute blinks, and was glad she had come alone. She busied herself; opening windows, tying back curtains, wedging doors, letting in the surprisingly sunny Norfolk autumn.

"Hal-oooo?" It had taken Mrs Crawshaw only five minutes to appear in the entrance hall. "I saw your car Lynne dear, I do hope you don't mind me coming over, how are you dear?" There was a pause for an enveloping hug, which untangled into a firm double handhold. "Oh, I *do* so miss your mother. Can I help you with anything dear? Such a terrible business, packing up. So sad. I'll make us a cuppa."

Shirley Crawshaw had turned 80 just four months ago. Lynne's mother, frail as she was at 83, had organised the party and for that Saturday afternoon most of the houses in Hickling stood empty while the gardens of The Pleasure Boat Inn, overlooking Hickling Broad were full of old tales, tall and true, laughter, pub food and ale. Wheelchairs and walking sticks had been in abundance, but so were strollers, nappies, kites, bikes, remote control boats, wetsuits and windsurfers. Four generations had gathered at Hickling Broad, aged 2 months to 94 years. It was the day Lynne wanted her mind to settle on, in memory of her mother, erasing the more recent months of hospital and palliative care.

Jean Drummond and Shirley Crawshaw had been friends for over 70 years. They were an institution at Hickling Broad; they knew everyone, and everything that was known about the district. When Jean reluctantly moved into the newly built retirement village because she could no longer manage stairs, Shirley did not hesitate to take up the villa next door as soon as it became available. All the ailments that had afflicted Jean, the compressed fractures in her spine, the arthritis in her joints, the delicacy of her digestive system and her increasing deafness, had bypassed Shirley. Shirley was a buxom, sturdy countrywoman who loved the bawdy humour of the pub and forgave Jean completely for having a more sensitive, intellectual disposition. Jean had ideas, and Shirley carried them out. It was the firmest of partnerships.

"Tony and Paula are going to Majorca next summer, they booked just last week. It will be lovely for them. Their first holiday together without the kids, won't that be lovely?" Mrs Crawshaw paused for a moment longer than it took for Lynne to offer the usual polite punctuation and then hurried on to the next sentence to belatedly fill the gap. "Well, what about *you* dear? You should get away in summer, would Tayla go with you, or Marcus? You should get away to some sun, you look very pale and I can see you don't eat enough, you spend too much time indoors at that university, how are you *really* dear?"

In another life, the one that had long felt like someone else's memory, Lynne had been a Crawshaw as much as a Drummond. She had chased Tony through a glass door in the Crawshaw living room; she and Wendy had shared a scruffy Shetland pony that lived in the Crawshaw's barn and she knew she had loved the Crawshaw's black Labrador much better than Tony ever did. It was Mrs Crawshaw's pillowy chest that she cried on when Tony started dating Hilary Webster, and it was to Mrs Crawshaw that she first confessed that she and James were living together in London. But just now, Lynne wished Shirley Crawshaw would leave.

"Well I know you'll be busy dear, how long are you here? Just the weekend? So much to do and so sad. You'll be too busy to cook for yourself, would you like a pie? I will bring you a pie for dinner tonight. Anything else you want? Just let me know."

Lynne closed the front door behind Mrs Crawshaw with steady precision. She walked into her mother's bedroom and pulled open the top drawer of the dresser to reveal the many and varied containers of make-up, powders, lipsticks and perfumes that she knew were there. She breathed the smell of her mother in deeply, sat on the edge of the bed and let the tears overflow.

~

Later that afternoon Lynne made up the sofa bed in the living room. It would be at least a month before ice would solidify Hickling Broad, but it was already cold enough to have the gas fire burning, to cover the sofa with flannelette sheets and a bulky duvet and to indulge in the comforting, warm trappings of winter. There were five piles growing on the living room floor: Oxfam, Martin, Lynne, Rubbish and Further Reading. Lynne tucked her knees up under the duvet, tucked several loose strands of blonde hair behind her ear, and started from the top of the Further Reading pile.

Jean Drummond had been active in her community in the years before frailty overcame her. She had been a keen member and patron of the Great Yarmouth Bird Watching Club, and much of the reading pile pertained to the preservation of endangered wild fowl and of the waterways around Norfolk that hosted the birds. There were copies of long letters she had hand-written to members of Parliament, pinned behind short word-processed replies. There were tributes that members of the club had written to her, copies of the *Birdwatch* magazine, and articles cut from the local papers supplemented with her notes to herself on the subject. Feeling some guilt, Lynne consigned all this to Rubbish.

Jean had also campaigned for the preservation of wherries, the traditional flat-bottomed cargo boat of the Broads. Her father had been a wherry-man. Before the Great War he had ferried coal into Norwich from the colliers that unloaded at Great Yarmouth. When he returned from the front he found there was little demand for his services any more. Road transport was taking over the wherry cargoes; 'dirty' wherries like his own were filled with rubbish, towed out to sea and scuttled. The decline of the wherry trade did to his heart as much damage as the gas in Flanders had done to his lungs. By 1949, the year Jean married Lynne's father, there was only one wherry still powered by sail. Any other wherry that could still float had been demasted and put into service as a lighter. Jean joined herself and her father up to the Norfolk Wherry Trust at its formation in the hope that it would give him an interest to pursue. In the Further Reading pile, amongst other documents about the Trust, there were photos of Lynne's grandfather, polishing cloth in hand, bent over *The Albion* on her first day of trade as a rebuilt sailing wherry and several group photos of boys alongside the boat in the short pants, long socks, wide-brimmed hats, and neckerchiefs that characterised the scout uniform of the 1950's.

Lynne knew these photos and stories. They were the furnishings of her childhood, but struck no more active chord in her memory. She remembered her grandfather sitting in his armchair, under a prickly woollen rug, dropping cake crumbs to Soot, the bristly black terrier that always lay alongside him.

She remembered him calling the dog a vacuum cleaner. Most of all she remembered him coughing. She couldn't pinpoint, in her memory, the day when he wasn't at Nanna's house any more.

Martin, born five years before her in 1954, would remember grandad and the wherry. These days *The Albion* was one of Norfolk's premier tourist attractions. Lynne began a subset to Martin's pile: Norfolk Wherry Trust.

At the bottom of the Further Reading pile, due its size rather than its chronology, was a wooden box that Lynne already knew to be Nanna's memorabilia. Having reached the limits of her own memory, and belatedly aware that she could never again ask her mother questions, Lynne opened up the box and went in search of the grandparents she had barely known.

~

"Chicken Pi-Eye," Shirley Crawshaw sang the words to announce her arrival at the front door. "Just the way you liked it best, dear. I might forget where I've put my glasses, but I still remember your chicken pie. How are you dear? Look at the size of those piles! You've done a lot already haven't you! How can you ever decide what to do with things?"

"Actually, I've some things I'd like to ask you about, can I offer you a cuppa?" In a better frame now that the task was underway, Lynne was prepared for Shirley Crawshaw. Nanna's memorabilia box was on the kitchen table. "Did you know my mother's mother?" Lynne fingered the edge of a black and white photo of a bespectacled, silver-haired woman, wrapped up roundly in a tartan overcoat and scarf, a handbag hanging primly from her folded elbow.

"Of *course* I did dear, how sad that you wouldn't remember much. She followed your grandad by only a year or so ... oh maybe more ... but you too young to remember."

"I remember her knitting. The same blue jumper, all the time."

"Oh no dear, not the *same* jumper. Your Nanna knitted ganseys for the lifeboat men. She turned out a jumper every four weeks easy." Shirley noticed that Lynne looked puzzled. "*Cromer* lifeboats dear, not Broads. *Broads* dint need lifeboats, they're a right paddling pool. Nanna Baxter was a Cromer girl, three generations of fishermen and counting. Missed Cromer something awful when she came to Hickling, married to a wherryman. Every six months she'd go back on bus, six ganseys under arm for them lifeboat men. I always wondered if one day she might *not* come back, but she always did. She weren't the eldest that were Nicholas dead at sea, and another brother, Thomas, dead in the Great War. *None* of Irene's siblings had children, so Jean had no cousins on that side of the family. Very sad. Your Nanna had a cousin in Cromer though, very close in age–they were more like sisters–and *that* cousin had children. They were younger than Jean, I remember her saying they hadn't much in common." A sip of tea and a bite of biscuit slowed Shirley down momentarily.

"We took the kids to Cromer for a beach holiday one year, I think Marcus was about 8 and Tayla would have been 6." Lynne remembered the holiday in photographs. James handsomely poised, knee-deep in water holding Marcus steady on a windsurfer. Marcus and Tayla, brown-skinned and beaming over a multi-stacked sandcastle with meticulously constructed pebble and sand walls. Tayla with a strand of blonde hair through her teeth as always, holding up the first crab she had caught from the pier. There was even a passable photo of herself, leaning against the promenade wall, tanned skin, late-summer sun stained and wind-tousled hair. The photo showed a slim, weight-lost profile; it was the holiday they had taken after they had made up the first time. When she thought they wouldn't make the same mistakes again, they had survived the crisis of his affair; they would now be happily married unto old age. She had been truly family-holiday-happy in that photo.

"Well you've seen the lifeboat museum then dear. Or maybe not?" Shirley continued. "Your mother organised a trip for the village just after it opened, only last year, so you wouldn't have seen it would you? Her grandad is in one of them big photos on the wall. Crusty old codger. Beard. Cork life jacket. Devil of a job getting lifeboats launched back then. No power, just oars, dint know how they did it. Them fishermen would all turn out to run the lifeboat down the beach into *huge* waves and a gale, doubtless, if a shipwreck was happening. And o' course none could swim. Fancy, but fishermen and sailors couldn't swim then. Int for the lifeboat in a shipwreck they'd be dead. 'Devil's Throat' they called the coast, always wrecks there on the sandbars. *Best* lifeboat men in the world your Nanna used to say. Reckon she were right, not that she'd travelled anywhere. Lovely lady your Nanna." Shirley paused to take another sip, but Lynne could feel her thinking.

"Well, truth is I was a bit scared of her. She was the intellectual, that's where your mother and you got it. Int knitting she'd be reading, or both at once. The Baxters could read 'n' write, way back. Your Nanna's grandad–he was also called Nicholas–*he* could write. It's in that box. You've seen it. Or maybe not yet? Your mum thought to publish, but even from her deathbed, your Nanna wouldn't let her. Dint know what happened, your mum stopped talking 'bout it. She were all fired up to go to Greece, but after that last argument with Nanna there was not another word about it. Greece, back then, imagine! But you young people dint think twice about going to Greece for a holiday these days do you?"

~

Lynne had intended to clear the bedroom wardrobe, but instead, as the night grew late, she was again cozied by the duvet on the living room sofa, picking through a selected pile of the things her mother had kept; things in cupboards, drawers, wooden boxes, tins and plastic bags. Forty years ago, when Nanna died, Jean had done exactly this. The thought sat eerily behind Lynne's shoulder, so much like a physical presence that at one point Lynne felt compelled to look around the room, checking the pictures on the wall, the photos on the buffet. Nothing moved, but that didn't lessen Lynne's certainty that her mother was with her, that somehow 2007 and 1967 were crossing paths.

The wooden boxes had the weightiest presence, and the fact that Lynne found nothing that she would throw away amongst them let her know that her mother has already sorted through them. In particular, the contents of the mahogany box that once held a cutlery set and now held Nanna's paper memorabilia evidenced a world very different to the one Lynne knew, and Lynne was surprised by the poignancy of the nostalgia that gripped her. The box contained nothing of the hardships of life: carrying water, cooking over a fire, patching clothes by candle light, mud from the fields, and storms from the sea. What it did contain were cards; mostly small in size, designed and cut individually, beautifully drawn with flowers and ladies in flowing Edwardian dresses. Inside the cards were hand-written messages-happy birthdays, congratulations, acceptances, invitations-sometimes just a note of appreciation for a lovely hour spent together, often closed with words from the Bible, or a psalm. Many of the cards were pieces of wisdom, quotations from Shakespeare, Coleridge, and many writers whose names were unfamiliar to Lynne. The cards were graceful and humble; there could not be a greater distance between them and contemporary social media and it made Lynne feel sad and guilty. Somehow, in just two generations, she and her peers had lost all this. Her own children would not even share her sorrow that it had gone.

Less well organised was the collection of cards and papers addressed to 'Jean', 'Mother', 'Granny'. They were all here, in plastic newsagency bags and cardboard stationery boxes.

Every birthday, every Christmas, every letter Martin had sent home during his four years at boarding school. A set of tiny handprints from Marcus, Tayla's first drawing of a daisy, a scout's promise written in Martin's careful, rounded school script, Lynne's Ode to a Shetland pony, more original but less well-written. There were many kindly tributes from people some of whom Lynne dimly remembered, and others she did not recall at all. Keeping the cards was a sign that these people mattered, that their words and deeds were too important to throw away, but what importance did they have now? Lynne kept just a few samples, cards anchored by a date, a richness of expression or precious handwriting, and she let the fullness of the years go. The meaning her mother read into the words had gone, the cards provided no more than a partial picture of her, like dots that have no joining line. As Lynne worked through the pile, consigning her chosen selection to a lacquered wooden box that Martin had made in a high school woodwork class, and the remainder to a recyclable waste carton, she reminded herself that what seemed ordinary to her now, would one day be interesting to another. Just as she looked closely at the few special cards that had been kept in Nanna's box from the early 1900's, so too would a grandchild look back on the selections Lynne was making now. That person would try to re-join the dots Lynne kept, with lines akin to those Lynne knew by heart.

Amongst the cards Lynne found a notepad of high quality parchment, beautifully embossed with one of her mother's favourite flowers, Lily of the Valley. The notepad was blank, it beckoned, and Lynne picked up a pen.

Mum,

I have wanted to immerse myself in the things you kept not in order to discover this legacy in the family lines. I expect it is to keep you–the sense of you–here at hand, for a little longer. It is to explore, as I have your things still here, what it means that you have gone. It is to look at the dots, before they go cold. To commit the life that joined them to memory, which was something I couldn't do while you were alive. Couldn't talk, or write, about a life as if it was over, when it wasn't.

So what does it mean that you have gone?

One of the rooms in my soul is empty. The sense of home, and nurture, and blessing is not active there. The walls echo strangely. My connection with you receives no answer, and I must go on in this world without it. I do understand, and I try to accept what feels so deeply unacceptable. I know I must keep the blessings that were emptied out of that room for me, and pass them forward. I will love you always. You will always be the foundation of the love I give to others, as I will be that foundation for my children.

Always. Lynne. October 2007

As Lynne placed the notepad on the top of the cards in the wooden box Martin had made, she supposed that it would be Tayla who would be next to sort through the family memorabilia. But she was wrong. It is Marcus who finds, adds his own words of loss and hope, and replaces the notepad for generations to come. But there are years between then and now and Jean points out that I'm ahead of myself.

~

Lynne was born for school. She made a career of university. She reads and she studies and she writes and she teaches. The Arts. As a child she nagged for Hans Christian Anderson; fairy stories about princes and princesses, fables with happy endings. She gravitated to the legends of Greece and Rome. In high school she loved Greek tragedies. Having abysmally failed audition, she made props for the school's staging of Antigone. She replicated Greek statues in papier-mâché and became fascinated by the characteristics that linked a sculpture to a certain time and place and artist. It makes sense that she became one of England's leading authorities in Greek antiquities ... she's driven to know the historical truth of things, the detail behind the surface impression. She prefers the past, a world she doesn't inhabit. The real-time world is too messy for her, too emotional. She makes better sense of things if she can stitch together all the detail with hindsight, with reason. She likes to know the ending before she tries to unravel the process. She likes to journey back to reinterpret paths already taken, not forwards to a future unknown. She likes the story to be already written, so she can safely read it again, and again. She sees beauty in things when she fully understands their composition, their meaning ... mystery does not appeal to her.

She hasn't fully understood why she and James failed marriage; she wants to find the Rosetta stone that is key to her own life; she wants to be given the moral of the story. But real life isn't like legend or fable. Real life is messy and sometimes what happens is ultimately nothing other than foolishness.

~

On Sunday morning, Lynne's exploration of the oak chest in the spare bedroom revealed Nanna's Baxter family archive; the family in large, yellowed manila envelopes. The envelope at the top, marked 'Thomas', included a number of letters written from The Front, marked 1918 but with no location. They were in an elegant script, addressed to 'My dear sister Irene', and signed 'Your loving brother Thomas'. There was a sepia-toned photo on thick board of a handsome, clean-shaven young man, standing proudly to attention in full army uniform with a rifle at his side. There was a typed letter from the War Office, buttery in colour with dark brown folding lines, and a hand-written letter from the Vicar of Cromer, expressing deep regrets on behalf of all in the Parish. Lynne felt the weight of it. What would that have been like, to lose a brother in the war, to keep his letters for the rest of your life, and why had she never heard of Thomas before today? There were no answers in the envelope, and nothing of Thomas elsewhere in the drawer.

There was a similar envelope containing Nicholas. The largest, most obvious item to remove first, was a sepia toned photo on thick-board which showed six men spanning at least three generations wearing dark ganseys, posing with hands on hips and the stern faces that were the norm before the photographic smile became ubiquitous. There were 6 names inked on the back. Nicholas was third from the left, and his father, Martin, was the last on the right. The date was 21st February 1919. There was a smaller black and white photo, with no date or identification, of Nicholas looking much more handsome in a smart Royal Navy officer's uniform, dark double-breasted jacket and white peaked hat, posing with a pretty blonde-haired girl in an elaborate white wedding dress, and a similar photo of them both, where the girl was wearing a stylish summer dress holding a baby in christening robes. On the back of this third photo, the inscription in the thickened black ink of a fountain pen read 'Nicholas Martin Robertson Baxter, 1 month old, 3rd May 1920.' Lynne gazed at the image of the handsome young officer, searching in her memory for the reason she found the photo puzzling. It didn't take her long to recall Shirley Crawshaw's remark that Nicholas had died at sea and had not had any children. The contents of the rest of the box revealed nothing further about Nanna Baxter's brother or the baby who should have been Jean Drummond's first cousin. Eventually, acknowledging that Mrs Crawshaw must have been mistaken, but mystified as to why she knew nothing about this branch of the Baxter family, Lynne put the 'Nicholas' envelope into Martin's pile for further investigation.

Shirley Crawshaw was right, however, about the manuscript written by the original Nicholas Baxter, Nanna's grandfather. At the bottom of the drawer was another large envelope; this one filled with pages of a journal, of sorts, dated 1827. Writ large on the first page was the title *The Genoa* followed by a short paragraph noting that the journal was written by Nicholas Baxter, a Cromer fisherman, lifeboat man, and Royal British Navy recruit about his experiences while serving on a Man-O-War, *The Genoa*, with the allied force that fought with Greece in their War of Independence against the Ottoman Empire.

~

The Battle of Navarino Story

October 1827: West coast of the Peloponnese peninsula

"*Genoa* Ahoy!" Admiral Codrington's voice boomed over the trumpet speaker, clearly audible despite the noise of the sea battle. "Send a boat with a hawser to swing my ship's stern clear of the fire boat that's drifting down upon us!"

The British seamen on *The Genoa* scurried in response. Nicholas Baxter was the first of six into the dinghy, holding fast against the side of the man-of-war frigate, while two seamen on the deck sent the hawser snaking down into a coil alongside his feet. He waited anxiously, eyes fixed on the two Turkish line of battle ships that were broadside to *The Genoa*. One of them, despite the fire raging at its stern, was reloading its forward portside cannons. Its last cannonball had fallen well short of the mark, but the wash rocked the dinghy violently.

Codrington's flagship, *The Asia*, was astern of *The Genoa*, engaging two enemy ships, a liner and a smaller frigate. An un-manned, derelict frigate set on fire by the Turks was 100 fathoms away to starboard, slowly ploughing through the water, on course to hit *The Asia* amidships. Nevertheless,

Nicholas thought grimly, *The Asia* had better chances than *The Genoa* did right now.

"Right-o!" George Finney, Captain of the Maintop, landed in the dinghy with a thud, the end of the hawser firmly in his hand. Within 2 strides he was in the prow, waving the crew forward. Nicholas and Seaman Fry took up oars. The water between the two ships was littered with floating debris and people who were desperately hanging onto flimsy pieces of wood, sail and rope, calling for mercy, grabbing at the oars. Nicholas strained his ears for English voices amongst the Turkish and Arabic.

The only English he heard, however, was Finney cursing abruptly. The hawser had run out with six fathoms to go. A cannonball struck the water nearby, knocking the oars from Nicholas' hands and into his jaw. He caught the gunwale just in time to save himself from being pitched from the boat. When he looked up he saw Finney strip off his shirt and dive into the water, striking out confidently. From the deck of *The Asia* a seaman was lowering a rope, and upon reaching the flagship Finney took the rope between his teeth and turned back. Nicholas felt his chest swell with admiration for his captain; he wished he had been the one to show such decisive bravery and skill. What he would give to be able to swim!

As Finney clambered back into the dinghy, two seamen were already joining the rope to the hawser. Nicholas and Fry turned and began to row back to *The Genoa*, chasing it as it started to pull *The Asia* out of danger. Nicholas, rowing backwards, had *The Asia* in full view as a cannonball hit and its mizzen crashed to the deck where the Admiral had been standing, flinging a body into the sea.

"Admiral overboard" he howled, startling the crew of the dinghy by backing the oars and leaping to his feet, his hand pointing un-erringly to the exact spot in the churning sea where he had seen the body enter the water. Finney scrambled to the oars so that Nicholas could guide them and this time it was

Nicholas who jumped into the debris-laden sea, grabbed the clothing of the sinking man and, buoyed by his life jacket, hauled the body to the surface.

Several hands reached out to fish the unconscious seaman into the dinghy, and Nicholas followed with a clumsy flop as the dinghy wallowed with the shifting body-weights. For a moment there was an incredulous pause. By his clothing this was not the admiral; it was an ordinary seaman. Nicholas was hit by the terror that he had made a dreadful mistake; he had let the admiral drown while he rescued someone else.

There was a life to save under his hands, so despite his fears Nicholas went to work, breathing into the man's mouth, pumping his chest. By the time the dinghy had caught up to *The Genoa* the seaman had vomited up a bucket of sea water and was hanging head-down over the gunwale, recovering.

Finney helped Nicholas pull the injured seaman up the final steps of the ladder and onto the deck of *The Genoa*.

"Look away," Finney waved towards the stern of *The Asia*, "ter be Admiral."

With enormous relief Nicholas saw Admiral Codrington on the poop deck, speaking trumpet in hand.

Nicholas nudged his toes into the slumped uniform that was wetly gasping for air at his feet. "Who be you then?"

"Stavros Kostis," came the whispered reply, and then, after another struggle for breath, realising that an explanation for his Greek name was required, Stavros gasped "pilot to Admiral Codrington."

Nicholas observed that the British uniform Stavros was wearing was leaking a watery flow of red onto *The Genoa's* deck.

"We'll take him to sick bay," Nicholas motioned to Seaman Fry, who helped pull Stavros to his feet and together the three stumbled towards the stairs to the lower deck.

"All hands aft!" Captain Finney roared urgently as they reached the stairs.

"You go, I'll be right there," Nicholas told Fry.

A moment later, as Nicholas was staggering under Stavros half way down the steps, a cannonball hit *The Genoa's* aft deck, blowing fragments of several sailors, including Seaman Fry, across the dinghy they had used to take the hawser to *The Asia*. Nicholas was catapulted to the bottom of the stairs, and Stavros landed on top of him. Nicholas felt an unbearable pain shoot up his left arm and immediately fainted.

Nicholas would later recount that he was grateful to Stavros, for having fallen on his left arm and not his right. It was enough to get him released from service, while leaving him able to write down the stories Stavros told him while they were recuperating in the temporary naval hospital set up at Fort Ricasoli in Malta. Stavros was convinced that Nicholas was a personification of Saint Nikolaos, who had come to save him a second time; Nicholas was inclined to think that the debt ran largely the other way, and that his fate, had it not been for Stavros, would have mingled with that of Seaman Fry. For four weeks they became the best of friends until the day came when they were discharged to their respective home islands, and never saw nor heard from each other again.

III

October 2007: Melbourne, Australia

George and David are crouched together over my laptop. George flinches as Skype burbles the incoming call.

"Loud," he objects, then "Is that her?"

"Dad!" David voices his disgust. 'Yes', he thinks, is too obvious.

"Where's the picture?" George has heard Claire's voice; he's looking for a key to push while David flicks the mouse.

"Can you see us?" David asks, and Claire affirms. Her word has left her lips long before it is heard through the laptop. George is still wondering what David did to make the video work.

They have a quick crossfire conversation on the merits of Voice Over Internet. George is underwhelmed. The picture drags across the screen as Claire moves out of shot. He is looking at a row of environmental economics textbooks on a white wall while she talks. Soon he tells her he wants to see her, and he wants her to sit still for the duration of the call. He speaks when she finishes her sentence only to find she is talking at the same time. He tells her she needs to say 'over' when she is finished and it's his turn to speak. Both of our children think this is tremendously funny, and neither obliges him.

Watching her face closely through more banter, George decides she looks happy, and tells her so.

I feel it sting her. I want to take her by the shoulders and shake her. *It's OK to be happy. I want you to be happy!*

This morning, in Boston-time, I found her happy. As her shoulder pillowed Leah's head; as their limbs mingled and the fingertips of their free hands wove lazy patterns of love on each other's palms; as the idea of loving another person forever struck its perfect chord in her and the resonance pushed every other thought from her mind.

Tell him! It will make him happy too.

But she holds back. It is so new. She is sure, but she is not sure. She needs time to know it's real. She needs to find the words to explain to her father why she's in love with a girl, not a boy. She needs to have a plan ready for his questions about the future. She enthuses instead about Boston's beautiful autumn colours, and her hopes for a white Christmas.

Invite him to Boston for Easter! I bend all of my will towards her; this one thing, if she says it now, can change the course of events.

But she holds back. She thinks that the right time to talk to him about Easter will be when she calls him for Christmas. She'll know more then. She'll research on the things they can do together in Boston in spring. She listens quietly while he tells her he is spending Christmas with Uncle Stephen in Brooklyn. She drifts away from the conversation on the music that is still in her head.

IV

November 2007: Cromer, Norfolk Coast, England

Lynne fancied she could see Nanna's craftwork in the stitches of the gansey that clothed the mannequin on display in the Cromer Royal National Lifeboat Institution museum. It could have been one of the jumpers she had watched Nanna knit, or it could have been the work of one of countless other wives, mothers or daughters of the lifeboat men whose bravery was heralded in this museum. Nanna's father was pictured, as Shirley Crawshaw had remembered, wearing a cork life jacket, and a stern expression almost exactly the same as the one on the craggy face in the photo Lynne had shown to Martin. The postings around the museum told of heroic successes and failures, of lives saved and lives lost at sea. The record since the launch in July 1923 of the *H.F. Bailey*, the town's first motorised lifeboat and the centrepiece of the museum itself, was understandably illustrated with many more photographs than earlier times, but nevertheless, the museum was a treasure trove of Cromer's history right back to the first lifeboat commissioned in 1805. So it seemed strange to Lynne that the information she had promised Martin she would find was not here. Could Martin have been wrong?

"Nicholas Baxter and his father Martin Baxter died on the same day, 14th January 1923, during a rescue operation performed using the boat *Louisa Heartwell*." Martin had almost been breathless with excitement, as he had told Lynne this in a phone call the week before. Lynne thought Martin's enthusiasm for family ancestry was potty, but of course, that was how she usually viewed Martin's intensely focused enthusiasms. The photo of their mysterious relative, the baby Nicholas, was a pathway to Pandora's box for Martin and he was thrilled by the intrigue he had so far found under the lid.

In Nanna's memorabilia there had been nothing about the deaths during the rescue operation. Lynne would have expected newspaper clippings, sympathy cards and citations for bravery perhaps, and she had come to the museum thinking that maybe her mother had donated these things to the RNLI. Instead, the museum claimed that only one life had ever been lost during a rescue operation, and that had been in 1941. The rescue operation on 14th January 1923 was only briefly listed as a having saved a trawler, the *Lord Cecil,* and there was no other detail. Thinking her quest would surely be hopeless but not wanting to waste her trip, Lynne eventually approached the small, middle-aged lady who was serving at the bookshop.

"Never heard that story," the woman declared cheerfully, after Lynne's lengthy explanation, "but if it *is* true then I do know who would know and if you *are* Irene Baxter's granddaughter, then Dot must be a relative of yourn. Dorothy Morris, dint you know her?"

Lynne shook her head, trying to remember what Shirley Crawshaw had said about Irene having a cousin in Cromer.

"Dorothy Morris is one of our main contributors," the woman tapped a promotional plaque that was announcing the imminent publication of a book: *Cromer Lifeboats: A Pictorial History.* "Sheila Baxter-Ford's daughter. I expect she'd just love to see you, she'll be back home after book club now - would you like me to give her a call?"

~

Dorothy Morris was standing in the open doorway of her narrow, peach coloured cottage, watching attentively as Lynne walked the 50 metres from the RNLI museum up The Gangway to meet her. Lynne felt embarrassed by the scrutiny as she opened the small wooden gate and stepped up through the aged mortar and pebble fence. With a more discrete glance, she made her own assessment of the many similarities between this frail, sharp-eyed, elderly woman and her own mother.

"Well, well. So you are Jean Drummond's daughter. After all this time. Do come in," Dorothy welcomed Lynne in to a small, musty living room on the ground floor of the three-story building. "Do sit down, I've put kettle on." Dorothy motioned Lynne towards one of the two armchairs in the room, and closed the door firmly against the cold wind that was blustering in from the sea front.

The living room was only 4 metres square, lined on either side of an electric fireplace with unvarnished pine bookshelves and a TV cabinet, while the wall on other side of the room was covered with family photographs of many different styles and sizes. Lynne leant towards the wall, examining the photographs instead of taking a seat and Dorothy paused beside her.

"This one is Martin Baxter," Dorothy singled out Martin's face in her own much smaller copy of the photo that Lynne had examined in the museum, "and this one next to him is his brother, my grandfather, Robert."

Dorothy pointed to another photo that showed two young women hugging each other and laughing, seemingly oblivious of the camera. Both were wearing simple woollen skirts, high-neck blouses and cardigans and they looked sufficiently alike in age and appearance to have been twins. "That's Irene on the left, and my mother Sheila on the right."

"How old would they have been?"

"Oh," Dorothy thought for a moment, "that were before the Great War, so they would be no more'n eighteen – they were same age you see, just a month apart, raised like sisters. Their fathers were brothers but also, their mothers were sisters. Did you know?" Sharon shook her head and Dorothy continued, her gnarled index finger pointing to dark grey-toned photos on the wall as she mentioned names.

"My grandmother Eunice. Sister to your great grandmother Isabella. Isabella were older, a spinster, and when your great grandfather's first wife died birthing Thomas, he were quick to marry again. Solving both problems, as done in them days." The whistle of the kettle summoned Dorothy into the small kitchen that was beyond the living room beside an incongruously modern spiral staircase. At the base of the staircase was an electronic chair lift, waiting to help Dorothy reach her bedroom on the second floor.

"We've met, you know," Dorothy continued as she made the tea. "I remember you at Irene's funeral. You were very little girl with pigtails then. Your big brother- Martin isn't he? After your great grandfather. Older than you by years? Martin were tormenting you about cremation. "They've burnt Nanna" he were saying-and my mother were very cross with him. My mother weren't well at the time, but she insisted, so I took her in wheelchair. She died a year later. That were only weeks after your mother came to talk to her. And now here *you* are. Milk? Sugar?"

"Yes, and no, thanks," Lynne accepted the cup and saucer from Dorothy's unsteady, purple-veined hand and set it down on the small table next to the armchair Dorothy had designated for her. She watched anxiously, wondering whether to offer assistance, as her hostess tottered to the other armchair, her own cup in hand, and she only sat down once Dorothy had successfully placed the cup on her own side table.

"My mother died in September," Lynne sipped at her tea, glad to feel the hot drink warming her veins.

"Ah, I didn't know. Is that why you've come?"

"I suppose it is, in a way," Lynne smoothed over a ripple of guilt. "I've been sorting through her things, and I was curious about some of the family's history. I came to Cromer to see the Lifeboat Museum ... I guess that you gave a copy of that photo of Martin to the museum?" Dorothy nodded, looking again at the photo as Lynne continued. "I thought there might be something in the museum about how he died," Lynne noticed Dorothy become suddenly still, the teacup poised in mid-air. "I understood that Martin Baxter and his son Nicholas died during a rescue operation by the *Louisa Heartwell*."

"Now Museum history doesn't say that." Dorothy was very quick and precise in her response. She put the cup down on the table.

"No, it doesn't, and I was wondering why not?" Something in Dorothy's manner convinced Lynne that Martin's information was correct.

"Well ... " Dorothy paused, filtering her thoughts for the right words. "Cromer Lifeboats had proud record of never losing a member of crew. In 1941 Walter Allen died during rescue of *English Trader*, only one in all the years. His citation is in Museum."

"So there's something different about what happened to Martin and Nicholas?" Lynne ventured helpfully.

"Well, yes." Lynne waited through another long pause before Dorothy was forced to continue. "Irene never wanted story told, you understand. But it's long ago, Irene and Sheila both gone, and here you are." Dorothy lifted her cup as if it were a heavy weight, and drained it slowly. Observing this dramatic procrastination, Lynne suspected that Dorothy had inherited the family trait of storytelling and was waiting for a further prompt.

"I'd really like to know what happened," Lynne pulled the two photos that she had of Nicholas out of her handbag and handed them to Dorothy.

Thalassa

"Oh my word!" Dorothy stared at the christening photo, the heavy lines on her face becoming suddenly taut with interest. "I've never seen this one," she swiftly turned the photo over and read out the name on the back. "Nicholas Martin Robertson Baxter." She shook her head in surprise, compared the handwriting on the back of the two photos and was apparently satisfied that the same hand had made both inscriptions. "How did Irene come by that?"

"I found it in a folder marked 'Nicholas', along with the photo that's in the Museum. There was no other information. I'm hoping you can tell me something about it."

"Well," Dorothy paused for effect, "best you read about it. Won't take you more'n twenty minutes if you've got time." She leant across the arm of her chair, struggling to reach the pile of papers that filled the lowest shelf of the bookcase.

Lynne stepped forward to help and Dorothy tapped a faded blue pocket folder with a sharpened fingertip. "That one, I think. Pull out that one if you can."

Lynne picked the folder from the middle of the pile and eased the remaining papers back into alignment while Dorothy looked inside and huffed in satisfaction confirming she had the correct file.

"This is original," Dorothy flashed a wad of flimsy paper hand-written in a tight, blue script in front of Lynne's eyes, "but typewritten version makes easier reading." She retrieved the next document from the folder and passed it over. "When I were in secretarial college, mother gave me box of family writings to practice my typing. She gave Irene originals and kept copies I typed. Except this on Nicholas. It were written after Martin and Nicholas drowned. Maybe Irene didn't want it; maybe Sheila thought Irene would destroy it. Or maybe Sheila wanted to keep it because it were her father, Robert, who wrote it and she wanted to keep his hand. Anyways, this is the only one where I have both copies. Even so, you can read it here, not take it with."

Lynne was not about to argue, she had settled back into her chair and was already turning to page two.

~

The Asia Minor Disaster Story

December 1918: Cromer, Norfolk Coast, England

Nicholas Baxter was 21 when he returned to Cromer just before Christmas 1918, having served on *HMS Iron Duke* since the latter part of 1916. It was the exciting news coverage of the Battle of Jutland in the earlier part of that year that had inspired him to join the navy when he was old enough to enlist, and he was greatly disappointed that during the rest of the war he was never engaged in battle. While history would record the blockade the British Grand Fleet imposed on the German Fleet in the North Sea as a critical factor in forcing King Wilhelm to the armistice in November, the seamen who waited on their vessels in Scapa Flow, playing cards, telling stories, scrubbing decks and begrudgingly following orders in countless drills, felt the war was passing them by. When Thomas was old enough to enlist at the start of 1918, he had been sent straight into action at Flanders and Nicholas felt something akin to envy when he invoked for himself, through a lack of information and a desperate need for consolation, a heroic account of his brother's death.

The stories told by the sailors who had manned the *Iron Duke* in the Battle of Jutland pointed away from the patriotic tale told by the newspapers towards errors of judgement, poor battle planning and indecisive results. It was the British fleet that was blockaded, they said, too scared to move south due to the mines and the German U-boats that patrolled the channel. The biggest threat to the fleet as it stayed in the North, it seemed to Nicholas, was their own fleet – on a stormy night in September 1917 the British submarine *HMS G9* had fired upon a destroyer, *HMS Pasley,* mistaking her for a German submarine, and the *Pasley* had in turn rammed the submarine, breaking it in half with the loss of all its crew bar one.

Nicholas emerged from the Great War with no plan for his future, a considerable disrespect for authority, a gift for imitating and lampooning rank, and a Lieutenant's uniform that he had misappropriated on the understanding, shared by many of his crew mates, that women love men in officer's uniform. In the early summer afternoons of 1919, while the crabbing boats lay idle on the beach by The Gangway, Nicholas put the uniform into use, wearing it fastidiously on his tall, athletic body, strolling the beaches at Cromer and Sheringham, finding occasion to flirt with young women, feigning the graces of a lieutenant and proving to himself that the theory held true.

Being a clown rather than a cad, Nicholas very soon tripped himself up by falling in love with a fair-haired beauty, the youngest daughter of the Earl of Caldbeck. Their fourth midnight assignation in the rotunda by the children's playground was even more exciting than the one before, which had been even more exciting than the two before it … and Nicholas was certain this excitement would just keep getting better. Cradling Bess in his arms, breathing her sweet perfume through the strands of her hair, replaying the passionate power he perceived in himself in each intimate move, he realised that he did not want it to be the uniform that this girl loved. Neither did he want to face her wrath when she found out he had deceived her, so he resolved to invent no new tales, but he did not retract the tall ones he had already told.

One uncommonly fine morning, when the crabs were late and Bess was early, Nicholas hoisted the heavy cane crab bucket up onto the quay that ran along the front of the colourful beach huts, and found himself looking up into the puzzled face of his beloved.

"What *are* you doing?" Bess asked innocently, examining his sea boots, his oilskins, his matted woollen jumper and his salt-laden brown hair as if she couldn't believe she recognised him.

Nicholas was quick ... indeed; he had already rehearsed his words in the event of such a discovery ... "I like to help out the fishermen in the morning. Gets me out to sea again, keeps me fit. This man lost a son in the war ... he doesn't have anyone else to help on the boat now. It's the least I can do."

"Nick!" the peremptory order that Martin Baxter shouted from the boat which was pulled up on the sand just 30 yards from them, grated on Nick's ears, out of harmony with the false impression he knew he had just given. He searched Bess's face for some sign of distrust, but there was none.

"How very good of you," she smiled. "Well ... don't keep him waiting."

When Nick brought back the next bucket Bess was still there, smiling. She had raised a parasol to protect her pale skin from the sun, and she had hoisted her skirts a little, concerned about the grime of the fisherman's wharf. She had a perfumed handkerchief in hand to help her endure the smells.

"You should go," Nick entreated, "it's filthy here, and I'm embarrassed that you're seeing me dressed like this. I'll see you on the beach this afternoon?"

"I like to watch you. What are you going to do next?"

Nick's pre-rehearsed script was running out. He started to sweat inside his oilskins. "We pull the boat further up, and then we get some buckets of water and scrub it down ... which really smells bad, I'm afraid. We might need to repair some pots too ... it will take a while. You should go, really."

"NICK!" Martin's order punctuated Nick's wheedling explanation.

Bess looked crestfallen–or was it sceptical? She dipped her head gracefully and moved away along the promenade towards the pier.

"Who was that?" Martin demanded.

"Just a girl interested in the crabs," Nick replied.

"Looks to me like you know each other," Martin observed dryly. "She's above your station bor, it'll only cause trouble. Get Bill 'n' Jack to help us pull boat up, and while you're at it, ask Bill 'ow 'is son lost 'is thumb the year ago. The Earl of Caldbeck ain't to be messed with bor."

Nick already knew the story, but until now he had not made any connection to the Earl. The spectre of other stories he had heard about the man's cruel methods of retribution prompted in him a newly fearful conscience.

The encounter had raised questions in Bess's mind too. That night, she was coquettish; she wanted answers to many questions before she would allow him to caress her.

"Where is your family? Where did you study? How come you are in Cromer?"

Nick's storyline, partly stolen from a warrant officer he had known on the *Iron Duke* was that his father was a retired admiral who lived at Marble Arch. Naturally he was following in his father's footsteps, and had studied at the Royal Naval College at Greenwich. His father owned property in Cromer–the fisherman's cottages on The Gangway–and during his furlough Nicholas was in Cromer to supervise some maintenance ... maybe extend the family holdings with some new purchases.

It was difficult for Nick to deliver this fabrication to Bess, now that he felt himself to be in love, but it was impossible for him to tell the truth and risk the consequences. Here in the rotunda amidst the scents and surrounds of their other nights, it seemed to Nick that the only right words to say were those that would be stepping stones to that tilt of her head which exposed her neck to his lips and that passionate sigh of permission that let his hand continue all the way up the inside of her thigh.

"When does your furlough end?"

"I fear it will be very soon, my love. Tonight could be our last night together for quite some time."

Discretion being undeniably the better part of dishonest valour, Nick acted to make this last part of his story true, and departed for Hull in the morning to re-enlist. Cowardly pretender that he was, he wrote Bess a passionate letter in which he said he had been called back to his ship, he could not bear the misery of having to say goodbye in person, he would love her forever, but that she should forget him because she was far too beautiful to waste her youth waiting for a naval officer to return.

This could all have been harmless enough–a dashing summer romance, keenly felt by both parties, and summarily over–but Nick had left behind more than the first cuts on a naïve girl's heart. Bess was pregnant, and when her father the Earl of Caldbeck came thundering into Cromer looking for the culprit, he found Martin Baxter, repairing fishing pots on the quay.

Once the truth had been untangled from Nick's lies and Bess's tears, and the recriminations and threats had settled down into an intense sense of shame and bubbling anger on the parts of both fathers, the Earl of Caldbeck oversaw a reputation-saving strategy.

Nick was immediately commissioned as a Lieutenant, and was brought to the Lakes District in England for a uniformed wedding to the girl he had not very long ago loved, who would now neither look him in the eye nor speak to him.

He was assigned to the docks for three months, and then returned to Caldbeck in order to have a presence at the birth and christening of his son. Immediately after the christening, the Earl of Caldbeck personally took his son-in-law to Portsmouth, saw him onto the gangplank of a carrier bound for Russia, and coldly farewelled him with words slick with deadly intent, "I have told the Admiral I want to see your death certificate before the year is out."

Thalassa

~

On a warmly sunny morning in June 1920 in the Sea of Marmara off Mudania, Turkey, Nick embarked again on the *Iron Duke* and was escorted directly to the bridge. He snapped crisply to attention in front of Admiral Sir John de Robeck, eyes aimed at a point somewhere slightly above the Admiral's head but, mindful of the Earl's parting threat, every nerve in his body was alert to the Admiral's attitude towards him.

The Admiral examined him slowly and evenly from the crisp brow of his white cap to the shiny black points of his black shoes. When the inspection was complete the Admiral gave a small grunt that Nick optimistically took as approval.

"Fortunately for you, young man," the Admiral spoke slowly, loading a pompous gravity onto each word, "the Earl of Caldbeck does *not* run my ship. Don't make any mistakes. Dismissed," the Admiral waved Nick, and the Earl's request, away.

Nick's record remained spotless until September 1922, when the *Iron Duke* was sent to Smyrna to stand-by after the retreat of the defeated Greek Army from that city. The Allies; Britain, France, Italy and America, expected that the victorious Turkish army would be hostile to the non-Muslim residents when they reclaimed their Anatolian city after three years of Greek occupation, and there were warships representing every one of those Christian nations in the port. All the ships were under orders to remain neutral in the conflict; they were permitted only to evacuate their own nationals.

Thousands upon thousands of Greeks and Armenians had poured into Smyrna, fleeing from the Turkish army, hoping for evacuation to Greece. All available small craft had already left the port before the *Iron Duke* arrived, bearing the early refugees away to nearby Greek islands. On-shore an ever-growing mob of refugees, in desperate fear for their lives, was clamouring to be rescued, while the citizens of Britain, France, Italy and America were staying in their homes, flying their national flags hopefully believing in the Turkish promise that the transition was not going to be violent.

By the afternoon of 13th September it was clear that their hopes were misplaced. The scale of violence in the city was escalating, spilling into European and American residential areas. A fire started in the Armenian quarter of the city that the Turks made no effort to extinguish ... indeed, it was said that they had deliberately started the fire and that they were laying paths for it by pouring petroleum down streets into the Greek and European quarters ... even to the front of the American consulate.

The evacuation of the British was ordered to start at 18:30 and Nick was placed in charge of a picket boat with a number of marines. His orders were to collect the British citizens from the quay and take them to the Merchant Marine steamer SS Bavarian. There was a great crush of people, bundles of belongings, goats and even donkeys with packsaddles on the quay. From what he could see of the Turkish soldiers on the streets, Nick knew that these people had every reason to be terrified; robbery, rape and murder of Greeks and Armenians appeared to be officially sanctioned. The Royal Marines were highly disciplined, holding off the mob with their rifles, marching the British onto the boats, knocking away those who attempted to swim to the picket boat and climb inside. Nick saw an elderly woman knocked off the quay into the water and he threw himself down quickly to pull her out, setting her back on the quay, only to find himself even more marked by the crowd as a likely recipient of their desperate appeals for rescue.

By 21:30 the British citizens who had been ready to leave had all been evacuated, and Nick was back on the deck of the *Iron Duke*, when he felt the wind pick up and realised that it was fanning the fire towards the sea-front where the crowd of refugees was now so packed that there was barely room to move. The heat was so intense he could feel it on the deck, 200 metres from the shore. He and the other officers watched in horror; knowing that the Admiral was in desperate consultation with Home Office; waiting for the order to commence evacuation of the people on the quay.

At 3 a.m. they were still at their posts, waiting, glued to the tragedy of silhouetted figures outlined against the bright flames leaping and folding back on themselves in the night sky. The fire had caught the old cinema on the sea front and had broken through to the quay. It was lighting the bundles of belongings that were spread amongst the crowd, catching the packs on the donkeys and sending those animals careening madly into the mob. There was pandemonium amongst people too packed to move out of the way, some were throwing themselves into the water. The screaming was digging itself into Nick's mind, burying itself so deep that he knew he would never be able to forget.

A decrepit boat, propelled by many hands because it had no oars, came alongside Nick's station, almost sinking as its overload of passengers grabbed at the side of the *Iron Duke*. Though he knew he was supposed to order his men to push them away, Nick threw down a rope ladder and as he helped up the first of the refugees there was no shortage of crewmen jostling to help him. Nick knew his Captain was watching him, hands on hips, lips firmly pressed into a grim line. He expected a countermand, but the Captain said nothing. More ropes and life buoys were thrown as another boat arrived, and then a third. The refugees huddled on the deck, weeping, hugging the crewmen and entreating them to rescue those who were still on the shore.

Finally the order came from the Admiral, 'Away all boats', and Nick leapt into his picket boat with six marines and headed for the quay.

The crush was so much worse than it had been in the afternoon. The crowd rushed the boats and the marines had to be brutal or they would certainly have been sunk. As the marines bullied the refugees into a steadier queue, Nick concentrated on fishing women and children out of the water. He pushed the men who swam to the boat away, justifying his actions with a cold contempt for their unmanliness. Nick took his refugees to *The Bavarian*, where again there was bedlam, as many boats tried to unload their human cargo as quickly as possible. He pretended not to hear the order to stop, returning with one more boatload that the already overloaded steamer did not want to accept.

The allied ships rescued a few thousand refugees from the quay that night, but it was only a tiny fraction of the number that needed evacuation. It wasn't until 10 days later that the Turkish authorities finally allowed Greek ships to evacuate women, children and the elderly. Greek and Armenian men aged between 18 and 45 were 'deported to the interior', words which most people took to be a death sentence. In all between 150,000 and 200,000 refugees were evacuated from Smyrna; between 10,000 and 100,000 were said to have died on the quay and during the massacres that took place around the city.

On the morning of 14th September, after only a few hours sleep, Nick was woken by his captain who brusquely ordered him to transfer the refugees that he had disobediently boarded to the *Iron Duke* the night before to the *SS Bavarian*, and to prepare himself to sail with the *SS Bavarian* for Malta where the captain expected that a disciplinary action would be brought against him. In the meantime, the *Iron Duke* would sail without him to Chanak, where the Admiralty was anticipating aggressive action by the Turks. Infused with a stinging sense of injustice, Nick packed up his belongings and gruffly supervised the transfer of the refugees. At 14:30 he stood on the deck of the *Bavarian*, feeling angry and bereft as he watched the *Iron Duke* and his crewmates steam away. At 15:00 the *Bavarian* left for Malta with 290 British refugees, and 460 refugees of other nationalities, mostly Anatolian Greeks.

As the sea's smoothly curved horizon replaced the Anatolian coastline, Nick realised he was being watched, timidly but surely, by a pretty, dark-eyed, dark haired girl who was leaning on the side of a lifeboat, amongst a group of female refugees.

When he returned her glance with curiosity she detached herself from the group and came over to talk to him, her head slightly averted in an endearingly shy manner, her gait uncertain on the moving deck. Nick didn't think he had seen her before, but she told him, in halting English, that she had been on the last boat that he had picked up from Smyrna. She touched his hand lightly and thanked him for pulling her out of the water, surely saving her life. She gave him a delightful smile, and then moved quietly back to her group.

The next time he passed her on the deck, Nick asked her name. By the time they were steaming into the Grand Harbour at Valletta in Malta, he knew much more about her than he had ever bothered to ask anyone before. Iliana Theodori had been working in Smyrna, apprenticed as a translator and aide to the British consulate; living in a boarding house on the Greek side of the Armenian quarter. Her parents and three siblings lived on a small farm in the hinterland, that they abandoned ahead of the Turkish advance, surging into Smyrna with a vast wave of refugees just as the Greek army left. Suddenly the boarding house was over-run with families; then came the Turkish troops; then came the fire. Iliana had been at work in the consulate when the *Chettes* raped and killed her mother and sister. One brother had been killed in a street skirmish, her other brother and her father had disappeared. They were either dead or had been 'sent inland' to almost certain execution. Iliana, like so many other refugees, had no family left in the world. She had followed the British consulate staff down to the wharf only to be pushed back by the marines. In the crush of the evacuation she had fought to retain her place near the front only to be told that the boats were full, and no more refugees would be taken off the wharf. In desperation she had jumped into the water and swum to Nick's boat.

Nick was proud of his role in her rescue, and he was ashamed of the uniform he wore; ashamed of the British government's abandonment of the Anatolian Greeks to the

Turkish army. When off-duty in his bunk he rehearsed a variety of noble-anger responses he could make to the disciplinary hearing, justifying his actions, but each time he put his uniform back on, he knew that anything other than a silent and stiff upper lip would land him in even greater trouble.

As they docked in Valletta, Nick scanned the wharf anxiously, expecting to see a charge sheet waiting for him ... would they come with handcuffs he wondered? Instead of Navy officers he found himself watching a chaotic melee of evacuees trying to find out what was to happen to them. The British were being shepherded off to Lazaretto, the quarantine hospital, where they would stay until alternative accommodation or a passage to England could be organised. The Greek refugees were being left to fend for themselves; most had been robbed of their money and their possessions had been burnt; there was no alternative to sleeping on the streets, and no plan for where they might go in future. Nick knew that another shipload was due into Malta in just two days; the situation was going to get worse. Iliana hovered close by his side, not moving as the other refugees shuffled off the boat, she had adopted him as her protector, and Nick felt himself to be properly fit for the role.

When Nick made his decision it was characteristically sudden, and not at all thought through. He told Iliana to follow him to his cabin, where he changed out of his uniform into civilian clothes, and picked up the duffle bag he had already packed ready to go ashore. He pulled a sailor's beanie over his head and walked down the gangway as a British citizen, holding Iliana's hand. He avoided the Lazaretto queue and walked along the wharf until he found a taxi-driver who knew of a hotel that still had some spare rooms, at a price. Within two weeks he and his 'wife' Iliana, 'unfortunately deprived' by the Smyrna fire of all the usual documentation proving their marriage and citizenship, embarked on a cargo ship for Britain. On 14th January 1923, Nick and Iliana arrived unannounced at the Baxter house on The Gangway, Cromer.

Thalassa

~

November 2007: Cromer, Norfolk Coast, England

On Friday 23rd November 2007, as Lynne watched, a 4.9 metre high tide was being whipped into the sea wall at Cromer by a vicious 38 mph North Westerly. Waves rolled in rapidly, their crests so high that they struck the underside of the pier before they crashed against its pylons and folded into two independent wave fronts, angling in to the shore. With little more than five seconds between them, white plumes of spray billowed over the corner of the sea wall and the pier, dumping seawater onto the promenade that was, not at all surprisingly, devoid of people. Each wave receded slightly, momentarily revealing the seaweed dreadlocks that dangled from the slick wooden palings of the breakwater, before the next wave roared in to take its place, swallowing the entire spread of the beach and slamming the wall again.

There were no crabbing boats on the beach. They had been safely pulled up onto the promenade and were colourfully parked in a line alongside the beach huts. The lower end of the Gangway was covered in white foam and as Lynne hugged her wind jacket tightly around herself, more frothy white patches came spinning in from the sea to land on the cobbled bricks at her feet. The sea looked dangerously high; it seemed to overhang The Gangway, threatening to clout the promenade with full force. It amazed Lynne that the pier, looking puny in comparison, stood firm as the waves raged beneath and around it; amazing that mankind had built a structure that, even though it could not tame the North Sea on such a day, could at least endure.

It was not hard to imagine, on a day such as this, freighters being wrecked by the waves, or blown off course and beached on sand banks. What was hard for Lynne to imagine was how, on an evening similar to this one, 14th January 1923, the Cromer lifeboat men, her own great grandfather and granduncle amongst them, had managed to launch their rowboat into such powerful surf. At the end of the pier, beyond the breaking waves, Lynne could see the steep launching slide of the modern lifeboat station, and she could replay in her mind the museum's video of the new power launch riding the slide and hitting the water in a massive bow-wave before racing away to the open sea. To help her imagine the experience of launching the *Louisa Heartwell* in 1923 history's prompt was a grainy grey-tone photo of a dozen or so men, weighed down by cork life jackets, carrying a wooden boat into white foam. The photo did not do justice to the fury of the sea, and the seeming impossibility of the task.

In Cromer in the 1920's, every fisherman had a responsibility to man the lifeboat; every fisherman who heard the siren ran to the boat, and those who were first to obtain a life jacket won a place on the crew for that rescue. Living here on The Gangway gave Martin Baxter's family a considerable advantage. The adrenalin rush of the rescue and the opportunity to deserve the approval of their community was enough reward for the men to be keen to brave the North Sea even on its worst days.

Nick had been home for just four hours. Irene had removed Iliana to Sheila Baxter's house while Nick and his father, Martin, argued vehemently on topics far too delicate for female ears. No one knew what had been said between them before they were interrupted, but it was assumed that they were in mid-argument when the flares went up from the coastal lookout, the siren howled and both men grabbed oilskins and ran for the lifeboat shed. Robert Baxter, who had been sitting in his armchair observing Iliana in a silence overhung with a dark scowl, arrived at the shed just in time to claim the last of the cork life jackets.

The argument between father and son continued after the lifeboat was beyond the breakers and the men had settled into their rowing stroke. At a precipitous lurch of the boat Robert looked behind to see both Martin and Nick standing. He could not see exactly, and neither did anyone else see who made the first lunge or threw the first punch, it could have been the roll of the boat as much as a punch that threw Martin over the side. But it seemed to Robert that Nick must have known he had knocked his father senseless. Nick was screaming 'DAD!' already pointing three waves beyond the boat, and even as Robert reached out to prevent him, Nick dived overboard.

Looking out over the brutal sea, Lynne was not surprised that the cork life jackets were not enough to save the men; that the lifeboat crew immediately lost sight of them and, despite hours of searching in the sea that night, and on beaches over the coming weeks, their bodies were never found. Fortunately the trawler they had gone to rescue had not been in grave danger of breaking up, it had been washed onto a sand reef, but the high seas had kept shifting it, and once the lifeboat did arrive it was easy to synchronise with a high wave and tow the ship away from the sand. The lifeboat's mission was classified as 'assisted to save vessel', and the deaths, while officially recorded, were not noted in the RNLI's records.

The wind was gusting along the promenade, forcing Lynne to lean into it firmly to avoid being blown backwards, spraying her with salty water. Her jeans were drenched below her parka; her hands and cheeks were icing up, and her inner ears were stinging from the cold air, the burn reaching along her sinuses and down the back of her throat. Lynne decided to quit the promenade and retreat to the narrow lanes that offered some shelter away from the seafront. She would follow their winding path back to her car, a heated driver's seat, a de-humidifying air conditioner, and a warm drive back to her London comfort-zone. At home she would pop a freezer-meal of salmon in white sauce into the microwave, and settle down within a few minutes to watch her favourite reality-TV show. After that, she would ring her brother Martin to let him know the surprising story she had learned.

As she escaped the wind, turning around the corner of a pub and heading up the street towards the church, hands buried deep in her pockets, Lynne was thinking of Iliana, waiting in a stranger's cottage with two hostile women in a country that was completely foreign to her, until the news eventually came that her saviour and protector Nicholas would never return. It was Lynne's grandmother, Irene, who had decided how the family was going to absolve its responsibility for this illegal immigrant Nick had befriended. It took several weeks to organise, but Irene had eventually paid the bribe required for Iliana to discretely leave England on a cargo ship bound for Greece. The closing statement of Robert Baxter's account had initially thrown Lynne's thoughts into a dizzy spell of coincidence, but her walk in the fresh sting of sea air had made the logic of it clear to her. Iliana had been sent 'to the family of Stavros Kostis, Milos' because this was the only Greek name, the only Greek address Irene knew.

As far as Dorothy Morris knew, the Baxter family had never heard whether Iliana Theodori had reached the intended destination.

V

I challenge Iliana. If our lives are predestined, and everything is God's Will, then surely she, of all people, must hate God. How can she thank God for sending Nick to save her? When logic requires that–if God exists at all–she should blame God for the terror wreaked upon her family; for the very fact that she needed to be saved.

Iliana, ever the interpreter, tells me I do not understand God's 'Will'. In the Greek Bible the word used is *'Thelema'*, and it means God's purpose, his wish, his plan for mankind. It is not something God directs against or for individual people. *Thelema* is the true path of our lives within the destiny of mankind.

Why then should people pray to God if their prayers cannot make any difference?

Iliana deflects this argument by telling me the Western interpretation of prayer is individualistic and egotistical. I protest and she concedes that the failing may be a universal aspect of human nature. She agrees that when she was young her own prayers were self-interested, which is illogical if God's Will is predetermined. In her older years her prayers focussed on finding her own peace of mind and trying to reconcile herself to the past.

Why then does she ask God's Mercy?

The Greek word for 'mercy' is '*éleos*', and Iliana explains that in ancient biblical use it properly means 'loyalty to God's covenant'. God, in His Mercy, will fulfil His promise to forgive the sins of those who believe in Him. We are misinterpreting if we think it means God will save us from suffering. What prayer should be, she instructs me, is an alignment of one's self to *Thelema*; a mindfulness of God's Will, and a faithful attempt to quiet the ego while we submit to God's plan.

Aretha is offended. She insists there is no place for such logic in our relationship with God. Through Christ The Redeemer we are able to have a personal relationship with God, through Christ our prayers are heard and if we truly believe then our prayers will be answered. Any failure points squarely to our inadequate faith.

Jean, as I've come to expect, has an irreligious perspective. What is there to either blame or thank God for? We humans are collectively responsible for the decisions we make, the switches we control, the instantiation of the universe that we're living amongst all the possibilities the Creator, has on offer. It is soothing, she concedes to Iliana, if through prayer or other means we quiet our ego and practise mindfulness of our self.

I am an atheist. I can't hate God. I can't love God. I can't blame God or thank God. But when I see Aretha praying-for George, for Stephen, for Mary–I confess, I wish there was someone-or something-I could ask for help.

VI

December 2007: Brooklyn, New South Wales

"This'll be the last Christmas for Pappous," Dimitry's tone was mischievous. "He is reminding us all, every day. Look out, because he's got something SERIOUS to talk to you about."

George asked, but Dimitry just shrugged and tossed his uncle's black canvas roll bag carelessly onto the neatly made queen size guest bed. "See ya when ya come down."

Through the fly-screened window George looked down on the lagoon between Long Island and the mainland, locally known as 'The Gut', with its colourful assortment of over-sized, expensive cruisers, old-fashioned rectangular houseboats, cheerfully decaying fishing boats, dinghies and pleasure craft. Sparse clumps of people, dressed in T-shirts, shorts and thongs dotted the several paling-grey boardwalks between the boats and the shore. Some youths were hooting at each other as they took it in turns to jump from the end of the Brooklyn marina wharf, bombing those in the brown water below. A teenage boy in wet board shorts sat atop a stubby pier on the next jetty, staring indifferently away from the group, across the water towards the abandoned oyster leases of Long Island. A gleaming white cruiser with navy trim was creeping towards

Brooklyn's fuel jetty through a narrow channel that was lined with moored boats of all shapes and sizes. A woman stood in the high, Perspex cockpit, craning her neck anxiously to detect any obstacles as she manoeuvred between the mooring buoys, lines and boats. A man stood on the foredeck with a boat hook, waving his arms in contradictory motions that the helmswoman appeared sensibly to ignore. Nothing else could be seen moving on the water in either direction. This was quiet for the summer season, George thought, but he supposed people were indoors, gearing up for Christmas Eve.

On the casement window ledge, alongside his hand, was a photo Liz had taken last Christmas. The Kostis siblings accidentally arranged from left to right in order of height. Stephen, at 6'1, was a little taller than George, and more than a little wider. Mary, a wholesome 5'7, was showing (to her horror) some post-menopausal weight gain. Her long black hair was shining with a lustrous brunette hue, falling well past her shoulders in dramatic contrast to Stephen's clean-shaven pate. In an over-reaction to comments likening him to his tufty-balding father, Stephen had appointed Dimitry to remove the evidence. The photo had been taken amidst much laughter, shortly after Stephen and Dimitry had appeared triumphantly from the bathroom. Margarita, after her initial shock, had decided she liked the new look. She and Liz had spent some time examining the photo on a laptop, zooming-in on the facial structure George and Stephen shared: generous eyebrows overhanging deep-set brown eyes; firmly chiselled, smooth jaw. They had photo-shopped the picture, substituting George's straight nose for Stephen's broken one. They had agreed that a moustache would be the best way to hide the scars above Stephen's lips, and giggled together as they shaded one in. Margarita had copied the moustache onto George, but Liz immediately undid the change, protesting 'No, never again!' Stephen must have fancied the image of his possible self, because he had kept his head shaved and now sported a neatly trimmed moustache and 3-day growth.

George ran his fingers through his hair, thinking that he should ask Dimitry for a number 2 cut again while he was here. The cut would leave him with a higher proportion of grey, he knew, but otherwise he didn't look very different now than he did in the photo. Which struck him as wrong. Terribly wrong. He laid the photo, and the memory of Liz and Margarita's laughter, facedown on the ledge.

Wanting to keep to himself for a little longer, George decided to explore the top floor before heading downstairs. Stephen had recently done a 'knock down and rebuild'. There was nothing of the old house left, and despite his own love for history and conservation George found himself admiring the newness of everything. It was a hybrid 'Cape Cod' house, built with Aussie resourcefulness into rocks at the rear, while exhibiting an attractive Cape Cod façade to the street, perched on suspended concrete and tall steel poles. The North-facing dormer windows to the upstairs bedrooms had a panoramic eyrie's view down on The Gut, and across Long Island to the wide Hawkesbury River beyond. The window frames were all aluminium, and the walls were made of HardiePlank fibre cement cladding on a steel frame. Admirable defences, Stephen had boasted, in the constant war against termites and bush fire. George felt less certain, knowing that to the West was the unruly scrub of the Marramarra National Park, and to the South, rising high behind Stephen's back yard, was the edge of Ku-ring-gai Chase National Park. The small township of Brooklyn was perched on a narrow strip of land sandwiched between Ku-Ring-Gai Chase and Sandbrook Inlet, its only access road dead-ending to the East on the banks of the Hawkesbury River. The fire plan here, George thought, should read 'run downhill and swim', but in the bushfire of 2002 Stephen and his young family had stayed. When the town's water lost all pressure they put out spot fires with buckets and wet towels. The fire came from the West but circled round to threaten Brooklyn again from the South when the wind changed in the afternoon. They were lucky. The updraught of wind from the river kept the fire on the ridge above them, and their desperate efforts over many besieged hours saved the house.

For the Christmas family assembly that year, Stephen had rented three houses on Dangar Island, a ten-minute boat ride away in the middle of the Hawkesbury River. The house in Brooklyn reeked of smoke and wet ash and their sister Mary had refused to even sit down in it for the Christmas meal. More importantly, from George's perspective, the back fence had melted and his dog, Tammy, would have headed home to Melbourne through thousands of hectares of burnt out national park before hitting the busy roads of the Northern suburbs of Sydney. Dangar, untouched by the fire, was the perfect solution, a bushy haven with a sub-tropical microclimate, marvellous vegetation, an abundance of birds, river beaches, endless photo opportunities and no cars. Liz had fallen in love with the tiny island. It was, she had said, the one place she could 'bear to live' if she had to move to Sydney. Since then, whenever they came back to visit his parents, George's family stayed on Dangar, and Liz had been much more willing to make the trip.

This year, for the first time in twenty-two years, George had come to Brooklyn by himself. The house Stephen had saved from the fire-the house where George had spent his own teenage years-was gone, and the new, architecturally designed mansion in its place was not in any way identifiable as 'home'. When George searched himself for a feeling about that, the best word he could find was 'disoriented'. He was pleased that Stephen and Margarita had a house that was now truly their own and in many ways he was glad the baggage cart of his memory had been disconnected. So much else was gone, it seemed fitting that the house should go too, just another chapter in the text of temporality. In other ways there was an unsettling dislocation - the same streetscape, the same place names, but a world of difference that reduced him to the status of visitor. Disconcerting.

Unlike the old place, everything in Stephen's new house was fresh, and clean and functional. The walls were a pure white from top to bottom, without watermark maps on the ceiling, or plaster cracks running down from the corners towards mould spotting above the skirting boards. The doorframes all boasted a perfect covering of white plastic paint, no edges had been scraped off yet and the doors opened and closed without that extra tug necessary to overcome the resistance of swollen plywood and dropped hinges. The mirrors on the built in wardrobes rolled smoothly and focussed clearly without any flaky rust dots. The bathroom was spotless; with gleaming white and gold tap fittings that didn't leak; a clear, seamless glass shower frame that closed with a satisfyingly tight squelch of rubber lining; clean white grouting between the shiny, modern tiles. The upstairs level was fully carpeted, and instead of feeling springy floorboards underfoot, George could pad silently along the hallway between rooms.

George pushed a bedroom door open to find Michael lying on his back, ears tethered to the boom box on his bedside table by a thin black cord. Michael waved cheerfully, pulled out one earplug and called "G'day Uncle George."

"Hey buddy, how are you?"

"I'm good, did ya have a good trip?"

"You make it sound like I came from Greece, not Melbourne."

"Didn't you?" Michael grinned. "Coulda, considering how long it's been since we saw you."

It had been not quite 8 months since the funeral. But the answer George gave was "I had to wait till you'd built the 5-star accommodation for me."

"S'orright isn't it."

"Very nice. You get back to your music and I'll go on exploring."

George followed the smooth curve of the staircase downstairs onto the polished hardwood floors of the entrance hallway, and walked into the noise of the kitchen. The granite top benches were covered with foodstuffs. He swept a finger around the edge of a bowl filled with a thick pink cream that he hoped was salmon in flavour.

"Look at you, just like one of the kids! If you aren't here to help, get out of my kitchen!" Margarita slapped the bench for emphasis.

"I'll help, what do you want me to do?"

"Your brother isn't helping. He's just back here with you and now he's going to bugger off for the rest of the afternoon."

"I have to open the shop." Stephen walked into the kitchen, patting his pockets in what George knew was a familiar leaving-the-house check-routine. Keys. Phone. Wallet.

"Christmas eve, he has to open the shop!" Margarita's voice pitched up a tone, her mane of black hair shook; her dark eyes flashed at Stephen and Stephen remained completely unfazed.

"For hire boat returns," Stephen explained for George's benefit. "I'm going now, want to come?"

"No ... he is more use to me here than he will be to you," Margarita retorted quickly. "There's a bowl of hard-boiled eggs George – peel and slice would you?"

Stephen shrugged, swiped a carrot slice from the bench and sauntered out the door.

~

After Margarita had caught up with the news of Claire (enjoying a year of overseas study for her economics degree in Boston) and David (working hard for peanuts at his first job in the Water Board), and after George had queried her reciprocally for news of Dimitry (working with his father in the boat hire business), Katherine (loving her nursing internship in Newcastle), Melinda (anxiously waiting confirmation of entrance to medicine at Sydney University) and Michael (lazy bugger, causing his mother complete despair), there was a lull in conversation as George mixed the egg slices into the potato salad and Margarita studied his work intently, waiting for him to finish.

Margarita patted gladwrap around the edges of the bowl and squeezed it into an improbably small space in the fridge. Having done that she launched into the conversation George had been expecting.

"And what about you? You've lost weight. Do you eat?"

"I'm looking good, don't know what you are complaining about." George patted his flat stomach and stretched a little higher than his official 5'11. He rolled up the sleeve of his T-shirt to exaggerate his right biceps and combed his left hand through his crisp pepper and salt-grey hair in a mock pose.

Margarita repaid his effort at light-heartedness with an ironic "you *are* just *too* good looking to be real" but George had failed to distract her from her line of questioning. "Are you really going to stay in Melbourne?"

"It's my home. I work there. I have friends. I do see David quite often and Claire will be home in October." George allowed some of the impatience he felt over questions like these to flavour his response.

"Dimitry says she has an American boyfriend." George raised an eyebrow so Margarita explained. "Facebook. She's changed her status to 'In a Relationship'." George knew enough about Facebook to know that meant the relationship was serious. "I'm sure she'll email you about it soon." Margarita had interpreted the crestfallen look on George's face. "We're always the last to know about our children's romantic life. It probably won't last long, she'll come back."

Margarita stole a look at the clock, and George mirrored her action without taking in what the clock said, his mind stumbling over the possibility Claire might not come back.

"Pappous will be finished his siesta in a few minutes. I have some *kourabiethes* for you both." Margarita opened the sleekly varnished door of a corner cupboard and took a tray from the top of a mix of silverware and soup ramekins. "If I didn't hide them they wouldn't make it through the day," she explained.

The *kourabiethes* were crescent shaped shortbreads made with almond meal and orange rind and dusted with icing sugar. A long-standing family treat. George's mouth started watering immediately.

"Coffee for you?" Margarita asked, pre-empting George's answer by retrieving the 2-cup *briki* from the cupboard, filling it with cold water and putting it on the stove. She loaded the *briki* with two teaspoons of coffee powder and two of sugar, and stirred it briefly.

"Pappous wants to talk to you about something," Margarita announced as they both watched the coffee warm up, until it started to foam. "He and Stephen have had a big argument, a *really* big argument."

"About?" George didn't find the conversation surprising so far; relations were often tempestuous between Papa and his eldest son.

"He wants Stephen to go to Greece, but Stephen won't – he can't, he just can't, he's got a business to run."

"Why go to Greece?" Now George was surprised.

"Pappous will tell you, it's about repairing the church. I just want you to know ... Stephen can't go, and I hope you'll take his side in it. It is such a silly idea–I think Pappous really is starting to lose his mind–he is so adamant about this."

The kitchen was rich with the strong aroma of coffee as the dark foam that the Greeks called *kaimaki* reached the top of the *briki*. On cue, George's father emerged from a door off the family room, which led to his own discrete apartment.

"*Yasou Papa.*"

Papa waved his hand impatiently and awkwardly turned his nuggetty frame back to the door. He oriented himself by holding onto the doorframe for a moment and then stomped heavily back into his apartment, leaving George smiling in bemusement at his back.

"He's forgotten his hearing aid," Margarita deduced.

Margarita shared the *kaimaki* out between two cups, and then filled each cup with the black coffee that was left in the *briki*. She motioned George to take the tray with the cups and the *kourabiethes* over to the coffee table and sit, waiting for his father's return.

~

Stavros Kostis the fourth, known as *Pappous* to his twelve grandchildren, and *Papa* to his three children, returned not only with a hearing aid secured in each ear, but also with a blue manila folder. He plumped the folder onto the coffee table alongside the *kourabiethes* and turned to give his son a gruff bear hug, ended by a shoulder-buried grunt that would have been '*ilie mou*', and a hearty slap on the back. George noted that, while still solid, the slap did not wind him, as it used to do, and it seemed to fall a few inches lower on his ribs. At 83, Papa's bulk was compressing into a more chunky space; he was shorter and rounder every time they met; his bushy hair was becoming frighteningly white but was still abundantly long where it sprouted from the two symmetrically deep pockets in his receding hairline. Papa's tufted eyebrows knitted together in the centre above his broad beak of a nose, and the deep creases on his weathered face dragged his eyes downwards as he scowled at George in what those well enough trained in his manner would recognise as welcoming affection.

"How are you Papa?"

"*Den boró na paraponethó*," Papa answered in Greek, as was his custom for family pleasantries.

George thought that Papa would have every right to complain – his knuckles were thick with arthritis, his elbows were purpled with psoriasis scabs below the short-sleeved cotton shirt, and below his khaki shorts his lower legs were tightly puffed up with retained fluid. Since the installation of a pacemaker three years ago, his heart had been beating steadily, and his blood pressure was good, but emphysema, the result of sixty years of smoking, was stalking him. The Angler's Rest at Brooklyn was now out of range for his daily walk and bending over to pick something up from the ground was a sure cause of dizziness to the point that it had already resulted in a couple of falls. Fortunately his bones were well padded thanks to Margarita's Greek treats and while he was on supplements for osteoporosis, he had not broken anything to date.

Papa sat down with a heavy puff of breath and reached immediately for a *kourabiethe*. Toffee, the family's short-haired ginger and white cat, appeared from nowhere and jumped onto the sofa beside him, reaching across his face with a paw to request a share in the biscuit. Papa transferred the biscuit to his other hand and let Toffee lick the almond sugar coating off his empty fingers.

"Toffee-*gata*, off you get," he said gently, pushing the cat off the sofa to the carpet where it checked for crumbs.

"Good flight?" Papa opened the conversation.

"Yes," George confirmed. "The flight and the train are easy. It takes as long as the flight just to drive from Warrandyte to Tullamarine – I wish we had a train line like you've got here."

"Christmas eve is busy. You've talked to Stavi?"

"A bit on the way from the station."

"About the church?"

"We talked about the business." The business, George thought, was a safe thing to talk about. All he had to do was ask "How's the business going?" and Stephen would then supply the rest of the conversation. George would hear about boats that had been bought and sold, new products that were revolutionising the boating industry, the Marine Board's authoritarian transgressions, onerous occupational health and safety regulations, annoyingly inefficient employees and amusingly foolish customers.

"I thought Stavi might have talked to you about the church."

"No Papa," George feigned ignorance. "What church do you mean?"

This was the prompt Papa was waiting for. He drained his coffee and opened up his manila folder, his breath wheezing noticeably with the effort of leaning over the coffee table. Toffee reared up on his back legs, put his front paws on the glass top of the table and inspected the *kourabiethe* plate, and Papa brushed him aside with the papers he had pulled out of the folder.

"The church hasn't been painted. This is terrible." Papa placed a photo that showed a cliff-side-view of the Church of Saint Nicholas in Firopotamos, on the table in front of George, followed by several photos that showed sections of the stonework in greater detail, evidencing disrepair and damage.

"This is the church in the picture you have in your bedroom?"

"Yes," Papa huffed as if George's question had been completely unnecessary. "You don't recognise your own church? Pah! Bicentenary Pascha. April. The church must be ready."

"Then we can pay someone over there to repair the church."

"No. One of us must do it. One of us, every generation, must do something of big repair for the church. This is the promise to Saint Nikolaos. Without this promise Thalassa comes for us. It is Stavros must do this, but if Stavros can't go, then it must be you."

George was momentarily struck silent with surprise. "Me?" was all he managed to say.

"Stavros won't go."

"Who painted the church last time?"

"Anton in 1983, and before then, Dimitry." Dimitry was George's uncle, two years younger than Papa, and Anton, his eldest son, was Stephen's age. Dimitry had two other sons and a daughter, some living in Milos and some in Athens, as George recalled. "Dimitry's family have done their share, it's our turn," Papa insisted.

"When did you repair the church?" George creased his brow, trying to squeeze some juice out of his memory. He did not recall that his family had been to Greece, and now that suddenly struck him as odd.

Papa was overly silent for a moment. He spotted Toffee's claw dragging a *kourabiethe* towards the edge of the plate, swatted the table and retrieved the biscuit, popping it into his mouth and excusing himself from making a reply.

"Did you do it before you immigrated?"

"I was soldier." Papa worked his mouth, clearing crumbs from his teeth.

"Did you and Mama ever go back to Greece?" Papa shook his head. "Why not? You had enough money." George persisted.

"We could not go. Your Mama not allowed."

"Why not?"

"You sound like five year old. Why? Why?" Papa was suddenly angry. "Government makes stupid rules. Your Mama not allowed back to Greece, according to *gamoto kyvérnisi*. We not want to go back anyway."

George decided to raise his further questions with Stephen or Mary instead of upsetting his father further.

"So … you never got to fulfil the promise to Saint Nikolaos for your generation …" George thought that he was beginning an argument towards the conclusion that it was not necessary to keep the promise any longer, but the statement had the reverse effect on Papa.

"And now you or Stavi MUST go or there is more bad luck. First Yia Yia, then Lizabeta, you MUST go, or it gets worse."

"It had nothing to do with not repairing the church!" George realised that he had raised his voice, probably not far above the norm for this household, but to a level unusual for himself. Margarita was hovering over a recipe book at the kitchen bench, casting an anxious frown over the top of her glasses towards them. "Saint Nikolaos is not in charge of the family's good or bad luck," he said firmly.

Papa dismissed George's opinion with a haughty wave. "You and your brother, you say exactly the same. You have been talking about this, I know. You are wrong. He MUST go and repair the church; this family has too much tragedy. I tell you this for your sake. It is too late for me, this is for you and your children."

From the kitchen Margarita watched both men fall into an angry silence, eyeing the cat as it licked the last of the almond sugar from the *kourabiethe* plate. They had the same dark stare from similarly deep-set brown eyes, she thought; the same determined, thin and straight upper lip, and essentially the same nose, though George's nose was still finely carved, while Papa's had become bulbous and red with age. George's shortcut hair was a signature of his role as an urban executive, while Papa's unkempt hair classified him as a nutty professor. The air between them was broody, pregnant with regrettable claims they might make on each other, and Margarita decided it would be prudent to interrupt.

"Toffee-*gata*! Get off that table!" Margarita ploughed into the middle of the ominous silence, flailing a tea towel at the cat. Toffee made haste off the table, but only so far as the door to Papa's room where he sat, calmly licking his paw. "Really men – why do you let him get away with that?" Margarita collected the plate from the table, and George took the opportunity to follow her with the cups, leaving Papa to return his photos to their folder, and puff his way back to his room.

~

The Kostis are storytellers. Not writers. The original shipwreck story has been retold through 3 generations to be saved in Papa's repertoire. Soon Stephen will be telling it to his grandchildren, and further across time, when it is 7 generations old, Dimitry will be telling it to his grandchildren, and still, no Kostis will write it down. Fortunately it is a simple story, not easily derailed by the ravages of time, changing customs or the narrator's personality. Some of the other stories that pencilled the contour lines on my husband's genetic map are more complicated and they tend to depart at one point or another from the truth for a journey through more captivating terrain ... even when they are still in the hands of the original storyteller. In all probability *mostly* when told by the original storyteller. Papa's story about his escape from Crete is a typical example - I personally heard it evolve over many tellings. The story is largely true, Aretha confirms, but when it comes to her own appearance in it ... well, she makes a disclaimer that Stavros had formed a different view of their courtship to her own, and it would not have been appropriate for her to correct him.

~

The Escape from Crete Story

May 1941: Rethymno, Crete

Frustrated and scared, Stavros kept pulling the trigger of his Mannlicher–Schönauer mountain carbine even though its rotary magazine was empty. It was the afternoon of May 28th. The 4th and 5th Greek Regiments had been fighting the German paratroopers for 7 days; gradually regaining the ground they had lost in the initial German offensive. Today the recapture of Perivolia should have been certain, but their guns were falling silent and it would be up to the Australians to take the town. The Greeks had no more ammunition and the allied bullets were useless in these much older Greek guns. Like some others in his own battalion, Stavros kept advancing, pretending to fire, making his way across the lines to blend in with the Australians of the 2/11th Battalion as they advanced on Perivolia.

The ruined streets of the town were only 100 metres away when Stavros made his last dash to the left to join the Australians. Shots shattered branches and leaves of the small tree he had tried to use for shelter and he felt a searing pain slice across his thigh, tearing his trousers. He rolled to the ground,

Thalassa

checking his leg and finding blood, but no disablement. The relentless fire from the town had him pinned down.

"Mate!" It was just one sharp shout to attract his attention and even as Stavros looked up, his right hand, in instinctive reaction, had caught the rifle the Australian digger threw at him. A magazine thudded into the ground by Stavros' knee and the digger ran on, weaving and firing for another twenty metres, before throwing himself into a crouch in front of a low stone wall.

Stavros was terrified for a moment that he would not know how to use the gun. But a quick glance at the Lee-Enfield's bolt action was enough. He stuffed the magazine in his pocket, lifted the rifle and let off a shot in the general direction of the village. Then he followed the digger's weaving course to the rock wall.

The Australian was loading a new magazine. Stavros took note of how it was done. *"Efharisto!"* he yelled.

"Don't mention it mate, I'm buggered if I'm gonna carry two." The Australian looked away to his left, where he saw the next signal to advance. "Keep the buggers off me!" he yelled, and ran for the town.

Stavros hadn't understood anything the man said, but the intent was clear. He lifted the gun and sprayed the already pockmarked walls of the village with bullets. Then he ran to catch up. In this way Stavros made his way into Perivolia, covering the digger and then running while the digger covered him. A part of him realised that he was carrying the gun that had belonged to the last man who did this, but there was no time to over-think that. He ran until the opposing fire had ceased. The Germans had fallen back.

The Australian stopped in a *platia,* where a number of soldiers were re-grouping. He stood square and tall in front of Stavros and gave him a measured look, taking in the sweaty black hair under the beaten metal hat, the stubbled grime on Stavros' face, the tattered uniform, bloodied pants and threadbare boots.

"You're just a spring chicken, what are you – 18 maybe? You're a mess, mate," he concluded, "but maybe I don't look that great myself." He wiped a smear of grease off his cheek and examined it with sharp blue eyes before sweeping off his slouch hat and letting a sticky wad of blonde hair fall free across his brow. "Nick Foster, AIF 2nd unit 11th Battalion."

Stavros didn't understand many of the words, but he did understand the extended hand and its firm grip. "Stavros Kostis, 4th Regiment."

"You need a Band-Aid, mate." Nick's advice was an understatement. Blood was steadily soaking through Stavros' trousers. "Let's find first aid." He motioned for Stavros to follow him, and Stavros did so, struck with considerable admiration for his new Aussie friend.

It took a long time for them to find any first aid, and as they worked their way amongst the increasing crowd in the battered streets around the square, Stavros noticed that the mood, at first jubilant with victory, was changing. The ANZACs were looking angry, talking to each other with voices ripe with disgust.

"Fucking hell!" (Stavros understood this exclamation from one digger who had engaged Nick in conversation.) "How can they order us to get here and then say we have to go back now? How can there be no more ammunition! Go back where? The fucking Greeks have left us? We're defending their fucking island and they've left us?" The Australian leant threateningly towards Stavros and Stavros shifted behind Nick even though he didn't know why he had attracted this anger.

"Leave him out of it." Nick pushed a hand against the other Australian's shoulder. "*He* didn't leave us. It's not his fault."

There were other Greek soldiers in the crowd and gradually Stavros learnt what had happened. The Greek regiments, having run out of ammunition, had been ordered back to yesterday's camp. There was a rumour that they were going to abandon their positions altogether. The Australian Battalions were also running short on supplies. While the battle for Rethymno and Heraklion had gone well, rumour had it that Maleme had been lost and the Germans had control of the airstrip. There would be German reinforcements on the ground tomorrow.

After a few hours, during which an Australian medical officer dressed and bandaged Stavros' leg, the ANZACs were ordered to fall back, abandoning the ground they had won that day. Not knowing what else to do, Stavros stayed close to Nick. As the rumours gained legitimacy overnight the Australians learnt that the British had left them before the Greeks. The British had been heading for an evacuation site on the South coast since the 27th – there was an angry undercurrent saying that the British had sacrificed the two Australian Battalions in Rethymno as a rearguard distraction. There was not going to be any air support. Stavros heard many new words from the Australian vernacular that night, and the way they were delivered let him know he should be careful about repeating them.

The next morning Major Sandover addressed his troops. The German reinforcements had arrived at Maleme, they had Panzer tanks with them, and the Australian Battalions at Rethymno were cut off from the other allied troops. Their situation was hopeless. The Allied Command had ordered surrender; but Sandover made it clear to his men that they had a choice. They could surrender or they could individually take their chances on an escape over the mountains of Crete, hoping for evacuation from the South coast.

~

Nick and his closest friends were huddled deep in conversation, lower backs against the rough clay sides of a trench, khaki-clad knees inter-leaved. Stavros sat a little apart, acutely sensitive to every glance the diggers made in his direction.

"I'm not fucking surrendering."

"We can't get through those bloody mountains!"
"We've no idea where to go."
"Wouldn't *he* know?"
"He's Greek, not Cretan."
"Same fucking language isn't it?"
"If Jerry catches us on the run they'll kill us."
"If the Greek surrenders they'll kill him."

The conversation went on for a long time, while Stavros waited for a verdict that he instinctively knew was going to be crucial to him. In the end, three diggers had walked away, and three remained. Nick beckoned Stavros to come closer.

"They're surrendering mate. *Paradosi.*" Nick didn't pronounce the word properly, but Stavros nodded that he understood. "Not us though mate." Nick indicated himself and the other two diggers who had stayed behind him. "*Ochi Paradosi.*" Stavros nodded again.

Nick drew a sausage shape in the dust on the floor of the trench and Stavros stared at it in puzzlement, waiting for Nick to make his intention clear.

"We're here," Nick dug a finger hole in the dirt on the Northern side of his map. "Can you take us here?" He walked his fingers across to the opposite side of the map. Stavros was still puzzled. "*Edo, Rethymno.*" Nick's fingers walked across the map again. "*Na edo, Sfakia.*"

Stavros thought he knew what Nick was asking, and even though he had been in Crete no longer than the other allied soldiers who had been evacuated from the Greek mainland just four weeks ago, he certainly knew which answer would be in his best interest.

"Yes," he said, nodding vigorously.

~

By nightfall Stavros had a backpack full of food, four water bottles, a camouflage blanket, a slouch hat, army gloves and a pair of pre-loved AIF boots, carefully chosen to be the right fit. He knew the Aussies wanted to go to a place called Sfakia on the South coast, where evacuees were meeting ships sent by the British and Australian navies. He also knew that German forces had control of the North coast of Crete to the East and West of them, and also of the road that led away to the South through a valley. The only way to go, he decided, was inland across the mountains that rose steeply behind the allied camp, and because the mountains were mostly exposed rock the only time to go was night. That night, 30th May, they set out.

Stavros had two significant advantages over the Australians. The first was language, of course, but the other was navigation. Like all Kostis sailors, he had grown up with the stars, and he had a map of the Greek islands implanted in his brain. Once he had seen a proper map showing where the Aussies wanted to go he knew exactly how to get there. The problem was the terrain in between … and there, the Australians showed their survival skills admirably.

It was 36 kms by line-of-sight from Rethymno to Sfakia. On an average sailing day the caïque that Stavros had been forced to hand over to the Germans in Milos could have covered that distance in 4 hours. At a brisk walk soldiers would be able to cover it in 6 hours. But this was a scramble by night over high mountains peppered with boulders and salted with gravel. Stavros was at first puzzled when the Aussies gloved-up and motioned to him to do the same, but within minutes of starting the first climb he found himself grabbing for holds amongst thorny bushes that severely tested even the thick gloves.

When dawn brought some definition to the landscape around them, Stavros reckoned they had covered only 4 kms in the whole night. They could not see either coast. While Stavros didn't want to leave his direct track, Nick insisted they take a detour to the East where there was a gully offering some shelter. The Aussies rigged a plastic sheet that dripped water from condensation into a bowl during the hot day; they strung their camouflage blankets between rocks and bunkered down to sleep as if they had no concerns in the world. Stavros sat nervously, shrinking from the German planes that flew overhead; watching the sides of the valley for German soldiers. But when no one had spotted them by mid-day, he finally fell asleep.

At night after a meagre ration of food and a share of the water collected in the bowl, the Aussies were ready to set off again, but they started in exactly the wrong direction. When Stavros stopped them, pointing the other way, a short but vehement argument ensued between them. A compass materialised, lit briefly by a match and the argument ended with laughter and backslapping. The men followed Stavros and didn't question him again. They tramped and scrambled across the mountain range all night without pause or complaint.

On the third night the group came upon a farmer's hut where they could see light beckoning through the windows. They crept near and lay in the field listening, and soon a burst of laughter and chatter told them that the occupants were German.

The Aussies weren't content to skulk away. Their water bottles were empty. A methodical search was performed; the farmer's well was located; in total silence the bucket was drawn and the bottles were filled. Stavros noticed a field of honeydew melons and picked four of them … not quite ripe, but a useful supplement to their rations. Two motorbikes were also found, which occasioned a flurry of hand signals. Nick shook his head and drew a flat hand across his neck, and the group silently moved on.

In the rest of that night they made virtually no progress at all. They had reached the edge of a gorge that was so steep that they had to wait until dawn so that they could see the best way to cross it. It took all of the next morning to climb down into the gorge, following what seemed to be a goat track, clinging to the craggy side wall, eyes glued to every footfall, praying that there were no German's watching. Their reward at the bottom of the gorge was a shallow creek of fresh water. They followed the creek for the rest of the day, which was much easier going than the mountainside at night, and when they reached a path that they could use to climb out of the gorge a debate ensued. Stavros argued with conviction-filled but inadequate English, that the gorge was not heading towards Sfakia, it was going to meet the sea somewhere well to the East. Nick argued that the Germans would be patrolling the gorges, looking for escapees. Then there was the probability of waterfalls and cliffs, and of having to retrace their steps. Not knowing if it was the right decision, they decided to climb out of the gorge, stay high and keep following Stavros in his unerring return to track.

It was on the morning of the 6th June that they finally looked down on Sfakia, and came to the grim realisation that there were no naval ships standing off the coast, and there were Panzer tanks in the town streets.

~

Stavros shed the trappings of the AIF and crept amongst the outlying houses of Sfakia in his grubby Greek clothing. He spied on the houses, listened hard for conversations, trying to decide which household to approach. After a while he realised that it was fear and procrastination that stopped him from choosing a house, rather than concrete reasoning. He sat for a long time alongside a hole in a low stone fence, watching a pretty girl with olive skin, dark eyes and long hair braids hanging out some washing. It was her beauty, he was to claim ever afterwards, that made him choose that house.

"Don't be scared!" he shushed her urgently when his appearance at the back door made her suck in her breath with a loud gasp. "I'm not going to hurt you. I need help, are there any Germans here?" The girl shook her head, wide-eyed. "Can I speak to your father?" The girl shook her head again. "Your mother?" The girl held up a hand to him and for the first time

Stavros detected some sympathy. He waited, looking around furtively, until a middle-aged Cretan woman appeared.

The woman was a larger, less attractive version of her daughter. She looked Stavros up and down grimly, saying nothing. Then she waved him into the house and closed the door.

"Sit," she told him brusquely, scraping a wooden chair on the wooden floor of the room that served as both a kitchen and living area. "Where have you come from?" She pulled a cloth off a loaf of bread and cut a slice for him.

"Rethymno."

"How did you get here?"

"Walked over the mountains." Stavros stuffed the delicious bread into his mouth, and immediately felt embarrassed by the girl's dark eyes watching him from behind her mother's back.

"What's your plan? The navy has gone."

"Are there soldiers in the village waiting for rescue?"

"Maybe." Stavros realised from the heavy caution in her voice that she thought he could be a spy. He too needed to be careful that she was not someone who would betray them to the Germans.

"We need a boat." This had not been discussed with the others; they were hoping that there was an existing allied escape route. Stavros hadn't thought the boat idea through.

"We?"

"Four of us."

For a long moment the woman examined him, evaluating the risks. "I can help just you." With that she disappeared into the next room, leaving him in an awkward silence with the beautiful girl.

"There are no boats," the girl broke the silence. "*They,*" she said the word with a contemptuous spit, "have control of the fuel. They give the old men only so much each day as they need to go out fishing, and bring the catch back to feed them."

"A sailing boat? An unused one?"

The girl looked thoughtful, but didn't reply before her mother called "Aretha, our friend needs to wash, get some water." Stavros fancied that Aretha flashed her eyes at him conspiratorially as she left the room.

Aretha's mother brought out a bundle of Cretan clothes. She hesitated for a moment as she held them out to him, but when Stavros checked her face for rejection what he saw was an indrawn sadness. She patted the pad of clothes gently and handed them over wordlessly, motioning him to follow her. She showed him into a laundry to the left of the back door that also served as a washroom. Aretha left a wooden pail of water alongside the cement trough and pointed out the bar of soap she had been using to wash the clothes.

Stavros thought it was the best bath he had ever had. He fancied Aretha was spying on him. The Cretan clothes were a good fit; he felt like a new man and he was sure Aretha gave him an appreciative look when he returned to the house.

Aretha's mother was sitting at the table in the chair he had previously occupied, staring at some papers on the table. She handed the papers over, watching him with the same air of despondency.

They were identity papers, and Stavros was surprised to find that the face staring out of the photo bore a passable resemblance to his own.

"Your son?" Stavros mumbled, realising what the offer meant.

The woman nodded. "Be careful, they take our young men and execute them so they can't be part of the resistance. Now you go," she said, "and don't come back."

~

Stavros disobeyed her, because of the beautiful girl. Aretha's wonderful eyes, he said ever afterwards, had begged him to come back, countermanding her mother.

With the identity papers and the Cretan clothes, Stavros was able to walk relatively freely in Sfakia, though he avoided contact with German patrols. He fetched water and food for the Aussies who made camp behind some straw in an abandoned goat shed some distance from town. He studied the waterfront intently, but his plan to steal a boat was not looking good. The fishing dinghies that were powered with outboard motors were not suitable for the 300km crossing to Egypt, even if he could get a few tanks of fuel it would not last the distance. There were only a very few sailing boats in the port, and they had been stripped of their sails. The locals would talk about the evacuation that had taken place already, but conversation stonewalled when he asked whether any more evacuations were planned.

After a few days Stavros appeared again as Aretha was drawing water from the well. This time he did not ask for her mother. He explained that he needed a sail so that he could take one of the sailing boats.

"I know which boat." Aretha surprised him, saying this before he had even launched into his excuses for stealing a boat, or a description of the type of sail he needed.

"In two days, I will come back from the market along the quay. I will put my bags down in front of the boat and tie my skirt. You can take the boat one hour after dark that night. By that time the sail and two oars will be in the boat. You bring water and food."

Stavros gazed at Aretha with deepened respect, realising that she must be working with the Cretan resistance to speak with such certainty.

"I will bring the boat back," he said lamely, knowing the improbability.

"You don't need to, the owner is dead," Aretha replied bluntly. "Now go."

At dusk on the day when he had watched her tie her skirt at the quay, Stavros appeared again at the back door of the house, surprising Aretha. He pressed the only thing he could give her into her hand ... a small silver cross on a chain.

"I will come back for you when this is over, I swear it." Stavros took Aretha's stunned surprise as acceptance. He planted a kiss on her cheek and disappeared over the stone wall.

~

December 2007: Brooklyn, New South Wales

When Aretha was still alive, it was at this point in the story that she would hold forward the silver cross on its chain around her neck, and flutter her eyelids dramatically at Stavros.

In her absence, on this Christmas Eve, Stavros raised his glass of ouzo to the empty chair at the head of the table and watched the candle flame reflections bounce off the angles of crystal. Then he downed the ouzo in one gulp and sighed loudly.

"This is the last Christmas for your Pappous" he repeated to no one in particular. "Those wonderful eyes, they beg me to come to her."

"You said that last year Pappous," Melinda and Katherine chimed together.

In response Stavros patted his puffy, purple-veined hands on the table, and sighed. He gestured to the empty, open fireplace. "Tonight, Saint Nick he will realise I am left behind." Saint Nicholas, patron saint of seamen everywhere, was better known to this latest generation of the Kostis family as the Saint Nick who clambered down chimneys on Christmas Eve.

"Nick Foster died in July," Margarita said as an aside to George, intending the remark as an explanation for Stavros' claim that he had been 'left behind'. "We got a letter from Sam, after the funeral had already been held." Sam, who had been one of Stephen's closest childhood friends, was Nick Foster's son. There had been many occasions when the 'Saint Nick and Escape From Crete' story had been told in duet with Nick and Stavros each contributing their separate parts in greater detail to the wider audience of both the Kostis and Foster families.

When on his own, Pappous would give a slightly different version of the story, which explained how he had met Yia Yia or why he had decided to immigrate to Australia after the war. The immigration story had a second half that ended with their arrival on Nick's home turf - Western Sydney. Usually these days the story ended with Yia Yia's wonderful eyes.

"That was sad news for Pappous, though it's such a relief really; Nick was in such a dreadful state, he didn't know anyone any more. We hadn't taken Pappous to visit him for more than a year, it only made him upset," Margarita continued. "For all that ... being friends for so long, the dementia, and even when he heard of Nick's death ... Pappous never wavered in his belief that the man was a personification of St Nicholas."

"Your Pappous *polý kaló náftis* – very good sailor. Thalassa, she is kind with me." Stavros confirmed this to Melinda and Katherine, since they were the only ones still listening to him. Dimitry and Michael were in the TV-room waging an interstellar war on their X-box 360, and Stephen had moved to the bar to look for a suitable port or whisky.

Melinda and Katherine nodded kindly, and Stavros pulled himself to his feet and kissed each of them on the cheek. "Goodnight Pappous" they chimed.

"*Kalinýchta,*" Stavros took them all in with a sweeping glance and a wave of his hand and headed unsteadily towards his apartment. A variety of goodnights and grunts followed him.

"Papa spoke to me about going to Greece", George raised the subject as Stephen handed him a glass of Glenfiddich. "I reckon we should just pay someone to paint the church and be done with it."

"That's what I said; but no." Stephen's response was gruff. "Apparently I have to do it myself, as the next generation Stavros, or Saint Nikolaos will turn his back on our family. Apparently I have to go for a whole month and I have to be there to participate in the bicentennial service and the Easter rituals."

Thalassa

George could see the problem. Not only was Stephen busy at home, he had completely eschewed the Orthodox Catholic faith. George knew for a fact that it was Margarita who had kept the Greek spirit burning in her family and had made it possible for Pappous and Yia Yia to come to live with them; Stephen–nee Stavros V–had wanted to renounce his origins completely. The fifties and sixties were hard years for the Australian children of Greek immigrants. It had been easier on George as the third child born to Stavros and Aretha; the weight of cultural expectation and the job of breaking their parents in to The Australian Way, had fallen very unfairly on Stephen and Mary.

"Well, he is insisting that one of us has to go. I'm not sure if he's asking me to convince you, or if he's given up on you and is asking me to go instead."

Stephen looked at George with new interest. "Would you go?"

"Look ... I'm busy too you know. I can't just go to Greece for a month. And what do I know about the Orthodox rituals, let alone renovating a church!"

"It's bullshit, whatever he said to you, about the bad luck." Stephen spoke vehemently into his whisky, not wanting to connect with George's eyes.

"Damn right!" The two men were silent for a long moment, stewing thoughts about bad luck that neither would vent. "We'll pay a painter." George concluded.

"Yep."

"So are Mary and Ian coming for lunch tomorrow?" George asked, even though he already knew the answer.

"Yep, in fact Mary's coming early, in time for church. Papa asked her as his 'last Christmas wish'. Ironic isn't it, they excommunicate her, and *now* he wants her to go to church with him!"

"It wasn't excommunication Stephen," George corrected his brother patiently.

"Whatever, same effect," Stephen underlined his point with a wave of his whisky glass. "It was a whole lot of shit."

~

It was almost Christmas day. Stephen had wished George goodnight at the bottom of the stairs and entered his own bedroom assuming that Margarita would already be asleep. Instead she had wrapping paper, trinkets, and knitted wool Christmas stockings scattered across their king size bed. He smiled at the trappings of old Saint Nick even as his heart sank at the un-readiness of his bed.

"Won't be long," Margarita, always adept at reading thoughts, promised him.

"Aren't they a bit old for this?"

"Never. And there's Sally and Leanne." Margarita pointed at the two larger Christmas sacks that she had made up for Mary's grandchildren and had propped against the wall alongside the bedroom door ready for their visit the next day.

Stephen watched Margarita drop a bag of gold foil covered chocolate coins into each stocking. "Five?"

"George."

"He is *definitely* too old. Where's mine then?"

"You've got to wait until morning to find out if you've been a good boy."

Stephen harrumphed at the predictable exchange and went into the ensuite for a pee and a wash. When he came back Margarita handed him the five stockings.

"Off you go," she gave him a brief kiss on the lips as she stretched up to put a red cap with a white tassel on his head.

With his Santa hat on Stephen crept up the stairs, into each child's bedroom and hung a stocking on the end of each bed. When he reached George's room he hung the stocking on the door handle. He then tiptoed downstairs again, enjoying his simple role for yet another year. All over Australia tonight, he thought happily, there were parents creeping around performing the Christmas stocking ritual, just like him. He knew he would be sad when the year came that Margarita did not send him off with an armful of stockings.

Back in his room, the bed had been cleared, Margarita was in it, and on his bedside table was a glass of milk and a Tim Tam biscuit. Stephen sat on the bed, munched his Santa reward and drank his milk obediently. He knew there would be no sex tonight. The customary cues hadn't been exchanged, it was late, and Margarita's mind was focussed on Christmas preparations. He slid under the covers, wrapped his arms around her in a hug and she gave him a long, friendly goodnight kiss. They lay there together, Margarita's mind running through her preparations for Christmas day, the Church timetable, the food, the presents, while Stephen was reminiscing on the Christmases of his own childhood.

It was his fifth Christmas when Stephen realised that Australian children exchanged Christmas gifts on Christmas day, while he had to wait until New Year's Day, as was the Greek custom. It was one of the earliest memories he had of the injustice of being Greek first, Australian second. The Fosters had come to visit on Boxing Day, and Sam had wobbled up the drive on a spanking fire-red bike. Whether his father had always intended to give him a bike that Christmas, or whether he rushed out to get one to match Sam's, Stephen would never know, but nevertheless, for seven days Stephen had to watch Sam learning to ride, trying to cajole Sam into letting him have a go, utterly envious of Sam's good fortune. When Stephen's bike arrived on New Year's Day it was a wonderful relief, but it was lacking the joy that would have accompanied it as a Christmas surprise.

It wasn't until George's second Christmas, when Stephen was 10, that the Kostis' Christmas was realigned to the Australian standard. Mama had been trying to persuade Stephen and Mary to join in the charade, so that George could enjoy the Santa story even though his older siblings knew by now that Santa was really Papa. Stephen's very firm trade-off was that Santa had to visit the Kostis family on Christmas eve, like 'normal Australians', and so it was until George's school friends apprised him of the shocking truth several years later. Stephen thinks of it as the first, and maybe the greatest, of several concessions he won for his little brother.

George has only the barest of memories of the Greek Orthodox Community at Earlwood in Western Sydney, whereas Stephen and Mary had been forced to spend much of their time outside school hours attending classes in Greek language and Orthodoxy. On Sundays when Sam was out surfing or just hanging out with the girls at the beach, Stephen was squirming on uncomfortable wooden pews, listening to old men in long black robes and square *Kalimafi* hats, moralising against the many sins that tempted young men in this wayward Antipodean culture. On festival Saturdays, when Sam was playing cricket or rugby, Stephen was required to dress up in musty traditional costume and perform Greek dances with other boys he did not like. He wanted to hang out with his Australian mates; he wanted to be like all the other boys at his school. He didn't invite his friends to the festival days ... indeed, he lied to them about what he was doing on the weekend to make sure they wouldn't come and laugh at him.

Twice a week after school Mama took Stephen and Mary to Greek classes because she thought their ancestral language needed protection against the subversion of the babble that was spoken at school. Stephen thought it should have been the other way round - he should have been taking Mama to English classes. At home she spoke nothing but Greek, and she had so little English and was so scared of the Australians around her that she had almost made herself a prisoner in her own house. She took them to Greek classes, Stephen knew, in order to enjoy a Greek-speaking social outing herself. Papa did speak quite reasonable English - he had picked it up well during his time with the British forces in Egypt - but at home for Mama's sake he continued to speak Greek. Stephen thought Papa hadn't done Mama any favours, he should have insisted on speaking English at home so that Mama learnt. Stephen didn't like to bring his friends home; Mama and Papa would carry right on talking in Greek even though his Australian mates couldn't understand and he would have to interpret for them. Stephen thought it was very rude of them. Sam was the only exception; Papa would speak to Sam in English. It was blatant discrimination, due Papa's wartime friendship with Nick Foster. Papa held a great prejudice against the Australians he didn't know; Nick's family on the other hand, were always welcome. Stephen had once shouted at his father words to the effect that if Papa could just get to know other Australians he would find that they were just like Sam's family, they could be good friends too. But Papa's views were seldom changed by Stephen's arguments.

There had come a day when Stephen was nearing 16 and he wanted to invite a mixed group of friends to his place for his birthday party, as many of his peers had done that year, but Papa had flatly refused. Papa would only allow a party with the Greek Community in the Earlwood church hall. Stephen had lost the yelling match, and had stormed out of the house with tears in his eyes and vitriolic swear words running from his tongue in both English and Greek. The impossible happened ... Papa reneged and Stephen had his 16th birthday party at home. It was years afterwards that Stephen found out from Sam that Nick had intervened on Stephen's behalf. There were, of course, some friends who brought dope and whisky, but surprisingly Papa simply sat smoking on the front veranda throughout the party and turned a blind eye to everything that went on in the house.

That party introduced Stephen to some of his first business contacts. One of the ways in which Papa controlled Stephen's social activities was to limit him to a near-to-nothing allowance and it made it impossible for him to keep up with his mates in cigarettes, whisky and entertainments for girls. Stephen started pocketing some extra money by being a go-between, exchanging packets of dope for cash, initially just at school, but by the end of his 17th year he was supplying marijuana to a large proportion of the school students between Marrickville and Bexley. He had told his parents that he was earning money from a mail delivery run, and when he bought his own bright red Monaro to facilitate his delivery business they thought nothing of it. Stephen still marvels at how innocent his parents were, that they believed he could afford to buy that car from the proceeds of a mail run. It disappoints him, at some level; he thinks they didn't love him enough to notice. He would certainly be on top of the matter if Dimitry or Michael started spending money they should not have.

In fact, Stephen had handed over his mail run to Mary … retaining a commission of only 10%, which he thought justified because he was running a cover for her with Mama. Mama had refused to let Mary be out on the streets without a chaperone, so supposedly Mary and Stephen were delivering local papers and junk mail together, while in reality Mary was filling up mail boxes while Stephen was running dope. Back then; Stephen remembers nostalgically, Mary used to do what he told her to do.

'Look after your *adelfi*?', Mama would say. 'She's your responsibility.' Stephen was only three years older, but from the day Mary had started kindergarten, he had been her caretaker. With his mother unable to speak English, and his father away from home for a 10-hour working day, it had been Stephen's responsibility to take Mary to her first day at school, find her classroom and introduce her to her teacher. For the rest of his primary years, and even when he moved to the high school over the road, it had been Stephen's job to escort Mary to and from school. When he had rugby practice he had to walk Mary home first, and run back to school.

Mary's worst enemies, in Stephen's opinion, weren't out in the street; they were in the playground. The other girls in her class bullied her. They didn't do it when he was around, but he would see her crying and she would tell him her story. One day when he was in year 5, he had given two of the bullies a hiding. It cost him a selection on the interschool rugby team because the wise-ass teacher, who had believed the girls' complaint, put him on a full term of detention on the rugby practice afternoon. It also, Stephen believes, cost him a prefecture in year 6, and he couldn't even reminisce that it was worthwhile, because when they all came across the road to the high school, Mary became best friends with the girls who had once been her bullies. They'd sit together behind the toilet block with their skirts pulled up around their hips, legs out in the sun, passing a cigarette around between them … and by that time, when he was telling her she mustn't do that … Mary wasn't obedient to Stephen any more.

The rugby forward from Boyle house who had the nerve to tell Stephen his fifteen-year-old sister was a slut was rewarded with a badly broken nose. Stephen was suspended for two matches, having successfully mitigated his punishment by calling in Sam as a witness to the provocation he had received. Stephen knew the truth behind the slur was that Mary had sensibly refused the dick-head's invitation to a party. It didn't help, the way Mary was behaving at school … but Stephen knew most of the other girls in her year were doing the same thing. Guys picked on Mary because she was by far the most beautiful and they all wanted her. Stephen had refused multiple requests for introductions … even when the requests came from his friends. If Mama had known anything of the attention Mary was attracting, she would have moved Mary to the Convent school.

It was Sam who had put Mary straight about not looking and behaving like a slut. In a thorough dressing down Sam had told Mary what he thought of her 'friends'; had told her bluntly what the boys in her year were thinking and that he himself thought she was 'pathetic'. When Mary had turned to Stephen in tears, expecting him to defend her, Stephen had told her Sam was 'dead right'. Mary had changed after that, and Stephen knew it was in order to please Sam. She wore only a fraction of the makeup, changed her hairstyle and looked much better for it. She dropped that troublesome group of girls and, having made friends with a girl that Sam had his eye on, she even started to take an interest in politics and became involved with the anti-war movement.

When Stephen was called up on his 18th birthday in 1970 Mary was beside herself with fear and rage. Stephen was upset too, not because he was anti-war, but because it was going to put an end to his lucrative business. A consolation was that Sam, already passed over by the draft, volunteered to go too. Stephen was soon back in business in Vietnam and there was so much easy money in that market that within a year he regarded himself as a substantially wealthy man, even if most of the money was lying untouchable in a secret bank account. When their unit was due home at the end of 1971, beginning Australia's withdrawal from the war, Stephen and Sam transferred to the Army training unit, AATTV, so they could stay in Vietnam. Stephen wanted to continue his business; Sam had a sideline writing news stories from the front, selling them to American magazines; neither was ready to leave. Stephen used some of his small change to buy Sam and himself a week of R&R between jobs at the right time to go to the Sunbury music festival-Australia's first Woodstock-in Melbourne in January 1972. Mary was desperately jealous when he told her in a letter ... more than anything else she wanted to go to that festival.

Mary, however, was firmly in Mama's control; Mama and her cronies at the Greek Club were planning Mary's life for her. The sons of those who Mama and her closest friends thought were 'good Greek' families had been thoroughly evaluated in the church kitchen, sifted through and appraised as prospective husbands. Mama had a list of suitors for Mary. Vasilis, Fabris, Christos, in that order. After a long time on the wait list she had succeeded in getting Mary into the Marist Sister's girls' school at Woolwich for years 11 and 12. Mama travelled by train to pick Mary up directly from school, supervised all invitations and chaperoned her to the very few events Mama sanctioned. Getting Mary to Sunbury took much more than drug money; it took Stephen's sincere brotherly-care promises and Mary's tearful remonstrations that traded on Mama's guilt that Mary would miss out on seeing her brother during his brief respite from the war if she didn't go to Melbourne. That escapade ended up in tears, Stephen admits, but on balance, he thinks, he did Mary an enormous favour helping her break out of the confines of Mama's Greek Community.

Back in Vietnam, and even wealthier towards the end of 1972, Stephen was treading on the territorial toes of some dealers much tougher than he was. One night he found himself face down in the streaming mud and shit of a Saigon gutter with the barrel of a revolver pressed into the back of his neck and a stream of Bronx invective pouring over his head. He was still struggling to work out what had happened when he heard Sam's voice, authoritative and precise.

"Step away from him mate, put the gun down and we'll all go our separate ways."

Stephen's neck was released, and he heard the gun clatter to the ground; saw Sam's boot swing; saw the gun slide away into a muddy sinkhole. He clambered warily to his feet, feeling dizzy, gingerly touching the back of his head and finding his hand wet with blood. He felt like everything that was happening was something he had seen before, and he couldn't figure out the timeline. His memory reboots, waking up in Sam's room at the barracks with the worst headache he had ever known.

That close call, Sam's hard words to him afterwards and, not least, the withdrawal of the AATTV in December 1972, ending Australia's troop involvement in the Vietnam War, made Stephen reassess his vocation. On departure from Vietnam he invested his secret account and remaining stock-in-trade in an ocean yacht with a discretely fitted hull cavity. He and Sam picked the yacht up from Haiti, where they had spent a month learning to sail with some American ex-marines who accompanied them as far as the little coastal town of Bahía Solano in Colombia. From there the marines travelled inland to take advantage of the opportunities they had heard of in the troubled district of Quibdo, while Stephen and Sam sailed across the Pacific to Sydney.

In Sydney Stephen sold the yacht for considerably more than he had spent. He could have lucratively traded drugs for years but, as a concession to Sam, he had made a one-off discount deal with a local rookie and drew a line under his drug-dealing career. Just days after that deal the shit had hit the fan over Mary, and Sam was gone. Back to Vietnam to be a freelance correspondent, leaving Stephen's plans for a joint business in ruins.

Stephen thinks of himself as someone who 'rolls with the punches'. His self-narrative has him fighting his way resolutely into an alternative life-plan. But he admits it did help that Sam had left without making any claim on the substantial profit made on the drugs. Stephen had spent half of the proceeds on a Marine dealership at Drummoyne, in the inner West of Sydney, which he ran himself. With Sam's half he rescued Papa from a tedious job in the Arnotts biscuit packing department at Homebush by buying, in Papa's name, a Marina boat hire and chandlery in Brooklyn. This sea change, when George was just 12, away from Earlwood to Brooklyn, rearranged everything about George's childhood. Papa was by-the-sea-in-boats happy, making it his business to collaborate with Australians, Mama was miserable without her Greek community. Mary, banished from the family home, stayed behind in Sydney with Stephen in a rented flat and George spent a typically Australian childhood in Brooklyn.

Thalassa

On this night in his new house in Brooklyn, Stephen has told George this story about his broken partnership with Sam, and about the origins of the business and the causal factors that determined much of George's life, for the first time. Stephen was gratified by George's evident surprise; he had not given any thought to what George knew or didn't know before, and now that George knows Stephen's side of the family story, Stephen smugly thinks George will be feeling indebted to him.

George is actually lying in bed feeling startled. It is not that anyone ever lied to him, he realises; it is that he had made childish assumptions. He had always thought that it was Papa who had heroically made a new and better life for them all. In an hour of whisky-flavoured family exposition Stephen has blown George's personal childhood story away, and George is unsettled by the new version; disturbed by his brother's admission to such high-order drug-dealing. How could he reconcile his ideal of the person who was his brother with the story he now knows? Did Papa know where the money came from? Margarita? Mary? What had Mama known about it?

He wonders what Liz would make of it, he wants to tell her how it makes him feel, he wants to give it to her to knit the fragments back together into something he can sleep on safely.

Aretha does not see Stephen's story because she does not want to. She suffers because George is aching for me and in this, I do understand her. Whatever our differences, she is the mother of the man I love.

~

Like the child he is, when we first arrive in Brooklyn and he is suddenly lost of his adélfia, my Giorgos is lying there silently crying into sleep.

Giorgos, he is a good boy, always a good boy. He did everything his mama told him, even when he was small. He always love his papa. When he was little and his papa was home being *melancholikós* for the packing of biscuits in the factory all day, he would go and sit at Papa's feet and stroke his legs which are so tired for standing still. And when my Stavi has stormed away after arguing, Giorgos he comes to ask 'Can I do it Papa?' even though he is not big enough yet. He watch all the things the other two do wrong, and he learns not to do these things. He never need to be told. He becomes good at things just by watching. He is a clever boy. Papa says he never teach him but one day he tie the bowline knot. Then he says 'I can do it Papa', and Papa is so surprised. That is our Giorgos.

He is not a hot head like Stavi, and he is not silly for attention like Maria. He never fights in school, and so I do not mind that he plays with the Australian boys. He is good with the bat in cricket, and he does not want to play this rugby game that I hate. Papa says he could win the top prize at cricket, but he doesn't try hard enough. Papa says he never wins the top prize in the sailing either, though Papa has given him the best Mirror boat. I think he doesn't want to win. I think he lets other boys win. I think he is a nice boy for this, but his Papa thinks he is weak.

We think that he will not try hard enough to win his girl. But he surprise us. One day he bring her home and tell us he is engaged, and we are not even knowing he has a girlfriend. Like tying the bowline. He does it when we are not watching. And even though Lizabeta is Australian, I am glad that Giorgos is going to get married and I make no fuss. But when I find out this girl does not believe in God, and they will be married in a garden, not the Church ... oh the pain it is dreadful, and I blame myself for letting Giorgos play cricket instead of going to church. I blame Papa that he does not know any Greek girls his age because we live here at Brooklyn. But Giorgos, he is not here and he does not know I think this. He never knows he breaks my heart over this. Papa tells me I must cope with this. I must not drive our Giorgos away like I drive Maria away.

But we lose Giorgos anyway, because he stays in Melbourne for Lizabeta, and for this Papa is to blame. Because Giorgos, he *want to be an architect. He watch the builders when we rebuild the Marina. He with them every afternoon after school and he learn the building by watching. He like the plans and he draw his own plans on play paper. But when he want to do that drawing at school, Papa make him do maths, because what good is drawing? In our business he need an accountant, he do not need an architect. Giorgos, he is clever with maths. His teachers say so, but he is not working hard enough to get the top marks, and the university in Sydney do not let him in. Instead the university in Melbourne agrees, and Papa says he must go there, because he must be an accountant. So this is Papa's mistake, because Giorgos meets Lizabeta and he doesn't come back.*

Except for holidays, and this is not enough. I love my engónia and want them here same as the children of Margarita and Stavi. It is no matter anymore that Giorgos and Lizabeta are not really married. This does not matter to me anymore. These are all my engónia, same, same. Papa is surprised I talk English with them. He thinks I have learnt no English in all the years. But the children have no Greek, which makes me very sad. I must speak to them, so I speak English. Papa says I am soft now with the rules, but so? It is for their parents to make the rules, and for me to be Yia Yia.

Giorgos, he is my last baby, the one who stayed inside me after the two I lost before they were born. He is in the very special place in my heart. It aches and aches, in this special place to see him suffer. He does not deserve this suffering. Papa says it is him who is to blame for this. The blessing of Saint Nikolaos has been broken. But it is because of me we cannot go home and the blessing it breaks, and the cancer it has already come for me. And this should be enough punishment. Why does Giorgos lose the one he loves? Arghhh, such a curse!

Papa says it is the firstborn son's duty to honour Saint Nikolaos through the Church, and now it is too late for him to make amends. It is Stavi who must go, before the curse falls on him, and on our grandchildren.

And like when they were children, Stavi is slamming doors, and I know Giorgos, he will ask 'Can I do it Papa?' But Giorgos, my moró, I pray he must not go to Milos, I pray God will stop this curse.

VII

Christmas Day 2007: Brooklyn, New South Wales

On Christmas morning George woke with a sense of dread. Today, above all other days, he would be obliged to be 'happy' while everyone was discretely feeling sorry for him. He wished the day over, he wished himself home alone with all Christmas and New Year insincerities already behind him. For adults, he thinks, Christmas is a time of mourning ... for lost innocence, for family members who were no longer at the table, for significant others who had failed to keep their promise to always be there. He felt angry with Liz for deserting him, and then angry with himself for thinking such a ridiculous thought. He toyed with a plan to take one of Stephen's yachts and sail out to sea for the day, but as the digital clock by his bedside flicked past 8:00 he dismissed that idea, and readied himself to go to church.

With the exception of his mother's funeral in March last year, and the weddings of a few friends many years ago, George had not sat down in a church in the 22 years he had been married to Liz. On the years when they had brought their secular family to celebrate Christmas at Brooklyn, Liz and George had usually stayed in bed while Margarita had marshalled Stephen and their four children off to the morning church service with Pappous and Yia Yia. Avoiding church was one of the things that staying on Dangar Island had made much easier for them. George cannot recall whether he had seen Mary in a church since he was a teenage groomsman at her marriage to John; he was sure she had not been to church since the furore over her divorce. Her marriage to Ian, the principal of the real estate agency where she had been working for a few years, had been certified on a golf course by a civil celebrant, witnessed by a few of Ian's preferred property developers and golfing buddies. Today, however, all three of Papa's children would honour his Christmas wish that they attend the Divine Liturgy at St Dionysios in Central Mangrove.

George checked his steely, 'I'm fine thanks' smiling-reply in the wardrobe mirror doors, opened the bedroom door and was stopped short by the Christmas stocking that plummeted to the carpet at his feet, spilling chocolate coins across the hallway.

~

Stephen had been checking his watch at reducing intervals, and he was visibly relieved when Mary swept in to the vestibule, just as the service was due to start.

"Really!" he growled at her, tapping his watch, as she gave him a generous lip-smack on the cheek and cheerfully rubbed off the waxy red mark. "Making a statement?" Stephen cast his eyes over her red satin dress, resting them on the split that was noticeably above her knee, approving of her appearance even though he did not want her to be quite so remarkable amongst the soberly dressed Orthodox congregation. "Don't expect anyone to identify you as The Scarlet Woman. There's no one here who knows you."

"Then I've dressed up just for you, darling." Mary turned to George and caught him in an enveloping crush as he was trying to escape into the church. She tucked him under one arm, beckoned Stephen into the other and sashayed down the aisle to the pew Margarita was guarding. She gave a cordial nod of her head as she squeezed past Margarita to stand next to Papa.

Mary was glad of Stephen's reassurance that no one from the Earlwood Greek community was at the church. Behind the bravura of her arrival she was beset with anxiety, just one unwanted thought away from tears as she stood alongside her father following the rituals of Greek Orthodoxy that had such a deep connection to her childhood and to her conflicted memories of her mother. During the ninety-minute service she was easily able to recite the Creed and the Lord's Prayer in Greek, accompanying Papa rather than the majority of the English-speaking congregation. George, on her other side, was neither singing nor speaking, though she could see he was following the order of service, turning the pages at the right moments. Most of the responses required in the Divine Liturgy of Saint John Chrysostom came into her head by rote, but during the hymns she mimed the words, not daring to open a path to her emotions by singing.

Cheerful with relief when the service was over, Mary entreated her brothers to share in the lighting of memorial candles. George paused with her at the table of candles; Stephen kept walking as if he had not even heard. Papa, who had lit candles with Margarita on the way in, left the church leaning heavily on Margarita's arm, directing her to take him across to the pavilion where his friends were gathering for coffee.

"Two candles each," Mary was not raising a question, she simply bought four candles and gave George two. "Doesn't matter George," she pre-empted the objection he had not thought of making, "this is for us, who are left behind. Doesn't matter what Liz believed."

"What about what *I* believe?"

Mary lit her thin beeswax tapers from the small flame atop a candle already burning in the rack. Since George was not moving to light his candles she took his hand with a light touch and steered his candles into the flames that were burning on her own.

"You still believe sweetheart. I *know* you do." Mary faced the icon showing Jesus in a white robe with His right hand offering a blessing, and His left hand holding a staff, and closed her eyes for a long moment, then placed her candles in the rack. George looked at her face closely as she turned back to him, expecting tears, but there were none. In the soft candlelight she struck him as agelessly beautiful, her mascara and her eyeliner were pencil drawn, her makeup perfect, her dark eyes glistened, but then again, so did her scarlet lips.

"Are you going to keep holding those until they burn your fingers?"

George put his candles in the rack and stared at them numbly, his mind automatically offering up his childhood bedside litany, "Dear God, please bless Mama and Papa, Stavi, Maria, Mávrosi, Tigri." He had forgotten the name of the rabbit. He was grateful when he heard Mary speak softly over his silence.

"Christ, the source of all Light, be ever present to strengthen us, instruct us, inspire us in the knowledge that Your Light will never burn out. Let us live in Faith without a shadow of doubt that darkness will ever defeat us."

They watched the candles flicker for a long moment, and then Mary patted him lightly on the arm. "Have you had ... a visit ... from Mama since she died?" George shook his head in the shadows, not needing any clarification to understand what Mary was asking.

"She came just once, about a month after she died. She came down the passage – I think it was our home at Earlwood – and she stood in the doorway. She looked well, her skin was unwrinkled, her breasts were restored, she was wearing her black skirt and that lilac top she liked so much, and she was holding a daffodil. '*I thought you needed this,*' was all she said. I knew it would end if I spoke to her, but I tried to hold her, and she disappeared ... even as I felt her in my arms, she evaporated. In one way it was *so* sad, but in another ... I was so glad that she had come. I wished I'd had the presence of mind, or the time ... to thank her so much for coming. I think it must be very hard to come, I know it won't happen again."

George nodded; accepting Mary's words without question, wishing he could have the same experience, wondering why it had been Mary, not him. Mary tugged on his arm and turned him into the light beam that was spreading into the church from the main door.

"That day, I looked up the meaning of daffodils on the Internet," Mary continued. "The symbolic meaning of the daffodil she was offering me, the one she said I needed. Do you know what daffodils symbolise?"

George shook his head.

"Faith and forgiveness. I had no idea until I looked it up. She was offering me faith and forgiveness."

"I thought you had given up on the Church."

"The Church and its hypocritical morality, yes, but never Faith, George. It's been a struggle, but I still believe, I can't *not* believe. Mama wanted me to share the daffodil with you, sweetheart, I know it."

They emerged from the dark church into the glaring sun of Christmas mid-day, arm in arm. George steered Mary across to the cement garden-edge where Stephen and Margarita were waiting in the sparse shade of some gum trees. Not having had the opportunity in the church, Mary officially greeted her sister-in-law with an embrace that lacked the warmth she had for her brothers.

To fill the awkwardness of the after-hug silence, George decided to ask the question he had been pondering since yesterday's afternoon coffee with Papa.

"Mary, do you know why Mama and Papa never went back to Greece?"

Mary looked blank; she passed the question to Stephen with an inquiring glance.

"Mama was exiled from Greece." Stephen spoke bluntly, which signalled that no further explanation would be forthcoming and George and Mary, both noticing the dark look Margarita shot at Stephen, simultaneously addressed their shocked demand to her.

"Why?"

~

Aretha's story

June 1941: Crete

The story Stavros IV often tells of the Battle of Crete ends in June 1941 when he left Aretha in Sfakia with a silver cross and a promise to return; and it is at this point that the story Aretha once told Margarita begins.

Stavros had guessed rightly that Aretha was a member of the resistance, and he had guessed rightly that the Cretan clothes he wore had belonged to her brother. Dymas had been executed by the Germans after he had been identified as one of those who had met the paratroopers upon landing, fighting and killing as many as he could with a pickaxe and a fishing knife. What Stavros didn't know then was that Aretha had two other brothers who had escaped capture, taking the German rifles they had seized, into the inhospitable White Mountains that Stavros and his Australian friends had traversed from Rethymno. Aretha's was not an uncommon story, most Cretan villagers resisted the Germans - sisters, mothers, children - the allied Battle of Crete had been lost, but the Cretans themselves never surrendered, and their war against the Germans carried on after the allies were evacuated and until the end of the war in 1945.

The Germans were brutal. The toll that the Cretan villagers, along with the under-provisioned allied forces, had taken on the elite *Fallschirmjäger* and the brutality the Cretans themselves had shown in defending their homeland had shocked the Germans and their reprisals were ruthless. Aretha's younger brother, Dymas, had been caught untangling fishing net with the help of a German gravity knife days after the invasion. He and other men similarly accused, young and old had been lined up in the plaka in front of the church, in front of a horrified crowd of villagers. The German officer had asked each of them if they had taken part in the 'massacre' of the paratroopers, and Dymas, when it came to his turn, spat in the officer's face. The officer pistol-whipped him and two soldiers dragged him into the execution line with others who had responded similarly. Aretha had held fast to her mother's convulsing body as the German bullets had mowed Dymas and the other sons of her village down.

As Dymas was being dumped in a common grave outside Sfakia, Aretha's older brothers, Galen and Mikolos, were learning how to use the rifles from the wooden crate they had captured from the Germans on the beach at Rethymno and had taken with them into the mountains. Their group of resistance fighters was growing at a steady rate as more and more dishevelled peasants climbed up the mountain paths, refugees from the German round-ups, rebellious men looking for an organised fight. Many brought pistols and rifles they had seized from German bodies, but ammunition was in short supply, as was food. For this they relied on the women and children from the villages. Aretha, her courage bolstered by hatred for the Germans and love for her brothers, became one of their most reliable suppliers.

Aretha soon found she had a talent for flirting, she knew she was very pretty and she knew how to flaunt her looks. The German soldiers were easy to distract with a saucy lift of her skirts, an inviting smile, wide eyes and a little of their own language, which Aretha picked up easily. When the children were nipping into the stores to steal boxes of ammunition-just a little at a time-Aretha and her girl friends kept the guards engaged. She used her intimate knowledge of the terrain to avoid German patrols as she hiked up the mountains, her thighs weighed down with straps of bullets, bags of home grown vegetables and packs of cigarettes under her voluminous skirt, but she had been stopped on three terrifying occasions. Each time her skill in flirtation, her protest that she was in the foothills looking for melons to feed her family, the invitation she offered to a party down in Sfakia with some of her friends who found the young blond-haired Germans very attractive ... each time these things brought a blush to the young soldiers' faces and an eagerness to let her go on her way without molestation. They were innocents, she realised. Much as she hated the Germans as invaders, these boys were more terrified of their own officers than the Cretan peasants were. They were keen to love instead of following orders, as long as an officer was not watching. They did not expect women and children to be fighting a war. Some women were not so crafty; as the months wore on the soldiers started to realise that the villagers were supplying the rebel groups and the job of courier became increasingly dangerous.

It was in the mountains, with her brother's rebel group, that Aretha met Manolis. While telling her story to Margarita, Aretha sat stiffened by hatred whenever she spoke of the Germans. Throttled emotion straightened her backbone when she spoke of her mother and brothers. But when she spoke of Manolis, Aretha softened to the point where Margarita felt that she was watching Aretha melt inside her heavy woollen robes. Aretha opened up her heart in the long-overdue telling of her story about Manolis; she glowed with the memory of their love for each other.

"Ahhh Manolis," she had sighed, "Oh la la, such a person to love." Manolis was tall and strong and handsome, "like our Stavi," Aretha had said. He had an abundance of black, wavy hair that she loved to set free from the constraint of his woollen beret. His rugged face with its prominent nose was separated from his wide-lipped mouth by a gallant, upwardly curved moustache. On her visits she loved using his cutthroat shaving blade to retrieve his handsome jaw and generous lips from under their shaggy coverings. The shaving always ended in a long, passionate kiss. He wore baggy farming pants held up by an ammunition belt and a cotton shirt held against his bulging muscles by the strap of the rifle that was slung across his chest. She loved taking the heavy weaponry off him and laying it down, exposing him for a lover not a fighter.

"We knew we were all going to die, you see," Aretha excused her transgression against the Orthodoxy that had ruled Cretan morality before the war, "we knew it was just a matter of time. In action in the mountains, or by starvation in the village, we knew the only way this could end was in death. There were no rules any more. We loved for the day. Ahhh, how we loved."

For Manolis it did end in death. The Germans sent a patrol of 400 soldiers into the mountains in a desperate bid to rid themselves of the troublesome bands of rebels. Manolis, Galen, Mikolos and their group ambushed the patrol. There were only 18 of them, but the Germans didn't know that. The mountains disoriented the Germans; they were hopeless in combat amongst the ravines and peaks, the caves and the rock crannies; they were easy victims to snipers. With only 18 men, the Cretans routed the German patrol, killing dozens of them, winning their guns and ammunition, sending the rest running for their coastal base. But at the end of the action, Manolis and Mikolos were amongst the seven rebels who were dead, and in the re-telling, Aretha's body became straight and stiff and expressionless again.

Aretha stayed with her brother Galen as political allegiances rearranged the links of friendship amongst the guerrilla bands.

Until 1943, while Crete was of strategic importance to the allies, the British had helped organise the Cretan resistance, equipping them with radios and intelligence about German movements, and the Americans had airdropped supplies when they were desperately needed, but by the end of 1943 the allies had a new enemy-communism-and this meant they were friends to some Greeks and not others. The leader of Galen's band, Tyrone, was a dedicated communist. On many nights around their campfires he had explained the Communist Manifesto, he had shown his band how the class struggle dictated their lives, he had convinced Galen and the other men that communism was the only way forward for Crete after the war. It was the Soviet communists who would ultimately push Germany out of the Balkan States, and then out of Greece, Tyrone predicted. The allies, not unlike Germany itself, were rotten with capitalism, they did not care about the future of Greece, and it was Russian communists, fuelled by their truly egalitarian sense of human rights, who would save Europe. Crete was a poor country, made even poorer by the war; the Cretan peasants would be dreadfully oppressed in a capitalist Europe, they would all be packing olives into jars that were sent to England or America where the factory owners would take all the money that was rightfully theirs. Crete would stay poor forever, full of downtrodden peasants if the capitalists controlled the government after the war. The arguments made good sense to Aretha; with Galen she committed herself to the communist credo of the EAM resistance movement.

In February 1945 the Greek government in Athens, supported by the British, signed a pact with the communist-led EAM, requiring the communists to surrender their weapons, reassuring them that they would be included in political dialogue after the war. When they heard the edict on their British radio, everyone in the band raged against the treaty, knowing that it would be suicide to give up their weapons while the Germans still occupied Crete. In May when Germany finally surrendered to the British,

Tyrone's prophecy was proved right, the capitalists joined ranks. The German battalions in Crete were allowed to keep their weapons in order to control the communist 'rebels' who remained in the mountains. The allies dumped German vehicles in the sea instead of handing them over to the peasants who needed them; they took the millions of litres of oil the Germans had stolen without offering any compensation; they fed anti-communist propaganda to the villagers, pitching Greek against Greek; Aretha's mother was tortured by a right-wing group from their own village in an attempt to make her betray the location of the band. She died from her broken soul, Aretha believed, as much as from her injuries. Galen died in a suicidal, mindless revenge-attack hours after Aretha had brought him the news.

It was at this moment in Aretha's story that Stavros had come back for her, as he had promised. He did not find her in the garden of her home near Sfakia as he had romantically anticipated, and weeks of inquiry revealed nothing of her. Instead, when he encountered her unexpectedly in Hania, he was wearing the British-provisioned uniform of the Greek army, and she was in prison, charged with treason and accomplice to murder. The first time he cajoled the guards into allowing him some private time with her, she told him she would rather hang than be saved from her fate by a pro-British capitalist Greek.

Aretha never knew how Stavros persuaded the Greek authorities; it was a story he never told. She supposed he persuaded her with his persistence - he simply wore her out, she came to accept his evidence that the communist cause was as misbegotten as capitalism, that all the suffering of both wars, German and civil, was a useless waste, that she could follow his determined lead to a world better than the rotten emptiness that was occupying Greece. Forty years later, she could remember only a handful of events between the day her mother and brother died, and the day she stepped down from the gangway onto Australian soil. She remembered the first sight of Stavros in the prison in Hania; she remembered the day he showed her Nick Foster's letter of sponsorship and its translation; she remembered signing the marriage certificate and the extradition papers on the same day; she remembered his relief and her sense of disassociation as he crisply saluted the white uniform on the other side of the signing table; she remembered how patiently and honourably he had waited for her to accept Australia as her only possible home and welcome him as her husband.

Pappous was a very good man, Aretha had assured Margarita, and over time she had come to love him very much. His version of their story had always been a happier, more romantic one, a better one for leaving out her personal tragedy. *His* version was the one she wanted her children to know.

~

Christmas Day 2007: Brooklyn, New South Wales

"So why did Mama tell *you* her story?" Mary challenged Margarita with puzzled resentment, and Margarita correctly interpreted that the emphasis was on '*you*' rather than '*why*'.

"She didn't volunteer the story; I grilled it out of her. She made me promise not to tell you. She didn't want to spoil Papa's story for any of you."

Mary set her lips into a disbelieving grimace and turned her accusing glare to Stephen.

"Marg didn't tell me until after Mama died." Stephen shrugged.

Mary checked George too, but the perplexed look on his face was enough to reassure her that he didn't know any more than she did.

"So when was this?" Mary demanded of Margarita.

"It was right after you rang to say you had left John. She was very upset, as you know. She said to me that she blamed herself, that you had inherited her reckless genes and that she had failed to protect you. She said she never told you her story because she thought it would be a bad example to you." Margarita looked up from her examination of her own hands and turned her apologetic gaze towards the sound of Mary drawing breath in a choking groan.

Mary pressed her palm across her right cheek, turned her head to the side and stood up. She muttered a word that Stephen and George were able to interpret as "Fuck!" and walked across the yard towards the back of the church.

"I've said too much." Margarita touched Stephen's thigh seeking reassurance.

"She had to hear it sometime. She'll be right." Nevertheless, Stephen launched to his feet, and set off with long strides to overhaul Mary as she reached the corner of the building.

George remained seated, musing on the fact that they all still missed their mother acutely, this second Christmas after her death. He thought he would like to have Mary's advantage, to let himself cry and be comforted. He made an announcement to the emptying churchyard that Margarita, who does not have my advantaged perspective, could not put in context.

"At least I'm not the only mushroom."

~

Maria, she looks like me. I did not know this when she was a baby, or even when she was a young girl, because there are no photos of me like these Australians have of themselves. There is no one from my family here to tell me. One day when she is dressed for church, when she is thirteen maybe, one day it suddenly hits me down and I remember, like I am seeing myself in a mirror. It is a feeling so strange, when I see myself in this other time, in this other person. And after that I keep seeing it, even when her skirt shows her legs right up to her panties, even when she paints herself to make boys look at her. I still see ... these legs are from my body, her face it is my face.

Her hair is maybe thicker than mine, but more looked after. With expensive shampoo, not soap, with conditioner for it to be shiny and silky. She adds foam to make it seem there is even more hair, to keep it where she puts it—sometimes curly and sometimes straight-and even on the boat it does not get messy in the wind. We didn't have these things in Crete. The boys used to say how they like my hair, but her hair looks much better. I know this though I don't like it when she changes the color. It is so beautiful, her hair, when it is black. I tell her she should not change the color.

And she paints her eyebrows and her eyelashes to match her hair, and she makes a dark brown ring around her eyes to make them seem even bigger and darker than they are already. Her teeth, they are very expensive. Stavi, he pay with his mail money for them to be perfect, like the other girls in the school. She has a smile she makes for the camera to show them off, and her lipstick, it is smooth and shiny and she spends much time in front of a mirror getting this perfect. I tell her she should not waste so much time in the bathroom; we only have one bathroom and she is greedy with it.

Her skin, it goes a golden brown in the sun, which makes her Australian friends jealous. She puts on creams so it looks good, and the creams keep the wrinkles away so she will never look old, like me. But this is still my skin, I remember, before my skin became like wrinkled paper. I like the way she looks after her skin, but I tell her she is costing her Papa a lot of money buying these creams.

Ahh, but she does look very beautiful, and this makes me scared for her. The boys, they are even more trouble to her than they were to me. Because here they are bad boys. They have no rules, they do what they like, they are not scared of the priest. Arghh, they are worse than the Nazi boys, and Maria ... she does not know what can happen.

When Maria is a teenager she wears such tight clothes, such short skirts and a top that doesn't cover her breasts. She excites the boys with this. I tell her not to do this, but she won't listen. The other girls do it, so Maria does it too. But Maria is more beautiful than those other girls, it is Maria the boys want – I know this. Even the Greek boys, their mama's don't want them to date Maria because they know she is too exciting.

When Stavi stops me from the washing up that night, and he makes me sit on the couch with Papa, I feel it along my spine. I know they have something bad to confess.

"Mama, Maria's got into some trouble." I knew it. Maria is not looking at me. She is far across the room. "She's pregnant."

I am wailing, and I would cross the room and slap her if Stavi is not holding my arm on the sofa.

"Now Mama, she could have had an abortion."

I am crying with both hands to my cheeks. How can Stavi breathe this mortal sin in our house!

"But we know you would never, never allow that." Stavi is now looking at Papa, who is staring at Maria like a deaf man. "So she is going to have the baby."

I cannot reach Maria so I slap her with screaming words. I say terrible things, I tell her to get out of the house and never come back. She is crying and running to her room.

"When is she going to have the baby?" Papa is finally speaking.

"Four months."

"Who is the father?"

"Vasilis."

I am gasping. It cannot be true. Later Vasilis' mama, Ariadne, she tells me it is not true, her son did not do this. It is one of those Australian boys Maria knows. Vasilis and Maria go to the movies like we arrange. Nothing else. Vasilis he swears on the Bible it is not him. But Stavi and Maria, they say it is Vasilis ... and still today I don't know who I believe except that Daniella, she looks like she is Greek and the older she is, the more she is looking like Ariadne.

"Then Vasilis will marry her," Papa is believing Stavi.

"Mary doesn't want to marry Vasilis," I can hear in Stavi's voice, the starting of a fight.

"Vasilis will marry her." Papa is going towards Maria's room to tell her this himself but Stavi is jumping up and stopping him. They stand there against each other, starting a fight, like so many times.

"This is 1973 Papa, and Mary does not have to marry anyone she doesn't want to marry."

They stare at each other for a long time, Stavi's knuckles are white and Papa thinks better not to hit first, so he insults Stavi instead.

"What sort of man are you that you let a boy do this to your sister?"

"Vasilis has three broken ribs and a black eye. Vasilis is not the sort of man you want to marry your daughter."

Papa is nodding because to him this is the right answer from Stavi. "Then you need to find a good man to marry her."

Then Papa is the most angry he has ever been with me. "These are terrible things, you said," he says. "Maria will still live here, if she does not marry. She will still be our daughter. You will tell her you are sorry."

And I make this promise to him, and I mean to do this, but in the morning, when I go to her room, Maria is gone. I confess my sins to our priest, but later when I see Maria with her baby for baptism, neither of us is wanting to speak of this fight and so I never tell her. I am always wanting her to forgive me, but I never say the words.

Vasilis' mama, to prove he is not the father of Maria's baby, she shows me a photo of Maria walking on the beach wearing bikini pants with no top part. In the photo on the other side of Maria, is a tall man and he has his arm around her waist, his hand on her stomach just under her breasts. I cannot see this man properly because he is looking out to sea. But he reminds me of Manolis. The photo reminds me of walking on the beach in Crete with Manolis, even though my clothes covered my *body, and Maria is wearing almost nothing at all. Somehow the clothes and the type of sand make no difference. I see it is me and Manolis and she is in love, and I am so scared for her.*

Her feet, they leave the same footprints in the sand. The same size, the same big toe, the same curve in the print where the arch is high. She leaves the same footprints in the sand as me, I can see this.

VIII

It is the afternoon of Christmas day, 2007. Stavros Kostis the fourth has gone for his afternoon siesta, and at 4pm he will return to the living room to have a cup of Greek coffee. Stavros Kostis the fifth, who has called himself Stephen since the first day of school, his sister Maria (Mary) and brother Giorgos (George) are walking along the footpath that takes pedestrians from Hawkesbury River Marina around the shoreline to the Parsley Bay boat ramp. Margarita, who is Greek, and Ian, who is not Greek, the surviving in-laws of the Australian branch of the Kostis family, trail behind the three siblings, loosely supervising Mary's two grand-daughters who are riding identical pink bikes with pink baskets and grey trainer wheels. The children are exaggerating the bumpiness of the path by issuing a guttural stream of vibration from the back of their noses, punctuating it with laughter and then starting over again. Danielle, the daughter Mary has with Vasilis (the Greek boy she did not marry), is taking a break from her children with a magazine on the grass between the playground and the marina. Dimitry and Michael have taken Danielle's husband Tom to try to surf on some mediocre waves that are breaking on the ocean beach at Terrigal. Melinda, Katherine and the two teenage daughters Mary has with Ian are lying by a pool at a friend's place a few blocks from the Kostis' home. Mathew and Robert, the two sons Mary has with her first husband, John, won't be seeing their mother until New Year's Eve when Mary has enticed them to bring their young families to watch Sydney's fireworks from a vacant apartment Ian has listed in Balmain.

Our son David is still at the dining table in the Melbourne suburb of Ivanhoe trying, despite the effects of roast turkey, plum pudding and an ample supply of wine, to stay attentive to the swirl of conversation between the many members of his girlfriend's family, none of whom are Greek. Claire is asleep in the icy Greater Boston suburb of Cambridge and will stay that way for another seven hours before the American girl George has not heard about yet, tousles her awake and presents her with a Christmas present. David and Claire are both happy and in love, but George aches. He looks out to the water as Stephen and Mary talk around him, wrapping him with a family solidarity that is special to this particular Christmas, and yet he feels completely isolated by his grief, just hanging-in there trying to numb himself against the day.

The swell of incoming sea is building small waves on the river's platinum surface, but the promised Southerly is not freshening the air yet. The fish are sheltering in the cool depths; the crabs are dug deep into mud-bunkers alongside the decaying boardwalk that encloses the old, oyster-shell encrusted river pool; nothing is going to bite the lines the Roebuck boys have dangled into the water – they will pack up in half an hour, take a swim and go home; all they really wanted was an excuse to get out of their house while the great Christmas dish-wash was underway.

The sky is that rich blue that makes photographers say they love Australia's light and at the edges, where it meets the gum-tree crowns on the ridge tops, it wrinkles into a crushed taffeta heat haze. The few wisps of cirrus are for decoration only; they fail to register a shadow as they move across the sun. The heat bakes the colourful plastic of the children's playground, and renders the exposed metal surfaces of the nearby pavilion untouchable. With the exception of seagulls, which have either no sense or no feeling and pester humans for food scraps right through the hottest part of the day, all the birds are taking their own siestas in shady hiding spots.

By the time the group has reached the marina, there is enough wind to have the glistening white and navy blue yachts that are berthed there knocking lightly against each other, lanyards slapping against masts. As they pass, Stephen points out the Farr 1104 that he sold two years ago to a member of the local Yacht Club. It is the winner of this season's handicap competition, still in top condition. Disregarding Stephen's interruption, Mary continues her assessment of the apartments above the marina and how the entire complex could be turned into a much better asset for the community in the hands of an imaginative real estate entrepreneur like Ian. George, barely managing to respond to her chatter, is remembering the day we sailed the Farr 1104 in the Three Island Race.

And I am watching the past, present and future of the people I love. I am thinking about the things they, in their busyness cocoons, don't take time to think about or don't want to think about. What they and the marina look like to a seagull. How the decisions they make - yesterday, today, tomorrow – are sifting them onto the train tracks of destiny.

IX

December 2007: London

While Stavros Kostis IV was retelling the shipwreck story to his family after dinner on Christmas night, Lynne Drummond was telling the same story to her brother as they waited for Christmas lunch to be served at Martin's terrace house in Gunnersbury, Greater London. Stavros was hoping the story would lead to a more fruitful conversation about family responsibilities. Lynne was brainstorming evidence for and against the truth of the stories Nicholas Baxter had written down, supposedly verbatim as told by Stavros I. The manuscript claimed that Stavros had told Baxter the stories when they were recuperating in adjoining beds in the Naval Hospital that had been set up at Fort Ricasoli in Malta for those injured in the Battle of Navarino. Lynne's research had confirmed the details of the battle, and the temporary existence of the hospital, and she had even been able to confirm the fact that there were some harbour pilots from Milos who had been selected to serve with Admiral Codrington at Navarino. The story she had heard from Dorothy Morris reinforced the connection between the Baxter and Kostis families, but could she be sure that everything Baxter had written down was true?

"What I don't believe," Lynne ruminated over the rim of her pre-lunch wine glass, "is that Nicholas could have translated all this from Greek. Surely a Greek fisherman turned navy sailor, would not have been able to speak much English? And an English fisherman from Cromer turned navy sailor, could not have spoken Greek. So ... it's a good story, but just a story ... our great great-grandfather built on some facts with a vivid imagination?"

As was often the case, Martin was pursuing his own line of thought rather than listening; he was spreading many branches of the Drummond family tree over the dining table, checking the dates on each page before lying it down in the correct spot. It was their grandfather, Robert Wallis, who had done the initial work assembling the family tree. His wife, Irene, had not been responsive to his enthusiasm for family details and as a result the Wallis side of the tree was in full leaf, while the Baxter side showed a bare skeleton of names, dates and occupations all related to sea-faring. Robert had entrusted the family tree to Martin many years ago, knowing it would be in safe hands, and Martin had grown the tree in all directions with the aid of Internet ancestry search engines.

Martin was disproportionally excited by the story of their missing cousin and had already invested many hours in blissful investigation of the mystery. His searches, confirming the story Lynne had heard from Dorothy Morris, had caused him to pencil in changes to the Baxter pages: Ethyl Wright, mother to Nicholas and Thomas, died giving birth to Thomas in 1898; Isabella Price, married to Martin 1899, mother to Irene 1901. The pages were messy at the moment, Martin apologised to Lynne, and he would fix them when he had got to the bottom of the mystery about baby Nicholas.

Martin had discovered Nicholas Martin Robertson Baxter in the birth register for April 1920, but could not find a corresponding entry in the death register or any other references to this name. Was their mysterious relative still alive? Had there been a name change? Martin had been insensitive enough to harass the modern-day household of the Earl of Caldbeck and had been discretely directed towards the Australian immigration register. The Lady Bess, it seemed, had continued to be a disgrace to the family name. She and the lover she had taken in the years Nicholas was away at sea, Michael White, had eloped to Australia in 1924. Martin was yet to follow up on the Australian records, but now on pages laid out on the dining table he was happily adding a new branch connected to the previously boring stump that was Nicholas Baxter b. 1896, d. 14/01/1923.

m. Bess Robertson of Caldbeck
line down to
Nicholas Baxter (1920-?), immig. Australia 4/6/1924 with assumed surname Foster.

Lynne, meanwhile, had picked up the first page in the family tree in order to see the original Nicholas. "Here he is," she said, assuming wrongly that Martin had been listening to her, "1st July 1808 to 28th October 1868." She paused, suddenly experiencing some family-tree excitement of her own. "Look at his mother's name ... Martin!" She raised her voice to finally attract his attention and when he looked at her she stabbed the piece of paper with her finger.

"Yes," said Martin, losing interest already.

"His mother was Greek." Martin already knew this, but he took a closer look at the paper, as if it would help him understand why Lynne found that exciting.

Nicholas' father was 'Robert Baxter, merchant seaman, b. Cromer 21st March 1793, d. Cromer 27th March 1819'.

His mother was 'Maria Konstantinopolous, b. Greece 1784? d. Cromer 24th April 1847'. She had come from nowhere, to join the Baxter family tree.

"Robert was getting old. He bought a Greek girl on one of his trading trips in 1807." Martin clearly found the idea entertaining and Lynne scowled at his chauvinism, even though she knew he would have diligently researched his facts.

"Nicholas' father died when he was only 11 – his mother lived much longer," Lynne fell silent, thinking over the implications.

"If you got your crap off this table I'd be able to set it!" Tayla marched into the dining room from the kitchen, and waved a hand full of cutlery in a sweeping motion above the table as if she intended to knock the papers to the floor.

"And now that Greek influence has been *completely* erased." Martin was casting an aspersion on Tayla's unfeminine behaviour as much as commenting on her looks.

Tayla's appearance changed regularly, but this Christmas her peroxide blonde hair had a very short, soft cut with a long fringe that fell to the right hand side of her face. Her eyes were naturally hazel, a replica of Lynne's, but Tayla wore such heavy mascara and eye liner that the overall effect was that her eyes looked very dark in dramatic contrast to her hair and the pale English peach of her skin. She had three earrings in her left ear, and two in her right, behind the veil of her fringe. Through her left eyebrow she had a slim black rod, and on the left side of her nose was a delicate nose ring. Lynne was actually pleased with Tayla's appearance of late; this look was much better than purple hair, the ear and nose rings had become more discrete, and Tayla was starting to use her make-up to good effect, enhancing the beauty of her cheek bones, her small, straight nose and delicate jaw. Lynne supposed it was the job that Tayla had held since she graduated from school last year-a receptionist in an up-market medical surgery in Clapham Junction-that had effected the change; she knew her own words on the subject had been wasted.

Unfortunately, Tayla's ability to behave in a demure fashion seemed to be restricted to the workplace; at family get togethers she continued to be bold and brash, enjoying the empowerment she felt when adults politely accommodated her etiquette-breaking behaviours and enjoying even more the confrontation she could spark with Martin who was incapable of such politeness. Today Tayla was wearing a black cotton top with prominent metal zips and studs and tight designer jeans with ragged tears at thigh, knee and bum-cheek pocket - an outfit guaranteed to disturb Martin. Lynne was drained by the not-so-subtle war that played out between the two of them. She hoped, desperately, that the hostilities already exchanged upon greeting would be enough for today.

As Tayla was loudly dropping silverware alongside placemats, Marcus brought two steaming plates of vegetables into the room and stopped, looking blankly at the table. "Where should I put these?" he asked with an archetypal male naiveté.

"In front of Inka's kennel!" Tayla retorted.

Marcus scowled at her with icy brown eyes and put the plates in sensible positions equidistant from the middle of the table. He rearranged his abundant amber-blonde hair with a shake of his head, turned brusquely on his heal and returned to the kitchen. It was natural for Marcus to be in the kitchen, helping with the preparation and delivery of the Christmas meal. Food–the purchase, cooking and, in particular, the eating of it–was his passion. Three years ago, when he was seventeen, he had decided to take over his father's kitchen during his alternate weeks in Chelsea. He claimed it was a matter of self-preservation. Before long he preferred his own cooking to his mother's as well, and Lynne happily found herself relieved of cooking duties, though she noted that with Marcus' enthusiasm for using the maximum number of pots and pans, this did not result in fewer hours that she spent in the kitchen.

Fortunately Marcus' fondness for food was balanced with his second passion – soccer. He trained with his university team three nights a week, and played on Saturdays. He also worked out at a gym, keen to keep himself as fit as he could be, with the result that he frequently reminded Lynne of the beauty she had seen in James when they first met. Tayla had spent some years scoffing at her 'gay' brother who liked to cook and keep fit, but a few months ago, worried by some extra pounds she noticed on her thighs, she had asked him to give her some personal training, and now they were regularly going to the gym together. Marcus was not gay and resented Tayla's proclamations. His confidence in relationships had taken a beating in the course of his parent's divorce, and he wanted to be absolutely sure he had found the right girl, someone he could keep his promises to. Now in his final year of economics he thought he had found her, even though their relationship had not yet gone beyond lunches together in the park, and holding hands at the movies.

"So, now, are you satisfied that the story written by old Nicholas Baxter is true?" Martin stowed the family tree in a manila folder and placed it on the sideboard as Tayla came back into the room with a stack of heated plates, Marcus followed with a heaped platter of turkey, and a pewter jug full of thick gravy.

"It does seem possible." As Lynne moved to take her seat, she was quietly considering how she would start the part of the story that she had not yet shared with Martin because it fell not into family genealogy, but into her own area of expertise–art history–and until now, Lynne had dismissed it as just another myth amongst many that existed around pieces of ancient art. The manuscript was written in English, evidently by Nicholas, but it was also illustrated, and Stavros Kostis had written his signature under the illustrations ... his way of co-authoring the story, Lynne supposed. Now that she understood how Nicholas Baxter had been able to translate the story of an illiterate Greek fisherman, the foremost question stirring Lynne's mind was how, if not through personal experience, a Greek fisherman had been able, in 1827, to faithfully draw the Venus De Milo, complete with two arms – an image that coincided almost exactly with the current consensus on how those arms were originally sculpted.

Thalassa

~

Most of the stories told by Stavros IV, like his father and the fathers before him, have a long and a short version. The short version of the shipwreck story ends with the promise to St Nikolaos ... the rest being so obvious to the descendants of Stavros I that the story did not need to be drawn out. The long version, which Stavros IV used on this Christmas night, tells of how St Nikolaos took Petros, but spared Stavros so that Stavros could build the Church, and raise a great family of sons.

St Nikolaos had sent Stavros the broken bowsprit to climb onto; St Nikolaos had instructed Thalassa to wash Stavros in to the beach. Stavros had staggered up the beach and into the nearest syrmata boat shed, where, with failing breath through shattered ribs, he had given the sympathetic fishermen of Firopotamos the very first rendition of the shipwreck story. All the fishermen in the harbour, and all the Kostis family in Milos were agreed that St Nikolaos had worked a miracle, and within weeks a site for the church was being prepared, as near as was possible to the spot where Stavros had seen St Nikolaos reach out to him from the rocks.

It was auspicious, the village believed, to lay the foundation stone on Holy Saturday, so work progressed at a furious pace to level the site in time. On the Orthodox Easter Saturday night in 1808, the auxiliary bishop of Milos led the villagers in singing "*Christos Anesti*" to the open night sky at midnight and blessed the foundations of the Church of Saint Nikolaos, Firopotamos, starting the spiritual life of the Church. It was another 14 years before the walls and roof of the Church were finally finished in the form in which it still stands today. Every year, as time and trading profits allowed, Stavros would replace another section that had originally been thrown together with the rotting wood and ropes washed up from the shipwreck, with quarried rock and mortar that would stand in testimony to St Nikolaos forever. It wasn't until 1825, when the interior had been lined with restored wood; icons of the Saint and the Virgin Mary which Stavros' wife had copied from those hanging in the Panaghia Thalassitra had been hung on the walls; and a solid wood altar had been put in place, that Stavros could finally inspect his church and feel that he had done justice to his promise. Truth be known, this was not quite the spot where Stavros had seen St Nikolaos ... but that spot was completely inaccessible, and Stavros hoped that lavish interior decorations and pristine whitewash would make up for geographical inaccuracy.

Stavros II and Stavros III continued to enhance the church. It was Stavros II, desperate to have a son after the birth of three daughters, who paid for the mosaic of the Christ Pantocrator to be installed in the dome - Stavros III was born the next year. The new altar was hand crafted by Stavros III and his wife Iliana when Stavros IV miraculously recovered from a childhood fever.

Stavros IV, the ultimate recipient of all this benevolence from St Nikolaos, had done the unthinkable. He had left the impoverished island of Milos, and the opportunity-forsaken village of Firopotamos forever, emigrating to the land of milk and honey that the AIF friends he had made in Crete had spoken about with so much longing. Too late, while Aretha struggled with breast cancer and his prayers were ineffective, he had come to understand that the welfare of his family depended entirely on keeping the promise with St Nikolaos. And if Aretha's untimely death was not enough, compelling proof could be found in the accident that had claimed the life of Giorgos' wife.

The story with which the Kostis family was familiar included one crucial piece of information – the location of the shipwreck - that was not specified in the version that was written down in the Baxter manuscript. Possibly Stavros was deliberately obscure because he didn't want to admit that Church was not in quite the right spot; maybe Milos had such an insular population in the early 1800s that specifics were not necessary; or maybe 'Milos' was a much easier placename than 'Firopotamos'. Lynne, however, was finding this lack of specificity a major nuisance. She had discovered that there were many Churches of St Nikolaos on Milos ... more, she suspected, than were documented anywhere, even in the records of the Greek Orthodox Church. The manuscript included drawings of the church but there were no conclusive similarities to be found on Google images. Despite hours frittered away on the Internet running every search she could think of, Lynne could neither prove nor disprove the existence of the church.

Why was Lynne so keen to know if the church actually existed? Because the story she told in London to the Drummond family over roast turkey, gravy, spuds, carrots, peas, ale and cider was even longer than the extended version being told in Brooklyn, New South Wales. It included some detail that Stavros IV either did not know, or did not think he should relay to a wider audience: a secret Stavros had told in 1827 to the incarnation of St Nikolaos who had come to save him from the sea a second time.

~

The Venus De Milo Story

April 1820: Milos, Greece

Stavros was plodding down the steep hill, mindful of the uneven cobbles under his sandaled feet but paying little attention to the sun as it spread a sparkling golden path across the Aegean Sea, or to people working in the brown and olive fields that lay behind the stone fences on each side of the path. His donkey, humorously called *Icthys*, which means fish, was following him in much the same state of mind. Six days of the week the pair trekked the same path: up to Tripiti with baskets carrying the catch of the day in the morning, and back down to

Klima with empty baskets slapping loosely against Icthys' thick hide in the evening. Icthys had trained Stavros to walk down the hill instead of attempting to ride. If Stavros walked, Icthys would follow placidly. Back in the days when Stavros had tried to ride, Icthys would simply stand still and ignore every shout, kick, whip – he would not budge. Icthys was not for riding, which was why he had been cheap.

During the day, providing he had managed to sell all the fish before the school run by the nuns of Aghia Nikolaos closed for the afternoon, Stavros would sit in the shade of the farthest tamarix trees, some distance behind the children. Maths lessons sent him to sleep well before siesta was due – he already knew how to calculate the price of a fish by weight, and the change he needed to give. Grammar had the same effect - he never had any problem getting his point of view across in the taverna did he? Theology invigorated him, especially when a saint was being discussed, but his main hope, in showing up at school each day, was that Sister Damopolous would be giving a class in Greek mythology. It wasn't just that he liked to watch her body movements, and loved the tenor of her voice ... he also loved stories of Gods and Heroes. He liked to imagine himself as Poseidon, the muscled, invincible God of the Sea. He would often fall asleep there under the tamarix trees and dream of the goddess Amphitrite who, looking very like Sister Damopolous, accepted the marriage proposal that Delfin the dolphin had delivered at Poseidon's behest. Sister Damopolous rode boldly towards him on Delfin's back, racing through the waves, with her legs astride and her robes flowing behind her, hiding nothing of her voluptuous figure. Fortunately, these dreams usually occurred during maths lessons ... when Sister Damopolous was actually present Stavros did not lose a moment to sleep.

After his siesta snooze, Stavros could usually be found in a taverna with a few other fishermen, telling tales of the sea over a glass of Raki and the grilled fragments of fish that had

Thalassa

not sold. Then, with just enough light left to make the journey, Stavros and Icthys would head downhill for Klima. After a few hours sleep in his cousin Dimitry's syrmata, Stavros would be ready to go out to sea again on Dimitry's boat, setting nets and trawling for fish until dawn crept across the water. Five days a week it was the same, but on Saturday once the fish were sold, Stavros and Icthys travelled down to Firopotamos instead of Klima, with Icthys carrying the provisions that the Kostis family would need for the coming week. Stavros spent the seventh day with his brothers and sisters, working on the church. Such was his life, now that his family no longer had a fishing boat of its own.

Today was Monday, 10th April 1820 and Stavros was on his absent-minded way back down to Klima when his life was suddenly put onto a new path.

"Stavros, Stavros, stop for a minute!" The call came from underneath a thorny bunch of bushes falling away down the steep side of the road Stavros was following. Stavros could hear feet scrambling towards him on the rocky slope. "I need your help!" Yorgos Kentrotas, Stavros' cousin (he had a lot of 'cousins') appeared through a break in the scrub.

Yorgos wanted Stavros and Icthys to help him take a piece of marble statue down to Klima. As Stavros slid down the embankment to take stock of the effort involved, Yorgos explained that he had found the parts of the statue on Saturday when he had been trying to widen his field by digging out rocks that lay here alongside the path. There were two large segments of marble: a naked torso, and the upper section of the legs and hips draped with a robe. The torso reminded Yorgos of a sculpture he had seen in the port one day as it was being loaded onto a French ship. Yorgos had heard that the French had paid money for that sculpture and was hoping that this one was also valuable. Did Stavros know anything about statues?

Stavros did not know anything about statues, but he did know some things about Greek mythology. Looking at the marvellous breasts on the torso and the legs, lying broken, but in place, Stavros was sure he was looking at Amphitrite. "She's the Goddess of the Sea, Poseidon's wife," he explained to Yorgos.

Yorgos looked confused. "The French officer said 'Venus'."

"What French officer?"

Yorgos explained that he had taken a small section of his find, the statue's left hand, into the port on Saturday night and had approached a group of French naval officers to ask if they would buy the statue. One of them had been interested and had come with Yorgos to look at the larger parts of the statue the next day. The French officer had become quite excited, he had helped Yorgos clear some more of the rocks away, looking for other body parts, and he had made a number of drawings. He said that he thought the French government would be interested in buying the statue, and that Yorgos should take the parts home and store them safely until the sale could be arranged. The officer did not say how much the statue would be worth.

Given the excitement he had seen on the officer's face, Yorgos thought the statue could be worth quite a lot of money, so he didn't want to store it in his own home at the end of the field, he wanted to hide it in their cousin's syrmata down at Klima. It would be a struggle getting it there, but at least it would then be ready to sail around to the port. Stavros couldn't fault Yorgos' logic, so he agreed to help.

The two large sections of the body were very heavy. Stavros and Yorgos agreed that there would be four trips involved, and the torso should go first, since it was the most valuable. Stavros brought Icthys down into the field and rearranged the fishing baskets, upending them and lashing them so that they formed a platform either side of Icthys' spine. Then, using all the strength they had, and partly crushing one of the fishing baskets as they struggled, Stavros and Yorgos hoisted the torso across Icthys' back. Icthys was good at standing still, it was one of the things he did best, and he showed little sign of objecting

Thalassa

to the weight on his back. He was reluctant, however, to move off when Stavros had finally finished securing the statue. With Stavros pulling from the front, and Yorgos using a branch to whip from behind, Icthys eventually gave in and the slow procession down the hill began.

The next day, Stavros reached the field earlier and helped Yorgos with some more rock clearing before they took the second section, the draped hips and upper legs down to the fishing village. On Wednesday they took the lower legs, and on Thursday they filled the baskets with broken parts – the arms and hands on one side, and the plinth on which the Goddess had been standing on the other. By candlelight in Dimitry's syrmata they put the parts together, reassembling the entire statue. When the French officer had drawn the statue she had no arms; Yorgos had found the left hand, which he had taken to the port, but the other sections of her arms had been flung wide in the fall. In Tuesday's digging Stavros had found the parts of the right arm while Yorgos had found the remainder of the left. Stavros, fancying himself as an artist, made some drawings of his own. He was more than ever convinced that the statue was Amphitrite, his own personal Goddess.

The French officers were divided about taking the statue with them before their Ambassador had confirmed interest in the purchase and asked Yorgos to wait for their return. No secret could be kept for long in Milos, however, and within a few weeks the Turkish governor to Milos had sent his representatives to Yorgos' home and had demanded that Yorgos turn over the statue. Yorgos could be relieved from this year's poll tax, or he could be charged double, he had 24 hours to decide.

On hearing this, Stavros, who had a deep genealogical hatred of their Turk oppressors, seized the part of the statue that he considered to be rightfully his because he had uncovered it – the right arm. The arm headed uphill to Tripiti surrounded by Sea Bream, and later that day it went downhill to Firopotamos with a few less family provisions than the baskets usually held. Yorgos, out of similar spite, hid the fragments that completed the left arm. When their cousin, Dimitry, sailed the statue around to the Port of Milos and handed it over to the Turks it matched the drawings originally made by the French officer.

As it turned out, the French ambassador's representative, Vicomte de Marcellus, arrived in port as the statue was being loaded onto the Turkish ship, destined for Constantinople. Dimitry, quick to see an opportunity to thwart the Turks and benefit his own pocket, told the Vicomte what was happening, and presided over the ensuing squabble between the French, the Turkish sailors and the Milian trustees to the Turkish Sultan. The Milian trustees were forced to annul the sale, the Vicomte paid Dimitry a handsome sum of money, and Yorgos was charged double his usual tax for that year. Dimitry compensated Yorgos generously for the tax payment, while keeping an undisclosed sum for himself. Meanwhile the Vicomte, seeing Dimitry's boat and impressed with Dimitry's handling of the political situation, asked Dimitry to recommend a new pilot for the French fleet when they put in to Milos harbour. Stavros reported for duty the next day.

Questions were asked, of course, about the statue's arms, and under the vengeful eye of the Sultan's trustees, Stavros and Yorgos could not possibly have brought them out of hiding. Instead Stavros and Yorgos fed stories to the Milos rumour mill. Their favourite was that Dimitry and his crew had fought the Turkish sailors as they were loading the statue, gallantly retrieving the statue for the French. In the struggle the arms had broken off, and Thalassa had claimed them, sweeping them away to the deep waters of the harbour.

Yorgos, scared of discovery and heavier taxes, had fulfilled the intent of this story by throwing the fragments of the left arm overboard to Thalassa. Stavros told Yorgos and Dimitry that he had done the same, but years later he confided to Nicholas Baxter that he had dealt with the problem in his own way. As an offering both to his benefactor, Saint Nikolaos, and his personal Goddess, Amphitrite, he sealed the statue's right arm permanently into the section of the church wall that he was re-building at the time.

X

December 2007: Brooklyn, New South Wales

By 8 am on Boxing Day the sun was strong and the breeze was missing. Hot white jetty edges lay above calm green water, and the motionless outlines of trees and rooftops stood sharply against the cloudless blue of the sky in promise of a baking-hot day ahead. Brooklyn was quiet, most of the town still sleeping-off Christmas dinner.

Mary was not amongst the still sleeping. She had been on the roadside outside the Marina cafe, waving goodbye to two carloads of family. Ian was on his way back to Sydney to spend Boxing Day with his son from his first marriage, Jacinta had to do a MacDonald's shift, and Rachel had a sleepover party. Danielle and Tom, and their two daughters would be spending the day with Tom's parents. Mary climbed the stairs to an apartment peacefully devoid of her family, for a day that she was supposedly going to spend quietly, catching up with George.

Inside her room, door quietly closed, Mary pulled her laptop out of the dressing table drawer, opened up the web browser and amended the default email logon to a private account that no other family member knew. She was not expecting any new email, she just wanted to re-read the last secret exchange; she wanted to switch her headspace out of mother and into lover. She wanted to know herself as the person who wrote the invitation, and she wanted to imagine Sam's thoughts as he wrote his reply. Today, six long months after their interlude in the Cook Islands, Sam would finally be here with her. This afternoon, tonight and tomorrow she will be under his touch, enclosed in his arms, stirred by the immensity of the love that they had shared for over thirty years. Then he would be gone, and she would return to her family life, until next time.

It hadn't always been an affair. In 1972 it was a teenage flirtation that would have flabbergasted Mama and Papa had they known, not because they didn't love their 'other son', Stephen's best friend, but because they had in mind for Mary a nice boy from a good family that attended the Greek club every week and because they had only allowed her to go to the Sunbury music festival on condition that Stephen 'look after' her. The flirtation was necessarily brief, Sam and Stephen were only in Australia for four days R&R; they returned to duty in Vietnam the day after the end of the concert. Mary's subsequent flirtation with the 'nice' Greek boy, Vasilis, came to a worse end when she fell pregnant and he and his good family disowned her. Stephen had pulled strings to appoint the best back-yard abortionist and, as Stephen generally put it, 'the problem would have been solved' if Mary's deeper Greek Orthodox beliefs had not made a surprise appearance.

Mary's pregnancy changed the family's view of Sam. Suddenly, he became a suitable husband for Mary in everyone's eyes except his own. Sam did not see why, aged 20, he should become a father to someone else's child. As Stephen well understood, having listened to Sam admit to his unrequited love for Mary on many a drunken Asian night since the Sunbury festival, Sam was furiously disappointed in his hope to marry Mary when the war was over. Stephen tried to talk Sam round, but Sam had come home from Vietnam darker, moodier, without the cheerful optimism and the forgiving nature the Kostis family had loved him for. He had come to love Vietnam even though he had hated the war, he had become addicted to the adrenalin in his blood, and his reaction to the responsibilities Stephen was trying to burden him with was to organise an immediate return to Vietnam. Vicious words were exchanged between Mary and Sam, an airing of anger and jealousy and wounded love from both sides. Passions raged and the night before Sam returned to Saigon to guard the Australian Embassy still lives in Mary's memory as the first of their truly erotic all-night love-making encounters, a night she likes to revisit whenever she anticipates their next assignation.

The third encounter was twelve years, a husband and two sons later. John was a good man, a home-loving 'Aussie bloke' who lacked the dangerous restlessness that kept Sam searching for new and challenging experiences. John had generously taken on his role as stepfather to Danielle, and he loved being a dad to his own sons. Cricket with a beer in hand was his great passion and, along with substitute TV sports in the winter months, it was his refuge whenever Mary was in a rage over a forgotten garbage bin, an unpaid credit card, children who were watching too much TV, or less than adequate romantic exertion on Valentine's day and anniversaries. John had the happy, but accumulatively infuriating knack, of never fighting back. Their relationship was a loving and safe place to raise children, a dispassionate ritual, and an easy disguise behind which she harboured her unfulfilled love of a man who, at least in fantasy, she found endlessly exciting.

On New Year's Eve, 1984, Mary's fantasy materialised at the large family and friends party Stephen was holding in the small weatherboard house he and Margarita had recently purchased in Five Dock. She had expected to see Sam at their wedding, held only three months earlier, but she had been disappointed. He was on assignment in India, reporting on the anti-Sikh policies of Indira Gandhi's government. He was convinced that something extraordinary was about to happen, and had declined his right of place as Stephen's best man. Having filed his reports on Gandhi's assassination and the subsequent anti-Sikh riots, Sam surprised them all by arriving unannounced at the party. The effect on Mary, when she saw him across the living room, was electric. He looked just as she remembered him, but with a longer, shaggier cut to his brown hair, a thicker but neatly trimmed beard and moustache. He was a head taller than most, and she watched his intense blue eyes scan the room, looking across and down at faces until he found hers. She could feel her face heating up as their eyes held each other much longer than would be appropriate; she nodded to him, and looked away, breathing deeply and busying herself with the emptying of her existing glass and selection of another drink.

He didn't move towards her, so she had to go and join the conversation he was in, allowing the crowded room to jostle her into his space, where they stood together and talked, acutely aware of every accidental touch. Eventually she pressed her fingers through his check shirt into his flank, an apparently light gesture accompanying a laughing comment, but laden with so much more contact than could be witnessed. She felt him pull away in shock and then he leant back in to regain her touch almost immediately. He lowered his mouth to her ear and whispered, "Don't do that or I won't be able to keep my hands off you." *What if I want your hands on me?* She whispered back the first admission of her intent, the words marking, in her memory, the moment their affair began.

John, sympathetic to her entreaty that she was having a great time and it was too early to leave, took their children home to bed and left her in Stephen's care. Mary and Sam discretely left the party and walked through the untidy, dark lanes of Five Dock down to the foreshore of Canada Bay, catching up on how much they had longed for each other through their widely different experience of the last twelve years. When they stopped and he gathered her into his arms under a tree that afforded them deep shadow, it seemed the most natural thing in the world to kiss him, search out his tongue in contest with hers, going deeper and deeper into the kiss until nothing else mattered. It was Sam who had the presence of mind to break the kiss as she started to undress him, pull her away from the New Year's crowd, hail a taxi and take her to his hotel.

When Mary breezed home the next afternoon she only faced Danielle's chagrin for having been left alone with two small boys all morning. John was at the SCG cheering with his mates for every Australian run, and that night he was keen to accept Mary's suggestion that he should go to watch the remainder of the match the next day. Mary spent eight wondrous hours making love with Sam, unlocking all the elements of him that she knew with certainty then, even as she did now, that he never shared with anyone else. The children survived their time home alone, though these days as she relives her memories, Mary seriously slates herself for deserting them, acknowledging that she was simply not in her right mind, so overcome was she with her ardour for Sam.

And Sam was overcome with his ardour for her. They talked of a future full of this love; they were soul mates; they had, in each other, found their other half and had been made complete; they would always have this passion for each other, it was inevitable. After the children were in bed that night, Mary interposed herself between the TV highlights replaying Australia's victory and the sofa where John was reclining and she confessed. John was dismayed, he suggested that maybe she was confusing lust with love, that she didn't have her priorities straight, that she should think about the children, that at twenty-eight years old she might be suffering a mid-life crisis, that he'd give her some time to reconsider, she should stay with him, keep quiet about this and they would work something out over time. Mary packed an overnight bag and returned to Sam's hotel room for the night.

While John had reacted with rational dismay, Sam reacted with horrified shock. He had not for a moment thought that Mary would leave John, indeed, Sam had a ticket back to India on Sunday, and he hadn't thought beyond that date at all. Instead of agreeing on a future full of love they now argued about practicalities, responsibilities, child custody, house and job searching, and the intransigent problem of how to align their two very different lives. With no workable plan in mind, Sam returned to India and Mary returned to John - to work something out over time.

It took almost a year, but Mary, sustained by passionate love letters and occasional visits from Sam, worked through the separation proceedings, dividing up property and children, and just before Sam was due to finish his last assignment in India she moved into a semi-detached in Rozelle and lovingly set up an office for him in the spare bedroom, ready for him to finally put together all his notes from Vietnam into a history of America's Lost War. Sam was thrilled with the antique writing desk she bought for him, and they were blissfully happy in the togetherness they had waited so long for ... until the 'honeymoon' John had kindly allowed them was over and it was Mary's turn to have the children.

Rob was three, but best described as still actively participating in the terrible-twos. He was capable of impressive tantrums and Sam was critical of Mary's accommodations. Sam believed in passing through the checkout without buying any sweets; he liked the phrase 'I Wants Don't Get'; he believed that the right response to a tantrum was a straddle over the knee and a sharp whack on the bum - even if the tantrum did take place at the shops in front of the neighbours. Rob was still wetting the bed, every night, and Mary was anxious that the divorce had made him insecure. Sam could do more to help, she said.

Matthew was five, eager to compete with his younger brother for attention - positive or negative. Matthew couldn't do anything the simple way. If he was supposed to walk to the car he would go via the back door, climb over the side gate, knock over the garbage bin and spill the contents on his way down, dirty his school clothes, tear a hole in his back pack. In the car he couldn't sit still, he'd be kicking the back of Sam's seat, taking off his seat belt to lean forward between the front seats, pinching his brother in order to start a fight. Only when Matthew was ill was there a respite, suddenly he would become an all too complacent child who would lie with his head in Sam's lap, listening to a story. Mary was so warm to such moments that Sam found himself ruefully wishing Matthew could be ill more often.

Danielle, who was then twelve, was overtly hostile towards Sam, taking every opportunity to cast snide remarks, ignoring every request he made. She monopolised the phone and the bathroom for hours; she drank fruit juices straight from the bottle, holding the fridge door open; she gouged the toffee bits out of the middle of the ice-cream and then left the pack on the bench to melt; she would keep him waiting beyond his endurance on days when he was supposed to pick her up from school, appearing on the side of the road as he finally left the car park, and getting into the car in surly silence; no apologies; no thanks. Sam thought Danielle needed a serious talking-to, but Mary was worried that Danielle was wagging school, her results had dropped off the radar, her teachers were expressing their concerns about her reaction to the divorce - could Sam just be kind to her? Could he just hold her, and love her until Danielle came to understand what a wonderful guy he really was and how much he cared? Sam gave Danielle a serious talking-to; Mary heaped rage upon him. Danielle continued just as she was, and Sam withdrew from the fight, leaving Mary's kids to Mary forever more.

The history of America's Lost War didn't get written. Sam found that Mary's well-intentioned offer to work while he wrote had made him a househusband instead of a journalist. He was frustrated by his inability to write, angry with himself for being unable to relate better to Mary's children, and he was angry with her for her unrealistic expectations of him. He knew he was disappointing her, and it crippled his desire for her; he had lost his place on the pedestal and he couldn't see that it was in his power to win it back. Mary asked why he didn't write love poems for her anymore and he could find no way to answer her, it certainly wasn't because he didn't love her, it was because half way through the poem a line would start with *But*. Within a year they decided their relationship would be better if Sam rented his own apartment, a space where he could write in peace.

And it was better, but in some ways it was worse. Finances were a big problem, maintaining two houses was a burden, the ever-unsettled arrangement of whose-house, which-day, where-the-children-were was particularly frustrating for Sam, who was fond of a degree of order that Mary simply could not muster. Mary was anxious over Danielle's increasing delinquency; Sam knew she wanted him to do something to fix the problem-even though she said no, she just wanted him to listen and sympathise-and he felt useless. Mary wanted an hour-long phone chat every night they weren't together. Sam, who hated the oversupply of trivial words, wanted a physical conversation in a space that was theirs alone. Phone calls often ended badly.

Towards the end of 1987 three publishers rejected the history of America's Lost War. Too late, they all said, unless Sam had a completely new perspective to offer, the reading public were bored with the Vietnam War. Mary was anxious that Sam was becoming depressed; she suggested counselling and anti-depressants. Sam had a better answer for himself; he quit his apartment and went to cover the Soviet withdrawal from Afghanistan. In 1989 he was back in his second-home, Indochina, reporting on the state of Cambodia after Vietnam's withdrawal. During his infrequent home visits Mary and Sam were as passionately in love as ever, but in between those times there were no love letters, and few phone calls. Sam simply exited her life, and Mary suffered the pain of abandonment over and over again.

There had been a long silence between them in the months before Sam turned up at the door, back from Cambodia in July 1990. Mary had been practising the words for some time, but still, as soon as Sam added his own words, the conversation departed from her planned script.

I've met someone else.
Have you had sex with him?
Yes.
How many times?
What sort of question is that?
Well.
More than once. Can we still be friends?
No.

As always, everything in her had wanted to pull him into her arms, to solve that little-boy hurt that was raw in his eyes. In that moment she would have given anything not to have slept with someone else, not to have started on this path, just to be with Sam, but the fact was that their relationship simply didn't work, and she had to take this opportunity to have a new life. She tried to strengthen herself with the belief that she was doing the best thing for Sam too.

The next week was hell for her, knowing Sam was just a phone call away, knowing she could reverse her course. Then Saddam Hussein took matters out of her hands by invading Kuwait.

It was five years, marriage and two daughters later when she heard from Stephen that Sam was in a coma in Westmead hospital. He had been flown home from Bosnia, critically injured in a mortar attack on the Markale Market in Sarajevo. He woke from taking the steps into the Market to find himself in the intensive care ward, with Mary asleep, her cheek lying on his hand. Mary-along with some of the Westmead nursing staff-is convinced that he heard her prayers, and stayed with her when the surgeons had ruled out his chances, when even his father had given permission to turn off the life support.

Ian is a kind, affable man, not unlike John, though his preoccupation is with his real estate business rather than with sport. He understood that Mary would be upset about her former partner's fight for life; he knew she was visiting Sam in hospital and, having heard from her how badly their relationship had fared before, he trusted her to prefer her happy family life with him and their two daughters. Ian is mostly right, Mary thinks as she habitually examines her body while towelling in front of the hotel mirror, she does prefer her family life with him-it is secure, comfortable, mutually beneficial, their two children have grown up in an ideal home-but there is something about Sam that Mary cannot be truly happy without. She needs to refill herself with it once in a while, and because she is wise enough now not to make any confessions, no one gets hurt.

Until today, twelve years since Sam was released from hospital, Stephen has been the only one in Mary's family to know that she and Sam continued to be lovers. Today George looks down as he is installing a new Bimini on Stephen's Caribbean 26 Flybridge, at the right moment to see her kissing Sam on the jetty, and there can be no mistaking the energetic intention between them. Later, George queries his observation with Stephen who laughs and replies with an offhand, characteristically imprecise generalisation that leaves George's head spinning.

"Oh ... they never stopped."

~

George was satisfied with his work on the Caribbean 26. When he looked around for something else to do, Stephen was with a customer and George knew better than to look for Mary. The day was hot and humid; working in the sun on top of the cruiser had made him sweat profusely and his light blue T-shirt was wet across the shoulders and as far down as the midpoint of his chest and back. He had wiped sweat off his brow several times into the neck collar of the shirt, which was now a greasy brown. He decided a swim was warranted, but not here in the murky waters of The Gut. He stepped into Stephen's Quintrex, which was berthed in front of the shop, cast off the mooring lines and motored slowly out of Sandbrook Inlet. A moment before he reached the 4 knot speed limit sign, he pressed the throttle forward and the Yamaha 60 outboard roared in response. The bow leapt and then quickly levelled out on the plane as George trimmed the prop. He stood in the wind that blasted through the open windscreen hatch, steered the boat with one hand around the Western end of Long Island and headed East along the Hawkesbury River towards the gunmetal arches of the Northern line railway bridge.

George was watching the shoreline as the Quintrex carved its way through the smooth water. He could see that the two red houseboat buoys offshore from the Long Island walking track were occupied, so he changed plan and pulled in to shore earlier, choosing a spot that had always pleased him, where two large sandstone boulders were perched on a rocky beach. Wind and water had eroded the river-faces of the boulders, exposing the beautiful swirling tones and gritty texture of the sandstone under the overhanging peaks of crusty grey, lichen spotted caps. As a boy, George had picked his way over the entire foreshore of Long Island, and he had hiked all the paths of its interior. Being just a short swim across The Gut from the marina it was a natural playground for him. Having chosen his spot for a swim now, he cut the engine and paused for a moment, measuring the push of the tide on the drifting boat.

There was no breeze, and the current was a slow outflow towards the railway bridge. Instead of fussing with the anchor, George took one of the mooring ropes in his hand. Just in time, balancing on the edge of the boat, he remembered to pat down his pockets and remove his mobile phone and wallet, dropping them into the cockpit. Then he jumped through the glistening, malachite surface of the river. The summer water was not cold, but it was refreshing and cleansing. With his free hand George rubbed the sweat out of his short hair and ineffectively tried to clean his T-shirt by squeezing and scrubbing it against his chest. Then he floated on his back, thinking blissfully of nothing other than the scraps of cirrus, hovering white against the bright blue sky, as the mooring rope tightened and the boat pulled him slowly towards the distant sea.

Five minutes later, as he approached the houseboats, George ended his meditative self-indulgence, and pulled himself hand-over-hand in to the back of the boat. He hoisted himself easily over the transom, sluiced water off his arms and his legs and squeezed water drops from the front of his T-shirt. The engine fired up at the first turn of the key, and George paused for a moment, suddenly unwilling to go back to the marina. Instead he pointed the boat towards Dangar Island and pushed the throttle forward. The apparent wind was deliciously cool on his wet body and the Yamaha made disappointingly short work of the journey. George pulled in to Dangar's public wharf, cut the throttle and let the boat nudge gently into the side of the jetty between two other dinghies. He threw out a back anchor and looped his bow line around a jetty post alongside a sign that said, 'NO TYING UP HERE'. The water level was well below the weathered planks of the walkway, and George had to pull himself up and over the white jetty railing, and jump lightly down to the wharf.

Not much had changed on Dangar in five years of Christmases. George walked up the hill away from the public wharf, past the small general store and café where he and Liz had ordered their usual–Cappuccino and a Long Black–on the last morning of their last stay. He paused to assess the line of wheelbarrows on the left hand side of the road - the local substitute for cars. The black wheelbarrow marked in burnished yellow paint 'Ella Bache' looked like it hadn't moved all year ... the weeds around it were taller than the upturned tray. The green wheelbarrow with the wooden handles marked '45G' was missing. Presumably there was a tenant in the beach-house he and Liz had come to call their own on Grantham St.

George veered to the left, up the narrow path past the community hall and then across the park. There were two girls on the swings goading each other towards greater heights while a large, untethered golden retriever watched them casually from a shady spot nearby. A young mother was helping her toddler up the playground's colourful plastic steps, across a slightly swinging bridge, down a short slide and around to the start again. On the bowling green–which was dry and brown–four bare-footed men in white and red team polo shirts were playing bowls. There was a blue esky near the Club's maintenance shed, and four beer bottles standing on the bench beside it. The Club itself was closed for Boxing Day.

When George reached the end of the sandy track between overgrown blue-flowered plumbago bushes, Bradley's Beach opened out in front of him. He looked first to the right towards the familiar beachfront of 45G, but then he turned left and stepped carefully across the broken-oyster-shell littered rocks at the Northern end of the beach. He sat down on a sandstone ledge at the point from which he could look across the wide, lazy sprawl of the Hawkesbury River to the high cliffs of Brisbane Water National Park. To his left were several private jetties, and to his right the river flowed south past Bradley's Beach before it re-joined its other half to head towards Jerusalem Bay. Liz had liked this spot because it was more private and more natural, than the beach at the front of the house. Last year they had sat here together on Boxing day evening, talking about Mary – or to be more accurate, in the aftermath of something that had been said at the Christmas gathering, Liz was complaining about Mary and George had said very little.

Thalassa

Mary's career, Liz had claimed, was to be beautiful, to attract people – mostly men. Mary had found a natural people-magnet role for herself, married to a high-end real estate broker.

Liz had asked him what it was that made Mary so attractive to men? And George was nonplussed. He volunteered that Mary had a great figure, very shapely, with generously sized breasts and she always dressed in clothes that showed her to the best advantage. When Liz had looked sceptical, he had gone on to compliment Mary's hair, which he liked when it was its natural black with just highlights of brunette to match her eyes. He liked the way she still wore her hair long, which made her look younger and she styled it in loose ringlets that made it look even more voluminous than it naturally was. Liz had been looking more annoyed with each comment and George had the uncomfortable feeling he was digging himself into a hole. He wanted an early exit from the conversation. It wasn't that *he* found that particular look appealing - but Mary always put a lot of effort into maintaining her figure, her hair, her clothes and her makeup. Men, George concluded, appreciate that.

Liz had countered that it wasn't just Mary's appearance that attracted men to her; it was her *need*. Mary had a craving for attention and she knew that she could get attention by giving it. She talked to Ian's clients as if they were the most interesting men in the world; she promoted herself as a very engaged listener. She asked questions, said outrageous things and laughed generously when her customers thought themselves funny. Men who couldn't normally hold a conversation found themselves talking to her for hours. They came away, almost invariably, feeling that she had been attracted to them, that maybe she had been signalling her interest in having an affair. Mary loved seducing men in this way – not to actually go to bed with them, but rather to trap their attention and feel her power over them. Mary, Liz had maintained, was very, very good at what she did, and it was not a shallow flirtation, it was a master of human interaction at work. Ian was a shrewd businessman, who knew how to best employ his wife's talent. He was also, Liz had declared, 'a saint'. He loved Mary steadfastly, without showing the jealousy that most men would feel, given her flirtations.

Last year, here on this rock, George had not taken that reference to 'flirtations' seriously, but now he is sitting here drying his clothes, watching the yellow cliffs turn orange in the evening light, and he wonders what Liz knew, that he had not known. He wonders what they, the in-laws to the Kostis family, used to talk to each other about in the in-between hours of family gathering.

~

It took me a while to notice George. He tells me he talked to me when I was running the Oxfam stand on the first day of uni, in our third year. But I don't remember that. He joined up on the spot, apparently, and came to a seminar I had organised with a few speakers talking about conditions in Bangladesh. I don't remember him talking to me there either, though he swears we had a long conversation. The first time I remember him was when he came to offer a sailing outing as a prize in our fund-raising auction for the orphanage. When he took the winner out on his boat he invited me to come too ... and it was only then that it occurred to me that he had an ulterior motive. We had a great day on the water and I've loved sailing ever since. He was funny, smart – I'd actually never come across a guy who wasn't totally self-interested. George, on the contrary, talked very little about himself, and seemed fascinated by me – I'll admit, it felt good. He was so quiet at uni that you wouldn't expect it, but out on the boat he was in his element. A very good sailor and a lovely companion.

But I didn't want to get into a relationship. I was going on exchange to The Hague for the European summer semester, and I didn't want to have ties at home. He was very hurt that I left him without making any kind of promise, but he wrote ... every week, I got a letter from him keeping me up to date with what our friends were doing. They weren't love letters, not really, just reminders that he was at home, waiting. There was a while when I stopped writing – I'd gone to Paris for the mid-semester break, and was hanging out with some intelligenci on the left bank and, well ... I'd made no promises to George and I resented his constant attention. Then he stopped writing ... I worried whether something had happened, and I realised I'd be sorry if I'd lost him.

I let him know when I was getting home, but he didn't meet the flight, which really upset me. Friends told me he had been dating a girl from his economics tutorial. George is handsome, in a smooth, urbane way. He dresses well, always looks neat and was clean-shaven ... as if he was already an office worker instead of a uni student. He's as far from radical as you could get. You couldn't call him charismatic, but girls did like his looks. He laughed at me later, after we were married. He said it was only to make me jealous. I wouldn't have thought him capable of such a manipulation ... 'desperate measures', he said. And it worked. We were lovers within a few weeks.

George is great in bed. Nothing is too much trouble, he'll do anything to please me, and that's made for some amazing sex ... but I've often wished he would just let me know what *he* wants. Always the answer is the same, he just wants to please me; he wants to give me what I want. I learnt to accept that. His entire want is about me, and our children ... about making us happy. Other people's wants overpower him. We had an interesting discussion after watching Titanic. He said he would stand back and let everyone else get on the lifeboats ... because they wanted to more than he did. As an afterthought he said he'd have to consider it, because of me and the kids ... that we might need him to save himself ... but apart from that he would have given way to others – not because he is a hero, just because their want is stronger than his. I know it's true, I can see that's what he would actually do, but I still find it a very strange state of mind. Wouldn't any sensible person compete tooth and claw for their own life?

The first time George brought me here to meet his family, we raced one of Stephen's yachts in the Three Island Race – rounding Lion Island, Dangar Island, Scotland Island. The start was off Palm Beach in Pittwater. The time and space make no difference to me now, I can watch the race again.

The start line is just thirty meters away, and I'm on the tiller of Stephen's Farr 1104, counting down to the gun. The wind is moderate to our starboard, 12 knots from the Nor-East, and George plans to tack across the line. He is standing tall and steady in the cockpit, watching the sail, watching the starting boat, watching the boat that's on a collision course with us. He has our sail trimmed to the max. I want to bear away from the blue Adams 45, but I have right of way and I mustn't disturb George's calculations. I'm angry with the skipper of the Adams. They have four on board. Yelling at each other, scrambling for ropes, unevenly filling and luffing their sail. On our boat the two of us are calm.

"Now," George gives the command and I push the tiller over while he unhurriedly pulls in the jib sheet, wraps it three times round the winch, brings the jib in tightly and casually leans forward to skirt the sail to the inside of the lifeline. On our boat, unlike the Adams, you wouldn't think a race was in progress. George looks up at the red tell tails spread across the white sail to satisfy himself he has the optimum pressure, cleats off the sheet on the winch, and then stoops to tidy up the ropes at his feet. He seems oblivious to the Adams, which missed our stern by inches, floundering in our dirty air as they tack behind us.

We haven't won the start. The new boat 'Serendipity', a Farr 42, is in front of us, having been shepherded by George, to some extent, to protect her from the foolishness of the crew on the Adams. Serendipity is being sailed by a middle-aged woman, Sally, whose husband died a few months short of realizing his dream to import this boat. George has given Sally the start, and it is only if she makes a serious mistake that he'll overtake her.

"Serendipity got that start well, don't you think? Look at the cut of the sails." George speaks favorably about Sally's skill at the helm and I agree with him, while keeping my opinion on the skipper of the Adams to myself – I've learnt not to annoy George with my negative views.

George is looking down Broken Bay, the crow's feet at the corners of his eyes creased in exactly that configuration that buries his white skin, and renders his tan continuous. His lips are narrow; evaluative; the dimple between chin and lower lip deepens while he considers his options. He tastes the breeze, noting the small cumulus tufts that are increasingly coming in our direction from the South. The wind, he says, is going to change as we go past Juno Point.

"Definitely the number 2 spinnaker", his comment is to himself, while keeping me informed. He bends from his boy-hips, ducks his head under the canopy and crabs his way down the steps to get the sail bag from the cabin.

I am left in the cockpit, one hand holding the tiller steady against the pressure behind the sail, and the other hand lying out towards the transom as I watch this superb waterway pass by. My job is no more than to stay behind Sally's Farr and in front of the rest of the fleet ... I must suppress my natural urge to win the race. I'm supposed, he has told me, to "relax and enjoy".

Our spinnaker run takes us all the way upriver from Juno Point to Dangar Island. Some boats round the island to starboard and some to port. In the middle, on the Northern side of the island, thirty yachts cross paths in an elaborate, inter-leaving dance driven by the wind on opposing tacks. George has briefed Sally in advance that in today's conditions she should keep Dangar to starboard. He is entertaining himself, flexing his sailing muscle by staying just a boat length to the rear and to port of her. He is taking photos of Serendipity, keeling majestically to port as the wind hits her hard from the Eastern corner of the island. When it hits us in the next moment-right across from the rock where we now sit, so many years later-he loses his footing, throws out an arm and swings back on one of the stays, landing athletically like a leopard.

Like a leopard, he is beautiful to watch, when totally unconscious of being watched. If he knows he is being watched, his elegance crumbles. When startled, he retreats to a safe hideaway, from which he can watch but not be seen. He's made a life of not standing out despite his abilities, of avoiding confrontation.

Unlike a leopard, he has no spots. The skin on his long back is unblemished olive, smooth to stroke all the way down from the hard bones of his shoulders to the soft rounds of his buttocks, which harden and flex impressively to my pinch. His black hairs thicken as my touch slides down to the back of his knees, and his bicycle-muscled calves are quite well covered – long enough to tease them with a comb; long enough to stream with water in the shower; as long as the hair on his head was when I first met him.

Now his hair is short cropped, a number 2 every four weeks is his habit. Neat, short and straight, streaked with steel grey, receding at the corners of his brow. It is strong hair, softened only by the conditioner I wanted him to use, and at bedtime, when the hair has broken out from his cheeks and jaw, it is distinctly abrasive, more enjoyable against some parts of my body than others – as he well knows. He tried a moustache for a short while, which looked quite debonair, as was his intention, but that had nasty consequences for my own face and I convinced him his lips were much better without it.

He doesn't smile widely enough. His lips bend without showing his teeth, his upper lip thins and stretches, turning up evenly at each end, while his lower lip pops out more fully … but his teeth stay hidden. There is no good reason for this, his teeth are perfectly formed; his bite is even. It's because he thinks too much of him will escape if he opens his mouth wide.

I saw much of him escape the moment he first held David, and it escaped again when Claire was born. He can give a smile that's wide enough to embrace the world when he forgets that someone is watching.

His wide smile crunches his normally straight nose, it turns his brown eyes into dark slits and accentuates the crow's feet wrinkles that stretch away to either side of his face. The creases in his tan become unhinged, showing up white in unusual places. The three deep lines across his brow multiply, and the scar across the bridge of his nose disappears. His thick eyebrows bunch into tufts, showing spikes of grey that were well hidden before. All this happens to his face when I tickle him, though soon he'll be protesting through clenched teeth. He is fiendishly ticklish, and I can use this to advantage in removing his reserve. Where the shaggy carpet of hair on his chest ends at his rib-line, and the bare skin of his flanks pares away to the bones of his boy-hips. The lightest of touches, a thinly drawn nail there will get him every time. And when he has made himself safe by wrapping the long fingers of just one of his large hands around both my wrists, he will unclench his teeth and give the laugh I love to hear.

And I regret every moment, when instead of that laugh we argued, we worked, we worried, we wasted the time we didn't know we wouldn't have. It's the worst thing, seeing him sad and being unable to touch him and make him laugh.

~

It is the night of Boxing Day, 2007. Having come in from a cold night swim at the Brooklyn baths, Sam has Mary pinned against the tiles of the shower wall in their apartment, the full water pressure of the hot shower spraying liberally over them both; she has been begging him for many minutes now to quit teasing and take her to bed, instead he laughs, twists her nipple harder, holds her up as her knees buckle, keeps her waiting and wanting until the moment he chooses.

On the other side of the railway line, in the Kostis' house, relations are more demure. After dinner, when Stavros IV started belabouring his sons again about the promise to which Stavros I had indentured them, Stephen summarily retired to his office, citing "paperwork", and George opened his laptop to read the days news from *The Age* website. Now Stavros has retired to his room and George is looking for his children first on email, then Facebook, then a hopeful look at Skype to see if Claire is online again. Margarita is gazing into the night, watching the lights of boats moored in The Gut glittering across the water, stroking the cat that has taken this opportunity to occupy her uncommonly still lap.

Claire is not on Skype. She is uneasily applying make-up in her Boston bathroom, preparing herself for introduction to her girlfriend's stepfamily, the second half of their Christmas obligations. During a quick call on Australia's Christmas night she deflected George's question about how she will spend America's Christmas day. She is procrastinating. She promises herself she will tell George about her sexuality later, when she has met both sides of Leah's family. She will invite him to Boston for Easter after she has gauged his reaction.

David, at home sleeping off a second consecutive afternoon of food and wine, has forgotten completely that Claire reminded him with a text message on Christmas morning, that he should call his father. Claire will be angry with David when she finds out (and she *will* ask because she expects the worst of her brother and seeks to improve him), but in fact, George is one of those easy-going people who expects little, and enjoys with surprise the graces other people show him. George regularly doesn't notice that he should be offended by someone's behaviour until Claire brings the transgression to his attention, and even then he struggles to agree with her.

"We do think about her a lot." Margarita, still watching the reflections from the water, speaks into the emptiness that follows Papa's departure and George knows perfectly well she is not referring to Claire. "Even if we don't say her name. Why is that do you think?" The question seems rhetorical, and George does not find an answer, nor does he feel he must find an answer. "Well, I miss her. Christmas isn't the same without sharing a bitch about the Kostis men while we're making the salads."

George has to smile at that, drawing back from the precipice that sympathy throws him towards, but still not trusting himself to reply. He opens an Internet tab on his laptop and absently finds something to click on. It seems helpful to keep the screen moving even though he doesn't know what he is looking at.

"Off you get Toffee-cat." Margarita lifts the cat from her lap and sets him gently down on the sofa, arranging his legs comfortably. Being a cat, Toffee won't accept being arranged and immediately jumps off the sofa and stalks towards the kitchen expecting supper. Margarita obliges by putting some kibble into his bowl.

"I won't hassle you then." Margarita returns to put a hand on George's shoulder and she squeezes gently. "Whenever you want to talk, *please* do. Goodnight."

George waits long enough for Margarita to be gone, closes his laptop, and slips quietly away to his bedroom, wanting to escape before Stephen emerges from the office.

A little later, lying in bed with the curtains open because he is not expecting sleep anytime soon, George is thinking about escape. For the last six months his goal post has been Christmas. Tomorrow he will return to his empty house in Melbourne and then what? Twelve months till next Christmas? Nine months until Claire returns, *if* she returns … what date can he keep his feet moving towards that doesn't seem too far away; doesn't seem too pointless? He has two year's of annual leave accrued, and the company wants him to reduce that … but how can he get excited about going on a holiday by himself? Should he intrude on Claire in Boston? Claire is 'parentifying', taking on her mother's role towards David and her father, and George is acutely aware that he needs to step out of his grief, be independent and set a better example to his children. Claire and David have their lives and he must live his own.

Should he move to the Central Coast to be closer to Stephen and Margarita? He does love the Hawkesbury. He experiences a great feeling of well-being when he is alone, out on the river, like he has been today. Should he offer to join Stephen in the boat hire business, expand it in a joint venture of some kind? George dismisses this thought immediately; tossing angrily in the bed to shed the bitter memory of the last time he and Stephen had tried to work together.

Thirteen years ago, when Papa had finally conceded that he could no longer run the Marina, Stephen's marine parts business had been based in Sydney, and George was working as an accountant with the Office of the Public Trustee in Melbourne. Initially they had installed a manager at the Marina, and-as part of the 'Papa's Business' charade, George now realises-Stephen and George agreed to share business decisions. Very soon it became obvious that they could not reconcile their very different ideas about how to run a business. Stephen was a combative wheeler-dealer, he traded boats and boat parts like he played football – check for the referee, dig in an elbow, grab the ball and run. Once in a while someone punched him back, but on balance he was a successful player. George was in favour of win-win deals, sticking to the rules, taking care of the entire supply chain long-term. It made George cringe to hear Stephen lie - George hated to even think of the word, but that's what he felt the sales-hype really was. When George protested, Stephen called him 'naïve' and cited his own superior experience in business. When George complained about the figures Stephen wanted him to report to the tax department, Stephen appointed another accountant who would report the figures he was given at face value. The end came when George refused to sign the returns and Stephen forged his signature.

The only way to preserve any brotherly-bond had been for George to remove himself from the running of the business completely and sell Stephen his supposed share in the company. Stephen had moved his importing business and his family to Brooklyn, sacked the manager of the Marina, and for several years now he had been running all aspects of the business himself.

Lying in bed, able now to see the crescent moon, George acknowledges that the injustice he had felt upon exiting the family business was, in newly exposed fact, completely unwarranted. Stephen supported Papa by giving him a job that made him happy for fifteen years through to a late retirement, and now he continues to support Papa by giving him a family home that will shelter him until the end of his life. Stephen is working himself at a brutal pace to keep up the business, and he evidently cannot go to Greece at Easter, one of his busiest times of the year. George realises, with heavy guilt, that it is himself who has neither met, nor been called upon to meet, any family responsibilities. Why should the responsibility of being Greek always fall on Stephen? George concludes that the reason is not tradition; it is that Papa rightly prefers his elder son.

As the idea of going to Greece dawns on George, as it starts to take over his thoughts and gradually turns itself into a decision, George does not take into account the promise that Stavros I made to Saint Nikolaos. He does not for a moment believe that Stavros was saved from the sea by Saint Nikolaos (twice), and he does not believe that his father owes anything to Saint Nikolaos for being alive at the end of World War II. He does not believe that any bad luck will come to the family if the church at Firopotamos rots, and he certainly does not believe any more than I do, that it was Papa's neglect of the church that caused a semi-trailer to veer onto the wrong side of the highway on April 8th 2007.

But George has always admired the photo of the church on Papa's bedroom wall, set against a beautiful backdrop of clear azure water, wooden dinghies and colourful syrmata. He knows he has 'cousins' in Milos – Anton, who sent the photo, and no doubt numerous other relatives who would welcome him if he visited. He speaks Greek, for God's sake, and he has never uttered a word of it in the land in which his father was born. He realizes that if he goes to Milos he won't be going on a lonely vacation just to use his accumulated leave; he will be amongst family, and his holiday will have a purpose. Destiny's predetermination of his decision is, as you can see, perfectly rational.

XI

February 2008: London

"I've found him!" Martin's excitement carried clearly over the phone and Lynne knew, despite the lack of preamble, that he was referring to their lost cousin. "In fact, I've found his son ... Nick Foster died in August last year in Sydney."

"How about you back up and tell me from the start," Lynne cradled the phone on her shoulder, closed the plastic cover on the student assignment she was marking, walked into the kitchen and took the kettle across to her sink.

"Well you know I've been researching the Australian databases for Nick Baxter or Nick White and getting nowhere."

Lynne hummed in accord, replaced the kettle on its electric base and flicked the switch.

"Well Sam Foster has been researching the English databases for Nick Baxter and he found us."

"And who is Sam Foster?"

"Sam Foster is Nick Foster's son, and Michael Foster married Bess Robertson of Caldbeck in Sydney in 1930."

"I think the start might be earlier, back up." Lynne liked to get an accurate chronological story; Martin frustrated her by reporting on events in order of personal importance to him.

Martin drew breath in preparation for the longer story. Lynne dropped a tea bag in a cup and watched the kettle as it started to rumble. She was much more interested in the Kostis family and the missing arms of Venus De Milo than the missing branches of the Baxter family tree, but she was prepared to humour Martin while she took time out for a cuppa.

"Nicholas Baxter the second drowned at Cromer in 1923 and his wife, Bess had a son, also christened Nicholas, who was not quite three years old at the time. You already know that much. The next bit was just gossip passed down from a woman who had been in the staff at Caldbeck Hall. Apparently, while Nicholas was away at sea, Bess had an affair with Caldbeck's horse-master, Michael White. After Nicholas died they told Bess's father that they wanted to get married. The Earl refused - Michael White was no more suitable for Bess than Nick had been, her father had someone else lined up - so Bess and Michael eloped, with baby Nick, to Australia in 1924. My problem in finding their immigration record was that they eloped under an assumed name - Foster."

"So how did baby Nick Foster find you?" Lynne poured boiling water onto the tea bag and opened the fridge to get milk.

"Nick Foster is dead" Martin corrected her impatiently. "He died in August, and when his son, Sam, was in Australia at Christmas, gathering the information needed to handle the estate, he was surprised to find the name 'Baxter' on his father's English birth certificate."

"So *Sam* looked up the English ancestry database and found us."

"That's the one, but there's more to it."

"Hmmm?" Lynne settled back at her desk, placed her cup of tea by the stack of assignments and re-opened the one she had been reading. She was estimating how many she still had to mark before tomorrow.

"Well, Sam saw a query that I had left on the community board on *Genes Reunited*."

"He's contacted you? You've actually talked to him?" Lynne had picked up on the familiarity with which Martin was talking about 'Sam'.

"Yep." Martin sounded smug.

"You said ... 'When in Australia' ... Where does Sam live?" Lynne was retrospectively paying attention.

"London. Want to have lunch with us on Friday?"

"You're a bastard. Why didn't you say so at the beginning?"

"You told me to back up."

~

Lynne absently wraps her index finger with strands of blonde hair as she watches an empty barge make its way up the Thames. It crosses her line of sight, obscuring Shakespeare's Globe, traversing the Tate Modern, and carving into the thick slug of outgoing tide under Blackfriars Bridge. At arm's length from her, rain adheres in small droplets to the expansive windows of the restaurant; fresh spits arrive, overburdening existing droplets and forcing them to the ground. It is overwhelmingly grey, which is no more or less than Lynne expects it to be.

Martin is chatty, as their mother Jean has assured me he would be. With Lynne he makes up for his fear of talking to other people. He thinks Lynne understands everything he says because she doesn't interrupt him; she doesn't test his meaning; she doesn't try to correct him. He takes this as a sign that Lynne is smart, and others are dumb because he cannot engage with the likelihood that Lynne, who has known him all her life, is not, in fact, listening to much that he says.

It's a rare event, Martin and Lynne together at a restaurant table. They used to meet every Wednesday night at the modest flat Martin could afford with income from the family trust. Since James moved out, Martin now visits Lynne at her house every Sunday, arriving promptly with his companion Labrador,

Inka, at 10am. Martin wants to 'fix things', and there is much in Lynne's house that needs fixing. Last week while Lynne baked the Sunday roast, Martin fixed a dripping tap in the bathroom, he replaced a down light in the hall, and he fixed a cupboard hinge in the kitchen because the cupboard door had to be lifted in order to close. Lynne had been living with that problem for weeks before Martin had occasion to close the door himself. Martin has already caught up with the long history of things James never fixed – including refurbishment of the ramshackle garden shed that was mostly buried within an overgrown niche in the hedge.

Martin remembers Pop's wherry shed, and fifty years later he has faithfully reproduced it in miniature, in Lynne's back yard. He still has Pop's tools, all hanging now in the outline he has drawn for each implement on a pegboard. The tools not suited to hanging are in drawers lined with felt so they won't rattle; the nails and screws are in compartments made to the right size, in order, left to right. Like Pop, Martin can put his hand on exactly what he wants the moment he wants it. He prefers Lynne does not try to fix things herself. She is careless, her work is makeshift; she returns screws to the wrong size compartment; she hangs the hammer between the wrong hooks. They have an agreement that Lynne should not enter Martin's shed.

Martin is glad James is gone. He never liked James. He likes Marcus, but suffers the same frustrations he has with Lynne. Marcus is vague, Marcus is careless, Marcus should fix things for his mother and instead he plays games on his PC. Lunch on Sunday only works because Marcus is out on Sunday morning at the gym, where he escapes Martin's critical attention. Tayla's preferred way to escape Martin's attention is to stay in bed, with Inka under the covers till lunchtime. But Martin and Lynne have an agreement that he mustn't talk about James or Marcus or Tayla, so at this particular moment, when Lynne is watching the barge move out of sight and Sam Foster walks into the restaurant, Martin is talking about anomalies he has seen in the 2005 financial year balance sheet of the Norfolk Wherry Trust. Before Martin finishes his train of thought, Sam announces himself with a light touch to Lynne's shoulder and is entertained rather than apologetic about her jolt of surprise.

Sam's stare is direct, appreciative. Having heard what Lynne would describe as Martin's 'over-sharing', Sam imagined she would look older; he thought she would be plain. She has come to lunch directly from lecturing; wearing light make-up, witch-hazel eye shadow and dark eyeliner that highlights the brown flecks in her green eyes. Her platinum sheen blouse is settled loosely across the shape of her breasts leaving her neck long, smooth and touchable. Her nose is small and straight and as he measures her, the pale skin on her cheeks is colouring quickly towards the red gloss on her lips. She blinks in recovery and settles her lips part way between generous and pert, in a controlled smile. She returns his gaze with a sceptical tilt of her head. They have looked at each other too long. Sam concedes and offers her his hand saying no more than his name. Their touch is brief and mutually constrained.

Martin has understood nothing of the exchange, but the silence weighs on him. He starts to tell Sam about the ledger of the Norfolk Wherry Trust, which prompts Lynne to swing into preventative action. Lynne has instructed Martin that she will do the talking.

~

Lynne's first impression was that Sam Foster was very tall. He was too close, and too sudden for her to stand to greet him, and before she could organise herself he had offered his handshake down to her. He was at least four inches taller than Martin, and the word that came to Lynne's mind was 'rangy'. Everything about Sam was proportionately large, his shoulders and chest were broad, his neck and head would have been half the size of hers again, but he was lean - the belly that featured large on most of the middle-aged male staff at the university was missing. Either Sam was so large he was impossible to fill, or he had a good exercise routine. Maybe it was both.

Through the small talk about commonalities and differences in their family backgrounds, Lynne listened to Sam's accent, trying to separate its Australian idiom from the many other accents she thought she heard in it. When she asked he gave a light laugh and self-effacingly said he had 'been around'. Later, when she asked directly about his job he said he was a journalist and his work had taken him many places. 'Home', it seemed, was either a war zone or the headquarters of whichever news network he was reporting for. At the moment that was London, but it had been New York, Baghdad, Sarajevo, Saigon ... he had spent more of his life away from Sydney than 'at home' there.

It seemed obvious to Lynne that Sam could not have a family and she felt too awkward to ask, but it wasn't long before Martin, unable to stick to the spirit of her instructions, covered off those questions. Sam unhesitatingly confirmed that he had never married, and he laughed while mooting the possibility that his genes might be continuing in Vietnam. When Martin turned a new page of his notebook to pursue the Vietnamese family connection, Sam had to recant and swear that the Nicholas Baxter line of the family tree truly ended with him. When Sam admitted to not wanting children Lynne thought that he must have been compensating himself; Lynne could not imagine anyone who, if they had the opportunity, would not want to have children. Sam must live a very self-centred life, she thought reprovingly. She was not surprised when Sam showed only a superficial interest in the photos Martin showed him of her family. Lunch, she decided, was dragging on too long.

When they had finished their main course Sam produced a silver laptop from his backpack and asked Martin if he had brought a USB. While Lynne searched her handbag for the little black stick, Martin briefed Sam on how disorganised she was and Lynne found herself uncharacteristically angry. Sam inserted the USB in his laptop, waited for it to register, and then went smoothly through the steps required to copy some folders. Lynne noticed that his two hands covered the complete spread of the keyboard, but unlike most men who had large hands, his were agile, poised like a pianist over the keys, long fingers striking keys quickly and accurately, confirming that he was an accomplished typist.

"Happy reading." There was smug condescension in his voice, and Lynne prickled with irritation as he dropped the USB stick into her palm. She had what she wanted; she could go now.

"Thanks, I hope it will fill in some of the gaps in my mother's record of the family story. It's great to have it."

"No problem. Call me if you have any questions."

"Thanks. I really need to get back to work, sorry - you two keep talking if you want." Lynne tried to excuse herself independently, but Sam did not want to stay for coffee and after the delay of settling the bill they all walked out of the restaurant together. At the door they fastened up their overcoats against the grey sleet of London's winter and parted company, Sam walking briskly in the direction of Fleet Street, and Lynne and Martin heading towards Blackfriars tube station.

"Well, would he be a good fuck?" Martin queried when Sam was quite possibly still within earshot.

"Oh shut up Martin, how many times have I told you *not* to say that!"

Lynne sped up and Martin had to run to catch up and harry her with other words for her opinion of their new relative. Knowing he would not be put off, Lynne soon stopped and faced him.

"I think he is entirely self-centred. He's got just enough curiosity to meet us, and he's not going to be the least bit interested in seeing us again."

"And if you've got what you want on that USB stick you won't be interested in seeing him again?" Martin dogged her.

"That's right."

However, the content of the USB stick was more than Lynne expected and it made her very interested in seeing Sam again.

~

Sam had, over the years, developed a journalistic habit of scanning 'primary source' documents and storing them on his computer. These days, his preferred database was 'in the cloud', so the documents were safe if his computer failed or was stolen or crushed or drowned-all of which had happened to him before-and so he could access his information from any Internet connection, anywhere in the world. At his fingertips in the restaurant he had not only the copies of his parent's birth and death certificates that interested Martin, he also had a scan of Nick Baxter Foster's written memoir of his service in Egypt, Greece, Crete and New Guinea during the second world war. Lynne had wanted a copy to add to her compilation of Baxter writings. What staggered her, when she read the memoir, was the sudden appearance in Crete of the name that had been plaguing her, Stavros Kostis from Milos. It was clear, in the New Guinea section of the memoir that Foster and Kostis had continued their friendship through correspondence. Lynne wanted more information; in particular she wanted an address.

When she had called Sam he had infuriated her by refusing to talk on the phone. It was clear to her from his reaction that he knew the Kostis family personally, but he would not give her their address. Instead he invited her to meet him for a drink after work. "I'll come to you," he had said, and now he was keeping her waiting at the Plume of Feathers, two blocks away from her office at Greenwich University. When he eventually opened the door he blocked out the light from the street and entered as a silhouette, ducking under the overhanging transom. His gaze fell on her immediately and he smiled with lips that stayed straight while his eyes creased and deep lines curved away from his nose.

"Drink?" he tapped the table lightly instead of shaking hands.

"Cider, Bulmers medium thanks."

"Sorry I'm late" he tossed the words carelessly over his shoulder as he went to the bar.

"Sure you are," Lynne muttered to herself, draining the remaining cider she had been reserving in her glass for several minutes.

"So why does Stavros Kostis interest you?"

At least, Lynne thought, Sam didn't mess around with small talk. It did seem brusque, and characteristically Australian, that he got straight to the point when he returned to the table, but she was glad of it, she wanted to get home.

"It is a big coincidence don't you think? Our great great-grandfather writes a story about rescuing a Stavros Kostis from the sea at Navarino, and then your father writes a story about a Stavros Kostis rescuing him from Crete. Is this 'Stavros Kostis' a mythical character who is resurrected in each generation's family story-telling?"

Sam had been leaning across the table, propped on his elbows, eyes fixed on her face while she studied her cider bottle, her glass or looked across to the bar instead of meeting his eyes. When called upon to answer he leaned back in his chair without breaking his stare, remaining silent until she actually looked at him.

"No, the Stavros Kostis from Crete is real. He's Stavros the Fourth, and he's going to be 84 this year. I don't know the story about the Stavros Kostis at Navarino. Tell me that one."

Lynne tried to relay the story briefly, but Sam pulled her up with questions at several points and by the end she knew he had extracted everything she herself knew about the Battle of Navarino. She had not, however, told him about the other revelations Stavros I had made to Nicholas Baxter during their hospitalisation in Malta.

"Sounds right to me," Sam concluded when it was evident Lynne would say no more. "Stavros the first was a fisherman in Milos, after the family boat was wrecked he became a ship's pilot in Milos harbour, and later he served as a pilot in the Mediterranean for the British admiralty. I didn't know he was injured at Navarino, but it's likely he was there."

"Coincidence then?" Lynne didn't find the idea of coincidence convincing.

"It does happen. I read a good saying on it – 'coincidence' is God choosing to stay anonymous." Sam played that straight-lipped smile again and Lynne wasn't sure whether he was being condescending. What she was sure of was that he knew more than he was telling her.

"So how do you know so much about Stavros Kostis?"

"As you know, my father and Stavros kept up after the war. Our families were close friends."

"Stavros Kostis immigrated to Australia?"

"That's right."

"Would you give me their address?"

"Why?" Sam watched her closely while she was unable to find a suitable answer. "You know the stories are true, what else do you want?"

"I'm interested in the church Stavros built for Saint Nicholas. I want to know where it is, I'd like to visit it."

For the first time Sam looked away from her. He studied the window to the street for a long moment. Lynne desperately wanted to know what was going on inside his head, but he was unfathomable to her.

"I think I can get what you want. Do you have a PC in your office?"

Lynne nodded, surprised by the question.

"Let's go then." Sam finished his drink and stood up, turning for the door. Lynne followed, not knowing how to refuse him, bewildered that she had been somehow duped into taking him to her workplace.

In her office, while she booted up her PC, his eyes explored everything in the room. He commented on her title, 'Dr Williams', and summarised the books on her shelves, 'Art History'. He flipped the book that was on the side of her desk to its bookmark, looked for a moment at the diagrams of the Venus De Milo with a range of structurally possible arms, but said nothing. He named the photos on her desk, 'Tayla and Marcus' making her realise that his interest when they had lunched the week before was not as superficial as she had thought. She felt anxious about the things she had lying around in her office, not having expected an inspection.

"Do you investigate everyone like this?" She thought the question would stop him, and it did succeed in making him pause to look at her directly.

"You would have to ask everyone," his smile was cheeky, "which could be hard."

"Meaning you are the best one to give me an answer," she retorted.

"I'm a journalist."

"That's a predictable reply."

"I'm sticking to it." Without invitation Sam leant over her and shifted the keyboard across her desk. His torso was so long that when he knelt beside her chair he was suitably placed to type. While she was wondering how to protest he had opened an Internet tab, and was deftly typing in user names and passwords. She found herself watching his hands in fascination.

"This is a letter Stavros sent from Athens when Dad was in New Guinea. 1945 - they figured the war was about to end." Sam was scrolling down to the end of the letter. "Last paragraph." He pointed to the screen, directing Lynne to read the faded, messy script.

"I can't come Australia mate. My family, my church, all

Milos. No commies get Milos. When we tell they will shut the churches everyone throw them out, no worries. Milos never change. I get another boat. I marry with Aretha and have many Kostis sons. Maybe never rich to see your Sydney, but you come see me. When war over send your letter to Stavros Kostis, Firopotamos, Milos. Here is how in Greek."

"Done?"

"Where is that stored ... have you downloaded it or could I have a print?" As Lynne asked Sam was already opening another tab and typing into the search bar. In a moment he had brought up a screen full of pictures of a colourful Greek seaside village. He tilted his head sideways to examine a photo of a church as if placing it in a different perspective.

"That's the church," he said confidently.

"How do you know?"

"There's a photo on Papa's bedroom wall."

"Papa?"

"Stavros the Fourth."

"Right. You *do* know the family well don't you."

"Saved. You can print it later if you want. I'd like to get a copy of the story our great grandfather wrote about the Battle of Navarino ... do you have that here?" Sam's hands were poised, ready to go in the folder direction she nominated.

"No ... I haven't scanned it in. I only have the original and it is with my mother's things." Lynne was dismayed by the ease of her instinctive lie.

"Well I'd like a copy, if you could."

"By email?"

"In person, if you would, I'll drop by to get it."

"Hmm." Lynne's suspicions simmered. Watching Sam's hands and the screen, she realised a few clicks late that he had erased her browsing history.

"What if I wanted that?"

"Sorry. You wanted to know about the church more."

Lynne didn't know whether to be angry or thankful. In a few minutes he had delivered to her the information that had evaded her for months. He stood and she followed him up.

"You are cagey aren't you - what are you hiding?"

"I'm a journalist." Said with that smile again. "What's your excuse?"

Lynne felt her face heating under his gaze. She stepped back from him.

"Time to go." Were his words a question or was she just alarmed by a normal Australian end of sentence inflection?

"Yes," Lynne replied quickly. "Thanks for doing this ... I'll let you out, I just need to finish up here."

"OK," Sam compliantly followed her out of her office to the university after-hours exit door.

"Goodbye, and thanks again," Lynne offered her hand formally.

"See ya," Sam gave the customary Australian farewell, held her hand still for a moment without allowing a shake. "You won't find any traces on your PC." He walked away without looking back.

For a moment Lynne was alarmed that he meant he hadn't saved the letter or the picture of the church. She hurried back to her office, but both files were there, safely in her downloads folder. She requested prints and while the printer was chattering she couldn't help but open her Internet browser to look around. What wasn't there, as he had promised, was any sign of how he had accessed his files. Neither was there any proof as to whether he had accessed any of hers.

Lynne found her mobile in her bag and selected Martin from the contacts list.

"Martin, don't tell Sam *anything* about the Venus De Milo, OK?" She said as soon as the usual pleasantries had been exchanged.

"Why not?"

"He's a *journalist*, OK? I don't trust him. He's the last

person we would want to know about this."

"Does that mean you think it's true?"

"It could be, it could be true."

"So what are you going to do?"

Lynne walked over to the university calendar that was stuck to her office wall with Blu Tack. "I think I'll go. This semester break after Easter, I think I should go and see for myself."

"Wow!" Martin thought for a moment, knowing from experience that he could be misinterpreting. "Is this a joke?"

"No Martin, this is not a joke. I think I should go to Greece."

"Wow!" Martin repeated. "Good luck finding the church."

"I don't need good luck, I've got the address."

XII

March 2008: London

During their settlement proceedings, James at one point charged Lynne with being 'a tit-for-tat player', and there is some truth in that. Being an over-hindsight thinker, the 'tit-for-tat' response often slips subconsciously into her plans. By walking into the Plume of Feathers, ten minutes late, she was intentionally keeping Sam waiting but she also intended to hand over the copy of the Navarino manuscript and make an immediate getaway. The strategy backfired, however, because Sam already had a bottle of cider on the table for her. As she conceded and removed her coat Sam leafed through the pages of the copy, pausing to read the last couple of paragraphs in more detail. Lynne sipped on her drink anxiously, waiting for him to ask where the rest of the story was, but he folded the copy into his pocket and said nothing more than "Thanks."

Keen to divert conversation away from the manuscript, Lynne rushed awkwardly into an alternative.

"I read an article you wrote about the US making undemocratic stipulations about the new government in Iraq," she began.

"You've Googled me." A teasing smile; an embarrassing exposure of her intent.

"Have you Googled me?" In defence.

"Of course," he laughed, making her feel easier about the exchange.

"Well, all you've found is a few journal articles and conference attendances - I'm very boring, I've done more teaching than publishing."

"Your thesis was on Roman and Greek sculpture, and how different techniques were used to uniquely identify mythical characters. You were arguing that even when different sculptors were at work, they used the same style of cut when carving Aphrodite, and they use a different, common style when carving Poseidon - for example. So when archaeologists dig up body parts, you've got a good chance of telling which character they belong to … you can verify that the find belongs to a particular statue."

Lynne was flattered that he had read her work in enough detail to paraphrase it even though she was concerned about the way he was steering the conversation. What did he know?

"Style of cut makes a contribution to identifying parts of the same statue," she elaborated, "even though it is principally used to identify the artist. I was arguing for the archetypal view - an artist cuts stone differently when carving Aphrodite than the same artist does when carving Poseidon. It's about the relationship the artist has with the mythical figure, and there can be more points in common between different artists both carving Poseidon, than there are between Aphrodite and Poseidon when carved by the same artist. Sometimes that makes it easier, and sometimes it makes it harder to identify parts of a statue … it is just something that needs to be accounted for."

"Do you do any work in identifying sculptures?"

"No, that was a long time ago. I was interested in archaeological art finds back then, but I got married, I had children … and teaching was a more suitable career."

"Laser scanning has endorsed your theory."

"Yes, that's been gratifying." How did Sam know that? "Are you interested in sculpture? Your news articles didn't lead me to think you were an art historian - you focus on war and politics."

"I am interested in art and sculpture, and there is a relationship to war and politics. Art has often been the booty of war and the proceeds from selling the stolen treasure have often been used to support corrupt regimes."

"Do you think that was the motive behind the theft of the paintings from the Zurich museum last month?" Lynne guessed Sam would know of the robbery.

"Yes, I think those paintings are headed for Serbia."

"They found the Monet and the Van Gogh in the backseat of a car a week later."

"They were lucky, and the thieves were careless. It will be a long time before we get the Cezanne and the Degas back."

"We?"

"Manner of speech."

"Are you working on an article about it?"

"No. I'm just alert to things Serbian because I was posted there during the war. What's paying my beer money now is news from Iraq."

"You're not optimistic about the Iraqi government? You think the US will fail in its 'puppet mastery'?" Lynne was genuinely interested in the subject; to her democracy was a treasure from Ancient Athens, and she had found herself in agreement with Sam's charge that the manipulation of government coalition parties in Iraq was an abuse of the concept.

"Headlines about the failure of the US in Iraq sell articles." Sam spoke so bluntly against his own work that Lynne's interest was sharply piqued, and when he caught a passing bar attendant to ask for another round of drinks she leant towards him across the table instead of raising any objection.

"Explain. Your writing doesn't read as if you're kow-towing to an editor?" Lynne surprised herself by flattering him, but it was true, she thought his writing was very good.

"You get your news from places like Iraq in sound-bytes. You get a headline, a few paragraphs and a picture in the paper, or on the Internet you can follow a link to a web page with just a few more paragraphs and an extra picture or 1 minute video … no background, no substance. You think you're getting the news but it's just a dribble of crumbs drawing you to the advertising, sucking you in to click on something that lets the networks fill up their databases with your personal 'interests'."

"But I read an actual article-pages-you wrote on why democracy will fail, or at least to be a very bloody road, in the Arab states."

"Because you Googled me as the author." Sam mirrored her in leaning across the table, so they could hear each other better amidst the hubbub if the pub. "That's what we write for our own sakes as writers, we publish it on blogs read by other journos. We don't get paid for that, and we're only preaching to the converted, we don't reach anyone who needs to know. I write an article, I put an editor-attracting headline on it, and the editor selects a fraction of the article to go into the news that people read. The editors are 'gate-keepers', you know, they choose which bits to serve up as news."

"Well, given that I've read the full article … you think democracy will fail in Iraq and in Egypt. Do you think there will be a blood bath over democracy in Syria?"

"I am in favour of democracy, absolutely, I just think people need to have generations of secular education, *and* freedom of association, to use it properly. Islamic 'democracy', at this point in time is designed to engineer public affirmation of a religious leader or coalition of ethnicities. It isn't about making an educated choice between political and social policies. Without strong, continuous advocacy from the full gamut of civil society democracy is vulnerable to the media, to business interests, to corrupt politicians, to fundamentalists … politics becomes a matter of identity not policy and people get led by the most powerful voice. There's a utilitarian argument that if everyone participates, government will arrive at the answer that is best for the greatest number, but for that to work, people have to be able to make an informed choice about what is best for themselves."

"You're a Utilitarian?" Lynne interrupted, wondering at a common interest in Philosophy.

"Part Utilitarian, part Consequentialist – the end result for the good of the majority," Sam continued smoothly. "People are mostly sheep - they'll follow the most charismatic voice-media, pop stars, fundamentalists-they can easily be made to vote against their own best interests. In Iraq the population has elected the leader the US wanted, and the US has to keep boots on the ground to keep their man in place. When Egypt votes it will democratically elect its next oppressor - watch this space. When Syria votes there will only be one candidate – *their* oppressor. What's 'democratic' about that? Any adjustment to democracy in the Islamic states will take generations, and there will be bloody resistance from those in power now." Sam's passionate response made Lynne wonder if he had been in the pub for longer than she had imagined, or had she hit upon his heart-subject? He was eloquent and vital, and she realised that while she might still be right that he was self-centred, he was centred in a big picture leftist worldview. She enjoyed listening to his opinion; she was unaccountably drawn to the sound of his voice.

Pub food and another round of drinks accompanied their exploration of their well aligned opinions on the possibilities of democracy in failing states, and of their different opinions on human rights, which Lynne argued were universally applicable against Sam's argument that they should be lost if the concomitant responsibilities were not upheld. "So you're in the 'drop a bomb on them' camp?" Lynne challenged him. "For the Khmer Rouge - absolutely," was Sam's response. "You can't do that and remain a civilised, humane society," she countered. "We're *not* a civilised, humane society anyway, let's just accept it," was Sam's unflinching response. Lynne decided to let Sam have the last word on that, even though in her view she had won the argument. She should stop talking to him and take her leave, she knew, but she wanted to change the subject to the one question she really wanted to put to him.

"So what is it you want to write about? News pisses you off, so what is the book about?" She was guessing.

Sam sighed and leaned back in his chair. "I write books too late to be of interest to anyone. By the time I reckon I've understood the big picture well enough, no one is interested any more." Lynne heard the bitterness in his voice and felt compelled to defend him against it.

"Surely that won't always be true. What do you want to write?"

"I'd like to pin down the idea that the oppressed rise up to be the oppressor. As journalists we report on it time and time again. It's what's behind most conflict, and conflict is what causes most poverty, keeps people in poverty. I'd like to somehow show it to people and get them to break the connection. People overthrow one regime, and when they get into power they start to behave just as badly ... oppression is the model they learnt, and even though they hated it, they repeat it. They see people who are in power as their role models ... we have to bring the powerful people who commit war crimes to justice, we have to make their disgrace public, we have to make governments and transnational businesses accountable. We have to show the ugliness of their abuse of power, we have to shame them so that the next generation does not want to emulate them. We journalists know what goes on, but usually we can't report on it because no one will print, or it's too dangerous to report on it, or it just dies an ignominious death because there isn't the political will to pursue it into the courts. It's not a new idea ... I don't have new ideas; I just marshal the facts to support old ones. To make a book I need a new hook to hang it on ... I've been told that lots of times."

"Keep looking for the right hook then." Lynne picked

herself up from the bench seat and eased her way carefully around the table, noticing how much she had had to drink. "I have to go."

Sam picked up her coat from the empty chair at the end of the table even as she was reaching for it, and opened it to receive her arms. She accepted his chauvinism graciously, acutely aware of his hands lingering on her shoulders, his arm behind her back as she went through the door into Greenwich's cold, clear night. Sam did not pause at the door to say goodbye, he simply set off in the direction of her house, a few blocks on the far side of the pub away from the university. She had little choice but to fall in step with him.

"I take it you know where I live," she commented after several paces.

"I do," he confirmed, the frosted current of his breath lit by street globes.

"Why?" she dared ask, but he gave no reply.

Lynne fervently wished she could read his mind. Her own mind was churning through possible words and decisions. Would she invite him in? Where were Tayla and Marcus tonight? What did she want from him? She couldn't deny the attraction, the excitement she was feeling. He seemed so sure of himself, but what was in his mind? What was he going to do?

There was a light showing through the curtains of her front room, a blurred television screen alive with colourful movement, and Lynne knew it was disappointment not relief she felt. "Tayla's home," she said softly to Sam as they reached the steps to her door.

"Right-o," he replied inscrutably, stopping at the bottom of the steps. With the barest of hesitations he put his hand behind her back and lowered his mouth to hers for a light, lingering kiss. Then he let her go and watched her face for her response.

"That didn't feel familial," she didn't move away from him.

"No, it's the most tenuous of family connections. I don't feel familial towards you at all." He understood her consent and leant down again. This time the kiss was powerful and she responded automatically. When their tongues met it sent a shock wave down her spine and she pressed herself against his body, regretting the bulk of overcoats between them. She no longer had any doubts what would have happened if Tayla had not been home. How were they going to organise some time together?

"I'm going to Iraq tomorrow," he answered her thoughts as soon as they broke from their kiss.

"Oh!" Lynne drew a deep breath of recovery from the kiss and from the slap of her disappointment.

"Eight weeks," he answered the unspoken question. "Maybe I'll be able to get back earlier."

"Well," Lynne regained her self control, "that will give us some time to think this through a bit. I'll probably be away for some of April myself."

Sam watched her quizzically, as if what he was thinking and feeling had him puzzled, as if she could give him an answer. "I'm sorry I'm going." He drew a finger down her cheek line, sending another shiver through her spine, cupped her jaw and kissed her again. This time her hands found his body through the part of his overcoat, under his jumper, and his hands knowingly followed suit, teasing her hunger so easily out of its deep reserve. Where did he live? Did he live alone? She would go with him now if he asked, but instead she was frustrated when he broke off the kiss and whispered "let's start this again in May."

Lynne re-buttoned his overcoat, "Let's," she breathed up at him and when he didn't accept her invitation to kiss her again, she took a step back and resolutely shook her door key from her pocket. "Thanks for dinner."

As Lynne closed the door, habitually hung her coat and un-habitually struggled to re-align her thoughts with her family-life, she wondered at the dilemma of having adult children living at home. How was it that Tayla could bring someone from a party-night home and have noisy, bed-rattling sex with

Thalassa

him in her bedroom, while she-the mother and owner of this house-was too embarrassed to bring her own man inside the door? Something was going to have to change.

~

"What's with BBC World Mum?" Tayla asked cheerfully a week later, snacking on the raw beans Lynne had on the kitchen bench ready to go into the pot for dinner.

"I think I should know more about what's going on in the world." Lynne had taken to having the TV on BBC World while she was at work in the kitchen. Iraq was mentioned in most bulletins and apart from learning more about the situation there, Lynne found herself compelled to know about the conflict. Had there been any suicide bombings? Had any journalists been injured? She thought she might be going crazy, her thoughts seemed completely overtaken, and-the worst thing of all-she knew that if something happened to Sam, no one would call her. She had no contact details for him, and no rationale under which she could justify trying to find him. She had asked Martin, much to Martin's amusement, but to no avail - an English phone number that was not answering. Sam was unreachable, and watching news about Iraq somehow brought him closer to her, even as it stressed her.

"Broadening your horizons with travel as well?" Tayla tossed a Greek Islands tour brochure onto the bench beside the saucepan. Lynne paused to look at the cover of the brochure, pondering the idea that her children never noticed a full garbage bin, an empty milk bottle, a list of jobs left on the bench ... but the brochure she had picked up from the travel agent that morning and had left sitting on the desk in her study had already grabbed Tayla's attention.

"I'm thinking about it - there are some very cheap deals around."

"I'll go with you."

Lynne was surprised. It had crossed her mind, as had many

other possibilities. She reminded herself not to feel flattered, obviously it would be she who was paying the bills, it was not so surprising that Tayla would make the suggestion.

"You really think you could bear to travel with your boring old mother?"

Tayla looked affronted, as if the idea that she did not think of her mother as her very best friend had never occurred to her. "Of course!"

"I presume I'd be paying the bills."

"It doesn't cost any more to have a second person in the room with you, and the flights are really cheap."

"So what if I have someone else in mind to be in the room with me?" Lynne couldn't resist.

"You do??" Tayla was suddenly fully attentive, as if it was the most interesting thing her mother had said to her in years. Lynne regretted that the implication wasn't true.

"No."

"Ha-ha Mum," Tayla said drily.

"Meals, entertainment?"

"I've got money. I'll chip in. Come on Mumsy, a mother-daughter holiday, how about it?"

"What about Marcus?"

"He can look after the house. Anyway, he and Dad are going to the EUFA Soccer semi-finals in Rome."

"When?" This was new to Lynne; her temper prickled as it usually did when she found out James had been making arrangements without her knowledge.

"First of April." Tayla knew she had played a winning card. She leant across the bench and showed Lynne a brochure page on Mykonos, the party island, pictures of windmills, pretty whitewashed houses, cobbled lanes lined with colourful shops and bars, beaches populated with silvery wicker umbrellas.

"I'm not going to Mykonos," Lynne said firmly, knowing this would disappoint Tayla's night-clubbing expectations.

"I'm going to Milos."

"Milos? Where's that?" Tayla studied the map in the front of the brochure. Lynne put a fingernail on the tiny island. Tayla squinted. "Like, it's still in the Cyclades isn't it? When are we going?"

Lynne sighed, thinking warily of the extra expense but knowing that she would feel much better if travelling in company. It was also, she realised, a suggestion Tayla might never make again. Maybe a mother-daughter holiday would be a very good thing for their relationship.

"Last two weeks of the semester break - I have to be back on 21st April."

"I'm on it! Let's see what Trip Advisor says!" Tayla crowed gleefully and waltzed towards her laptop in the living room, keen to research the net for flights, ferries and accommodation.

XIII

April 2008: Greece

Sitting on a plane-*going* somewhere-had Lynne reflecting morosely on her life. The seat held her captive; there were no escape paths to busyness; no way out of thoughts about journeying and belonging. She had brought a book, thinking 'holiday-read', but on this first outward-bound day she couldn't bring herself to begin it. She was not accustomed to reading, much as she had loved doing so before she had children. She was accustomed to dipping-in to newspapers, magazines, academic articles that related to her job, and of course there was the never-ending stream of student writing. She wondered if she would ever be able to get beyond the thought of reading as a chore. Could she let go enough on this holiday to get lost in a book?

Tayla wouldn't be getting lost in a book, much to Lynne's regret. Tayla's leisure time was fully occupied with movies, video games and social media; she was witness to reading as a lost art. Tayla came prepared for the trip with the laptop her father had given her for Christmas and the iPhone he had given her for her birthday a few days ago. Most interactions Lynne had had with Tayla since Christmas had been in competition with *Farm Frenzy* – Tayla was breeding sheep and cows in virtual reality. The herd, Lynne mused, had recently been hit with a potentially fatal disease called iPhone mania. In the Wi-Fi free zone of the plane cabin Tayla had surrendered her iPhone to her handbag and had returned to her farming duties to find that predators had attacked her unprotected herd. She couldn't buy faster dogs because she hadn't been taking her milk and wool to market. She was absorbed in her laptop visuals, trying to make amends. Lynne regretted having surrendered the window seat while Tayla ignored the spectacular coastline, the feathery clouds and the expansive blue sky that Lynne would like to have escaped to. She wondered how long she would cede her rights to her child and the answer, she thought, was *'maybe forever'*.

Which brought her to the moving-out conversation she had not yet had and now felt not so compelled to have. One night's conversation, one kiss and then nothing, not even a text. Sam had not given her any lasting reason to think about rearranging her life. In contrast with Tayla who seemed to be in daily micro-contact with the lives of five hundred friends on Facebook, Lynne found herself in no communication at all with the one person who, for these six weeks, had been at the centre of all her thoughts. She countered her angry humiliation with the self-argument that one kiss gave her no claims on him, but that didn't help much when she relived the accompanying passion. The evidence remained that he was a self-centred bastard. Lynne found herself even more set against Sam than she was before their last meeting and yet, remembering, she knew how easily he could dissolve her opposition.

James had dissolved her opposition - the first time she caught him cheating. His explanation: an office affair, started after too many drinks at a party, continued over drinks and lunches, a dalliance that was meaningless once exposed. He loved her and the children, it wouldn't happen again. Was it really so clichéd? Or was it his imagination that was limited, and she was no wiser to the truth for his words? We all believe what we want to believe; she knew she had been no exception. Some counselling, some solemn promises, an extra effort on both parts to make the marriage more exciting, an inevitable drifting back into routine. But trust had not come back. She had watched for the signs even though she hated herself for doing so, she had heard the possibility of it in every hushed phone call, seen it in every late stay at the office, every closure of a computer window as she walked into his den. By the time of his second affair-at least the second she caught him in-she felt as if she deserved it, she had been waiting for it, she now only had a nearly-love for her husband, the father of her children.

But there's the rub. The children who loved him and looked up to him; assumed for themselves the ideal of a happy family. It was for the children's sake, mostly, that she had compromised herself, but there were other reasons. They could not afford to own separate homes, the house did not have a spare bedroom, they had excused themselves to the same bed at separate times of the night for over three years until Marcus finished his A levels. Lynne could not stand to let James touch her, not because he had, or was still touching someone else, but because he was a liar. James said he lied so he would not hurt her feelings, but Lynne knew he lied simply because it made his life easier. Sometimes-when they had had a few drinks and James' lies were somehow so much more convincing-Lynne's opposition temporarily dissolved again. How could she justify that to her children? How to reconcile it to her own self-image? James was still her husband; she still found shelter in the fact of her marriage and had no wish to flirt with other men. Sometimes she still needed to believe he loved her. Sometimes sex was more important than her ego. Some things just don't bear explaining - especially not to the children to whom you want to offer a better world than the one you made.

It was now 30 months since James had moved out, and Lynne still heartily relished the empty bed to which she retired every night. It had been such a relief to end the stress of their relationship, to stop pretending to the world. And yet ... her life, her household, her wholesome busyness had been reduced by his departure, none of his clothes in the wash, none of his personal favourites in the shopping trolley, no one to pass responsibility to, no one to call her husband. Lynne thought she had coped well, no small thanks to her work life at university, but she did wonder what would happen when both children had finally left home. How empty would life feel then? Why would she hurry Tayla out the door? Why would she let Sam in?

As the plane flew along the Ionian coast in descent to Athens, Tayla was glued to her window, talking animatedly about islands that Lynne couldn't see. Lynne caught the PC just before it slipped off Tayla's lap and stored it with her own unopened book. Tayla, if she noticed at all, did not see fit to thank her. Lynne remembers that she seldom thanked her own mother, and often didn't pay attention to her mother's words. It doesn't mean she loved her mother less.

Lynne focused intently on the clouds outside the window and breathed mindfully for as long as it took to steady her wish for her mother and force her tears safely back inside. She wondered *'how long does this go on?'* And the answer, she felt, was *'forever'*.

~

Tayla changed the family dynamic – overnight. Marcus had been such an easy baby and Lynne was supremely confident that she had motherhood–her life-perfected. Married to a handsome, high earning lawyer, with a delightful 18-month-old boy and a brand new baby girl. Tayla came into the world at 11 am and they came back home that night at 5. I was there, ready with a hot pot, Marcus was in his 'jammies, ready for bed, and all was well with the world. Except that Tayla bawled all night.

The next morning Lynne was exhausted, I could see it, but she told me to go home, 'we can take it from here thanks Mum', she said. The very next day, despite being on parental leave, James was called away to negotiate with the striking workers in the English Tunnel dispute. 'A few hours' turned into fourteen days and he was exhausted and short tempered whenever he did come home. 'Never mind Mum, it's not his fault,' she said, 'I can manage.'

Tayla was a very unsettled baby. She kept on screaming, night after night. She would feed a little, sleep a little and wake up screaming again. Lynne kept insisting that she was managing, but after ten days of it she broke down on the phone to me. Post-natal depression came as a complete shock to her ... that it could happen to her, I mean. I rushed down there with a breast pump, and Martin's Valium. She was horrified, but I can be forceful when it's needed. With three 8-hour sleeps she turned the corner, and Tayla improved a bit too.

1989 was a busy year for James. He was making a name for himself as a hotshot negotiator. British rail went on strike, the Underground's workers, the Dockers ... it just went on and on. Lynne had intended to go back to part time teaching at the university, but she gave up that idea. She said James needed a lot of her attention when he was home and it was best no one else was there in the house with them at nights. Which made it hard to help her ... it is a long day-trip from Norwich. I'm sure Tayla went on being very demanding, but Lynne stopped telling me about it; she didn't want me to know.

And poor little Marcus was sidelined. No attention from anyone ... Tayla stole all the attention, one way or another, and that didn't change as she was growing up. Lynne tried to put her in pre-school when she was two, but Tayla wasn't having any of that – even though Marcus was there. She caused such a fuss that Lynne took her back out again, and had to cancel that semester's lecture program, which the University never forgave her. Lynne took the blame on herself – 'Tay's too young, Mum, it was silly of me' she said.

But it was after Tayla had been in school for a year or so that the trouble really began. When she learned to talk back to James, when she learned how to push his buttons to get his attention. By then James was negotiating football contracts, and he often had free tickets to the games. He liked Marcus to go along with him, and Marcus took to soccer like a duck to water. 'The crowd's too rough, Mum, I don't want Tayla to go to the games', Lynne told me ... and there was no doubt some truth in that, but I know she didn't want Marcus to go either, and there was no doubting, even then, which of his children James preferred to have with him.

Marcus is such a sweetie ... just like Lynne was ... while Tayla is very challenging. You don't see it in James at first, he is so charming ... but as Lynne once said to me, she learnt a lot about James by watching Tayla grow up. Character traits that are right out there, on Tayla's sleeve, are in James as well, just better dressed, glossed over. They're both manipulative, they can be very unfeeling towards other people, ruthless about taking what they want and really, honesty is not a high priority to them. James was involved in something that discredited him at the football club, Lynne wouldn't say anything about it, just that he got moved into a less public role and his career took a backwards step ... that happened when Tayla was about seven, I think.

But on the positive side, also like James, Tayla is socially appealing. She can look very pretty when she tries, and she can talk to anyone so easily, so nicely when she wants to. It's such a pity she doesn't behave that way with her own family. She is a natural, it seems, at the latest job James has organized for her - a medical receptionist at a center owned by one of the board members of the football club. She was also 'a natural' of course, waitressing at the golf club cafe for six months until the manager fondled her bottom and she broke his nose with what I can imagine was a very powerful right hook! She won't get any more jobs through James if something like that happens again; she was on her last chance, he told her. You'd think James would be angry with the manager and protective of Tayla – she was only sixteen then and the manager would have been in his forties ... but maybe I don't know the whole story, so I'll keep my thoughts about James to myself.

It's not as if Tayla would not have been in some ways responsible for what happened, given the way she dresses and behaves, but still, it's inexcusable. There are always boys hanging around Tayla, and she makes a sport of teasing them. Children grow up so soon, they are sexualized so early. How could they not be? The television shows for teenagers are full of sex, swearing, drugs and alcohol. I don't know why Lynne let Tayla watch such shows, but she said she had to, otherwise Tayla would not be 'in-step' with her peers at school; she said she often sat down with Tayla to watch TV and commented on the issues that were brought up in the shows ... and maybe so, but it strikes me that Tayla was listening much more to the TV than to what her mother said.

It strikes me that Lynne–and James too, for that matter–have tried to be Tayla's friends, not her parents. Tayla needed firm boundaries, responsible role models, parents who presented a united, disciplined front. If parents give in to everything children want, they won't grow up – why would they want to? Tayla has a very comfortable life at Lynne's expense – why would she move out of home?

I know Tayla becomes a freethinking, intelligent, beautiful young woman. But maybe the shock she is about to get; the challenge she is about to face has a vital part to play in that. There's a saying that life doesn't present you with more than you can handle. It's not true. It depends who you are.

~

In Mykonos after nightfall, even in April, months before the peak summer season, party people stream into the town from the New Port on one side and from the bus station on the other, steadily filling and then over-flowing the night clubs, spilling out to obstruct the passing foot-traffic in the narrow lanes. As the night wears on the average age decreases and the drunkenness increases. People her age, Lynne realised, were leaving, and she thought that would be a good idea. Tayla, however, wanted to stay. Tayla was just getting into the mood. Lynne was divided, should she suppress her motherly fears and let Tayla stay or should she insist they were both going back to the hotel? It wasn't just that she was scared for Tayla's safety in town overnight, it was also that she didn't feel confident about her own bus ride back to the hotel. Perhaps conceding to this second point, Tayla agreed to call it a night and mother and daughter shouldered their way against the in-flowing crowd towards the bus station.

The bus station was a rickety ticket box, not much bigger than a phone booth, a parking area for several buses and a large turning circle populated with a mass of wandering people and several scantily clad night-club touts who were handing out free drink vouchers to the tourists disgorged by each incoming bus. Having bought their tickets Lynne stood to the side of the turning circle, watching in horrified fascination as each incoming bus pushed its way, very slowly into the crowd, spewed out its passengers, and then gradually manoeuvred itself backwards into a bus bay. Added into this frightening mix of buses and people moving through the turning circle were motorbikes and private cars, letting people off, pushing through in transit. Around the edge of the bus turning circle were stalls selling cheap jewellery, watches, sunglasses and tourist-ware. People stopping to browse were pushed along by the bumper bars of cars, handlebars or feet hanging off bikes. While Tayla happily perused the display boards of a nose ring stand Lynne kept vigil beside her, ready to pull or push depending on which way a vehicle approached.

There was a timetable, but the buses weren't running to it. Fill up and go seemed to be the principle. When a bus with a 'Platis Gialos' card in the front window arrived, there were as many people, mostly families with children, waiting to get on as there were sweat-oiled, tattooed youths jostling down the narrow steps and jumping boisterously to the roadway. Lynne defended their position in the queue forcefully, determined to get a seat instead of waiting another hour for the bus to make its return trip.

Back in the cool, crowd-free lobby of the Hotel Acrogiali Lynne was finally able to let down her guard. Her sudden weariness nearly overflowed in tears as she struggled up the smooth granite stairs. One a.m. was way past her bedtime.

~

Eight a.m., on the other hand, was much too early for Tayla to wake up. Lynne slipped out of the hotel room quietly and took a long, refreshing walk around the promontory to the West of the hotel. Looking down from the dirt track on the headland, Lynne marvelled that the water was indeed that beautiful azure colour the tourist brochures promised, patched with the dark underwater shadows of submerged rocks. The waterline stretched out in a band along the sandy beach that was Cavo Psarou, and then made a right angle turn along the steep headland on the far side of the bay. Covering the headland, in extensive patches around steep rocky drop-offs, were masses of purple and white wildflowers. The only trees to be seen were planted in green patches amongst the white buildings at the head of the beach. Lynne paused at many vantage points along the path to take photos with her rather old and in recent years regrettably unused digital SLR.

As Lynne walked along the beach, her sandals in hand, sandy shell-grit underfoot, cafe attendants were casually going about their business, rolling sun beds into position near the water's edge, setting up large silvery cane umbrellas, fitting breakfast menus into plastic holders on the umbrella spikes. On the far side of the beach she followed a narrow path up the hill towards a church she had seen from the headland. The church was pure white, evidently recently painted; perfectly formed with arched crevices that looked like they should be windows but were instead sculpted into stone. The arched doorway was real, but the recessed wooden door was bolted closed. Several flat ledges rising to the dome were decorated with grey ceramic pots growing Aloe Vera. Visions like this were what Lynne enjoyed about travelling; she took several photos to show Tayla what she was missing.

Tayla also missed an early morning swim, breakfast on the beach in front of their hotel, and an hour's reading time during which Lynne did start to re-enjoy the experience of a novel.

"Water is very good," Lynne confirmed when Tayla eventually arrived on the beach and made a half-hearted inquiry. "Get in," she encouraged.

Tayla dropped her sarong and the hotel towel and waded into the water up to waist high, holding her arms above the surface making out the water was alarmingly cold. She eventually sank herself to shoulder height, keeping her hair dry, and was shortly back on the beach.

"Some swim that was," Lynne remarked mockingly.

In response Tayla flopped into the beach lounge Lynne had saved for her and helped herself to Lynne's orange juice. "I had an email from Dad this morning."

"Yes?" Lynne replied dubiously, wondering what was coming.

"Joanne has moved out." Joanne had been James' girlfriend for three years, which, in Lynne's reckoning, was probably the average duration.

"And how's your dad feeling about that?"

"He didn't say really. Just something about the relationship having run its course."

Lynne suppressed a response expressing her total lack of surprise.

"Would you take him back Mumsy?" Tayla had the misconception that Joanne had been her father's first extra-marital escapade; that the family world had been wonderful before Joanne. There was a childish yearning in the question. Lynne toyed with the idea of disabusing Tayla of her belief, but reminded herself that there was nothing to gain and much childhood happiness to lose.

"There's no going back Tay," Lynne intended her voice to be soothing. She knew that for all her brash, sexy maturity, Tayla longed for a return to the united family in which she had felt secure and happy; she didn't want to be divided between Mum and Dad, and who could blame her?

"But you're lonely. And now he's going to be lonely too. Isn't it better to forgive and forget?"

"I suspect your Dad will find someone else Tay," Lynne thought it probable James already had someone else, "and I'm perfectly happy the way I am. I don't have to have a man in my life you know."

"Who's going to look after you when you're old?"

"That'll be your job," Lynne smiled, "is that why you're worried?"

"I'll put you in a nursing home," Tayla mustered a serious tone.

"Make sure you save lots of money. I deserve a nice place."

"I'll have a *rich* man in my life."

"How traditional of you," Lynne was amused, "I think you might be better off to start university in September and get a degree so you can look after yourself."

"Perhaps I should. The boys I meet are all dick-heads. The boys at university would be better wouldn't they? Like when you met Dad."

Lynne thought that any basis for discussion about university was better than none. "Yes, like me and Dad. Does this mean you've thought of what you would like to study?"

"The right guys would be in law do you think?"

"I think maybe you should aim at arts, Tay," Lynne sighed.

"What are we doing today?" Tayla changed the subject.

Lynne suppressed a reply to the effect that the day was half over. "Want to go into town and explore when there are less people?"

"Can we hire a quad bike?"

Lynne was not so sure about that. The quad bikes looked like fun, and all sorts of people seemed to be driving them, she supposed she should be able to do it ... but what about the other mad traffic on the roads? "We can see what they cost," she equivocated.

"I want to go to Super Paradise tonight," Tayla announced. "There's a boat from here at 9."

Super Paradise, Lynne already knew from Tayla's pre-trip briefings, was a disco beach - mecca of Mykonos partygoers.

"OK, but I'll give it a miss," this evidently was the response Tayla expected.

"Here Mum," Tayla squeezed onto the sun-bed with Lynne and held her iPhone at arms length to snap a photo of them both with ranks of sun beds and umbrellas in the background. Lynne protested mildly, she could not understand why Tayla's generation were so keen to advertise themselves with ridiculous 'selfies' on Facebook. She knew she would look awful in the photo, and reminded herself to police Tayla's Facebook page for the next week.

"Right, let's go then," Tayla picked the key off the sun-bed table and headed back into the hotel.

Lynne lingered for a moment over the open pages of her book, reluctantly dog-eared her place, and followed.

~

"What about Personal Training Mum? I could be a Gym instructor." The next afternoon, Tayla was examining the muscular torso of the magnificent Artemision Bronze statue of Poseidon in the Archaeological Museum in Athens. "Guys would kill for a body like that wouldn't they? I think I'd like to know how to make one of those."

"Then maybe you need to learn to sculpt," Lynne gave her riposte absent-mindedly as she circled the statue, looking up at the pose of the right hand. More than two thousand years ago, before the shipwreck that committed the statue to the bottom of the Aegean Sea, that hand had held either a trident or, if the statue actually represented Zeus, as many latter day scholars were arguing, it would have held a thunderbolt. The argument for Zeus said that a trident, held in that position, would have obscured Poseidon's head. "Not if he was holding the trident nearer the fork," Lynne spoke aloud, shifting her shoulders into javelin-throwing position, imagining a heavier head on the stave. No, it wasn't the trident argument that persuaded her towards the Zeus camp, it was the beard. Poseidon's beard was normally sculpted with knotty curls, as befits a salt encrusted sea-God. The beard on this statue was long, made with straight strokes of a chisel, the beard of Zeus, ruler of the skies, married to Hera, father of many out-of-wedlock children including Aphrodite - better known as Venus, the Goddess of Love.

"I like going to the gym with Marcus, I've learnt a lot of stuff from the fitness instructors already, and it's really interesting. I could study anatomy, and nutrition and motivational psychology. Do you think I got good enough marks in biology? What else would I need to get into a degree in Personal Training?"

"I haven't heard of a degree in 'Personal Training' Tay, I think you'd need to look it up on the web."

"Mum ... fuck ... we came from there!" Tayla protested vehemently as Lynne left the Artemision Bronze, heading back towards the statue of Aphrodite, Pan and Cupid for another look even though she had already spent fifteen minutes in that statue's presence, trying to engrave it on her memory.

"Tay, *your* pick on the trip was two nights in Mykonos, and *mine* is an afternoon in the Archaeological museum, and tomorrow at the Acropolis, OK? Don't rush me." Lynne was in her element, she wasn't thinking about Tayla's study options and she wasn't thinking about either James or Sam. While she was looking again at the sculptural composition of Aphrodite's arms she realised with certainty that the arms were joined to the torso with metal pins, and this had her imagination excitedly focussed on how she could find the treasure that lay within the walls of the Church of St Nikolaos at Firopotamos.

Sam, at that very moment, was also thinking about Aphrodite's arms and the Stavros family church, as he stood in the check-in queue at Athens airport for his 45-minute flight to Milos.

XIV

I challenge Iliana; can she not see that religious belief is the source of intolerable evil in the world? I ask her where the blame lies for the ethnic cleansing of the Asia Minor Disaster, the Greeks or the Turks? The Christians or the Muslims? Does acceptance of God's will mean that we should make no effort to understand history and try to prevent the horror from happening again?

Iliana blames politicians. Her family were Turks who spoke Greek as well as Turkish and practiced Christianity. They lived peacefully alongside Turks who spoke Turkish as well as Greek and practiced Islam. They hauled in their fishing nets together. They sat on the side of the village well telling jokes and tall tales. They cut chunks of locally made cheese and ate it on handfuls of bread torn some days from fat loaves and some days from thin loaves. They toasted each other with the juice of grapes picked from the straggly vines on the hillsides – choosing to fill their jugs from the aged and fermented vat or from the freshly crushed vat according to their conscience and taste. They went to each other's churches to jointly celebrate special occasions. They were different but complementary parts of the same small community and their squabbles were far more likely to be over ownership of a goat found standing on a cliff side tree branch than over religious or ethnic differences.

The politicians, she says, were preachers of fear and hate. They were not faithful members of their religious belief – Christian or Muslim. They were power mongers who wanted to divide the common people and grab land and booty for themselves.

Encouraged by the British the Greeks had grabbed the Asia Minor shoreline after the first war, pushing greedily into Turkey and behaving abominably towards the Turks in their path. Led by the Ataturk the Turks had fought for their land, driving the Greeks back to the Mediterranean and behaving abominably towards the Greeks in their path. Neither of these actions had been taken with the wellbeing of the people who lived in Asia Minor in mind and regardless of what the troops may have been shouting, both sides acted in the name of Man, not God or Allah.

After the Asia Minor resettlement of Christians to Greece, and Muslims to Turkey, World War Two saw Nazis try to cleanse the world of not just Jews, but homosexuals, gypsies and the disabled. The Greek Civil War was a political battle over economic theory that pitched Greek Christians against Greek Christians. In Yugoslavia a State that had been held together by a forceful politician shattered along ethnic fault lines as soon as he was gone, and a new generation of power mongers whipped up genocidal rage in pursuit of their own goals.

Iliana believes that it is God's Will that we should learn from the suffering we bring to ourselves through our mistakes. If we were to properly and humbly follow His instruction to forgive others their trespasses then wars would not be born of our genealogical hatreds.

Aretha is content with this explanation, and reminds us of the sacrifice Christ made so that those who believe in Him and follow the way of the Lord can be saved from their sins. She is horrified, however, by my next challenge.

Would we not have more chance of avoiding war in a secular world? Is it not the task of the next generation to put religion and its divisions behind us?

To which Iliana replies, would we not have more chance if we were all white with blond hair, if we all agreed on the same political, economic and social theory and no-one was allowed to express dissent, if we were selectively screened at birth to ensure the breeding of a super race, if we all spoke German? How would secularity resolve the problem of mankind's brutal quest for ascendancy?

And it is at that point in our debate that Jean lets us know that Sam will write on the difficult subject we are exploring. She surprises us by implying that she, who neither met him nor fell in love with his grandfather, knows him better than the rest of us.

XV

Wednesday 9th April 2008: Milos

Sam swung his featureless black rucksack onto his left shoulder as he stepped off the sand-dusted tarmac of Milos airport and through the door of its small terminal building. He extended his right hand and a cheerful smile to George.

"Hey buddy," their common family greeting swapped sides simultaneously.

"How's the church renovation going?" Sam asked.

"Not far yet - I've only been here a few days, just introductions and drinks all round so far. In order to sign up a tradesman I have to spend an afternoon in a bar." George laughed. "I didn't realise I had so many relatives here! Bags?"

"No, this is it." Sam bounced the rucksack on his arm and the two men headed straight through the terminal.

"Just as well," George gestured towards a motorbike parked at the end of the empty taxi rank. "You don't mind not having a helmet do you?"

"Well and truly used to it, mate."

"I'm still adjusting, but I admit - it feels good." George started the bike and Sam stepped easily over the passenger seat and folded his legs to bring his feet onto the rear foot pegs.

"Hotel? Or Tripiti to meet the family?" George asked before moving off.

"Lagada Beach Hotel in Adamas, I need to check in and organise a car."

"Not a bike? It's easier on these roads, I can tell ya."

"Can you imagine your sister on a bike?"

George laughed. "Point." He kicked the bike into gear and took it slow as he moved out of the airfield, getting used to Sam's weight on the back before he sped up along the coastal road from the airfield to Adamas.

Sam directed George through the hectic portside streets of the town, between restaurants and the seafront, past the ferry terminal and through the port car park to the entrance steps of the Lagada Beach Hotel.

"Want to wait and have a drink here or in town after I've checked in?"

"Sure," George kicked the foot stand down, pocketed the key and followed Sam into the large foyer of the hotel. While Sam checked in he cruised past the doorways to the lounge room, where a couple of young women were using the hotel's PC, and the dining room where staff were setting up tables for dinner. He browsed the tourist guides arrayed in the rack on the table beside the dining room door. Sam clacked his room key against its wooden tag as he walked past. George replaced the brochure he was reading, and followed Sam out of the foyer and along a pathway lined with pockets of green shrubs encased in low, whitewashed walls, delimited by short steps that led up to the door of each unit.

"Nice," George surmised as Sam unlocked his door.

Sam waited until he had checked the unit before he agreed with George's comment. He threw his rucksack into the wardrobe, put his money belt into the safe and closed it with a combination, then stepped into the bathroom. George cast his eyes over the double bed, scowled deeply, and quickly moved

Thalassa

to the balcony, looking out over the hotel's pool yard, trying to suppress his thoughts about his sister's ongoing affair.

"First green lawn I've seen in Milos," George commented when Sam emerged.

Sam looked up to the barren hills behind the hotel. "Yep - dry isn't it. Giving you a thirst?"

"I reckon."

"What does a beer cost here?"

They agreed on a drink in town rather than at the hotel, and walked the short distance, stopping to book a car for Sam from the next morning. Night was falling and the town's lights were on, as they settled into a table on an elevated balcony a street back from the main road, with a view over the port. There were few people on the streets or in the bar, it was too early in the evening for the locals, and it was too early in spring for the tourists. At a temperate 20 degrees it was a very nice time to be in the Greek islands, they concurred.

"So what's the schedule with the church?" Sam asked.

"I've got plaster coming in to the port tomorrow afternoon and the plasterer starts on Friday. I'm going to do the painting myself - whitewash and Cycladic blue get here on Monday. There's a couple of beams to replace and the wall panels - we've got some timber coming from a building in Sifnos that's been demolished. That should be here on Friday. There's a community working-bee planned on Saturday to fix the walls and get the beams up."

"What's on for you tomorrow?"

"I've got a few chairs in Dimitry's work shed at Klima. I've nearly finished repairing them, gotta sand them back and stain them. I was going to go on with that. What do you want to do?"

"I'll finish my dispatch on Iraq and get a few things organised. I'll front up for the working bee and the painting - how's that?"

"That'll be great."

"Do you need help picking up the plaster? What time does it come in?"

"I've got Dimitry's ute for that, it'll be right. It's due in at noon, but you know Greece ... could be anytime later in the afternoon."

"Sounds like you're enjoying yourself," Sam commented on the enthusiasm he could hear in George's voice. "You seem a lot more relaxed than you were at Christmas."

"I didn't think you saw me at Christmas." The tone of George's voice switched to a semi-sarcastic jibe.

"Well ... I heard about you." Sam paused for a moment, estimating George's remark. "So how are you sitting with this?"

"You and Mary?" Sam nodded. "It's hardly for me to judge mate. Whatever makes her happy." The stiffness in George's tone belied his words.

They fell silent for a moment, each resorting to a swig of beer and a perusal of the waterfront. George was thinking about the years he had hated Sam, first for breaking up Mary's marriage and making their mother so miserable, and later for walking out in spite of all Mary had given up for him; for breaking her heart. George had been twenty-five when Sam and Mary started living together, thirty when they split up. They had come to Melbourne as a couple in 1985, cutely holding hands as they watched George and Liz take their vows in the autumn-covered gardens of Montsalvat. Liz had thrown the bouquet so that Mary could catch it.

Sam was thinking about the same years, acutely aware of George's unspoken anger.

"So why have you come a few days before her?" George asked the question that had been puzzling him since Mary had last phoned.

"It's just worked out that way. I was in Athens. No point going to England and then coming back here a few days later. Mary wants to stay till Pascha on 27th April, but I'd rather help with the practical stuff and skip out before the religion begins. We get a week together in the middle."

George accepted the explanation and looked out to sea again, finishing his beer. "Do you know Mary came here with Ian and the kids several years ago?" Sam nodded. "Well ... the family here remembers it, you know."

"Yes I know buddy," Sam sighed. "I'm used to it, we'll be discrete. I'm the Kostis Foster-son, I know the rules." They both smiled at the long-standing pun on Sam's surname, but I know that beneath his smile George cuts himself with the knowledge that in their shared sibling life, his had been the lesser part.

XVI

Friday 11th April 2008

Lynne nudged Tayla awake as Speedrunner 3 passed the Northern headland of the Port of Milos and powered past the steep hillsides and narrow valleys at the Eastern edge of the horseshoe-shaped island's central caldera. The ferry had taken just over four and a half hours to cross the 86 nautical miles between Piraeus and Milos, with short stops at Serifos and Sifnos to transfer passengers. Long enough for Lynne to read a quarter of her novel, while Tayla slept off the effects of the party that had found her overnight. Athens had come up in Tayla's estimation. The Greeks they had met in the Plaka after climbing down the narrow track behind the Acropolis had been very generous hosts. While Lynne declined the after-dinner invitation and returned to their hotel, Tayla partied on through a number of bars without ever having to pay for a drink, and at 3am she arrived safely, but very noisily, at the hotel door. Lynne's relief had made her angry about her own loss of sleep, but Tayla was an oblivious target. Within a few minutes of dancing in the door, Tayla was snoring - lightly, but enough to keep Lynne from getting back to sleep until 4am.

The 6.30am taxi ride to Piraeus and the wait in the ferry terminal had passed in relative silence. It was all very well for Tayla, Lynne thought, just follow Mum and at every stop lay your head on her shoulder and fall asleep. Not a care in the world. Mum had ordered the taxi, Mum knew where to go and how long it would take, Mum was watching the luggage and the passports, Mum would wake her up when it was time to move on. Not for the first time on the trip Lynne had asked herself ruefully, who would look after Mum? She supposed she had been looked after in the past, but she really couldn't remember it and she guessed it would never happen again. Lynne put those thoughts aside, pointed Tayla towards the purple roller-suitcase on the luggage racks and carted her own silver suitcase down the stairs that led to the vehicle deck. Tayla caught her yawning as they stood amongst the colourful assemblage of travellers, watching the lowering ramp give way to the bright afternoon sun.

"Tired Mum? Not enough sleep?" she mocked cheerfully.

"Funny," Lynne said flatly.

"We're in Milos Mumsy, aren't you excited?" Tayla linked arms with her and pulled her in the direction of the ramp as it grounded on the concrete pier.

~

"Firopotamos is next right," Tayla was reading directions from a map she had looked up on the Internet in the hotel lobby and had saved to her iPhone.

Lynne looked dubiously at the Greek lettering on the small road sign, and felt a new appreciation for the Internet's GPS mapping. Around her usual haunts in London she felt that more often than not she had to override the directions given to her by an Internet search, but here in Milos it was very useful, not least because there was no road map and no GPS in the hire car. She steered the nifty little Panda into the narrow, paved street, braked hard-up against the side of a building behind a parked car while a small delivery truck passed in the other direction, and then continued, glad she had the smallest car in the hire fleet. Sidewalks, it seemed, were for main streets only, and often they were used for parking or deliveries rather than walking. Away from the main street, Lynne shared the strip of bitumen carefully with pedestrians, dogs and at one point they even passed a donkey that was asleep in front of a store, empty baskets hanging over its back. Tayla stretched her hand out of the window, above the roof of the car and clicked the camera app on her phone. Lynne was not surprised to hear her complain, upon review, that she had missed the donkey.

The distances in Milos were small; just a few minutes later Tayla instructed, "go left, and then right."

"Down there?" Lynne was alarmed by the steep track that led down to the sea. The road was made, but it was very narrow and the tarmac on each side crumbled into gravel. On one side was an uneven rocky cutting, on the other a precipitous drop into a deep gorge. There was nowhere to pass. If she met another car or truck, one of them would be reversing until a suitable passing bay was found. Lynne studied the road for a long moment, turning only when she felt confident there was no vehicle on the way up.

A few hundred metres down the road they were rewarded with the beautiful vista of a horseshoe bay filled with superbly azure water, lined on the left side by a chalky white cliff, and on the right by a higgledy-piggledy cluster of white buildings with flat grey concrete rooves. At the far end of the rocky peninsula was the ruined wall of an ancient temple, and between the temple and the buildings, perched at the edge of the cliff, was a pretty white church with two bell towers and a small dome.

"Aghios Nikolaos," Lynne announced.

"That's so pretty," Tayla exclaimed. She took some blurred photos through the windscreen.

The road widened to provide a few parking spots and a turning circle. Lynne stopped the car alongside a workman's utility truck and two motorbikes. She reached for her bag from the back seat, took out her DSLR camera and joined Tayla at the edge of the road, leaning over a low, whitewashed wall to take photos of the gaily striped little fishing boats that were speckled across the vivid blue of the water. Concrete steps, rimmed with white paint, led down from the level of the road and the flat rooftops, between each boathouse to the wharves where the boats were tied. The flat top of the low walls was painted Cycladic blue, as were the wooden doors of the boatsheds. A fisherman sat in the stern of one of the boats; untangling a mess of ropes and on the wharf beside him a longhaired black and tan Alsatian lay on a bright yellow fishing net, indolently licking at its groin.

Preoccupied with her camera and the many different perspectives she could get on the pretty fishing village, Lynne temporarily forgot her reason for visiting Firopotamos. She and Tayla explored the rocky harbour front for viewpoints, clambering over the heaped rocks of the breakwater to take photos back towards the cliffs. Tayla took selfies and posed for photos at Lynne's request, while Lynne herself avoided being in front of Tayla's camera. Eventually they worked their way around the rock to the front of the church.

Aghios Nikolaos had seen better days. Unlike the brilliant white of the churches in Mykonos, the walls of the church were yellowed, and in many places the plaster had fallen away, exposing aged wooden posts and a motley assemblage of stones, bricks and mortar. The heavy wooden door at the village side of the church was standing open but, despite its beckoning power, Lynne decided to walk around the outside of the church before going in. The Northern side of the church, facing the sea, had been recently plastered, but not yet painted. The surface was a rough, but thick covering, hiding the inner structure of the wall. As Lynne turned the far corner of the church she came across three workmen, one on a scaffold and two others bent towards the lower part of the wall, their clothes and caps covered with plaster dust. They were absorbed in their task, and she watched them for a moment wondering whether she could make herself understood if she was to ask them where she could find the family who owned the church.

"*Me synhoríte*," Lynne attracted the workmen's attention with 'excuse me'. The workman on the scaffolding looked down at her briefly and immediately returned to his task. The two workmen at ground level straightened up and looked inquiringly at her. "*Miláte angliká?*"

The two men could have been Abbott and Costello; one was short and round, the other was tall and lean. The short, round one slapped his hand against the tall, lean one's elbow with a burst of laughter and turned back to his work. The appointed spokesperson stepped towards her.

"G'day," George said cheerfully.

"Oh," Lynne was taken aback.

"Can I help you?"

"You're Australian."

"Indeed. You're English. I'm George, but I won't shake hands." George showed her his plaster-caked right hand.

"Lynne," she replied, making some quick mental adjustments. Could she be so lucky? "I don't suppose you are a member of the Kostis family?"

Some plaster powder fell from George's eyebrows as he lifted them in surprise. He blew a puff of air up his face and wiped his eyes with the back of his hand, failing to make any improvement.

"I am. In disguise. I'm not naturally this white."

"Plastering is not your normal day job?" Looking past George, Lynne noticed Tayla observing them from the rocks of the headland; saw her turn away towards the temple ruin rather than join them.

"Whatever makes you think that?" George said with a generous laugh. "Christos here is wearing just as much of it as me." The plasterer turned and gave a dusty salute upon hearing his name.

"Do you own this church?" Lynne asked.

George looked puzzled. He scuffed some more plaster off his face. "I suppose you could say that – I own it as much as anyone else does, I guess. Do you want to know something about it?"

"I'd like to talk about its history, and actually, there are a few things I know about your family that might interest you. Our great great-grandfathers fought together at the Battle of Navarino in 1827."

"Really? Where's Navarino?" George sounded only politely interested.

"On the coast of the Peloponnese peninsula, the West side of Greece. Stavros Kostis from Milos was a pilot for Admiral Codrington of the British Navy. My great great-grandfather, Nicholas Baxter, fished him out of the ocean after a cannon ball hit the Admiral's ship."

"That rings a bell," George said thoughtfully, trying to remember how that family story went. His memory traces were associating the story with his high school days and history homework.

"My great great-grandfather wrote it down. I have the manuscript."

"Really!" Lynne thought George seemed genuinely pleased. "My family has nothing written down. Everything is word of mouth, handed down through the generations, and … you know how it is … we can never really believe anything. It's probably been changed out of all recognition."

"Do you know the story of the shipwreck and the promise Stavros made to build the church here?"

"Yes! Is that written down too?" Lynne nodded. "I would like to see that … I wonder if it is exactly the same? Dimitry would love to see that. Do you have it here?"

"I have a copy at my hotel."

"How long are you on Milos?"

"A week."

"You should meet Dimitry. He'll want you to come to dinner, I'm sure. He knows more about the history of the church than I do."

Lynne weighed up her next question. George struck her as a very open, honest person. She felt she could trust him. "Have you ever heard a story that connected your family with the Venus De Milo statue?"

George searched his memory. "I don't think so ... but Dimitry would be the one to know. Is that your interest? Are you here to research the statue?"

"Yes - I'm an art historian, and it tweaked my interest to see what was written in that manuscript."

"Which was?"

"One of the arms of the statue could be concealed somewhere in this church." Lynne watched George closely for his reaction.

"Seriously?" George's face crinkled its while layer of plaster, his deep brown eyes shone at her in complete surprise. He looked at the church as if Venus de Milo was about to wave at him. "Where?"

"I don't know. The manuscript says that at the time the arm was hidden Stavros was re-building the walls of the church. It leads me to think that he sealed the arm up inside one of the walls. Any ideas where that might be?"

George shrugged. "The walls are about twelve inches thick - there could be a cavity anywhere. How are we going to tell?"

Lynne was pleased that he was considering the idea so seriously, taking a common ownership of the mission with her. "I *do* have an idea about that."

~

George looked entirely different when Lynne next met him, in the village of Triovassalos, which was up on the central ridge of the island, half way between Firopotamos and Adamas. He was, as he had hinted, much less white after a shower. His skin was a deep brown compared to Lynne's pale English-peach and his washed hair had been abundantly tousled dry by his helmetless motorbike ride.

"I need a haircut," he said apologetically, noticing her gaze. As he ran his hand self-consciously over his head Lynne noted his wedding ring. "You found the hire-shop alright I see."

Lynne gestured towards Tayla, who was still sitting in the car, iPhone in hand but her attention openly fixed on George. "I have a navigator with directions on screen," she explained.

"I'm surprised that works here on Milos," George's smile creased his face with kind wrinkles.

"It's not live GPS ... it's a map saved from the Internet. We can't get any Wi-Fi away from the hotel, and there are plenty of black spots where the phone doesn't work," Lynne replied. "Mainly down the bottom of those scary coastal roads."

"So you went round to Plathiena - via the headland?"

"We made it to Plathiena ... if you hadn't told me the road was okay I would never have followed it, mind you. I had to back up a hundred metres to let another car get past me."

"Only once?" George interjected with a grin.

"And the road to the headland ... alright for your dirt bike maybe, but I'm not taking the hire car out there."

"I better take you on the bike then, because the view is spectacular." George's easy familiarity made Lynne wonder about his wedding ring, and her own too readily suspicious nature.

"All the scenery is spectacular, it just seems as if every road is worth going down, there are so many wonderful lookouts over the sea. Plathiena was lovely, though I like Firopotamos more."

"Glad you like it. Shall we?" George invited her to enter the store he had nominated as their meeting place.

Lynne looked around the one-room hire-shop, thinking it looked remarkably small and empty. There was a bench saw behind the grubby waist-high counter, and a router sitting on top of the bench next to a hire contract pad and a tattered red diary. She supposed that the shelves that led away into the dark recesses of the shop must be holding more tools, but they appeared empty at the shopfront end. A middle-aged man came out of the shadows to stand under the fluorescent globe that was above the counter. He had a strikingly shiny pink pate and bushy grey hair on each side of his head and his brown eyes were fixed on her as George made his inquiry in Greek. She looked away from him; turned to check on Tayla in the car.

"Fifty euros for a three day hire," George reported his preliminary findings to her, his voice indicating his disapproval. He turned back to the nuggetty, greasy-apron clad shopkeeper without waiting for her reply, and after a short incomprehensible exchange he turned back to her. "Thirty euros special for you, doesn't matter if you have it for one day or three." Lynne reached into her handbag. "But - it's out at the moment, you can book it for Monday."

Lynne felt impatient, she was anxious to search for the arm, to get on with her mission. "Are you sure this is the only hire store on Milos?"

"I've been reliably informed that not only is it the only hire store, it's the only metal detector."

Lynne sighed. "Monday then. Deposit?" She handed over a ten Euro note and wrote her name and phone number into Monday's page in the diary.

"What will you do tomorrow?" George asked as they left the store.

"I guess we'll have a drive around and see the sights."

"You should go to Klima, and take a walk around Tripiti. Or you can go out to Pollonia and take the car ferry to Kimolos." George recommended the coastal villages that had been suggested to him only a week ago. "Dimitry is very interested in the manuscript and he wants you to come to dinner tomorrow - would you be able to do that? We'll be working on the church during the day, but Dimitry won't be there, it's too

Thalassa

much for him. He stays at home in his armchair and waits for us to come back and tell him stories about our day."

"Who is 'we'?" Lynne was expecting George to name his wife.

"My cousins Anton and Petros are helping out when they can. And tomorrow their wives Elena and Rose will be there too. But you'll meet them all if you and Tayla come to dinner."

"That would be very nice, thank-you. I'll bring the manuscript - can you translate for Dimitry?"

"I'll try. My Greek has improved ten-fold since I first got here. I couldn't have done that a week ago." George jerked a thumb in the direction of the store. "I'm amazed how well I get by."

"Thank-you very much for helping me find the hire-shop and negotiating for me - I don't know how I would have done that by myself."

"My pleasure," George's eyes shone, polished by even such small praise. "Any time after seven o'clock - here's the address for your navigator," he dipped his hand into the pocket of his cotton shirt and handed her a folded yellow square of paper.

"Thanks, I'll see you tomorrow then." Lynne settled herself into her car and fastened the seat belt.

"See ya." As George sauntered to his bike his farewell struck Lynne a poignant blow of recognition. It was exactly the same in delivery and intonation as Sam's.

XVII

Saturday 12th April 2008

"Oh shit!" Sam howled, but did not drop his end of the load of pine panelling.

"Mind your head," George failed any criterion of empathy.

"Bastard," was Sam's rejoinder.

"These are going to the far wall." George navigated the door with only a slight inclination of his head and used the straight panels to push Sam's backward steps in the right directions until he gave the instruction, "here." George ran his hand across the bare plaster wall of the church, showing Sam the work he had already done. "I've taken the rotten panels off, and cleaned up the wall. These have been cut to size - they should go straight up - but I've put that off till Tuesday. Today we're working on doors and windows."

Sam followed George around the church while George introduced him to their fellow workers. Rose and Elena were on a scaffold, high in the dome, touching up the colours of the Christ Pantocrator. Rose was delicately inking the script in the open bible Christ was holding in his left hand, while Elena was refreshing the blue in the cross behind Christ's head. The sound of their constant, happy Greek chatter rebounded from the dome and echoed though the church. Anton and his son Theo were arguing over the best way to replace a broken windowpane in the bell shaped window that faced the ruined temple of Apollo. Petros and his son Colum were carrying another load of pine panelling in from the boat Petros had moored to the concrete wharf in front of the church. Neither of them, Sam thought ruefully as he rubbed the back of his head, had to duck to avoid the overhang above the door.

"If you want to have another go at that beam with your head, that would be fine," George grinned, "because we're going to knock it out and put a fresh one in."

"Can we make it higher?"

"No. Come and get the beams with me."

Sam followed obediently, trailing George around the front of the church, down the steps to Petros' cäique, and across the gangway to the stack of wood piled on the deck. They hoisted an Oregon beam onto their left shoulders and retraced their steps to the front of the church where they dropped the beam next to a bench saw. After they had brought the second beam up from the cäique George produced a tape measure, notepad and pencil from the pocket of his beige work trousers and motioned Sam towards the church door.

"When does Mary actually get here?" George asked casually, his voice lowered, as he noted down the width of the top of the door.

"Today's flight. Five-fifteen."

"They think she's arriving tomorrow."

"Yes."

"So, I'm guessing I pick her up at your hotel at about five-fifteen tomorrow?"

"We can meet you somewhere if that's easier." Sam said smoothly.

George was silent for a moment, measuring up the side of the door. Sam waited uncomfortably. "She was bloody upset after you left at Christmas," George eventually spoke in a soft, accusing growl. Sam studied the line of the church wall, making no reply. "Doesn't make me feel you *are* making her happy."

"What did she say?"

Mary had said, "Don't worry about it George, it's always like this. I'll be fine tomorrow, really. I just hate to see him go, but I get over it and life goes on as normal till next time. Never mind me."

He had asked, "So who do you love? Sam or Ian?"

She replied, "I love them both, George - of course I love them both."

To Sam, at the door of the church, George recounted, "She said she hated to see you go."

George took his measurements over to the bench saw and together they positioned the beam and marked the cut. "So do you have any plans beyond this week?"

"If you mean, am I going to bust up this marriage as well, the answer is no. Mary's never going to leave Ian; she and I will never live together again. Apart from that, I don't know what happens beyond this week, and neither does she."

George started up the saw and cut the beam. He measured again; they repositioned the beam and George marked the next cut. "So if the two of you couldn't live together, if you had to walk out on her like that because it was so *bad* being together, then why didn't you just stay out of her life?" Sam did not respond, so George changed the question. "Or ... if you two were so much in love, why didn't you ask her to marry you?"

Sam was not in the mood to ignore the critical tone of George's questions. "I *did* ask her to marry me."

George's fingers froze on the saw's trigger. Here was another family-truth he didn't know. "When?"

In the early hours before dawn, under a clear sky with a partial moon, in a paddock some distance away from the encampment at the Sunbury festival. The third night they had spent together, overwhelmed with the wonder of love, sure the feeling would last forever, feeling responsible for this very beautiful girl he had in his arms, in his care. When she was seventeen; and he was nearly twenty. When she had been too young to make the promise she made, but he had meant every word he said. When they had thought her parents would stop them seeing each other if they knew. When he had to go back to Vietnam to finish his tour, but would be back in just a few months. When he was experiencing the horrors of a war abroad, but still believed he was safe at home. Before she broke her promise, before she slept with Vasilis and fell pregnant, before she crushed his ideal of a future built around her, before the night Stephen had lifted the army revolver from his tongue substituting just enough heroin to see him to the morning, before he learnt to save himself from the black dog by forgetting his anger in the reassuringly worse world of war.

Sam had stayed away long enough, or so he thought. He couldn't make it to Stephen's wedding, so he dropped into the New Year's Eve housewarming. He presumed she would be there, but it had been so many years, she had a husband and children, he had his own life. He sincerely hoped he would look at her and think, "What the fuck was that all about?" and the bitterness would fall away from him for good. Something he should have done years before, he rationalised to himself, time to let it go. But far from letting it go, she had taken him over again and suddenly he found himself responsible for breaking up a happy family, suddenly he had three children who weren't his own, suddenly he was trying to hold them all steady through a divorce. He had wanted to stay with Mary as much as she had wanted him to stay. She had whole-heartedly offered to support him so that he could be with her and write his book. But sitting in a den, writing a book doesn't feel like valid work; it doesn't look to others like valid work; it doesn't bring money in and when the publishers rejected his work Sam gave up on any hope he had of deserving respect. Mary kept trying to love him, but he didn't believe her, all he could see of himself in her eyes was a lost cause. Every compliment she tried to give slid off him; every critical word hollowed him out until he felt he could do nothing right. He shrank into himself. Her claws savaged him as she tried to dig him out; and he savaged her back.

He had taken the contract in Cambodia to try to restore his self-respect. To try to be again the person she had loved. He had suggested that she could travel with him; try to live his life, or at least to try to find a compromise that would keep him alive and would suit her as well. But it was an impossible ask - her shared children, her job, her fear of change, her love of family and home. He understood why she hadn't gone with him, and he understood that he had left her alone to make her decisions in the thin hope that she could favour him. He could hardly blame her for deciding against him, but the manner of her betrayal had reopened old wounds. Given the opportunity, Sam believed, people repeat their crimes. She was sleeping with someone else, and Sam had walked out of her life vowing never to return, telling no one why he had left, too ashamed of himself and his failures to keep any contact with anyone until Stephen tracked him down in Iraq.

When he had woken, years later, to find her in his hospital room he had told her to leave. When she came back, day after day, he told her she shouldn't be there. But when she demanded to know if he still loved her he couldn't say 'no'. When she had kissed him he had no way of stopping himself from kissing her in return, kissing her the way they had always kissed. His time in hospital was nearing its end when she put her proposal to him. They couldn't live together, that was certain. She couldn't travel the world with him, she loved her home, loved her family, loved Ian and he had to accept that. But they could meet. Two or three times a year. When he came home for Christmas, when work brought him to Australia, when she had an excuse to travel to him. They could be together and simply love each other, no strings attached. What if he met someone else? He had asked. Then the relationship would be equal, she promised. She wanted him to be happy. Sam had his doubts that Mary would be equable if he *did* have a serious relationship with someone else, but she knew better than to ask, and it had been easy to keep their lives widely separate for all but their few precious weeks each year.

Within the first couple of years, Sam had lost his reservations about the arrangement. The fact was that it worked. Mary was happy in her family life, excited and loving whenever they were together. Parting from each other was always hard, as Mary had told George, but the next day life *was* back to normal. George had encountered Mary in a worse than usual state last Christmas because Sam had told her that since he no longer needed to visit his father, he would not be coming back to Sydney for Easter. Mary, ever a demanding taskmaster, had not been impressed by his arguments from thrift, time or duty. Why was even a single day with her not worth crossing the world for? Sam knew he had been brusque with her; he hated that line of argument from Mary and over the years he had developed his own ways of shutting any discussion down when it took that direction. What he had hoped she would accept, even if he hadn't said it properly, was that he had no plans to ever return to Australia. By March Mary had found a way round his attempt to withdraw: she had arranged to visit the family in Firopotamos while George was renovating the church; she was going to stay for Pascha, the Orthodox Easter festival; and he could meet her in Milos. Sam had nearly refused. He knew he *should* have refused, but her plan gave him an opportunity he needed. So he agreed - one last time.

She would be on the 5.15 plane from Athens.

~

George was sitting on a crusty pink mound of rock, the Temple of Apollo at his back, the Aghios Nikolaos in front of him, and a view across four fishing boats to the arc of the beach of Firopotamos. On the right hand side of the beach were eight boatsheds - *Syrmata* - that had been converted for tourist accommodation. They were freshly painted in brilliant white with egg-blue shutters and boatshed doors. Their flat rooves sported a matching blue water tank and dark grey solar panel. George had chosen the same blue for the shutters and doors of the church. Now, surveying the church from his rock, he had decided on a brush-width blue edge to the church walls and roof, and he was hoping he had ordered enough blue paint.

Behind the tourist Syrmata was the cliff, stratified by colour and texture: powder-white to roof-height, rocky-orange, earthy-brown, scrubby-olive, wildflower-sprinkles, and finally a line of tarmac-grey where the cliff ended and the road lead to the Northern headland. There were some houses above the road, then more rocky scrub and then the setting sun, still well above the sea as it perched on top of the hill in George's view, and began to turn the sky a faint red. The shadow of the hill had fallen across the Western side of the bay, and the dark edge of shade was steadily advancing upon him. The temperature was falling and George knew he would be more comfortable in a jumper, but he stayed on his rock waiting for the shadow to insist upon his departure.

He had picked a lump of pink rock off the edge of his seat and was rubbing it absently between his palms, wondering what sort of rock it was and where its colour came from. It was light, easy to crumble into grit, not powder. He thought it probable the promontory was formed by a lava flow; the rock seemed volcanic, maybe pumice, while the hills behind the beach looked like granite. He wondered which member of his new found family would be the most likely to understand his untranslatable question, and know the answer. Maybe Theo who worked each summer as a guide on one of the tourist boats that circumnavigated the island, weather and waves permitting.

George was feeling happier than he had felt in many years. He had been welcomed to Milos in the warmest, most heartfelt of ways. His Greek family had opened their arms and taken

Thalassa

him in without any reservations. They asked him about Australia, about climate, about jobs, about supermarket prices, about kangaroos. Rose asked the question about the accident early on the first night, when the whole family was around the table. They talked openly, the women hugged him; the men thumped him on the back. His grief had been shared with the family and they had moved on to talk about his children and their children. Before long they were arguing about Greek politics and the failing economy, cheering and downing another glass of ouzo with each argument they resolved in favour of themselves and against the government. George had been greatly enjoying his renovation project. He had thrown more money into the work than he intended - but he wanted to do a really good job; he wanted the church to look beautiful when he was finished. He enjoyed sitting on his rock at the end of each working day and gazing at the church, pleasing himself with the things he had done and planning further improvements. Nothing about his accounting job fulfilled him like this work did. He had realised he should have been a builder or an architect and wondered if it was too late to start a second career. He wished he had thought to bring Liz here; he wished he had known–or had at least acted as if- they didn't have a future.

At 5.20, as the shade reached George's feet, he heard the Dash-8 circle in to Milos airport. He considered Sam's side of the story; rethought the judgements he originally made twenty-five years ago. He regretted the lost time and lost love - his own for his big brother Sam, as much as Sam's for Mary. He looked along the dark, crumbling trail of tarmac that led up the cliff-side towards Tripiti, shivered with cold, and straightened up from his rock to go home for dinner.

At the Milos Airfield terminal, Mary took her last few steps at a run and launched herself at Sam, smothering him with kisses. He shook her off eventually, smiling Cheshire cat wide inside a red ring of lip stamps.

"Take me to bed," she murmured dramatically.

"Don't want to wait for your luggage?"

"Can't we send a boy?" She was acting the memsahib in the wrong country and he revelled in the vivacious colour of her. Was it just three months ago he had tried to tell her-and had promised himself-he wouldn't see her again?

"It's a very short drive. Ten minutes."

"Did I mention I've missed you?" She took his arm; tugged on it.

"I didn't hear you."

Mary used his arm to push herself upwards and bit him sharply on the neck.

~

Iliana is not interested in Sam. She is only nominally interested in Mary. She has no concerns about the morality of their relationship. I think, to some extent, that's because she relishes her opposition to Aretha, but her rationale is that the morality is trivial. What harm do they do? Ian is having two weeks off, happily at home leaving the dishes in the sink and his clothes on the floor. He's expecting, on the basis of her past digressions, that Mary will come home refreshed and conciliatory. He will be careful to ask her no questions that might lead her to lie.

I suggest to Iliana that her view is modern, and she says to the contrary. It is old. In a world haunted by genocide, where rape is an accepted act of ethnic annihilation, where slaughter is the answer given when God is called by the other's name … from the perspective she gained in that world, why would she hold a judgment against someone who is doing no harm? The human race, she assures me, is easily capable of so much worse.

Iliana has, understandably, retreated from the human race. She likes nothing more than to stay by her immediate family in Milos, absorbed in the minutiae of their humble, daily life. She particularly likes to be near the evening meal.

My son Dimitry is two years younger than his brother Stavros. Dimitry's son, Anton, is fifty-six like Giorgos' brother Stavros. Petros is fifty-one, and Nicoli is forty-eight with his twin, Angela – they are the same age with Giorgos. Nicoli works in Athens as a ferry pilot. Angela is also in Athens, and will be coming for the Easter weekend with Nicoli to meet Giorgos. Anton and his wife Rose have a son, Theo, who is twenty-one and lives in a little flat above a shop in Adamas. And they have a daughter, named Iliana for me, who is nineteen and lives with Angela in Athens except she is on university vacation now at home with her parents. Petros and Elena, who live here in Tripiti with Dimitry, have two sons, Colum also twenty-one, and Alex who is eighteen. Soon after her arrival, Lynne is realising that the person being called 'Giorgos', which sounds to her ear like 'Your Gos', is actually the George she has met at Aghios Nikolaos. He doesn't hear it, he tells her, his mother always called him Giorgos. Lynne is also noticing that when Giorgos speaks Greek he is much more expressive in his voice, his face is alive, and he moves his hands so much. He tells her it's an essential part of the language, but she is telling herself he is joking; she is suspecting that before she mentioned it he hadn't realised it himself.

Dinner is starting almost as soon as Lynne and Tayla arrive at 7.30, but the dishes are coming to the table for the next three hours. There are many plates being passed around, a great variety of food of different colours and flavours and textures. Battered tomatoes, fried zucchini balls, yellow fava paste, calamari, octopus, stewed greens, beetroot ... Tayla, who has managed to be sitting between Theo and Colum, is enthusiastically trying everything, which is amazing to Lynne. Lynne is more careful, the octopus looks too much like octopus and she is saying she never has liked beetroot, though she is thinking she must take a small serve and is surprised to find our beetroot tastes sweet rather than being a bitter pickle. Giorgos is speaking Greek with many English words to the older members of the family and he is translating for Lynne. To the young people he speaks English, because Anton has asked him to, but now Tayla is doing the speaking for him. She, Theo, Colum, Alex, Iliana and Tayla's fancy movable phone, are in their own entertainment at the far end of the table.

Knowing the meal will take all evening; Giorgos has been reading the story of the Battle of Navarino in bits and pieces. At intervals he eats while Dimitry comments on the story in Greek. Dimitry has heard a story like this but he is thrilled to see it in writing so that he can know it is true. He is also thrilled that a woman has come from so far away to bring him the manuscript. When Giorgos is telling Dimitry that Lynne teaches art and history at a university in London, that her title is 'Doctor Williams', Dimitry is even more impressed. He is instructing Anton to refill her glass of wine and is toasting her with an extra welcome.

Dimitry is swearing on the Bible that the shipwreck story is accurate; it has been passed down through the generations without any alteration. He is adding some detail about Petros, who was the eldest in the family and had no children before he drowned. After the shipwreck the name Stavros is given to the first-born son of each generation. Lynne says in England this was the same, and for her family before her grandmother the name was being 'Nicholas'. She is explaining her brother Martin's obsession with family ancestry, but this challenges the translation of Giorgos, and they have to be satisfied in saying this information about Lynne's family comes from the Internet. Anton and Petros have not thought to look up the family on the Internet; they doubt there would be anything to find. Lynne is agreeing that there isn't because she looked herself. Dimitry is toasting her for her modern understanding of the Internet, which must be because she is a Doctor.

After she has talked so much about her brother, her two children and her ex-husband, Lynne tries to be talking about

Giorgos' family in Australia, but instead three char-grilled fish arrive, with side dishes of Greek salad and the eating starts again. Tayla, who has not, Lynne is saying, ever looked a fish in the eye, is gleefully taking a portion for herself while chiding her mother for being squeamish. The fish is delicious and Petros is toasting his wife, Elena. Lynne is not noticing the third time Anton is making a refill of her glass.

Giorgos reaches the words in the manuscript that tell the Venus De Milo story. Dimitry is nodding happily. He loves this story; he is toasting the donkey. He particularly loves the part played by his namesake; to him his great grandfather Dimitry is the hero of this tale and the version passed down in his family by Para Pappous Dimitry is different at sometimes to the manuscript. Dimitry is not knowing that Stavros fancied the Nun; that is good reason to be toasting Stavros with much laughter. Dimitry is knowing a lot more about the fight at the Port of Milos, and this story from him takes a long time and many toastings; how Pappous Dimitry is fighting hand-to-hand with the Turks to prevent them from loading the statue to their boat; how he has so much cleverness and courage. Dimitry is overwhelmed to tears when he sees Pappous Dimitry's name in the old English script; he is toasting Pappous Dimitry and is sad for some moments even though they never met.

The story is wrong though, Dimitry is soon telling Giorgos, where it says that the statue is Aphrodite. The statue is really Amphitrite, the Goddess of the Sea. He is wagging his finger at Lynne while he is explaining in Greek to Giorgos. The academics of her art world, the experts at the Louvre, they are getting it wrong. What need did the people of ancient Milos have for Aphrodite? Their goddess was Amphitrite. The name Venus De Milo brings tourists to the island, but the old fishing families are knowing better. Amphitrite's arm is keeping Aghios Nikolaos safe from storms, volcanoes and earthquakes, while Saint Nikolaos, whose home is the church, is protecting all the generations of the family. Lynne starts with excitement to say that she would like to take the arm to the Louvre, but Giorgos is placing a hand on her arm below the table and shaking his head. He is making no translation, so Dimitry does not learn from these things Lynne has said.

Baklava is being served, and Anton now is filling glasses with ouzo instead of wine. Dimitry is not knowing where the arm is buried; no one is ever caring to find out where. To him all that matters is that it is there to protect the church. Papa told him, and he has told Anton and Anton has told Theo about this. There is no plan for the building of the church, no record of when each wall was rebuilt; the manuscript is the only time he is seeing any drawings by the first Stavros. Dimitry is toasting Para Pappous Stavros for being a great artist. Lynne is realising too late that it is best to take much smaller sips of ouzo. Tayla is saying how much she is loving Elena's Baklava which is the Pontic recipe she learned from me.

As Lynne is coming back from the bathroom she is tripping on the uneven cobbled stone paving of the hallway steps, she is trying to get steady by holding the wall, and is caught by Giorgos to stop her falling. They laugh together and Tayla makes this an excuse to show off to Theo and Colum that she can embarrass her mother. It is time to leave, Lynne is saying, and when Giorgos is offering to drive them back to the hotel Lynne is saying 'no' and Tayla is saying 'yes'. Only then is Lynne learning that Tayla has arranged with Theo and Colum, Alex and Iliana to go on a sailing trip around the island next day. Giorgos is inviting her to join him and go as well. He is saying everyone he has met on Milos has told him he must go to Kleftiko, and the only way is by boat, so this is his opportunity. Lynne is thinking she is over-indulging in their hospitality, but Tayla and Giorgos insist, and before Lynne has agreed she is learning that Giorgos is driving them to the hotel tonight and picking them up in their car in the morning to go to the boat. Not too early, ten o'clock.

Thalassa

~

In the car Lynne enticed George to speak of his two children. As they reached the hotel she asked about his wife.

"She died in a car accident in April last year."

It was a calm, and very sobering statement, and not at all what Lynne was expecting to hear.

"I'm so sorry." Lynne could find no other words.

"Yes. Never mind - at this point no one ever knows what to say." George stopped the car and pointed his finger across her nose towards the hotel. "Do you think you can make it up those steps or should I escort you?"

"I've got her," Tayla opened the door and pulled at Lynne's arm. "Come on now Mumsy, lets pour you into bed."

Lynne shook Tayla off angrily, got herself out of the car easily and turned back to George to thank him.

"No worries," he replied with a cheerful smile. "I'll be back at ten a.m. See ya."

As George drove away Lynne stalked up the stairs independently, with Tayla giggling behind her.

XVIII

Sunday 13th April 2008

Theo held Tayla's arm for longer than was necessary, Lynne thought, as he helped her from the beach into the aluminium dinghy. Tayla contributed by feigning a helplessness that was not a normal part of her demeanour. They remained occupied with each other, giggling as they stowed picnic food in the stern alongside the raised outboard motor. Lynne stepped over the gunwale unaided, and George pushed the dinghy off the shore before he levered himself onto the prow and crab-walked on wet feet and hands to the bench seat beside her. Theo started the motor, powered up more than necessary through the turn, and within a moment had the dinghy's bow down, speeding towards the double-masted, black-hulled boat that was waiting off the beach.

"Thalassitra is a *Trehantiri*, a traditional wooden sail boat with a curved bow stem," George leaned towards Lynne, bumping her shoulder as the dinghy bounced over waves. He raised his voice above the over-stressed pitch of the motor. "Greeks have built *Trehantiri* since the middle of the 17th century. They're very stable in rough seas because they're wide compared to their length. They're ideal for the wave frequency on the Aegean. That's *rantopsathi* rigging," he pointed to the boat, "two mainsails and two jibs. Anton is hoping to run up all the sails today to check them out. The first booking for the season is next Monday. Three families from Athens get together to book the boat for that same week, the week before Pascha, every year. There are five cabins, and for day trips-that's most of the high season-it can take about fifty people."

"How old is it?"

"This one was built in 2004 - don't worry, it's almost new!"

"It looks very expensive?"

"It would be ... my uncles and Dimitry have a share that adds up to fifty per cent, and there's an investor from Athens who owns the other half. Anton and Petros operate the boat, and Nicoli and the investor manage the business side of things. It's built to Dimitry's design - apparently it is like the one his grandfather had in Milos harbour in the late eighteen hundreds."

"What happened to that boat?"

"The Germans took it when they arrived in 1941 and scuttled it when they left in 1945. That's part of the reason my father moved to Australia after the war - the family's livelihood was gone. It took Dimitry's family sixty years after the end of the war to get back to the point where they could afford to even part own a boat like this again."

"Dimitry didn't think of immigrating to Australia as well?"

"I think they couldn't immigrate unless someone sponsored them. Papa was fighting with the Greek army in Crete, and after the German invasion he escaped in a sailing boat-with three Aussies-to Egypt. One of the Aussies sponsored him to immigrate."

"Nick Foster," Lynne's insertion of the name made George look at her with astonishment, but he lost the chance to question her when the dinghy slowed alongside Thalassitra, and he had to grab the ladder rail to stop the dinghy's drift.

Lynne and Tayla climbed up the ladder, cheerfully assisted over the gunwale by Colum and Alex. Picnic supplies were passed up, and the girls took them to the ship's galley where they met Rose and Iliana and soon became involved in a ship's masterchef class, helping prepare a Greek lunch. George walked astern, dragging the dinghy by its rope to tie it to the back of the boat. On his way back to the galley he noticed a loose batten on the jib Anton was raising, and soon he was inspecting the other sails, having forgotten his intention to question Lynne about Nick Foster. Colum had the wheel, and with one jib half-raised he motored slowly away from Paliochori and set a course West along the South coast towards Kleftiko.

Theo summoned Lynne and Tayla out onto the deck as Colum steered the Thalassitra alongside the stunning moccasin-grey coastal cliffs at Gerakas. Tayla's iPhone camera was ready to put to immediate use, but Lynne had to go back into the galley to get her DSLR when she realised that a wonderful photo opportunity was at hand. Behind, and to each side of a fifty metre long strip of gravel the island's edge soared abruptly for over forty metres to meet the sky in a clear, treeless edge. The cliff was laddered with sedimentary layers, and smooth snakes of rock slid down shallow gullies, fanning out as they reached the water's edge. The pure aquamarine of the water lay invitingly still in superb contrast to the pale rock.

"Stunning, isn't it," George arrived beside her at the deck rail, watching the coastline with an affecting enthusiasm. "There is a road at the top there, but you can't get down from it. You have to see this from the water."

"Have you been out here before?"

"No, this is my first time. They tell me Kleftiko is even better. Want me to take a photo of you and Tayla?" Lynne agreed and George took their photo with the deck and wheelhouse to one side, and the sea cliffs to the other.

Anton shouted *"Ela"* from the bow and as George left he told them "We're putting the sails up now." Lynne followed and snapped photos of Anton out on the bowsprit rigging, clipping a halyard to the head of the foresail, and George perched on the shiny lacquered rosewood of the prow, freeing the lower edge of the jib from its red sail bag. Anton hauled on the halyard to raise the foresail, and then George waved to him to indicate he could raise the jib as well. Each sail billowed noisily as it was pulled up its stay; then arched in a pleasing curve ensnaring a bundle of wind as George tightened and clamped the halyard through a cleat on the opposing deck rail.

"You've done this before," Lynne commented as George passed her on the way to the main mast.

"Nearly every day of my teenage years, and a lot of days since" George replied with an in-his-element grin. "It's the family business in Australia too."

Lynne was attracted by the furl of the sails. She lay on her back on the glossy prow and took photos up through the white angles and curves of the sails to the bright blue of the sky. She was contentedly lying in the sun, half asleep when George returned and asked to see her shots. Shading the camera's LED display he flicked backwards, moving on from the scenic ochre cliffs of Paliochori to the many artistically composed photos she had taken of the narrow pathways, arches, stairs and pleasingly shaped buildings she had found during yesterday's walk around Tripiti.

"You've done this before," he commented, and continued to browse Friday's photos from Firopotamos.

"Every day in my early twenties, and not many days since," Lynne smiled.

"Do I detect the sad loss of a favourite hobby? An alternative career that never got off the ground?"

"Indeed. Travelling the world taking amazing photos of art, sculpture, architecture, cultural sites and ancient ruins for National Geographic would have suited me very nicely. Alas, not to be."

George offered her the camera, but caught her extended hand instead. He turned her palm upwards. "I see ... a man, and children, and lots of baby photos, and then a camera ageing quietly in the back of a dark cupboard."

"What an uncanny knack you have," Lynne laughed and took her camera. "You, meanwhile, were not interested in following in the family business?"

"I had the privilege of being the only one in the family afforded a tertiary education. They thought the family needed an accountant, not another sailor."

"You're an accountant in the family business?"

"No, that was a fail. I'm an accountant in a private practice in Melbourne ... the family's boat hire business is near Sydney."

"You ran away from home then?"

"Sort of. The course I got into was in Melbourne, so it seemed like a good idea to live there."

"Did your wife sail?"

"Yes," George didn't seem to mind the question. "That's how we met, actually. I persuaded her to come sailing with me and when she liked that I joined her up to the university's sailing club. We did lots of sailing in the first few years."

"I see..." Lynne took up his hand, "then came children, weekends taking them to football and netball, nobody using the boat and nowhere to keep it, not enough money to do everything, fewer trips back to Sydney."

"That's the story. We always thought we would get past all that and sail again."

"So now ... a part share in Thalassitra maybe? Sailing the Greek Islands?"

"It's crossed my mind this week, I'll admit," George looked away towards the coast and Lynne lost his attention to a large pinnacle of white rock jutting out of the water less than fifty metres from the boat. "Wow! Look at that," he jumped up and went to the deck rail.

"Kleftiko," Theo the tour guide announced, "Snorkelling and lunch."

~

Theo was assuring Tayla that the water temperature was a balmy twenty-four degrees Celsius - perfect for a swim. Tayla- who had stripped to her bikini to sun-bake, not swim-was not sure she should believe him. Lynne knew not to believe Theo because she had seen George's face after he had turned away from Tayla's view. The deck of the boat was too high to test the truth of the matter. Tayla was eyeing the ladder, but Theo shepherded her along the deck to the bow, which was riding at anchor some fifteen feet above the waterline.

"No, I'm not going in," Tayla's voice rose in pitch as they approached the limit of the boat. Somehow Theo had separated her from her iPhone. She was water-ready.

Tayla tried to make a break under Theo's arm but he scooped her up easily, lifted her over the deck rail and dropped her into the sea.

Tayla came to the surface thrashing and choking with outrage rather than water-blockage. "It's fucking freezing! I'm going to fucking kill you!"

Theo found that enticing, not threatening, and jumped into the water beside her. Tayla landed two punches on his surfacing head before he pinned her arms to her body and held her relatively still while he trod water. He yelled something in Greek and Alex reached under the bench seat and threw down two mask and snorkel sets. When Theo let Tayla go and offered her one of the sets she turned and started swimming for the ladder. Alex ran along the deck and pulled the ladder out of reach to which Tayla responded with another tirade of street vernacular. Theo floated on his back idly, a safe distance away, holding the mask and snorkel towards her. Within a minute she had asked Alex to also throw down a pair of flippers; she had put the snorkelling gear on and was finning alongside Theo towards the arch of a cave where the azure water flowed far into the underside of the cliff.

"Sixteen degrees, at best," George advised Lynne. "Feel like a swim?"

"It looks beautiful, but no," Lynne smiled. "I feel like lunch," she went to the galley to help bring the plates of food out onto the table that was set up in the stern of the boat.

Like last night's dinner, lunch was presented in an array of appetizing dishes, with a plate of Pita bread cut in bite size triangles, ready for dipping. There were bowls of the familiar yogurt tzatziki, hummus and tabouli, and there were also bowls of eggplant melitzanosalata, fassolia beans, a filo pastry slice Rose called *spanakopita*, and a rice pilaf.

"How lucky are we?" Lynne remarked to George when she brought her selection of dips to the bench-seat in view of the coast. "A delicious lunch with what must be one of the world's most beautiful views from the restaurant deck. Thank-you very much for the invitation, I really appreciate it."

"Thanks to Anton and Petros, not me."

Hearing his name, Anton came to sit beside them and after waving away their gratitude he launched into an exposition about this South Western corner of Milos. The rocks had originally formed underwater, three million years ago, through volcanic eruptions that laid down sediments of pumice and breccia. The coast had started to emerge from the sea not more than one and a half million years ago. Regional uplift had accelerated the regular underwater deposits, and Milos was still volcanically active like the other islands linked by the South Aegean Volcanic Arc, including the more famous tourist destinations of Santorini and Poros. The pumice and breccia had been easily eroded by wind-forced waves, driving deep caves into the cliffs, isolating dramatically sculpted islands of rock from the mainland. Pirates had once used the caves to hide their boats, and shelter from storms, these days tourists snorkelled through them to lie on hidden sandy beaches.

Lynne began to imagine what might be keeping Tayla and Theo out of sight for so long, and when George suggested a tour of the caves in the dinghy she wasn't sure she wanted to find them. George seemed to understand her hesitation as she viewed the cave into which the couple had disappeared. There was no other reason for him to tell her "the outboard motor will echo loudly in the caves – they'll hear us coming."

George was right, the noise of the outboard was almost deafening when they first entered the cave, but within seconds George had cut the motor, raising the outboard so that the propellers lifted clear of the shallow sand bar underneath. As the ceiling of the cave lowered, he lay down on his back across the dinghy seats, motioning to her to do the same and they laughed together as they moved the boat forward, passing hand-over-hand along the roof of the cave until they had head-room again, the momentum from George's last push drifting them into the sunshine of a small cove. Together they lent over the side of the boat, almost tipping the dinghy, admiring the clarity of the azure water, the rise and fall of the shallow, plant-less seabed. George lamented the fact that there was no coral, and no fish, but he did agree that the structural beauty of the cliffs and the caves made Kleftiko worthy of the acclaim he had heard. They crossed the cove into another cave, paddling lazily with their hands instead of engaging the oars, and pulled themselves through the cave using hand-holds on the wall, pausing to read love heart dedications, laughing at English misspellings and at the absurdities George invented when he couldn't read the Greek lettering. After ducking under another low cave-rim, they found Tayla and Theo masking-up in the shallow water in front of a narrow strip of sand.

"We've been listening to you two giggling all the way through the cave!" Tayla smoothed her hair away from the rubber seal on her mask, filled her mouth with the snorkel, and sank into the water. Theo held the side of the dinghy pointing out to George an alternative route back to the Thalassitra. While Tayla and Theo swam back through the caves, George and Lynne motored on around imposing stalagmites of layered white rock, weaving a longer course back to the boat.

They met an impatient reception. Anton wanted to get George back to Adamas in time to meet his sister's plane from Athens at five-fifteen. George had seemed unconcerned about the deadline, but once on board he followed Anton and Alex's lead in rapidly hoisting the sails and getting underway. They sailed back to Paliochori as if they were in a race, with much shouting in Greek, imperative gestures towards Colum in the wheelhouse and to each other, manning ropes and adjusting sails, a sense of urgency in the air that Lynne sensed was more about testosterone than the time of day. In contrast, Theo was sitting cross-legged on the raised deck in front of the wheelhouse, playing pop songs on an acoustic guitar and singing the well-known words as if he was a native English speaker. His long brown hair was tied back in a bun on the top of his head, showing off the heavy enamel earrings he wore in both ears and highlighting his sparse goatee beard. Tayla lay stretched out on a towel alongside, and the other women sat around them, enjoying the music and making suggestions for Theo's next rendition.

As Thalassitra dropped anchor at Paliochori, the Dash-8 could be heard circling overhead, on approach to the airport. After the dinghy's outboard failed to start for Alex, then George and finally Anton, oars were located, and the dinghy was rowed to another mooring to be swapped with a similarly sized boat with an engine that worked. Eventually they were ready for Lynne and Tayla to disembark.

"I'm staying with Theo Mum. We'll be having dinner at his place and then we're going to a night club in Adamas," Tayla called down to Lynne instead of getting off Thalassitra into the dinghy. "I'll see you tomorrow sometime."

Lynne was not entirely surprised by Tayla's plan, but neither did she have a ready response. She bristled with indignation more for being suddenly dumped as a travel partner than from moral outrage as a mother. She was acutely aware of George's attention to the exchange, and struggled with the 'right' response. "OK" was the weak outcome.

George stepped smoothly into the breech as the dinghy took them to shore. "We didn't get through all your storytelling last night," he reminded Lynne. "You started to say something about a woman from Asia Minor who was called Iliana ... but we got distracted and never came back to that part of the conversation. What I didn't get to say is that Iliana from Asia Minor was my grandmother. Is that who you were talking about?"

Lynne couldn't remember saying anything about Iliana last night, but now George's words excited her. "It probably is! My grandmother's brother rescued an Iliana from the fire at Smyrna, and my grandmother sent her to Milos to look for the family of Stavros Kostis." Lynne saw that George was looking puzzled. "It's a long story."

"Well ... Dimitry wants very much to hear it, and so do I, and so will my sister Mary. So can you join us for dinner again tonight?"

Lynne was certain now that she was accepting much too much hospitality from the Kostis family, but Tayla had deserted her, there was a story to tell, and George jumped from the dinghy onto the beach without waiting for her to protest.

"Give me a lift back to your hotel, I'll go to get Mary, and you drive to the Kostis place when you're ready ... dinner will be late, sometime after 8pm," George set out the plan as they walked up the beach to the car park.

"What about picking Mary up from the airport? How are you getting home?" Lynne was puzzled.

"Mary has her own arrangements, and she's got a car – so I'll just walk over to her hotel and we'll be right."

Discrepancies between Anton's idea of the plan and George's execution of it, sprang to Lynne's mind, but she sensed that George was not taking questions on the matter, so she kept quiet. As it was, George still had her car keys in his pocket and without negotiating on who had the wheel, he drove them to her hotel, parked the car, handed her the keys with a cheerful 'See ya later' and strode away from the car park in the direction of Adamas.

As she climbed the steps into her hotel Lynne pondered cultural differences. James would always have asked her "do you want to?" "Should I?" "Are you sure?" "What if?" It could take a long time to negotiate a decision towards any modicum of certainty. George, conversely, decided in favour of his own suggestion before she had time to think it through, as if he was too impatient to wait for her, or was already certain of the answer. With James she had felt as if she had to make all the decisions. With George, it seemed as if he was making them all for her. Conversely, when she compared George with Sam, Lynne found their similarities striking. Was it Aussie chauvinism? It felt nice to be the recipient of it right now, but she wasn't sure she would enjoy it long term.

While Lynne was preparing herself for her shower, analysing the character of Australian men, the Kostis-Foster brothers were cracking a beer together on the balcony of Sam's room at the Lagada Beach Hotel. Mary would not be ready to go to Tripiti for dinner for at least another half hour. She was having considerable difficulty managing her makeup routine in front of the cloudy mirror in the much-too-small hotel-room ensuite.

XIX

Iliana's Story

September 1922: Smyrna, Asia Minor

On September 13, 1922 when a Turkish militiaman put a match to the petrol trail his band had laid from the Armenian quarter towards the American Embassy in Smyrna, Iliana Theodori had just celebrated her eighteenth birthday. The Great Fire of Smyrna left her without family, without a home – indeed, with nothing but the clothes she was wearing

Iliana's parents were Turkish-speaking Pontic Greeks, who had lived all their lives up to 1920 in Trabzon, where the Silk Road met the edge of the Black Sea in North East Turkey. Her father, Ekrem, was a relatively wealthy landowner who had grown his fortune, and his influence in the community, by taking foreign traders and Smyrna's diplomats on summer fishing trips in the Black Sea. From a young age, Iliana had been given the job of entertaining the visitors' children, usually in the company of their nannies, and over the years she gained many random chapters of education and a handy array of languages. Comments from his clients drew Ekrem's attention to her language skills and, by the time she was 15, Iliana was handling all foreign language transactions in the family's popular business by the sea. By the time she was 17, her beauty had become an attraction equal to her quaintly melodic English, and the Attaché to the British Consul proposed to Ekrem that Iliana should return with him to Smyrna to work as an aide at the Embassy.

Ekrem would like to have refused, because he realised that Iliana had become a vital part of his business. Iliana's mother, Irem, did refuse, shouting and weeping at Ekrem for hours because she did not trust the British Attaché's intentions. But at that time, in Trabzon, there were compelling reasons, of which the British Attaché and Ekrem were all too aware, that Iliana would be better to leave Pontus for the protection of the Embassy in Smyrna. Indeed, the Attaché tried to persuade Ekrem to relocate his entire family to Smyrna. Ekrem was still procrastinating, not inclined to bring his wife's wrath down on his head, when the Turks trussed Leonidas, Iliana's older brother, head to feet and left him tied to one of Ekrem's wooden fishing boats as they torched it. The good citizens of Trabzon, led by their Metropolitan, Chrysanthos, acted boldly under the ribald view of the Turks to save the boy from bodily harm but Leonidas was so traumatised he retreated to the house and refused to step outside again. He did not even go to the station to bid Iliana farewell on the day she left for Smyrna with a German family Irem had been led to believe was of some relation to the Kaiser.

To Iliana, cosmopolitan Smyrna was a magical, marvellous city. She loved the Levantine community with its swirl of Italian, French, English and Greek words speaking of the wonders of other parts of the world that she desperately hoped she would be able to visit one day. In the prim, white cotton and lace dress and the dainty shoes that the Secretary to the British Consul had bought for her to wear when attending the Embassy's functions, she was able to visit the shops along the Cordon, feeling the fabrics of the dresses that came from France, picking up the shoes that came from Italy, tilting the hats that came from England into the many angles that flattered her face. She dreamt of a future when she had a wardrobe full of such clothes, shelves strewn with shoes, bags and hats. From the wardrobe she would choose the outfit she would wear to garden teas where she was a valued guest, instead of an aide and interpreter. One day she would have a garden as pretty as the one the wife of the British Consul picked roses from, and a house as grand as the one where she waited in an imposing entrance hall of dark English wood and lightly coloured Florentine tiles, as the carriages of foreign ministers rolled to a halt and disgorged their cargo of importantly suited men and their fashionably dressed wives.

Outside her working hours, Iliana's life was somewhat different to her dreams. When off-duty she would carefully fold her white dress into its shallow and wide cardboard box, store her shoes in their squat rectangular one, and tuck both boxes under her bed in her corner of the room she shared with three other Greek girls who had all come to Smyrna from varying parts of the Pontus. Then she would don her own, heavy skirt of hemp, a cotton blouse and a woollen jumper in the colder months, and she would report for duty to the head of the household, a Greek widow in her mid fifties who ran an efficient boarding house where each girl had to complete a set of daily chores as well as paying their weekly rent.

Mitéra Iasonidis, highly valued her standing as an approved boarding house matron in the Levantine community, and she knew that if she was to keep these young girls away from the temptation of the smartly uniformed consul guards in particular, she must keep them busy with chores and strictly monitor their comings and goings. Several times a year, she reported young men to their superiors, and confined girls to their rooms for a fortnight as the statutory first offence, or a month for a second offence. Two girls, so Iliana was told, had been sent home in disgrace in the last twelve months for their disobedience.

Iliana particularly admired one of the American consul guards, Richard, but she knew she was just one of many girls whom he flattered with a wink from his post, or an arm and an offer of a cocktail at the Grand Hotel Huck if he was walking down the Cordon when off-duty. She doubted that her dreams of a grand house would be satisfied by a consul guard and she knew she should reserve her coquettish humour for the son of the Duke of Marlborough, even if he did not look so handsome and had never invited her into the hotel with him. In August 1922, as the leisure of the summer season was spoiled by the increasing alarm in reports of the Greek Army's retreat, the Duke of Marlborough's family returned to the safety of England and Richard ardently tried to persuade Iliana of her need for protection from a military man such as himself. Iliana could not see that need, but she was nevertheless willing to be persuaded. Mité Iasonidis had sent Iliana's roommate home to the Pontus while Richard, guilty of the same illicit liaison, had remained unscathed. Gossip said his impunity was because he was the son of someone very important in the States.

Walking down the quay-front, between the schooners and the fancy hotel and shop-fronts of the Cordon, arm in arm, blending whites with her crisply uniformed consul guard, Iliana felt well protected from the bedraggled, vulgar men of the Greek Army who were starting to accumulate along the sea front, waiting for boats to evacuate them to Athens. Like Richard's guard squad, her roommates, and all the Turkish people she knew in Smyrna, she was contemptuous of these grubby, defeated Greek soldiers who were retreating from the Ataturk's force – a militia that numbered only a fraction of the Greek Army's size. What cowards the Greek soldiers were, and how dare they let a civilised town like Smyrna be threatened by the advancing Turkish army! There were reports that the Greek Army were pillaging and destroying all the villages they retreated through, ruining the livelihoods of villagers such as the families she had known in the Pontus, and turning the Turkish Soldiers into vengeful rapists and murderers who would assault Greeks on sight. Questioning her national identity for the first time in her life, Iliana realised that if these men were Greek, then she was Turkish. Her native language was Turkish; her Greek was not much better than her English, French or Italian. The only distinction between her and her Turkish girlfriends was their religion, and that had never caused an issue before – indeed, she felt she had more in common spiritually with her Muslim friends than she had with this very un-Christian Greek mob that was piling up on the waterfront. She wished the evacuation would be over quickly and Smyrna could return to normal.

In the Embassy the staff were tense. Iliana recognised it in the despatches she translated, in the tone of the Consul's voice and the sweat that beaded on his brow as he paced the floor while talking on the telephone. Iliana assumed the tension was all about events in other parts of Asia Minor because she knew that the Ataturk had guaranteed the safety of Smyrna. She trusted completely that nothing bad could happen here, under the auspices of the consular buildings and trading halls of the Levant. It was only when news arrived at the boarding house that the roommate who had been sent home to the Pontus had been raped and murdered by Turk soldiers that Iliana felt the first shock of fear and personal outrage. She dumbly watched Mité Iasonidis weeping, waving a crumpling letter in the air as she admonished her girls to say nothing, to not even glance at any soldier–Greek or Turkish–to go directly between the house and the Embassy in groups of at least four, and never to be out on the street alone.

Within days of that news the families of the girls in the boarding house started arriving in Smyrna. Mité charged around the house, wringing her hands, calling out the orders that would make more room, create more beds, serve up meals in shifts, complaining but turning away no one who had a family connection to her girls. Soon Iliana's younger brother, Bajram, arrived, only 16 but nominally in charge of both her mother and her sister of 14. Leonidas had stayed in the house; his fate was unknown. Ekrem was dead or 'transported to the interior', to which Irem attributed the same meaning. Iliana gave up her bed to her distraught mother; she and Sevde slept on the floor, Bajram was ushered away to a boys boarding house in exchange for the girl from another refugee family. Iliana's family was lucky; within a week there was simply no more room and Mité was turning people away with an implacably hard face at the door, and wrenching sobs in the kitchen. Iliana believed it could not get any worse; her beau assured her that the Americans would not let any harm come to them. The overburdened Mité Iasonidis was no longer a risk to the young couple, and Iliana's anxiety slipped well into the background when Richard was kissing her amongst the pallets and boxes behind the fruit and vegetable store, claiming his reward for the misappropriation of part of a delivery reserved for the consulate.

Richard's food deliveries soon petered out. There were no more supplies coming in to Smyrna, and the Greeks along the waterfront had resorted to looting the stores. There were ships in the harbour evacuating the foreign residents, and the American and British consul staff had been given the option to leave. Iliana became alarmed when the Consul's secretary asked her what plans she had to leave Smyrna, and then recommended that she should seriously think about where she could go. Iliana heard Mité sobbing woefully behind the locked door of the bathroom after she had spent the afternoon first at the British, then at the French, Italian and finally the American embassies. Richard nobly said she should leave with the British ... he would find her, somehow, some place.

The Greek Army was gone and the Turkish army arrived, all on the same weekend, and Smyrna was quiet, as the Ataturk had promised. On Sunday Mustafa Kemal himself rode into town, with a disciplined Turkish cavalry regiment following him, and on Monday as the Turkish flag was hoisted on what had been the Greek Occupation's headquarters along the quay the safely housed population of Smyrna welcomed their reprieve. Thank God the Greek Army had evacuated in time and the war had not been fought in their streets. Three crates of food arrived from the British Embassy, which had unlocked an abandoned grocery store in order to provide food to the hospital: one of their guards had seen the opportunity to divert some of the surplus to Mité Iasonidis. The house was hopeful all would be well.

For the rapidly growing number of Greek refugees miserably encamped on the wharf, waiting for the boats to return, it was another story. Mité said nothing to the families under her roof, but reports steadily trickled in. The Turkish irregular army, the *Chettes* as they were known, were working their way through the refugees, bayonetting men found wearing Turkish boots, dragging away teenage girls who had looked passably pretty and would now never be seen again, demanding that the refugees hand over what money and goods they had in exchange for their momentary safety. From the boarding house the girls could not see the wharf, but they could hear the general commotion and at times, most often after dark, a gut-wrenching screaming would rise above the noise that made the people in the house grab their nearest family member and hold tight as if that could protect them from the sound of unspeakable harm.

On the night of Tuesday 12th September the British Consul sent two guards to escort Iliana to the Embassy. The office of the Consul was hectic. There was talk of evacuation, there was talk of war, there was confusion–at least in Iliana's mind, but she thought in general–as to whose side the British were on. She translated intercepted reports where the Turks were using the word for 'cleaning', and the Consul fiercely, almost hysterically, corrected her to say that what the Turks really meant was 'murdering', and that the 'dirt' they were sweeping from the villages of Asia Minor were Greek and Armenian souls. These undisciplined Turks would reach Smyrna that night, the dispatches suggested, and the staff of the European embassies were arguing whether to order an evacuation or an allied military response.

It was breaking dawn, and Iliana was fitfully asleep in a chair outside the Consul's office when a consul guard shook her by the shoulder and advised her that she was to be escorted home, and exchanged for a fresh interpreter who could work through the day. As she was escorted back to the boarding house, flanked on either side by a guard with his rifle anxiously at the ready, Iliana saw several bodies in the streets. When one of the bodies moved and groaned the guards would not let her stop. Instead they pulled her forward by the arms and picked up the pace until she had to take short running steps, stumbling in her high heels, to keep up with their stride.

The front door of the boarding house was partly open. Its hinge was bent so that it could not close properly, and the wood was splintered at the door handle, exposing the lock. One guard held Iliana back, catching her before she even had time to register the significance of the broken door, while the other guard entered the house on full alert, sidling along the walls of the entrance hall, and turning into each room, rifle first. When the first guard left the room Iliana's family had occupied, motioning them forward along the hall, and the second guard was looking along the corridor behind them, Iliana darted for the door. The first guard lunged back to try to stop her, but she beat him into the room. When she saw her mother's bayonetted body on the floor she screamed and fell to her knees.

Knowing that their advantage of silence was gone, the guards left her, running quickly along the hall, checking the other rooms until the door at the end of the hall was thrown open in their faces and their rifles met a shotgun held by Mité Iasonidis. The guards were so well trained that they held their fire, and they were safe from Mité because the shotgun was empty. Beyond words and tears, Mité waved the guards aside and marched down the hall to where Iliana was keening and rocking over her mother's body.

Mité had emptied the two barrels of her shotgun into two Turks who were lying in bloody bundles in the third bedroom along the hall. She had then picked up one of the Turkish rifles even though she didn't know how to fire it, and she had ushered the other two trouser-less Turks out of the room while they yelled obscenities and promised to return. Hearing the commotion, the Turks in the front two bedrooms had made an escape, dragging four of the younger girls, including Iliana's sister Sevde, away with them.

In the two bedrooms at the front of the house, all the older women had either had their throats cut, or they had been bayonetted in the stomach. The girls of Iliana's age had been roughly tied, ready for rape. Two of the younger girls had already been raped, and their throats had been slit afterwards. The carnage was horrific, but Mité Iasonidis did not pause over it. She gathered up the traumatised girls and ordered them to quickly get dressed in their boarding house clothes. She brought the food delivery cart up to the back door of the scullery and directed the girls to bring their work dresses and whatever valuable possessions they had, and stack them onto the cart. While they were doing that Mité raided the kitchen for water, bread and any other foodstuffs that could be eaten without requiring cooking. They were almost ready to go ... not that Mité knew where she was going to ... when she had heard Iliana's scream.

Initially, Mité asked the Consul guards to take Iliana back to the Embassy, but Iliana couldn't be moved, she was wrapped around Irem's body, and blood was soaking into her white dress. So Mité turned to Demetria who was waiting by the cart, told her to find her embassy dress, put it on and go with the guards, in accordance with their original orders. Before the girl and the guards left, Mité had another set of instructions for them: they were to tell the Consul what had happened-in every gory detail-and they must ask the Consul to send the guards back, and escort the rest of the girls to safety at the Embassy.

Mité busied herself and the girls thinking of things they might possibly need and stacking them carefully onto the cart so that it would carry as much as it possibly could. At intervals she checked on Iliana, waiting for her to surface from the trauma, as the other girls had eventually done.

"I'm going to find Sevde," Iliana asserted, when Mité's check found her hunting ineffectively for her boarding house clothes amongst the chaos of the bedroom.

At the time, Iliana thought Mité told her that Richard, her American Consul guard, had gone to search for Sevde and the other girls. There was no need for Iliana to go, Richard would have a better chance of finding them. Much later, rethinking the events, Iliana knew that it could not have been true. Richard would have been fully occupied at the American Embassy, just as the guards at the British Embassy had all been called to duty. Yesterday's kiss behind the fruit and vegetable store had been their last.

Mité pulled a heavy overcoat from under the bed Iliana's family had used, and forced it onto Iliana's arms, wrapping it around the blood-stained embassy dress. She found Iliana's flat shoes and pushed Iliana's feet into them. She put the high heals in their box and managed to open up just one more spot on the cart for them. She pushed Iliana into the middle of the throng of girls where she was held fast in a huddle of desperate hugs.

When the guards had not returned by mid-day, Mité Iasonidis gave the order to her miserable band of women to ship out in the direction of the British Embassy. She walked ahead, and the girls took it in turns to push the overloaded cart behind her. There were several stops in order to readjust the load, but they reached the Embassy without incident.

As they approached the gates it was apparent that the Embassy was being evacuated. There was a squad of marines lining the street in front of the gates. Other groups of people, with carts like their own, were milling around, arguing with the marines and trying to gain access to the Embassy. The Marines were checking identity documents and only those with British papers were allowed through their lines. Women and children and suitcases were slowly accumulating in the driveway of the Embassy, and when each group reached a certain size it was escorted down the road to the wharf, where the British were being boarded onto picket boats and transferred to *HMS Serapis,* which was at anchor in the harbour two hundred yards off the quay.

Mité had lost her argument with the marine who was checking papers at the gate. She appointed Iliana to watch from one side of the cart and shout to anyone she recognised from the Embassy to solicit help. It was Mité, however, who recognised Demetria and instead of asking Demetria for help when Demetria saw her and started towards her, Mité did the opposite. She ordered Demetria to stay in the group, ignore them and go to the wharf with the British. Iliana tried calling to the Secretary, but it was no use. Her voice was either drowned out by the many, or that usually very kind woman was too overwhelmed to respond. The Secretary kept her head down, looking neither right nor left, and shepherded her own children through the marines towards the quay.

Perhaps because she could see the hopelessness of their efforts at the gate; or perhaps because she wanted to keep sight of Demetria - Mité ordered the girls to push the cart on towards the wharf. With Mité at the apex of a triangular phalanx of girls, they gradually forced the cart down to the waterfront. At some point, after the line of marines defending the Embassy had ended, they managed to fall in behind a group of British, gaining easier passage, and when they were halted by the queue at the wharf they could still see Demetria about fifty yards ahead. Mité held her hand across her mouth as she watched the marine shaking his head at Demetria and waving her away. Then the British Secretary pushed her way forward, one arm around a daughter of her own, and wrapped her other arm across Demetria's shoulder. The marine dipped his head to the lady and stood aside as she motioned all the members of her family through the checkpoint towards the picket boat. Mité drew a sob of relief.

When it was their turn, however, Mité lost her own argument with the marine. Instead of leaving, as the marine had ordered, Mité told the girls to drop the cart and stay put, slightly to the side of the queue, refusing to budge until the marine gave up and returned to his duties, re-checking the documents of the arriving evacuees. Soon there were so many people behind them that there was no way they could have moved the cart anyway.

"They have to embark all the British staff first," Mité explained to her girls.

The quayside at Smyrna was two miles long, and as wide as a football field, but by the time dusk fell on that afternoon, it was a shoulder-to-shoulder crush of refugees. The Turks who were 'cleaning' the countryside had pushed two hundred thousand people, and the meagre belongings they had been able to bring from their Anatolian villages, right up to the seafront. Greeks and Armenians were also crowding onto the wharf from Smyrna itself, as Turkish brigands ransacked their houses and stores, killing, raping or brutalizing anyone who stayed behind. Houses in the Armenian quarter had been burning since early afternoon, and now there were fires in the Greek quarter, approaching the wharf. The sky darkened prematurely, overhung with the black, acrid smoke that comes from the burning of petrol and household goods. The crowd watched the thickening smoke uncertainly, huddled together in protective family circles over their belongings, looking outwards in preparation for the *Chettes* who now, thankfully, had little chance of pushing their way through the dense throng.

It was night when the last of the staff from the British Embassy arrived at the embarkation point. The suited men, and the consul guards were all carrying document boxes. Even the Consul himself had his arms full as he brought up the rear, his eyes fixed resolutely on the picket boat, his ears closed to the calls from the crowd. The marines promptly closed in behind him, forming a shield of blue chests crisscrossed with rifle barrels.

Mité's renewed efforts met a rigid, intractable silence. When the picket boat returned it was the marines who embarked on it, and the seafront was left without a single guard.

"They'll come back for us in the morning," Mité Iasonidis assured her girls.

Mité told the girls to eat a ration of the food they had stored on the cart. She ordered three to keep watch, and told the others to try to sleep – they would change shift at one am. Iliana was so exhausted that she fell asleep in a huddle of overcoat alongside the cart.

When Mité roused her, Iliana was startled to see that the fires had come much closer while she slept. The European quarter was now burning, and horrifyingly beautiful red flames leapt out against the night sky, only a few blocks from the quay. Iliana could feel the fire's heat, but Mité would not let her take off the overcoat – it would protect her from sparks, Mité had said. At 3 am the roof of the cinema-an elegant building that faced proudly onto the Cordon only a hundred and fifty yards away from the cart-caught fire. Other buildings along the Cordon also started to burn and the crowd pushed even harder towards the waterfront as ash started to fall on them. When their belongings on the cart caught fire, Mité and the girls tried to beat out the flames with their overcoats. Their frantic effort was useless, and the flames soon forced them and the rest of the crowd back into a wide circle. Within half an hour all that was left of their belongings was ashes, and before those had even cooled, the crowd was pushing in over the top of them. Mité made the girls put their singed, smelly overcoats back on.

"The boats are back," the words spread faster along the quay than the fire was jumping between rooftops on the Cordon. It was black out in the harbour, while the fire was lighting the wharf. Iliana stared hard to see the gloomy shapes of the picket boats pulling up to the wharf. They arrived quietly, but within minutes the crowd had surged towards them. The marines jumped onto the wharf, fast, athletic, the metal of rifles glinting red in the firelight. They fought the crowd, bullying it into a queue that could board the boats as quickly as possible without overturning them. As they filled, the boats left for the ships that were lying in the harbour, and after a seemingly interminable wait they returned to repeat the process.

By determinedly holding their own against the push of the crowd, Mité's band of girls had reached the waterfront and, by Mité's reckoning should have been next to load, but the boats were taking longer to come back. Eventually just one boat returned. Others in the crowd interpreted this in the same way Mité did, some were desperately jumping the queue and when the marines closed the entry point the girls had missed out.

"Who can swim to that boat?" Mité urgently asked her girls. Iliana nodded, and before she had time to object, Mité had ripped the overcoat off her shoulders and pushed her off the wharf into the debris-laden water. Iliana was not sure afterwards, but at the time she thought Mité had pushed a couple of the other girls in as well. With her hand on the boat, feeling it start to tow her away from the wharf, Iliana saw the water was full of people, struggling to swim or just to stay afloat in their heavy peasant clothes, and she couldn't recognize anyone. On the wharf Mité was standing resolutely, staring intently at the boat, willing Iliana to hang on. As Iliana thought that was going to be impossible she felt a hand grab her wrist and hoist her upwards. Another hand caught her under the armpit and she was wrenched over the gunwale to land inelegantly on top of the multitude in the boat.

~

From the moment she boarded the *Iron Duke* until the onset of dementia in her ninety-third year, Iliana had never given up her mission to find out what had happened to the other members of her family, to Mité Iasonidis and to the other girls from the boarding house. But it was to no avail; all she had was supposition, and the tenor of that was largely dependent on her mood on the days when her idle thoughts returned the past. Through her questions she learned that the British Consul staff had been transhipped from the *HMS Serapis* to a merchant steamer that took them to Athens, so she supposed that Demetria had made it safely to Athens and had been resettled there. None of the other girls from the boarding house had made it to the *Iron Duke* so she chose to think that they had swum back to Mité Iasonidis at the wharf; she imagined Mité fishing them out of the black water. She had been told that most of those on the wharf had survived the fire that kept burning for two weeks and eventually left all of her beautiful, beloved Smyrna in ashes. Iliana liked to think that Mité had found Sevde and Bajram; that Bajram had managed to scrounge food and water and that Mité had managed to position the group at the front of the evacuation queue.

In her mid-fifties, Iliana began a friendship with a woman who had been in that evacuation queue, and had made it to safety in the last days before the deadline that Nureddin Pasha had publicly set for the massacre of any who remained. Timothea had moved to Milos from Athens to live with her new son-in-law's family, and within days of her arrival the families had brought their Pontic mothers together. Timothea knew nothing of Iliana's family and friends, but she did recount a horror story that was worse than anything Iliana had imagined before then.

After the *SS Bavarian* left Smyrna with her relatively small cargo of passengers, the less fortunate refugees who still numbered more than two hundred thousand waited for up to three weeks on the wharf for Greek ships to evacuate them, living in terror of persecution from the Turkish soldiers and infection by the typhoid and smallpox that was spreading as the days wore on. During the day the Turkish soldiers would select young men of fighting age, rope them into human chains and march them away 'to the interior'. At night Turks would push into the crowd again, selecting girls and dragging them away to rape them.

After hearing Timothea's story, Iliana's imaginings placed Mité's band at the first of the checkpoints for the evacuating ships. A Turk would demand money and jewellery from Mité in order to let her group pass and Mité would reach into the depths of her underwear to produce the valuables she had cleverly concealed till now. At the next checkpoint the Turks would push back everybody's hoods and scarves, strip off their overcoats and Bajram would be found and dragged away 'to be cleaned'. At the third checkpoint the Turks would order the women to take off the rest of their clothes. The girls were all young and attractive, they were herded away and when Mité threw herself on the soldiers to stop them she was wrestled to the ground and bayonetted. In Iliana's nightmares no one ever made it onto a rescue boat. In reality, over three hundred thousand refugees were evacuated from Smyrna, a hundred thousand were killed, and over one hundred and fifty thousand were deported to the interior, never to return.

~

Sunday 13th April 2008: Milos, Greece

They have all been telling the story of Iliana while they eat dinner, this is the Greek way. They tell, and they argue ... which day it is, which place, which person is saying which thing to which other person and who will eat the last of the Fava. It takes much time, but it is important to make the story right and so many tellers help each other's memory. In the end what Giorgos learns is right. I never tell Dimitry about Richard in Smyrna, I only tell Elena when I am much older and sad in my remembering, and now Elena does not mind telling my secrets so she is being important in the story telling. Dimitry is surprised when Elena is adding that part of the story though he is not angry because Elena makes my feeling for Richard sound more honourable than it was then. What Dimitry does not like now is the part Lynne is telling about my Nikolaos. This I never tell to anyone because they would see a disgrace. This Lynne knows because I tell it all with tears to Nikolaos' cousin in England who is kind to me in the weeks after he dies in the sea and before his sister sends me to Milos.

So Dimitry is upset. He is not making any toasts. He is scowling with his thorny eyebrows meeting in the middle and his fat nose scrunched up in folds. His mouth it is a thin line with no lips and all the creases on his face move tightly up and down as he is chewing his kebab. Lynne sees she has upset him, and is unable to know how to make him better because it is too late to take back the words of the story. Giorgos is not noticing because he enjoys his kebab as much as Anton and Petros. Maria is noticing because no one is talking and so she saves the happiness of the evening by asking Dimitry to tell the romance story of his papa Stavros III and Iliana - my Stavros and me - here in Milos.

~

Dimitry would like to, but cannot argue against Lynne's telling of his mother's brief trip to England. He realises there is a gap in the logic of the story he knows. Iliana had indeed arrived in Milos on an English container ship, and she had not explained how or why she had come to Milos when she had no money and no family or friends on the island. Dimitry had never questioned the storyline that his father told with manly pride while his mother sat by with a quiet smile. It was the ship's pilot who had found Stavros III in the port tavern and had insisted that the English captain wanted Stavros to take responsibility for Iliana. She was bad luck on his ship, the captain had said, she was causing trouble among the seamen who lusted after her, he could not keep her even a day longer, he had been paid to bring her here to Milos, and would take her not one fathom further. Stavros coyly retold that he had been intrigued by the Pilot's lavish description of the girl's charms, and when he had met her on the ship it had strongly occurred to him that the captain's bad luck was his own good fortune even if she was more Turkish than Greek. When the captain told Stavros that the girl spoke English and French and Italian as well as Greek, Stavros was pleased that he now had a business-like reason he could give to his parents and Uncle Dimitry for bringing the girl home.

Over the next few years, in accordance with the Treaty of Lausanne, 1.2 million Christian Greeks were forcibly relocated from Asia Minor to Greece, in exchange for some 360,000 Islamic Turks. Most of the Greeks spoke only Turkish, and the Turks spoke only Greek. They left homes and livelihoods they thought they would return to one day, but that day never came. While the economy of Greece staggered under the strain of the influx of so many impoverished, unemployed, homeless people, Milos was largely spared from the refugee resettlement program. The few Anatolian Greeks who came to Milos were nearly all linked by kinship, and they integrated into their extended families without suffering the same hardship that was felt by the massive numbers of refugees who had no link to anyone on the mainland. Even so, the Anatolian Greeks, divided from the Greeks of Milos by a seemingly insurmountable language barrier, were viewed with deep suspicion, and it was in helping them overcome this barrier that Iliana made her greatest mark on Milos.

Iliana sought out the Anatolian Greeks in the hope of news of her family from Pontus, and her friends from Smyrna. It was news no one was ever able to give her. Soon Iliana was sought out in return for her abilities as an interpreter and language teacher, most often to help the new family members communicate with their own Greek kin. Iliana never asked for any payment, but the families she helped were soon buying all their fish from Stavros and Dimitry, and Uncle Dimitry became the freighter-of-choice when deliveries were required. The fish stall was always busy when Iliana was on duty. Stavros understood that Iliana was behind the increase in the family business, and he possessively refused when the tourist operator in Adamas asked his permission to offer Iliana a job. There was no question in Stavros' mind that altogether too many men in Milos were yearning for a closer relationship with Iliana.

Initially Stavros' parents were flatly against any suggestion that Stavros should marry Iliana. In their eyes Iliana was Turkish, she had no family, no dowry, and a union was completely unacceptable. But in time, as they were drawn into the approval that some members of their society were giving Iliana, and as they begrudgingly became fond of her themselves, their resistance lessened. When Stavros, who was worryingly more than fifty years of age, did not pursue any other girl for the year after Iliana's arrival, his mother relented. Better to have children with a Turkish girl than no children at all, she told him brusquely. As for Iliana, her sole thought when she first arrived in Milos was that she would find a way to return home to Smyrna or Trebzon, but as more refugees from Asia Minor arrived and she heard their stories she gradually accepted that there was no going back. She had to make Milos her home, her dreams of a cosmopolitan life were buried in Smyrna's ashes, and she knew she was very fortunate that the Kostis family had taken her in. Stavros was a kind man, of modest means and a reputable standing in Milos, and when he asked her to marry him she graciously accepted.

As soon as she had arrived in Malta Iliana had painstakingly bleached and repaired her white embassy dress. In Milos she added lace to its long white sleeves, and sewed a bridal train to match using fabric provided by an importer in Tripiti in exchange for her services interpreting foreign contracts. A metalworker from Klima whose surviving family had recently arrived from Anatolia, made a delicate, bronze Grecian leaf headband and presented it to her with awkward protestations of gratitude that Stavros viewed with suspicion. Not to be outdone, Stavros spent three years of his savings on two gold betrothal rings while his mother, unimpressed by this expensive fuss, wove two marriage crowns from lemon blossom. From the small cache of belongings Nick had bought for her in Malta, Iliana produced a beautiful pair of white, high-heeled Italian sandals, and the wedding-story never put a question mark over this part of her trousseau.

Stavros II and his brother Giorgos made several chairs to line the walls of the church so that the elderly members of the community could sit through the wedding service. His sister, Leda, refreshed the Icons that had become weary after almost a hundred years of veneration. The Christ Pantocrator that had been installed over fifty years earlier to persuade the Saints to favour the family with the birth of Stavros III, smiled brightly and benevolently down on the people of Milos as they packed Aghios Nikolaos at Firopotamos. The crowd spilled out of the church door, filling the courtyard to the harbour walls. In Dimitry's more expansive retelling of his parent's wedding, the crowd even covered the rocks behind the church, all the way past the pillars of the ruined Temple of Apollo to the sea-cliffs. In just one day, the new gold-leaf paint on the Holy Book in the right hand of St Nikolaos had been kissed away, revealing the wood underneath the Icon that welcomed worshippers inside the front door. There were so many candles burning in the church that it was amazing it had not burnt down. All a testament, Dimitry said, to how popular his mama had become.

In fact, it took many more years of service to the community, pious devotion to the Church, and the birth of four children, before the people of Milos forgot that Iliana was a Turkish orphan and her popularity grew to the level that Dimitry so fondly remembered. On the wedding day, in April 1924, most guests came to satisfy their curiosity and join in the biggest party the island was likely to hold that year. In these prosperous times the Kostis family, with the blessing of St Nikolaos upon them, did not disappoint the community's expectations. The bride was hauntingly beautiful despite her origins, the church service impeccably traditional, and the feasting and dancing after the wedding spread out along the harbour and beachfront of Firopotamos well into the night. Dawn's light found dozens of men and women, including Stavros II and his brother Giorgos, asleep in their dishevelled Sunday best on the sandy beach - proof of a most successful event.

His own wedding, Dimitry lamented, had not been blessed by the same extravagance, the same optimism about the future. In the years immediately after the Second World War, after the Nazis had destroyed their boats, the family had been too poor, too disheartened. His own brother Stavros had not attended Dimitry's wedding, nor had Stavros had a wedding of his own – unthinkably, Stavros IV and Aretha had just signed a piece of paper and eloped to Australia. It still brought tears to Dimitry's eyes, and gave pause to his storytelling, to remember the loss of his brother to the under side of the world.

~

"*Para Yia Yia* was 102 when she died - not quite 2 years ago. She was ninety-four when I came here with Ian and the children in 1998." Mary leant sideways into Lynne's shoulder as Rose squeezed a plateful of Baklava through the narrow gap between Mary and Dimitry. "She had dementia, but she remembered the Smyrna fire quite clearly and she told me about it … in Turkish. I couldn't understand much she said, but I could tell when she was talking about her family because there were tears pouring down her face. Sometimes she would say whole sentences in English, or French, perfectly clearly, then go back to Turkish. She showed me her white dress and the shoes she still had even though the leather had perished. The bridal train had been separated from the dress, and she said she had worn it again, but it didn't fit her after she had her first child. She told me the dress had saved her life, but I didn't understand how – it was obviously very precious to her.

"Think about it," Mary continued, cutting herself a sizeable portion of Baklava, "*you're* looking into your family tree, and you've got stories, photos, cards, things your relatives owned ... *Para Yia Yia* had absolutely nothing but the dress and the shoes. No photos, not a single thing handed down through the family, not even her own birth certificate. Just terrible, terrible memories. She kept crying and talking in Turkish. I just kept nodding as if I understood what she was saying. She could have told me about your Nicholas and the trip to England ... I wouldn't have known if she did." Mary pushed the Baklava towards Lynne and, after Lynne shook her head, Mary offered the plate across the table to George who had been in conversation with Anton and Dimitry.

"I'm sorry," Lynne glanced at Dimitry, feeling dismayed that she had upset him, "there's nothing to say that Iliana actually had relations with Nicholas ... they could have been just pretending she was his 'wife' to get her past immigration into England."

"I doubt she would have found a husband here if she had told the full story," George responded, "I'm not at all surprised she didn't tell anyone ... even if the relationship was entirely platonic."

"Of *course* she slept with him," Mary picked up the photo of the uniformed Nicholas, Bess and baby Nick that was lying on the table in front of her. "He's *gorgeous*. I'd sleep with him." She smiled conspiratorially as she passed the photo back to Lynne. "Don't translate me," she instructed George.

Lynne noticed George's wry smile as he and Mary locked eyes momentarily. A barb had been thrown, she realised. She saw George catch it and prepare to throw it back in a form Mary could hardly have expected.

"You said something this morning about Nick Foster sponsoring our father to immigrate to Australia. I was wondering, how did you know that? Where does that connection come in?"

Thalassa

His question was directed at Lynne, but George was intently watching Mary, while he waited for the answer. Lynne wondered at the sudden thickening of the air between them. "Nick Foster is the baby in the photo. He's the son of Nicholas Baxter and Lady Bess Robertson, daughter of the Earl of Caldbeck."

Mary gasped and clamped a hand across her mouth. Other conversations around the table quieted, while everyone looked Mary's way. George, evidently less surprised, distracted the table's occupants by picking up the photo and explaining in a mix of Greek and English while he took an extra, long look at Nicholas Baxter III.

"So this man, who drowned after the fight in the lifeboat leaving my grandmother Iliana high and dry in England, is Sam Foster's grandfather, and this baby is Nick Foster, Sam's dad. I take it the Lady Bess married again?"

"And immigrated to Australia," Lynne completed the story for him.

"You found all this out from the ancestry records in England?"

"We only got as far as immigration to Australia, the trail reached a dead end because of the change of name. It was Sam Foster who contacted my brother Martin earlier this year. They ran into each other online – both looking for records concerning Nick Baxter-Foster. Sam told us the story about how his grandfather met yours in Crete, he gave me the address of the church from a letter your grandfather sent Nick not long before the end of the war. I gather, from Sam, that he knows your family very well."

~

This mention of Crete, in English, is attracting Dimitry's attention. He knows this is introducing one of his favourite stories. He thumps the table, making the honey-sticky baklava plate jump, and demands that Giorgos make translation. Giorgos is taking a moment to explain to Lynne that Sam Foster grew up as a Kostis, after the death of his mama when he is only six. Maria is excusing herself and going to the bathroom with her handbag for recomposing. Then Giorgos starts the story of the Escape from Crete, but Dimitry takes over this story because he loves to be telling about his heroic brother Stavros IV. He only tells briefly how Stavros falls in love with the impossible communist Cretan, Aretha. She was brave, he admits, for resisting the German occupation. But it is Giorgos who adds to the end of the story the news he is learning only recently, that Aretha was deported from Greece and can never return. Dimitry nods to let Giorgos know it is true, but his lips are clamped thin and shut. He is not toasting Aretha. Like me, he is always so sad his brother never comes home.

~

It was almost midnight but Adamas was brightly lit and buzzing with people, cars, boats and bikes as Mary and Lynne drove back to their respective hotels in their separate hire cars. Lynne was a little under the influence despite her restraint, but she had rationalised to herself that it was only a very short drive down the hill from Tripiti. She had declined Mary's offer of a lift because she wanted the car with her just in case Tayla rang. She had declined George's offer to drive her because she didn't want to be sitting in the passenger seat wondering whether she should invite him into her empty room.

Tayla was dancing with Theo in a nightclub just one block behind Adamas' waterfront boulevard. In a couple of hours, both thoroughly under the influence, they would scramble, giggling, up the stairs to his small bed-sit above a shop that sells beach toys, sandals and postcards. They would start to make love again, but alcohol and exhaustion would defeat them, and they would fall asleep snuggling instead, promising each other satisfaction in the morning.

Mary found Sam asleep, as she expected, when she quietly slipped into the hotel room. He was lying across the double bed, his arms and legs splayed as if someone had flung him down. He was not trained in the art of sharing a bed. Even if he started on his own side, he would soon spread himself more comfortably across the width of the mattress. She was well accustomed, on their occasional nights together, to gently relocating his limbs. While she preferred her chance of a good night's sleep on her own in a king size bed, she had never resented waking to find herself pinned down. There was something child-like and vulnerable and completely hers about Sam the sleeping giant, and she enjoyed rearranging him without his notice. He would never accept her rearrangements while he was awake. It was a guaranteed way to start a rough and tumble, which was fun, but it was a whole different Sam. Indeed, Mary knows there are many different Sams, of which the sleeping giant was definitely the easiest.

She laid her clothes over her bags on the luggage rack, and went into the bathroom to prepare herself for bed. The bathroom mirror was hopelessly inadequate, too small, with dark spots and swirls across it where the reflective surface had been scarred, but it was enough to sponsor her self-comparison with Lynne. She thought (inaccurately) that Lynne had the substantial advantage of being more than ten years younger than her. In the last ten years since menopause began, despite the many diets she had tried, and the exercise routines she pursued, Mary had gained at least a kilo a year, most of it on her hips. She was losing her looks, and she hated it. In her youth a toss of her abundant hair, a flutter of her artful lashes and a full-lipped smile could make any man turn his head to smile back. She was still alert to the head turning of men as she walked into a gathering, a bar, a shop ... but these days she realised that her expectations were not met unless she wore, did or said something outrageous. The attractive young men would be looking at young women or other young men; the unattractive men of her own age would be absorbed in their drink, their food, the sport on the big screen, or at the very least in themselves. Age had ruined the game.

Ian told her not to worry about it, he loved her exactly as she was and he would be horrified if she were to ask a plastic surgeon to alter anything – even Botox was out of the question. She checked with him regularly, and at every request he unhesitatingly confirmed that she was beautiful. She knew Ian meant it, but she found it an empty reiterative reassurance, albeit one she demanded. Sam, on the other hand, had never told her she was beautiful. Sam was dissatisfied with the surface of things; he viewed beauty as a veneer to be distrusted, overturned, examined underneath; he suspected it was a pleasure that would be taken from him when its real nature was revealed; he believed he would lose the beautiful things he admitted to appreciating. Mary had learnt long ago not to ask Sam. He would reply 'why do you ask?' or 'what do you think?' And yet, when Sam touched her, when he made her wait while he worked his hands over every surface of her body, he made her feel completely beautiful, she loved every bit of herself as it burned for him, she loved to win him, to make him surrender himself to the desire she could provoke in him. In his best moments he would playfully touch the dip between her collarbone and her jugular vein and answer her "I like *this* bit." In his worst moments he would tell her "Julia Roberts is beautiful" as if she needed an epitome of the word to understand its correct usage.

Mary didn't think Sam would find Lynne beautiful. Lynne didn't look at all like Julia Roberts; more like the Cameron Diaz look that George favoured. Not that Lynne and Liz had much in common apart from short blonde hair and even on that they differed between platinum and natural. Liz had a lean boyish fitness, tall and straight through the waist and hips, while Lynne was softly curvaceous. Liz wasn't into food, so it was most unfair that she had one of those metabolisms that let her eat whatever she liked without gaining weight. Liz was into sport– sailing, netball, tennis–she even ran marathons, a masochistic exercise Mary couldn't begin to understand. She had been constantly on the move when her children had been in school; taking them to sports and activities, and when they had left home she had just kept going. She had been in Ballarat that weekend, at an interstate schools netball tournament. Still coaching the high school team even though Claire was now in university. She had played in the seniors final with her fellow coaches before getting in the car for the long drive home. The team had surrounded Claire in an uncommonly tall female cluster, talking about that last game, on the steps outside the funeral parlour.

Lynne hadn't talked much about herself over dinner, but Mary had already surmised from the academic credentials George used that Lynne was the bookish type. Mary could imagine Lynne in twenty years time, rounder, with short grey hair, a cardigan and reading glasses, writing a research paper in an oak-panelled study. It was getting harder, already, to bring Liz to her mind's eye, but Mary imagined that in twenty years time it would still be just the hair they had in common. Liz would have been thin and straight, leading a group of environmentalists on a bush walk in the high country, arguing with the cattlemen over whether their cows were damaging a rare plant. Lynne, Mary expected, would have conservative views on politics and religion, more suited to George's nature, in fact, than the radical atheism Liz upheld. Mary can't accept that Liz believed there was no God. Surely, Liz had to believe there was something beyond human existence? Liz had been laughing as she used the cliché 'When you're dead, you're dead', but it was nevertheless what she believed. Mary finds the emptiness of it unfathomable. She fears for George's soul if he believes the same.

But tonight George had seemed enervated. Relaxed, refreshed, talkative, open. It was the first time Mary had heard him laugh–

really laugh-since the accident. Mary, who attributes too much to sexual attraction, thinks it must be Lynne's doing. A holiday romance, whether a few days or even just one night, would be perfect for George, Mary thinks. Enough to break down the barrier, to show him that it's possible to enjoy another person's body, to love more than one.

Mary, robed in a red satin nightshirt, stood over Sam in the hotel room, massaging moisturising cream into her hands and reimagining, for a few moments, her enjoyment of his body that afternoon. She knelt on the bed beside him and lifted his arm, placing it across his chest. She slid his left leg across, next to his right. Then she tucked her hand under his left shoulder and lifted it, pushing towards the far side of the bed. He groaned in protest and tried to lie back in his preferred resting place, but she resisted him with the firm assurance of experience until he gave in and rolled over. She rewarded him with a soft kiss on the shoulder, and lay down, supporting his back with hers so that he would stay on his side.

XX

Monday 14th April 2008

In the clear and sunny Milos morning, Mary sat on one side of the breakfast table looking across the still chlorine-blue water of the pool to the wild flowers on the hills ringing the side of their hotel, while Sam sat opposite her, covering slices of toast with ample slabs of butter.

"I met your cousin last night."

"Who?" Sam thought Mary's remark completely random.

"Lynne Williams."

The ice-bucket cold chunk of butter broke through Sam's brittle toast, spreading the surface of the plate. He made a growling noise at the butter, then repeated Lynne's name with a question mark.

"You met her in London, you gave her the address of the church."

"She's here?"

"She's visiting Milos with her daughter. She has been a guest of the Kostis' for the last two nights, apparently her great great-grandfather, and my great great-grandfather knew each other, and that's only the start."

"What's the rest?"

"You would know the rest, darling, given what she said." Mary paused, watching Sam silently opening a strawberry jam packet. "You gave her your father's account of the escape from Crete. She said your father had a letter from Pappous, that's where the address came from. Where did you meet?"

"I had lunch with her and her brother Martin at a place near Blackfriars Bridge. I'd been emailing with Martin, and he asked to meet me in person. Lynne has been collecting things the Baxter family has written over the generations. She wanted a copy of Dad's story. Then she was intrigued that the name Kostis cropped up again … in Dad's war story as well as in her great, great grand-father's story about the Battle of Navarino."

"It *is* intriguing, don't you think? And in between, *your* grandfather actually rescued a woman from the fire at Smyrna, the Asia Minor Disaster. He took her home to England, died in a boating accident and then Lynne's grandmother sent Iliana, *my* grandmother, to Milos to look for the Kostis family."

Sam had stopped slathering his toast. He was staring at her, knife in mid-air.

"Ah … something you *didn't* know, I see." Mary was outlandishly pleased with herself. It wasn't often that she could surprise Sam with a fact, and a fact that evidenced the workings of fate that Sam disdained was even more pleasurable. "And now there's us. Four generations on, our family fates are still entwined, aren't *we* amazing."

"Is that written down?"

"It's word of mouth, but it's from both sides … we compared stories last night and it all fits. *You'll* need to research it and write it down, but I already believe it." Mary squeezed her tea bag and dropped it in the small coupe plate on the centre of the table. "I think it's a great story, and it's not finished yet. Lynne's daughter Tayla is fucking Theo as we speak, and George has been squiring Lynne all over the island. If only those two were as quick to make up their minds as Gen Y is! It's obvious they're going to get together, they're wasting time being coy with each other."

"Lynne and George?" Sam sounded incredulous.

"I know George thinks he can't get over Liz, but he can, he has to. This is a great chance. I was thinking, we should invite both of them to have dinner with us on the waterfront tonight."

"You're match-making." Now Sam sounded angry.

"Well why not? George needs a push ..."

"George does *not* need a push," Sam cut in.

"He needs a push, he is too hesitant, he needs to know she likes him and wants him so that he'll make a move on her."

"*Does* she like him and want him?"

"I can tell she does ..."

"You can't tell anything about her! You spent ... what ... two hours in her company? While she told this story about your grandmother? I bet she hardly said anything about herself and you've made up an entire persona to link her romantically with George."

"Alright, if you know her better, then you tell me."

"I'm saying *you* don't know her."

"What type of cousin is she to you?"

"Half second ... or third ... some number of times removed." It was the hesitation that gave Sam away. Sam would have known exactly, Sam always knew exactly. Mary detected in him the feelings her suspicions were looking for.

"You know her better than you're saying. You're not thinking of her as a cousin at all are you? What is she to you?" Mary glared at Sam accusingly while he tidied up his breakfast plates and glanced around at the other guests, knowing their heated words had reached flash point. "Have you slept with her?"

"You have *no* right to ask!" Sam pushed his chair back and rose sharply to his feet. In an angry bound he was gone from her, striding around the edge of the pool and onto the path towards their room.

Mary rose to follow him, and then sank back in her chair, counting her breaths, disciplining herself, knowing that he had left and she must stay because the argument would escalate if she made the further accusations that were crowding out rational thought. How fast it was, when arguments like this blew up between them. Just one minute ago they had been happily eating breakfast, but she had unknowingly walked their chatter into one of the minefields that lay between them. She dropped her head into her hands, closed her eyes and beat her intuitive understanding down with a mantra: *You have no right, you have no right, you have no right*. When she thought she had convinced herself and could talk to him calmly, she made her way to the hotel room.

She found Sam on his way out, a large black duffle bag in each hand. She pressed her hand flat against his chest and pushed hard to stop him in the doorway.

"Don't go, put them down." Sam resisted her tug at the bag in his right hand, but for the sake of privacy he let her push him back into the room until she was clear of the door and could kick it closed. "I'm sorry, I have no right, please put the bags down." Sam wasn't convinced yet. He was swaying from one foot to another, a sure expression of his divided opinion. As he swayed to his left side she managed to take that bag from his grip and lower it to the ground. He put the other bag down himself, but then raised his arms up, locking his hands behind his neck as if he didn't trust them now they were empty. He was swaying between holding her and hitting her and she understood that he was resisting both options equally. She wrapped her arms around his waist and laid her head on his chest. "Hold me Sam, I know you love me, I know it's my fault, I know I promised not to do this again. It was a shock, I'm sorry."

Eventually, Mary felt Sam's body ease, and she knew she was winning the fight. "I didn't know she was here," he said.

"OK."

"She doesn't know I'm here?"

"OK." Mary didn't hear the faint question mark. She reached up behind his neck and worked her fingers into the inter-locking of his own. She kissed him, pulled his hands apart, and brought his arms down and around her back.

"I know," she whispered, "that you couldn't possibly do what you do to me, if you didn't love me completely. You are the most extraordinary lover. Of course I'm jealous, but I know I can't say anything, I know we agreed." Now that his arms were holding them together, Mary had released his belt, unzipped his fly and had taken him in hand. She flexed her fingers individually around his penis, when he hardened she stroked the length of him. He groaned in submission and lowered his head searching out her lips and her tongue. She pushed him further into the room, alongside the bed, moving back from him for long enough to pull off her blouse and unhook her bra, dropping them on the floor as he kicked off his jeans. She hooked her hands behind his neck and pulled him down towards the bed, lifting her mouth urgently to his well before his weight had come down onto her, making him fall the last few inches.

Essentially the same fight, the same breakages, the same impassioned remedy, they had been enacting for thirty-five years. A game age had fine-tuned, not ruined.

Later, his body fully released after orgasm, his mind unresisting, Sam confessed to Mary that he had not slept with Lynne yet. Mary let his assurance pass without comment, despite the enormous relief she felt. She became all the more determined that she must make a match between George and Lynne.

~

The metal detector looked as if it was used in World War II, but it did work. George had pulled the wand across a metal bracket he had laid on the ground and the earphones had delivered a shrill tone that caused Lynne to promptly tear them off her head. Placed on the other side of the thick wall of the church, the metal bracket was not detected, but when underneath a brick, the tone could be clearly heard. Lynne and

George agreed that a scan of the walls from the inside, and another from the outside should do the trick. Lynne started in the Western corner, behind the altar, and she hadn't made much progress when George checked on her half an hour later. She admitted to a shoulder aching from the khaki strap that took the weight of the wand. She confessed that she was only scanning the wall to her shoulder height; she couldn't keep the wand raised for long. They agreed that the treasure they were seeking was unlikely to be stored above George's shoulder height, so George took half hour turns, scanning the higher section of the wall. By mid-day they had scanned inside and out to George's shoulder height, with no results. They sat together on George's pink sitting-rock, drinking from water bottles, taking stock of the situation, and reviewing their logic.

The arm had been joined to the statue with a metal pin at least 1cm wide, and several centimetres long. The drawings showed the arm in one piece, so the metal must still be in it. Dimitry had confirmed that the arm was buried in the church wall. Lynne was concerned that the renovation of the church was falling behind George's schedule. George insisted that the arm must be there and they must find it before he secured the interior panelling. Lynne said her shoulders were too sore to go on holding the detector today, but she could sand and paint the window frames. George erected a scaffold and started again in the Western corner, scanning the upper section of the wall.

George was scanning across the top of the Northern window when Lynne's phone rang below him. The earphones where emitting an empty hum, so he could hear her conversation clearly. Tayla and Theo had been touring the island on his motorbike. They were going to meet some friends of Theo's for dinner, Tayla wouldn't be back tonight, but she'd see Lynne tomorrow. George spied on Lynne from above as she shoved the phone back into her pocket with an impatient shake of her head that sent her blonde hair into a momentarily swirling eddy before it fell back into place. She continued with her work without commenting on the call. He was on the other side, outside the church and outside Lynne's earshot, when Mary rang him. What were his plans this evening? He confessed to having none apart from falling into bed. What were Lynne's plans? He told her with some amusement that Tayla had dumped Lynne again, so he supposed Lynne had no plans either.

"George, you are an idiot." Mary surprised him by hanging up.

A moment later she rang back. "I have booked you a table for two at *Fournos Artemis* at 8 o'clock. Sam and I had dinner there on Saturday, and it was really good. Don't be a berk; take her to dinner. It is on the main drag, almost directly across from the bus station. *Fournos Artemis*, 8 o'clock."

"Mary," George started to protest, but Mary had hung up again.

~

As dusk fell, George was again sitting alone on his rock, but this time he was scowling unhappily at the church, concentrating his glare on the walls, as if the arm of the Venus De Milo would show itself in x-ray. Their soft-approach with the metal detector had revealed nothing. To find the arm they would need to bring in heavy artillery that would scan the walls for cavities or irregularities. Equipment that was not available in Milos. A palaver that would inevitably mean he had to let Dimitry and his family know what they were looking for, and what they intended to do when they found it. An expense Lynne would have to convince the university research department, or the Louvre itself, to underwrite. Was the arm of the Venus De Milo worth all this? Obviously the answer was yes, if they *did* find it, and if it *was* the real artefact. Still, George regretted the nuisance it was causing him. At any rate, none of this would happen before the Easter celebration, so now he had to catch up two lost days and complete the work. Lynne had apologised profusely for wasting his time, she had offered to help with the painting over the next two days before she returned to England. She had accepted his dinner invitation, but only on the condition that she was paying.

George was happy for Lynne to repay his hospitality with dinner at her expense, but he was unhappy that instead of this being Lynne's idea, or his own, Mary had arranged the booking. He was feeling the anxiety-itch of manipulative intentions towards him. He was disgruntled that his easy-going, far-from-home family church renovating holiday in the Greek Islands had become complicated: by Lynne and the fruitless search for the stone limb, by Mary and her secret liaison with Sam. He knew the obligation to have a new partner in his life was being foisted on him, and he wished the world–principally his sister–would just leave him alone. The simple pleasure of his daily thinking-time on his pink rock had been spoiled. He stood up and scuffed his way across the gravel turning circle to his bike, thinking of inventive reasons for cancelling his dinner date.

~

At eight o'clock George and Lynne, both people who like to be reliably on time, were walking along the waterfront boulevard of Adamas past the sailing boats that were tied to the wharf behind hoardings advertising 'Around the Island' sailing trips. George had been commenting on the types of boats, the facilities on board, their suitability for sailing the Mediterranean, what type he would like to own, but his prattle stopped when he saw Mary and Sam step out together from a group of people who had been listening to the spiel of a boat-tout. Mary had Sam by the arm, she pulled him in to her, wrapped him up in a passionate kiss.

"The restaurant is right across here." George promptly directed Lynne across the road, but he knew it was too late. Her eyes had followed his, she had seen and recognised exactly what he had seen. She had watched for a moment longer.

"So, Mary and Sam have a relationship." Lynne said the words flatly, as they navigated between cars, crossing the boulevard.

"They do" George admitted, "they have had for more than thirty years."

"It sounds like you don't approve."

"Call me old-fashioned."

"Did you know Sam was here?"

"Yes – but it's meant to be a secret."

"That didn't look like Mary was keeping it a secret."

"No, it didn't look like that did it."

A waiter met them at the canopied entrance to the street-side restaurant. "Kostis," George confirmed the booking, and was puzzled to see that they were led to a table made-up for two. When he had seen Mary he had thought that it must have been Mary's intention that she and Sam would join them for dinner. Now he was wondering why she would show herself with Sam here, when she knew he and Lynne would be in the same place. As he took his seat at the far side of the table he searched the shadows and light-wells of the road, but the couple had disappeared. Again he felt the prickly discomfort of knowing that Mary was manipulating him, aware that he didn't understand her motivation.

Lynne, more attune to Mary's probable motivation than George, had only one question she felt compelled to ask. "I thought Sam was in Iraq?"

"He was. Mary persuaded him to come to Milos to meet her before going back to London. They see each other a couple of times a year like this, for a few days. Then Mary goes home to her husband and children, and Sam goes to some other assignment, somewhere else." George looked up from the wine list to meet her eyes. "Red or white?"

"Whatever you would like," Lynne demurred.

"There's a good Australian cabernet sauvignon here."

"That would be great, because I think I'll have the lamb."

When the food was ordered and the wine was poured, Lynne offered her thanks as a toast.

"Thank-you very much for your hospitality, and for the effort you've put in to search for the arm. I am sorry it's been a waste of your time, and I really appreciate you taking me seriously."

"No problem. The interconnection of our families is really interesting, it's great to hear the stories you have, and if it does turn out that the arm is in the wall there – well, that will be an amazing thing. Pity I won't be around when you and The Louvre come back to discover where it is!"

"You'll be here," Lynne smiled. "You're going to buy a share in Thalassitra and spend the rest of your life sailing the Greek Islands. You'll buy a little whitewashed house in Tripiti, with narrow steps down to a courtyard surrounded with a blue wooden fence and an overhanging pink bougainvillea, and steps up to a tiny kitchen and a bedroom that has views across the sea. You'll have a motor bike chained to the front fence and you'll drive the wrong way out of the one-way street whenever it suits you – like everyone else does."

George laughed and raised his glass to the idea. "Doesn't that sound great! And what will you be doing?"

"You need to tell me. I've pictured your future – now you picture mine."

George swilled wine through his mouth thoughtfully, evaluating his possible answers.

"You'll be at The Louvre, leading tour groups of British seniors who come to gaze at the Venus De Milo and her one arm, and listen to you, the famous Dr Williams, telling the story of the arm's recovery. You will have authored several papers on the subject of the statue, and people in the street will recognise you from a TV show on Great Historical Finds of the World. Your account, including photos of Firopotamos and the church, will have been published in National Geographic, and they will be negotiating with you for further articles and photographs on artefacts from antiquity."

"Oh yes! I knew my future would look so much better if you imagined it for me! Can you make that come true?"

"I'll do my durndest. Step one is to assure The Louvre that the story is true – yes?"

"Yes." The conversation paused while Lynne dipped some bread in the shallow plate of oil, then dark vinegar, then dukkah. George followed suit. Lynne shifted the conversation to family by asking about Claire and David; then talking about Marcus and Tayla. Dinner passed easily and it was after eleven when they started back along the still busy boulevard towards Lynne's hotel, and Lynne's phone rang with the ring-tone reserved for Tayla.

"Mumsy!" Tayla's voice was exhilarated and loud enough for George to hear. "Theo and I are at the *most* magical place and you've got to come out here now."

"It's after eleven Tay – where are you?"

"Sarakiniko! It's moonlit, and it's white and it's stunning! You've got to come out here now!"

"Saranikito? Where is it?"

"Sara*kiniko*. It's just five minutes from Adamas on the South coast, white rocks looking over the water, and it's all lit up by the moon. It's the most beautiful thing ever – you have to come!"

"Well – let me think about it." Lynne looked up, past the lights of Adamas to the clear sky and nearly full moon.

"Just come!" Tayla hung up.

"I've heard about Sarakiniko," George offered. "I'm told it is amazing under a full moon."

"It's so late," Lynne wavered, "Tay never thinks it's late."

"It's not too late." George stopped alongside his bike on the street outside the hotel. "My chariot awaits. I know where it is. Shall we go?"

Lynne hesitated. She thought about not having a helmet; she was glad she was wearing jeans instead of a skirt; she analysed her heels and decided she could take them off if necessary;

she wondered about holding George's waist. She thought she shouldn't, and then swung her leg over the back of the bike.

"Ready?" George asked after she had slung her bag over her neck and shoulder. "Hold on then," as he said it he reached behind, took her left arm and pulled it round his waist. She wrapped her other arm round him and slid down the seat to settle comfortably small against the windshield of his back.

~

The car park above Sarakiniko beach was deserted except for Theo's bike. There were no lights at all in the rocky valley that led down to the sea, and yet the footpath from the car park down to the beach was clearly illuminated by a very bright, nearly full moon. Shortly after they had started down the path Lynne paused to remove her shoes. George, ungallantly, missed his opportunity to offer either his shoulder or hand in support as Lynne wobbled on one leg at a time. They continued down the path, with Lynne marvelling at the smooth, powdery texture of the white rock under her feet, and George breaking pieces of rock off the sidewall of the path, testing the rock's texture with his fingers, trying unsuccessfully to crush it by closing his fist. Lynne thought the rock must be a limestone because of its colour, but George thought otherwise because of its texture. A 'white lava mousse', he had heard the locals say. On the right hand side of the path, silhouetted against the moon, were mushroom-shaped rocks that George found compelling. He clambered up the low cliff and set off to investigate, assuming Lynne would follow. It took him a few moments to realise she had stayed behind on the path, and he returned to look down on her and ask quizzically why she had stayed behind.

"How do I get up there? Aren't you going to help me?"

"Oh," George was taken aback. "Sorry – I just assumed," he offered his hand and competently pulled her up the cutting.

"Should I take it Australian girls don't need help climbing cliffs?"

"Well ... Liz was very independent. She never accepted my help in things like that. She'd be more likely to say 'I can do it myself, thanks!'"

"Was Liz your only girl?"

"From the day we met – yes." George's response was gruff, and he turned away from her as he spoke, re-initiating his expedition to investigate the oddly shaped pinnacles. She followed, gradually falling behind as she picked her bare-footed way carefully across the rocks. "Now *this* is pumice." When she caught up to him, George handed her a piece of the dark rock that formed the mushroom caps. It was dark in colour but light in weight, aerated with large streaky breaks in the rock. "And it's perched on top of sediments of this hard white lava mousse. Don't they look weird?" He waved his arm across their view of a dozen or so mushroom pinnacles sprouting from the luminous white surface of the rock between them and the sudden edge that fell in darkness to the sea.

"It must be the closest thing I've seen to a lunar landscape," Lynne replied, turning to look at the view behind them, where white rock flowed smoothly down to a crinkled, rounded drop off into the sea – as if the lava flow had come to a sudden, nose-curling stop. Against the glowing white rock she could see a moving black shape. A shape that separated into two figures, and then merged again as she watched.

"Tay and Theo, I think," Lynne drew George's attention, and started back towards the path to intercept the couple.

"Isn't it just magic Mumsy!" Tayla tugged enthusiastically at Lynne's arm with one hand, while leaving the other arm inseparably linked to Theo. "Follow the path all the way down, round to the left and you'll come out on the side of the beach. It's gorgeous, and there's *no one* down there. We're going back to Theo's now. Enjoy yourselves!" Tay and Theo's two figures merged into a one again as they headed up the path towards Theo's bike.

Lynne looked hesitatingly towards George, and he answered with a gesture down the path to the beach.

"It's so easy for them," Lynne said after a few moments of silent walk.

"What's so easy?"

"'Hooking up', is the term I believe. Meeting each other, feeling an attraction and getting straight into bed with each other. Call *me* old fashioned, but I can't feel comfortable with it. I keep feeling like I should counsel Tayla to be more prudent … but then, I'm hardly qualified to give her advice. Whatever they do, I sometimes think … whatever they do has got to be better than our generation."

"Our generation has not done so badly," George's tone was consoling.

"*All* of my peers are divorced. Not the fifty per cent statistic the social pundits quote. *All* of my work-mates that got married have got divorced. I was actually the last – I got a 'join the club' reception. It's hardly a good example for the kids."

"So do you think your kids won't get married?"

"Tayla says she's not going to, she's already proclaimed that she simply couldn't be monogamous. Marcus is quite the opposite. He thinks he can set the world right, he's not going to have sex before marriage, he's going to choose the right girl, have a traditional wedding, and be faithful to her for the rest of his life."

"I'm guessing he's trying to make up for the sins of the father?"

"Maybe – but I don't want him to feel that way. I just want him, and Tay, to live normal happy, fulfilling lives – not some extreme anti-reaction to what they saw their parents do."

"Maybe it doesn't have as much to do with your divorce as you think," George had a gentle smile in his voice, "because the way you describe them sounds much the same as my children. Maybe they're just reacting to the society they find themselves in. The girls have liberation and they're exercising it, and the boys are seeking security. David will be very happy to be married, I think, while Claire is not planning to marry any time soon … though I'm sure she'll be changing her mind, I'm sure she'll want children, just not until she's got her career going."

George and Lynne both paused at the same moment. Standing to stare across the dark sliver of sea that stood between them and the astonishingly beautiful moonlit rounded cliffs and pinnacles of the other side of the gorge.

"That's stunning," Lynne breathed. "I'm going to have to sit and look at that for a while." She moved to the edge of the cliff and sat down, and after a moment, George followed her.

~

Unlike Theo who asked Tayla, 'Wanna fuck?' as they swam in the crystal waters at Kleftiko, and Tayla, who replied 'here in the cave or have you got a secret beach nearby?' Lynne and George are not keen to have sex. Lynne is thinking angrily of James and Sam, though she talks only of James and of her feelings about the divorce. George is thinking sadly about Liz, though he makes the right responses at intervals to encourage Lynne to keep talking.

There comes a point in the conversation when Lynne bravely takes George's hand, and feels him stiffen, as if she had made a threatening move. She sighs and squeezes George's hand instead of letting it go.

"It's alright George, there's nothing we have to do. I know you're just wishing Liz was here instead of me."

George lets his breath out heavily, turns his face away and smooths his free hand through his hair.

"That's okay. I think you are a really lovely man, it's been great to have your company, and it's fine that we're just friends. I wonder if you've talked to anyone about Liz's death and how you feel?" George shakes his head, but remains silent, so Lynne continues. "My mother died six months ago. She was old and frail; she had been in decline for many years. In the end it was a relief. It hurts to be without her–more than I ever guessed it was going to-but her illness gave me time to prepare, to say everything I wanted to say, to be able to let her go." Lynne pauses to control the quaver in her voice. "I've been thinking about how different it would be – to lose the person you love suddenly, before time. You must feel very angry, I think. Tell me about her – start with what she looked like?"

George doesn't feel angry. Unlike Lynne, he has no one to be angry with. George feels empty, he feels like his existence has been vacuumed out of him. He feels pointless; he is just putting one step in front of the other, with no sense of where he wants to go. His life plan had been comfortably vague, powered by Liz, steadily growing old with her and with no other thought in mind. Liz left him no instructions, and still all he wants to do is love her forever. He needs people to talk to, to act with; he needs the warmth of human company and a joint purpose like he has had here, renovating the church. He does not need people to make him feel obliged to take another lover, but he has enjoyed Lynne's company. Thanks to Mary's interference, he has spent some time imagining how it could be to put his arms around Lynne, to kiss her, to undress her, to make love … but at every point, he struggles to hold Lynne in mind. Every passionate touch, every gift of love is to Liz. The end of his imagination is always to be inside Liz as he falls asleep, wrapped in arms, hers and his. He would rather keep Liz like this, than traumatise his memory by touching someone else.

It's not that their marriage was perfect. They had had fights and they had been disappointed with each other at times. Liz had often accused him of being too complacent. At times he had been 'gutless', 'spineless', 'a social chameleon', a patsy for everyone else's opinion instead of having a firm view of his own. At other times he had been 'uncaring', 'an ostrich', 'oblivious' to the sorry state of the world, the corruption of politicians, the evil of consumption, the damage to the environment. George had learnt, over the years, to make himself knowledgeable and support her causes when they were in company, and when they were alone he would soothe her frustration, reminding her that the 'silent majority', of which he was one, were good people who were balancing her views amongst the many others, and were gradually making the world a better place. Liz was often angered by his unfailing optimism, but he knew she needed to come home to it. He loved taking her away from her concerns, feeling her mind and body relax under his fingers, pouring all the love he had over her, and feeling it soothe her angst.

Their biggest argument, and one in which he had surprised himself when it happened, was over religion. George had been very happy to go along with Liz's views in their early years together. He had no need to attend church, or observe any religious ritual. Liz's professed atheism had seemed strident to him, but he had no need to either agree or contest her view. What surprised him was his own reaction when he heard Liz telling their three year old, David, in no uncertain terms, that there was no God. It was indoctrination, he argued with her. No less than the indoctrination his mother had given him in the Catholic faith. If he was not to tell their children the story of God, then equally, she was not to tell them that there was no God. He wanted his children to grow up with open minds, and to decide for themselves, on the basis of their own experience of the world whether there was a God, and what they thought God might be. At the time she had ridiculed him. He had prevailed in the argument, but in the long term, not surprisingly, her more circumspect transmission of doctrine had prevailed with the children. Liz thought George was a fool for holding a primitive, irrational faith. George thought Liz was poorer for not understanding the spiritual comfort that came with secure belief. He thought she suffered unnecessarily because it was up to her to save the world, instead of having trust in God's overall plan.

Even now, when he can't find a reason for a semi trailer

being on the wrong side of a highway at the pinprick in time that will cause him the most grief, George can't turn his thoughts against God. To George, the accident was not God's doing, any more than to Liz it could have been God's doing. As he had argued with Liz, he did not have to conclude that God did not exist just because he did not know what God was, or why God was. It was enough to believe in the possibility and hope to know the answer after death. Liz had labelled him an 'agnostic' as if that were a pejorative label, George had responded 'and proud of it.' The issue had sat unchanged between them, rarely discussed. Now Liz was gone, and George was still hoping to know the answer she might have found.

No, George is not angry with God, nor with Liz. At moments in his thinking he is angry with himself, for not going with Liz to the netball tournament, for not phoning her just before she left Ballarat … for not being that minute of delay, that flap of a butterfly's wing that would have meant that Liz and the semi trailer did not connect. And sometimes he wonders if, conversely, he was the agent of her death. Did he put too much or too little petrol in the car? If she had stopped for petrol at some different point in her trip, then he wouldn't be thinking these thoughts.

George knows that no sense can be made of any of it, but his thoughts keep returning to our last moments together.

~

"No George, that's too much! They can't ask you to do that, it's not right." I'm standing at the kitchen bench alongside tote bags packed with food and drink to go, and I'm furious.

"I'll get time off in lieu." He tries to placate me. He adds a couple of items into an already firmly packed bag.

"You always say that, and when has it actually happened? How much time off in lieu have they actually given you? None.

Have they paid you for the time? No."

"Jimmy can't do it, he's taking his son to an interschool football carnival in Shepparton, and we have to get it to the client on Monday."

"Then why didn't Jimmy get it finished by Friday?" George's answer is to shrug, he doesn't engage with the possibility that his peers are inefficient. "I'll tell you why … he knows he can ask you to finish it for him, and he didn't bother. He went to the pub on Friday evening, didn't he?"

George doesn't want to confirm my accusation, but I wait and force his response. "Well, yes, he did." George is looking down to his feet, one hand on the bench, the other anxiously stroking the hairline at the back of his neck.

"They use you George, they fucking use you all the time and you let them!"

"Look, I can still come to Ballarat on Sunday. I'll get it done today and I'll come in the morning to watch your game on Sunday."

"We're not going to take two cars to Ballarat."

"I could get on a train and we'll drive back together." I know by his tone that George doesn't for a moment expect me to agree to this option.

I am momentarily tempted to say yes, ok, you do that, but instead my momentum carries me on. "Don't be stupid, George, I can drive myself back. You don't have to come to Ballarat, it's not as if I'm going to be alone, and you've seen enough netball games. We mightn't even make the final on Sunday. I'm not angry because you can't come with me, I'm angry because they take advantage of you like this." I know that isn't entirely true.

"We won't have to leave Tammy with Roger."

Now George is finding positives, as he does. The dog can stay home with him, which is good. We have been worried that Tammy is unwell, her old hips are giving way and she doesn't get herself up to ask to go out. She has had a couple of *accidents at home, and there is a danger she'll disgrace herself in Roger's house. I know George didn't really want to leave her for the weekend, and maybe George didn't really want to come away for a weekend with my netball team either – in which case he should just have said 'no' in the first place.*

"So I'll call Roger?" *he ventures.*

"You do that. Fucking call Roger. And then call Jimmy back and tell him you'll do his fucking work for him IF he gives you that pay rise he's been promising you since last July." *I do a good job of skipping over tears with anger.*

"I'll come on Sunday," *he knows about the tears and he tries again.*

"No, you won't come on Sunday. You're making me late." *I push him out of the way of a cupboard and pull out my water bottle and some picnic ware. He hovers, and when I ignore him and go to the fridge he slips out of the room. I don't bother to call him to say goodbye before I walk out to the car. I don't ring him on Saturday night to tell him we had won the semi. I wasn't angry any more – the girls and I were having a great night out at the Commercial Club. I was just making my oh-so-petty point.*

~

George can, and once did, empty a bottle of Glenfiddich to drill the depths of his pain seeking a catharsis ... but in the morning his world was the same. He can, and twice did, talk to a psychologist seeking help with 'his feelings' ... but by the umpteenth 'and how do you feel about that?' he was sickened by the shallow, professionalised empathising and came away longing for a meaningful conversation with someone who really cared.

George's solution, by happenstance rather than a design, is to keep himself busy. Being busy passes the time. Sometimes being busy even brings moments of relaxed joy, like sitting on the rock looking over his work on the church. He is waiting for something, but he is not sure what. Maybe he is passing the time until the day he doesn't think of me. Maybe he is waiting for the day I come back. Maybe he is waiting for the day he comes to me. But he has the sense that he is waiting, and with no sense of how long it might take, he thinks that one day he will know.

Lynne also hopes that one day she will know. Like George, Lynne feels her mother's continuing presence. Unlike George, she assigns her feelings to her memories; her brain's reconstruction of the image and presence of the thing she subconsciously desires. Like George, Lynne is an agnostic, but where George arrived at his position by the unravelling of his childhood faith, Lynne arrived at hers by gaining an education in history and philosophy. Lynne, like her mother Jean, sees the possibility of God in the fact that billions of people across time and geography have believed, and still believe. She sees the differences in approach as human and immensely flawed, but she sees the commonality of a belief in a reality beyond human perception as evidence. The Temple of Apollo, and later the Church of St Nikolaos, were flawed attempts to communicate with God and attract his favour; the Venus De Milo was an ancient attempt to depict a Goddess in human form, making the idea of God more approachable. What interests Lynne most, apart from the works of art themselves is the idea that the architect and the artist were reaching out to a greater power, in the firm belief that such a power must exist. The motivational power of belief is too dominant in the course of human history to be dismissed. In it, Lynne thinks, we see the face of 'God', but we can see no more than that. Everything else is human kind struggling for a semblance of control, over nature, and each other.

On the soft white rock, under the full moonlight, George has fallen asleep. He denies it when Lynne nudges him, and he supplies evidence in the form of a reiteration of something she said a few minutes earlier. She lightly un-smudges some white rock-powder from his cheek and instructs him to get up and take her home. She holds him more comfortably on the way back to the hotel, lying her head against his shoulder and snoozing more that she had thought would be possible on the back of a motor bike.

"I really enjoyed that," she tells him sincerely at the steps of the hotel. She takes his head in both hands and kisses him on each cheek, tousles his hair with a smile and walks into the hotel.

I watch him ride his bike home through empty streets to Dimitry's house in Tripiti, night wind in his hair, the warmth of friendship in his heart, and the happy grin of freedom on his face.

~

Sam had been edgy during dinner. He had taken the seat on the far side of the table, so he could watch the door; his eyes were looking past her to the street during most of the main course. Mary lost patience with him.

"She's not going to see you here, you know. She's at dinner at *Fournos Artemis* with George."

Sam glowered at her. "How do you know?"

"George told me he booked them a table."

Sam spread the remaining piece of his steak with red wine jus and potato mash.

"Why does it bother you so much?" Mary continued, despite her resolution not to badger him over Lynne. "What are your plans when you get back to England? Are you going to go on seeing her?"

Sam pointed his knife at her. "I do *not* want to talk about Lynne Williams."

"Then what *will* we talk about? Because you haven't exactly been chatty this evening."

Sam filled his mouth with food and chewed slowly.

"We could talk about Rob and Matthew, since you didn't ask," Mary continued sarcastically. "I'm worried about Matthew, he works too hard and he's always away from home. Fiona's raising their child all by herself, and she shouldn't have to. Matthew should be home to help her; he should get out of the Malaysian side of the business and stick to Australia. What's the point of all that ambition if you lose your family? Do you suppose you could venture a few words?"

Sam swallowed, set down his cutlery and wiped his mouth. "How's Rob?"

"Rob broke up with Lisa just before Christmas, as I think I would have told you. He was heartbroken. Anyway, they're seeing each other again. They got back together at a party last month. It's no good; I'm not encouraging it. Lisa is a bitch; she just uses Rob up between her other dates and her work abroad. He's just an accessory. Rob needs to move on."

"And Jacinta?"

"As undecided as ever. She is talking about doing a gap year in Europe and she just doesn't understand that we can't afford that kind of thing. If she doesn't want to go straight on to uni she should be looking for a job. If she doesn't want to work in real estate then she has to find her own job, and support herself don't you think? Ian and I can't go on supporting her forever."

"And Rachel?"

"That dick-head English master won't apply for a reader to help her during the exams. Her dyslexia is not enough of a disadvantage and she 'should learn how to handle her impediment'. As if! Doubtless the prick is expecting me to pay him something before he'll agree, can you believe it?"

"I doubt the English master is a 'prick', and I doubt Lisa is a 'bitch'," Sam growled.

"Oh, you are in a right mood aren't you!"

"Just disagreeing with the way you put things." Sam motioned to the waiter for the bill.

Mary's anxiety festered during the walk back to the hotel. Sam had taken her hand, which was positive, but he was taking long, tense strides, which was not. She could feel a fight brewing … or maybe this morning's fight hadn't really gone away ... and conflict was the last thing she wanted. Was this all because she had mentioned Lynne or had three days together already been too long?

But as soon as the hotel door clicked shut, Sam slid her cotton jacket off one shoulder, held her still by the other shoulder from behind and lingered the fingers of his right hand down the buttons of her blouse. She felt a wave of relief.

"A massage, I think," Sam offered, pulling back the bed coverings.

"Oh – yum!" Mary shed her clothes and lay face down, adjusting a pillow under her stomach while Sam picked the massage oil out of her toiletry case.

Sam began with her shoulders, his hands sure of the exact strength required to bring her muscles to that limit of feel-good pain and no further. He turned her arm up her back so that her shoulder blade was exposed, and worked his thumb along the edge pressing flesh into bone and as he held her she let her fantasy run, imagining her helplessness against his strength should he force himself on her in any way he pleased. He enclosed her whole shoulder in one hand, lifting and stretching it, then ran the edge of his palm down the soft side of her breast, tucking his fingers underneath to elicit a moan from her. She could feel him smile at her response. He let her arm go, and massaged the small of her back and her flanks for a while, before repeating the shoulder massage on the other side. This time his fingers caught her nipple and twisted it as they brushed down her side. She gasped, brought a knee up and tried to turn over, but he held her down.

"If you insist," she breathed with delight as his massage continued over her buttock to the inside of her thigh. Stroking smoothly down the length of her leg, pausing to tease the inside of her knee, bringing his fingers up firmly along the inside of the leg until his finger tips spread the lips of her vagina.

'Oh come on ...' she entreated him as his fingers retreated, returned and retreated as he kept her constantly on edge while kneading her thighs and her calves.

"I've missed this bit," he said when she gave up the game and tried to pull him towards her. He pinched the tendon at the back of her ankle, picked up her foot and drew his fingernail along its soft underside, provoking a shriek.

"You're vicious tonight," she laughed, and he promptly rolled her over, laid his weight on her and covered her mouth with his, challenging her to a duel with his tongue. Sometimes he gave and sometimes he took. She met each challenge with her tongue and raised his energy with hers until they were both breathless. He game-changed by pulling back, and taking her nipple into his mouth instead. When she moaned too loudly he clamped a hand across her mouth, and sucked harder. When she could take it no longer she shook herself free, and reached for him.

"Now, come on, now," she commanded and finally he conceded.

XXI

Tuesday 15th April 2008

In the morning Mary woke to find Sam already dressed, sitting on the side of the bed.

"What time is it?"

"Quarter to seven."

"What are you doing?"

"My flight is at 7.45."

"But …" Mary struggled to work out the days, had she lost one?

"I changed it, I'm leaving today."

Mary was suddenly wide-awake, and suddenly outraged. "Why?"

"I have to go. There are a number of reasons."

"So tell me!"

Sam was looking at an envelope he had in his hand, he was tapping it on his knee. She saw that it had no address on it, and she knew it was for her.

"Sam, don't."

"We have to stop doing this, Mary. We agreed last time."

"No, we didn't agree."

"Then you weren't listening, or you didn't let me say it all. I've written it down so that it's said properly. This is the last time."

"Because of Lynne?"

"No, it's NOT because of Lynne."

"No ... you have a *number* of reasons. You always have a *number* of reasons. I have just one. Last night ... you love *me*."

Sam stared at her for a moment. "Yes, I already know that." He gave her the envelope and stood, looking irresolute.

"We *don't* have to stop doing this. It works."

"Not for me, anymore. It's in the letter, please let me go."

Mary felt like a blade was scraping out the inside of her chest, and from the look on Sam's face she was sure he was feeling the same. She scrambled out of bed to take him in her arms and stop this madness, but he caught her by both shoulders and sat her down.

"I love you, and I'm saying 'goodbye' now. This is where you let me go, like you promised you would." Sam released her shoulders and stepped to the entrance hall of the room. He held the door open with his foot while he picked his waiting duffle bags up in each hand, nodded to her and stepped out. Mary heard his first steps echo unevenly down the tiled hallway and then the door closed out the sound of him.

It was true; she had promised she would let him go if and when he asked.

To My Love, Mary
  Because this has to be the last time.
  You have brought me to your presence again, despite the words we said on parting at Christmas, despite our agreement–or is it mine with myself alone–that we must not do this anymore.
  I have loved you more than life. You have been the keeper of more joy and spirit and beauty for me than any sunset, any moonrise, any glorious view in any exotic

land. And yet, it is not in my power to give myself up for you, any more than you give yourself up for me, not for any more than our deepest moments alone together. We cannot do life together. We lose ourselves in each other so intensely that day-to-day living is just too disappointing. I cannot bear not being everything you want me to be; I cannot bring to you everything you need.

It has been lonely, this life of loving you. I cannot share my heart, the way you have shared yours. It belongs to you and cannot look to someone else while it belongs to you. While you return to your comforts of home and forget me until the next time, I ache and ache and ache and just when I've gone numb you call. This place of steady love you call home is a place I've never known. You offered it to me, I know, and I couldn't do it then. Probably because of me ... but at least in part because of you. I think I have missed out. I want to change my life now. I think my restlessness has gone.

I don't want to see war any more. Once I felt that I could make a difference. I thought we were changing the world. Now there are new wars, new ways of waging them, new ways of reporting them - but all the same human hatred and greed. We've changed nothing that mattered. Now I want to stay home in the hope of finding redemption on a smaller page. A sense of community; a sense of where I belong. While I want to retire from journalism, I can't give up being within reach of the world, in the centre of the News. I think of myself as a Londoner now.

I know that even if I were to ask you, you would not leave Ian. I know you do not trust me; you will not change your life again for me because I already failed you once. I know I am for excitement, not 'home'. And I will not settle in Sydney in order to stay in your orbit as you might suggest ... I do not deserve it, and neither does Ian. There is actually nothing we need of each other any more, other than to end our relationship and deal honestly with ourselves, and the others in our lives.

I will always love you. I will always treasure the amazing connection we found in each other. But I need a new life, and given everything we know about ourselves, you must let me go, and I must not return.

S.

~

Mary was in the bathroom, applying eyeliner and critically checking that all the puffiness under her eyes was smoothed out by her makeup when George knocked on the door and called out to her.

"Sam called me from the airport and asked me to come over." As he came in George cast his eye over Mary, and around the bedroom, but found nothing alarming.

"Thoughtful of him," Mary commented flatly. "I'm alright, George, I'm not a teenager." She returned to her makeup.

"He said I should take you to pick the car up. He put the keys under the passenger foot mat."

"He took my car to the airport? Of course. I'm *not* going to ride on your motor bike."

"I brought Anton's ute."

"Well, I'm glad of that. How was dinner with Lynne?" Mary pouted at herself in the mirror and carefully applied gloss to lips that still felt swollen from last night's passionate kissing.

"It was very good, the food was excellent. And the answer to your next question is 'No', and I wish you would stop meddling in my life."

"Lynne doesn't want you? Or you didn't ask?"

"Both."

"When does she go back to England?"

"Tomorrow."

Mary was silent in the bathroom, packing away her makeup and stowing the toiletry bag in the cupboard under the sink.

"I'll come and help out at the church today," she announced as she came out of the bathroom and looked for her handbag. "But take me to the airport first to get the car."

~

As Mary was following George from the airport to Firopotamos, Lynne was returning the metal detector to the hire shop in Adamas. The shopkeeper watched her with the same discomforting gaze, but this time, without George to talk to him, there were no words exchanged. Instead he silently pushed the hire book and a pen across the counter to her and tapped the cover of the book.

Lynne leafed through the book looking for the entry she had originally signed, and stopped with surprise before she reached the right page. She put her index finger under the name and read it again.

"Sam Foster."

On the next page she found her own name, and by a comparison of the Greek lettering she confirmed that Sam had hired exactly the same piece of equipment that she had.

~

"Martin, *did* you tell Sam Foster the arm was buried in the church wall?" Lynne shouted into her mobile phone in her hotel room. Reception was not good.

"I could have," Martin conceded.

"I told you to say nothing about it!"

"Yes, but that was later. I did talk to him for quite a while before the day we had lunch together … he was very interested. He asked a lot of questions – that's why he said he wanted us all to have lunch together. I told him everything he wanted to know."

"Then why didn't you tell me? When I told you to say nothing, why didn't you tell me you already had?"

"Because you didn't ask me *that* question. What's wrong with telling him? He doesn't write for the tabloids. Have you seen anything in the papers?"

"No, but Sam is here in Milos, and he searched for the arm in the walls of the church before I did."

"Did he find it?"

"I don't know – I only know that I *didn't* find it."

"Then you must ask him," Martin said reasonably.

"I *would* if you could tell me how to contact him. He never answers the phone number you gave me. Any other ideas?"

"You said Milos is a small place."

Lynne growled in exasperation and hung up.

~

Lynne found George high on a scaffold in the sunshine, painting a line of Cyclades blue along the edge where the whitewashed dome of the church roof met the freshly plastered and whitewashed wall. Colum was further up on the roof, painting a blue line down each join in the hexagonal tower in the centre of the church, the tower that supported the dome that overlay the Christ Pantocrator. Lynne had seen Mary inside the church with Rose, their heads bent over the white altar tablecloth, and she had, with a discrete inspection, decided that Sam was not in the church. Preferring to speak to George privately, but with some embarrassment, she signalled for him to give up his paintbrush and come down.

"I need to speak to Sam."

George vacillated momentarily between "Why?" and a more cooperative response, and settled on telling her that Sam had left Milos that morning.

In the car as she drove to Firopotamos Lynne had already analysed George's possible involvement with Sam in a scheme to spirit the arm away without her knowing, and she had rejected the idea. George struck her as totally honest, and none of the alternatives that she could think of made any sense at all. George, and even Sam for that matter, had more claim to the arm than she could make, so if they had found it why would they not just tell her? If George knew Sam had already searched for it, he would not have searched again.

Reading the dismay and indecision on her face, George now asked "why?"

"Sam hired the metal detector before we did. I think he searched for the arm in the walls before we did. Would that have been possible?"

George viewed the church walls for a long moment. "Yes. He came two days before Mary. Before we put the plaster on." Lynne watched George's deepening scowl. "You had told him about the arm?"

"Well, not exactly. But I now think he knew. Why else would he hire the metal detector?"

"No other reason. Fucking hell!" George fumbled under his overalls and pulled out his mobile phone. He punched a contact, held the phone up to his ear and they waited expectantly until the dial tone ended. "Fucking hell!" George repeated. "He's probably on a flight back to England now."

"Could I have that phone number?" Lynne intercepted George's hand as he moved to put the phone back in his pocket. George turned the face of the phone to her and Lynne copied the number into her own phone.

"Did you take him to the airport? Did you see his luggage?" Lynne asked.

"No, he drove himself." George pulled the overalls off his shoulders and let them drop around his feet, revealing a T-shirt and shorts. "God, it's hot in those!" He stepped out of the overall pile and stomped around the end of the church, heading for the door.

Lynne was not at all sure that she wanted to confront Mary, but after a moment's pause she ran to catch up.

George separated Mary from her discussion with Rose by tugging on her shoulder. He directed her to a cooler, dark spot at the back of the church.

"Do you know anything about Sam searching this church for a relic? Or a part of a statue?" George demanded.

"No," Mary looked completely bewildered, "why would he do that?"

"It's the arm of the Venus De Milo, it's a priceless artefact," Lynne contributed.

"It's not the kind of thing Sam would be interested in." In being so assured, Mary was laying a claim on her man, she watched Lynne with firm contemplation.

"Why did Sam leave early?" George's question did not shift Mary's eyes.

"I don't know. Maybe Lynne has a better idea than I do."

"Did he know I was here?"

"He did. It seemed he didn't want you to know *he* was here."

"You have the wrong idea about our relationship." As she said the words Lynne mocked herself that she had also had the wrong idea about her relationship with Sam.

"Oh, probably not," Mary said dismissively. She turned back to George. "So what are you saying? Are you accusing Sam of stealing this relic?"

"Did you see anything in the hotel room? What luggage did he have with him?"

"I didn't see anything. He had nothing special with him, just his duffle bags."

"How big were the duffle bags?" Lynne asked.

Mary made an approximation with her hands.

"Two?" George asked. Mary nodded.

"Were they heavy?" Lynne followed up.

"I didn't lift them."

"He only had one bag when I picked him up last week." George's words were a judgement.

Mary looked from George to Lynne and back again. "You're wrong, it's ridiculous."

"Where is he going to?" Lynne asked.

"Home – well, I assume he's going back to London. I didn't see his tickets. Look – whatever it is you think he's done it's ridiculous. He is not going to steal a relic, or an artefact or whatever it is from this church. It doesn't matter what it is or what it's worth. You should know that George, really!"

Mary turned a mockingly sweet smile on Lynne. "You're going back to London tomorrow – just call him when you're back and ask what's going on. I'm sure he'll set you straight." She turned her smile back to George. "Now George, you *were* saying we were behind schedule and there was a long day's work ahead of us, so will we get on with it?"

~

It had been a long afternoon for Lynne. She had spent much of it in the hotel lobby where there was Internet reception. She had looked at flight schedules; she had Googled 'Sam Foster' all over again; she had quizzed Martin again; she had learned nothing useful. She had used the hotel phone to ring the phone number George gave her, only to hear Sam's voice issue a curt "Can't answer, leave a message." The sound of his voice stirred her, but now her imagination ran to tearing him limb from limb rather than threading his limbs amongst hers. She wondered at the vehemence of her feelings; she didn't appreciate being made a fool; mainly she wanted the answers and while she was now impatient to get back to London, she was well aware that she might never find him. Her bags were packed, waiting by the door of the hotel room. She didn't have a good answer when Tayla breezed into the room late in the afternoon, cheerfully greeted her with "Hi, Mumsy" and asked how she had spent the day. Fortunately, Tayla wasn't interested in getting an answer.

Tayla wanted Lynne to go to dinner with her and Theo. "I want you to get to know him better, Mum." Lynne found the words worrying, but she agreed, and waited without further comment to see what the evening would reveal. She told Tayla to make sure she had everything packed, ready to go early in the morning. When Tayla complied Lynne was relieved that at least the response was not "I'm staying in Greece." Tayla surprised Lynne by saying she wanted to go and see the church, and say goodbye to the Kostis family before going to dinner.

As the car climbed the central island ridge that lay between Adamas and Firopotamos, the plan she had made with Theo bubbled out of Tayla in a happy, irrepressible stream.

"Theo and I are going to go to Australia in October. We're going to go to Uncle Steven's place and take one of his boats on a charter trip up the coast all the way to North Queensland and the Barrier Reef. Theo is the skipper and I'll be the cook. We'll be getting paid for being on holiday!"

"Does 'Uncle Steven' know about this?"

"Not yet ... but George said Theo should do it. George said Uncle Steven had a boat Theo could take, and it was just a matter of advertising the trip and getting paying customers. Isn't it a cool idea?"

"How long does this take?"

"Six months ... we would miss the European winter. Theo could do this all the time ... like sail the Mediterranean for six months of the year, and Australia for six months of the year."

"What about your job? What about university?"

Tayla scattered Lynne's objections down the roadside slope, across Adamas and out to sea with a wave of her hand. "This is the chance of a lifetime, Mum. Everyone I know would *kill* for this. Even you, Mum. You would have done this if you had the chance at my age."

"What about money?" Lynne was still posting objections even though she knew Tayla was right. She knew Tayla would not have thought the issues through.

"We'll be earning money!"

"The flight over there?"

"I'm going back to work now, and I'll work until October, and I'll save the money. And Dad will give me some money towards it, I'm sure."

Lynne felt an internal groan at that phrase. It meant a 'matching grant' would be expected. She wanted to challenge Tayla over the solidity of her relationship with Theo and whether it could last their next six months apart, let alone spending so much time together in a small yacht on a big sea serving expectant customers. But this was what tonight's dinner was for, she realised. Getting to know him. So she held her tongue.

"It's a great idea Mum! Isn't it a great idea?"

Lynne inclined her head slightly and took the easy way out. "Maybe. We'll see what Dad has to say about it."

~

George was on his rock. He liked the blue trim that now highlighted the edges of the church. The church looked loved. From his vantage point, he could see nothing left for him to do. The walls and roof were brightly white; the window frames were smoothly blue and all the hinges and latches worked, as they should. The other sides of the church were also complete, and the heavy wooden door was swinging true, and locking easily. Just inside the door, in the Narthex, Petros had hung the renovated icons of the Crucifixion and Saint Nikolaos side by side, and he had placed a table on the left hand side where Elena was setting out bundles of thin, cream-coloured candles on each side of an ancient wooden tablet dotted with candle holes. Rose was in the Sanctuary checking the Epitaphion, the linen shroud she had pulled out from the cupboard under the altar, for moth damage. She was looking critically at the embroidered outline of the body of Christ, testing loose strands with a brush of her thumb. Anton and Colum had taken their caïque back to Klima for the night. Mary had returned to her hotel some hours ago in order to 'freshen up' for tonight's dinner in Tripiti.

Next Saturday a Holy Communion would be held at the church, opening Holy Week with a celebration of the resurrection of Lazarus. During the afternoon the children of Firopotamos would decorate the church with palm leaves in preparation for the Palm Sunday Divine Liturgy the next morning. The church would be open for worship every day, but there would be no further services held here during the week of Lent until Vespers on Good Friday afternoon. All of Milos would attend the midnight mass at the Panaghia Thalassitra on Saturday night, but there would be another Vespers here at Aghios Nikolaos on Easter Sunday morning.

George was confused by it all. He preferred to avoid the discussions that were taking place inside the church. He was embarrassed that he didn't understand the symbolism of the icons, he didn't know the order of services, he didn't sympathise with the rituals. Today, when Mary had arrived at the church, automatically crossing herself as she walked through the door and immediately throwing herself knowledgeably into the business of the sacraments of the Eucharist, George had been dismayed by the gulf between them in religious education. George found it hard to reconcile this Catholic Mary with the sister he knew. Where had she learnt all this and why had he been excused from that learning? George thinks that his mother excommunicated the whole family through her own shame at Mary's 'downfall'. He feels a yearning towards the comforting security of the communal belief of his Greek family, but he can't find in himself any motivation to learn the customs of Orthodoxy. His role in preparing the church has been entirely practical, and he is glad Mary is here to represent the family on religious matters. It has taken the two of them, he acknowledges, to stand in for Stephen.

Stephen, as George had discovered during their heated phone conversation after Lynne's departure this morning, knew about the church's talisman. Like Uncle Dimitry, he knew Amphitrite's arm was sealed in the church wall but he didn't know where. Stephen agreed with Mary that Sam would not have stolen the arm, and he had directed his ire at George for even presuming to help Lynne find the arm and take it from the church. Papa and Dimitry would be furious, Stephen had said. They must never know, he asserted. Alerting The Louvre and letting them dismantle or even x-ray the Church for the arm was out of the question. Papa would never allow it. When Papa and Dimitry were both dead maybe Stephen and Anton would have a talk about it ... but that was a modest concession - Stephen did not intend to allow it. Amphitrite's arm had to stay in peace, wherever it was in the wall of the church. George's thoughts were still muddied with disbelief that Stephen had taken this position. He was still mulling angrily over the likelihood that it was another instance of Stephen asserting his patriarchy. Mostly George was wishing he had never heard about the arm. Here on his rock he was trying to push the issue out of his mind so he could recapture the simple beauty of the renovated church against the backdrop of Firopotamos.

When George saw the little black Fiat winding its way carefully down the cliff-side he didn't immediately associate it with Lynne. There had been a dozen or more of these ubiquitous hire cars on the road today. They would creep down the track, steering away from the cliffs, arriving with relief at the gravel turning circle, parking in random spots because there were no markings to guide them. Forty-five minutes, George figured, was the average time for a tourist to spend at Firopotamos. There would be a correlation, George thought, between the weight of the photographic hardware they carried, and the duration of the stay. The visitors wandered across the harbour rocks in front of the church, clambered out to the far side of the Temple of Apollo and trekked back around the Eastern end of the church to the turning circle. Some ventured up to the church door and poked their heads inside, retreating as soon as they saw people at work within.

George did not move off his rock until he saw Tayla get out of the car, and by the time he reached the front door of the church, Tayla and Lynne had already met with Petros, Elena and Rose, and Lynne had expressed the intention of their visit, offered her thanks for their hospitality and was bidding them farewell. It was Petros, Elena and Rose who got into their car and departed first, leaving Lynne and Tayla to say goodbye to George.

Saying goodbye was made easier by Tayla wanting to talk to George about Australia, about Sydney and the Charter business, about sailing a boat up to North Queensland. George was enthusiastic about the plan and, as was Tayla's intention, his encouragement largely won Lynne over. George had absolutely no reservations, as far as he was concerned this was something Theo and Tayla *must* do, and he would look forward to welcoming them to Melbourne as well. George and Tayla settled the plan for their reunion with a hug.

"And what about you?" George asked Lynne as he locked the church door. "Can we persuade you to visit Australia?"

Lynne agreed that she would love to visit one day; she said all the things travellers classically say when they part company, not wanting to acknowledge the imminent end to their friendship, but knowing that there is little likelihood they will meet again. George was glad Lynne said nothing about the further search for the arm. He intended to email her to let her know that the family had refused. They walked to their cars. George offered his hand. Lynne shook it and then gave him a hug and a kiss on each cheek. Tayla and Lynne settled themselves into the Fiat. George climbed up into Anton's ute and led the way up the road towards home and hotel.

~

Paulos Stefanides was to land transport in Milos what Dimitry Kostis was to coastal freight. He had four trucks, one laden with gas and water bottles, one with a septic waste tank, one for deliveries of general groceries and hardware, and this afternoon he was driving the water truck. All the trucks were old. Paulos had not made enough money from his business to upgrade his fleet in the last thirty years. Over the last two years, Paulos had not had enough money to service his trucks with anything more than an oil change in his own garage. He knew he was due to spend a significant amount of money either repairing or replacing his trucks, and there was no way he was going to be able to do it. Long ago Paulos had laid off his other drivers because he could not afford to pay them, and he had lost business as a result of the competition they set up, running adhoc deliveries in whatever vehicles they could adapt to the purpose. He still had a monopoly on septic waste removal and bulk water deliveries, but those two heavy trucks, in particular, were long past retirement age. Every morning he said a prayer to the Virgin Mary to keep his trucks running through the day.

This winter had been dry, which had been good business for the water truck. With the Easter week approaching, Paulos had been running bulk water deliveries to several hotels and townships. Today he had been out to the island of Kimolos, but there was no profit in that for him once he paid the fee for the barge he had to take from Pollonia. He knew he should either increase his own charges, or he should refuse to service Kimolos, but the manager of the hotel there was his wife's cousin, and their business was also running at a loss. They had to have water, and how could he refuse? He was hoping they would be able to pay their account after the tourist season.

Firopotamos also needed fresh water before its population tripled during Holy week. Paulos was finishing his working day by bringing a full tank down the road into the township. He preferred to come down to Firopotamos late in the day, when he was less likely to meet tourists driving up the single-lane road. It could take them a long time, and often an abusive stand-off before they understood that he could not reverse and he could not pull his heavy truck over to the cliff side because the road was not reinforced and the cliff could collapse. On roads like this one-and there were many around Milos-other vehicles must simply get out of his truck's path, even if that meant backing all the way down to the sea.

Paulos could smell his brakes burning as his truck lumbered slowly down the steep sections of the road. The smell had been getting worse over a number of trips; he knew the footbrakes were badly worn and he was using his handbrake to compensate. He was a third of the way down the hill when the handbrake lifted in his hand with no resistance at all. Paulos stared at the lever through a moment of shock and inevitability. He had known that this would happen eventually, he had just assumed, somehow, that it would not be at the worst possible moment. He held his foot down hard on the brakes, and the truck slowed slightly, but it could not be stopped, it kept pitching its weight inexorably downhill. Paulos called to mind the end of the road: it would be sacrilege to run into the church so Paulos planned to turn the wheel and head for the rocks to the East.

Then Anton's ute appeared around the bend in the road immediately below him and Paulos and George had a moment to look at each other.

George reacted by pulling quickly to the right, taking the ute all the way to the edge of the cliff, for which Paulos could have been grateful, but there was still not enough room to pass and no way Paulos could stop or even get his line right for the approaching bend with the ute in the way. Paulos sputtered a curse, insulting George for not reversing, fractionally before he saw the black nose of the second car arrive at the bend.

Lynne saw the brake lights of the ute, and she saw that George had pulled over. When she then saw the truck she assumed it would stop while the three vehicles sorted themselves out. She halted the Fiat in the middle of the road and, knowing that her only option would be to reverse she looked down at the unfamiliar gearbox to change gear. It was Tayla's scream that warned her that the truck was not stopping. Lynne took her foot off the clutch and reversed sharply into the high side of the cliff in a desperate attempt to get out of the way.

Paulos aimed between the two cars. His truck hit the bluff of the bend, blasting rock and sand into the air, and careened towards the cliff drop. He frantically pulled at the wheel turning the truck's nose towards the Fiat pinned against the cliff, while the truck's tail caught on the tray of the ute and started to drag the ute backwards. The truck slewed sideways, the ute's back wheels pulverised the rock, fighting hard, and the cliff edge crumbled beneath the weight of both vehicles.

As Lynne and Tayla watched the truck and the ute disappear over the rim of the road, rocks started to rain down on the Fiat from the bluff of the cliff above them.

~

When the deluge of rocks stopped, Tayla took stock of the situation. The Fiat had been crushed on the left hand, driver's side and Lynne was somehow flattened under it, semi-conscious, bleeding from her head - pinned by her legs, so Tayla thought. The windscreen was shattered, creased along long cracks, but still holding onto its buckled frame. Tayla's skin reacted with pricks of blood as she wiped glass chips off her clothes, but apart from that she was unharmed. She couldn't open her door, so she pulled her sleeve over her hand and tried ineffectively to break the windscreen. She turned herself sideways, leaning against Lynne so that she could deliver her strongest possible kicks to the door and eventually she succeeded in breaking it open. She retrieved her phone from the floor and stepped out of the car. Her knees buckled, but she steadied herself against the door and firmly pushed shock away to a more convenient time. She walked unsteadily to within a metre of the edge of the cliff and tried to focus through the evening light on the truck that had rolled to a stop at the bottom of the cliff. Anton's ute had torn away from it, part way down, and had ended up some distance away. There was no sign of movement at either vehicle, but across to the right Tayla could dimly see a small group of people hurrying towards the truck. She sat down with relief knowing that the townspeople had been alerted, but then she realised that they may not know there was another vehicle up on the road.

Tayla had to walk a hundred metres or so down towards Firopotamos before the reception bars lit up on her phone. She sat down again, and only realised that she was crying when Theo answered and she could not speak.

~

The steep scree face that fell from the side of the road down to the gully that led to the beach at Firopotamos was pockmarked with boulders, and loosely held together with thorny scrub. The townspeople scrambled their way awkwardly in the twilight toward the spot where the truck had come to rest. They knew already that it was their long-standing island friend Paulos, and they were certain already that he would be dead. They found him in the driver's seat. A sack more than a man, with an unnaturally loose head and a red chest deeply creased by the seat belt. After a moment's silence they looked up the gully towards the other vehicle that they couldn't yet see properly. There had been a suggestion that it was Anton's ute. There had been talk that Petros, Rose and Elena were at the church today. Either way, the townspeople were certain that what they found would be deeply distressing for them. But when they reached the ute they found it empty. The driver's door had been torn off; the seat belt was hanging loosely as if it was un-clipped, or never fastened. They began to hope that the occupants had escaped the car safely. They pulled out their torches and fanned out across the slope. One person returned to the town to get more people and more torches; they would start from the road and work downwards along the swathe the truck had ploughed down the hill.

On the road the new search party was surprised to find Tayla, waiting for them to reach her, standing guard by the Fiat, which was almost invisibly black and squashed in the shadows of the rock-fall. They dug their way into the car with the intention of getting Lynne out, and Tayla pulled them away, yelling as if she were berserk. They didn't understand her English protests of 'crush injury' and 'spinal injury', but they did understand her ownership of the situation and they pulled back to discuss amongst themselves. Headlights winding down the road announced Theo's arrival, and a moment later the white Kombi with the diagonal green and yellow stripe that identified it as the paramedic's vehicle, pulled up alongside. There was much excitable discussion in Greek, and when Tayla saw a uniformed man approach her, carrying a neck brace and a medical kit, she finally admitted him to the car.

Night had fallen. The townspeople left Lynne and Tayla with Theo and the paramedics. They stood on the edge of the road, sweeping their torches over the scree slope between the edge of the truck's tracks and the torch beams that were criss-crossing the hill from below. They found nothing, so they spread out and started carefully picking a path downhill. They knew now that they were looking for George. Anton and Petros arrived, and after brief words with Theo they plunged down the hill after the search party.

There was no 'jaws of life' in Milos, no rescue helicopter, and the Kombi van was the only ambulance. The paramedics stabilised Lynne, and monitored her condition as Theo cleared the rocks off the top of the car and eventually managed to free her by levering the car's control column off her waist. Tayla watched suspiciously as they carefully lifted Lynne out of the car and onto a stretcher – Theo had explained that this was the best care Milos could offer under the circumstances. They would take Lynne to the medical centre and if necessary they would call in an air ambulance to take her to hospital in Athens. Tayla was daunted by the differences between this and the medical TV series, *ER* that she liked to watch at home. She resolved to get her mother taken to hospital in London instead.

It was 9pm in Milos, and 7pm in London when Tayla called her father from the medical centre. At the sound of his voice she broke down and her description of events was only partly sensible. James quickly stopped her, saying he was at a restaurant and would call her back, but it was Martin who rang her back, and she had to deliver the story again. By the time they finished the phone call Martin had a comprehensive description of Lynne's condition, and he had promised Tayla he would go to their house at 10 the next morning and find the travel insurance documents that would be under 'I' in Lynne's filing cabinet. He could not go tonight because Lynne had told him not to go out on the streets at night. He could not go before 10am because Lynne had told him he should never turn up at their door before 10am. Tayla did not even try to persuade him that these were special circumstances. She tried to ring Marcus instead, but his phone went straight to voicemail.

Tayla wondered whether to call her father again, rethinking the sound of the female voice she had heard confer with him in the restaurant. Instead she pushed the Internet button on her mobile phone and checked out the Wi-Fi signal.

"Ask them for their Wi-Fi password," she held her phone out to Theo, nodding in the direction of the paramedics. After some consultation one of the paramedics took the phone and typed in the required response. "*Efharistó*," Tayla said gratefully as the paramedic gave the phone back to her.

As Tayla made her second password attempt and successfully gained access to her mother's email account, the CB radio at the front desk crackled in Greek and the two paramedics scrambled, leaving the medical centre unstaffed, and Tayla aghast.

"What the fuck?" she demanded of Theo as he returned to the room where she had remained sitting beside her mother's stretcher, watching the readings on the monitors that were watching Lynne.

"They've found George," Theo replied.

~

George is lying under the night sky with hundreds of light stars shining in on him from beyond. He cannot move away from the sharp rocks that are under his back, but the pain of them has gone. He can't free any part of his body, but his mind feels that it can move anywhere and everywhere. Not that it wants to, because Liz is here, being with him, holding his mind and talking with him. He can see her, though that's not quite the right word, they are in touch, they are communicating with each other and it is a warm and joyful homecoming.

"Am I dead?" he has asked, and she has told him *not yet*.

It makes him fear that this is temporary, that he will not have her for long, that he must commit this to memory. The world will intrude on them with the idea that it is rescuing him. This magic will end and when they wake him up she will be gone and, even worse, he may not remember. Time may be short, so he rushes to tell her everything he has wanted to say. About missing her, about love, about the measure of his loss. She is smiling all around him, and simply tells him *she knows.*

He tells her about David and Claire, their reactions to her death, their lives since, but again, she leaves him without much news because she already knows much more. Indeed, she tells him with certainty that Claire is going to marry her American girlfriend in Boston next fall, that Claire will have a son, and Leah will have a daughter. David and his future wife will have two daughters and one son.

"How do you know?" he has asked, and she has told him *I couldn't resist looking.*

George struggles with the information, aware that there is so much wrong with knowing this, but he understands that what she saw made her happy, so he is happy too.

"What's going to happen to me?" he asks, and she asks in return *what do you want?*

"I want to be with you, is that possible?" but this she either doesn't know or doesn't tell, so he is alarmed again. "I don't want to live if I'm disabled," he says firmly, and she fully understands.

"What's it like?" he asks, having spent a while contemplating the possibilities of his own continued existence. She tells him she doesn't know yet and he feels she is holding out on him and wants an explanation. *I've been waiting*, she says.

"So have I," he replies. "What has it been like waiting?" *Smartarse,* she gives her customary reply and he feels so inordinately pleased to hear her that he starts to cry. He is sure her fingers brush his cheeks and he feels her give in. *Not much longer,* she reassures him.

After a while he recovers and decides it is safe to ask her the big question. "Does God exist?" He can feel her amusement; she has been expecting this. *If she does, then I haven't met her yet.* George thinks of that as an encouraging shift in her thinking, he would have expected her to give him an outright 'No'.

"We'll meet her later then," he replies. "Thanks for waiting."

George can hear the voices searching for him but he shuts them out because he fears it will be the end of his time with Liz. Eventually he can no longer ignore them because they are over the top of him with their talk and their lights, reminding him of the pain in his body as they move him. He retreats from them, trying to follow Liz, even though he didn't see where she went.

~

"The paramedics are back," Theo announced as he came through the door of the room where Lynne and Tayla had spent the night. "George is alive ... but ... they're going to airlift him to Athens, the plane is already on the tarmac and George is on it. They've come back to pick up your mum now."

Tayla nodded, wondering if the insurance company had acted so promptly or if her mother would have been transferred anyway. The two paramedics marched purposefully into the room, checked the monitor readouts and started disconnecting Lynne from the machines. All was well, Theo relayed to Tayla, her mother was still unconscious only because of the sedatives they had given her, and it was better that she stayed that way for the moment, keeping completely still until the hospital could run tests. With the words 'completely still' in mind, Tayla watched critically as the paramedics eased the stretcher into the van, and she felt every bump in the road on the way to the airport.

On the tarmac there was a sleek Hellas Wings air ambulance jet waiting to receive them, glistening white under the moon. Lynne's stretcher was loaded through the normal passenger door and eased down the narrow body of the jet, into a medically equipped stretcher bay on the left hand side. George was in the further stretcher bay at the rear of the small cabin, tied by many tubes to the machines that were mounted on the aircraft frame. He was wrapped in white cotton blankets and Tayla could see bloodied handprints where the paramedics had folded the rugs around him. What Tayla could see of his face around the opaque rubber of the oxygen mask was purpled and blood streaked. His hair was matted and the pillow under his head was smeared with dark blood.

"It's not good," Theo stroked Tayla's back as they both looked down on George. Then he directed her to a seat across from Lynne and sat himself in the seat behind her, leaning forward over her shoulder to distract her with the arrangements he had made during the transfer from the medical centre.

"I have given the paramedics your hotel key. Mary will get the key and pack up your room. She'll be on the 7.30 morning flight to Athens with all your things. She'll meet us at the hospital."

"I want them to take Mum straight back to London," Tayla has said this before, and it made Theo cross, but he was patient with her.

"The hospital in Athens is a good hospital. Believe me. It can look after your mother. That's where we have to go. They will decide when you go back to England. For now, you have to switch off your phone," he pointed firmly at the phone, ever-present in her hand. "You have to wait now."

"You're staying with me?" Tayla checked fearfully, even though she had asked him this on the way out of the medical centre.

"I'm staying with you," he promised.

The passenger door closed with a firm suck of air and the reassuringly solid sound of a levered lock. The co-pilot hovered over them, speaking in Greek and pointing towards Tayla's phone and her seatbelt. The air ambulance officer made a final check of the drip he had plugged into Lynne's arm, and moved back down the cabin to take up a seat behind them. He thought of giving Tayla a reassurance about her mother's condition on his way past, but assuming that George was her father, he opted to hide his diagnosis behind the supposition of a language barrier. Best to leave the confirmation to the hospital.

~

Dimitry was asleep in his armchair, but Mary was anxiously awake and jumped to her feet as she heard Anton open the front door.

"He is alive, the air ambulance is taking him straight to Athens, but I have to tell you Maria …" Anton's pause was heavily burdened, "they say he does not have much chance."

Mary sighed in a burst, as if the air had been crushed out of her lungs, and pressed herself into Anton's chest. He hugged her awkwardly with his biceps and elbows, holding his hands clear.

"I have to wash," Anton manoeuvred his way out of her arms and towards the bathroom. Mary followed, asking for particulars and then falling into silence, her hand across her mouth as she watched blood wash off Anton's hands and swirl down the basin.

Anton returned to the living room and gently shook his father awake. Rose arrived, bleary eyed from her bedroom and pulled Mary down onto the couch next to her, holding her there with a firm arm around her shoulders. Mary's weeping rose and fell as Anton sat facing them and recounted the search for George: his condition, the transfer to the air ambulance and the plan for the next twenty-four hours.

A while after Anton's narration had finished, Dimitry broke the silence by telling Anton to bring him the phone because he must ring his brother Stavros. Anton looked at Mary who marshalled herself with a tissue and replied that she would ring her brother Stavros instead. Dimitry inclined his head and gave a wave of concession.

It was a little before 1 am in Milos and almost 8am in Australia when Margarita came in from the back yard clothes line to answer the insistent ring of Mary's call. Because it was Margarita she was talking to, Mary was able to give a clear account of what had happened. The call was brief. Margarita got off the phone quickly in order to ring Stephen and ask him to come home from the office.

When Stephen rang back fifteen minutes later, he already knew the bones of the story. He had already thought through the alternatives of his flight to Athens, or George's flight home for medical treatment; he had already stung himself with the many guilts of superstition; he had already sampled the words he would use to break the news to Pappous. He rang Mary for the details, which she failed to supply through her gasping tears, until Anton took over and the phone conversation switched to Greek. Dimitry was listening to it all, and after a while he demanded to speak to Pappous. Stephen refused to facilitate the connection, and promised to call back.

Toffee-*gata* was waiting hopefully by the bench when Margarita came into kitchen, leaving Stephen with his father in the privacy of the office. She squeezed the cat close to her chest, her tears falling steadily on his fur as she listened to the low rumble of Stephen's Greek followed by Pappous' angry, disbelieving howl of grief.

Eventually Stephen came into the kitchen, and told Margarita in a hollow voice that Pappous was now talking to Dimitry. She dropped Toffee-*gata* to the floor, and offered herself up to a long hug.

"What time is it in Boston?"

Margarita had already prepared for this question. She rechecked the kitchen clock and did the maths. "6.30pm."

"Should I wait?" he asked her for her empathetic wisdom to seal the decision he was reluctant to make.

"No. There may be time for Claire to get there."

"Should I go?"

"No. Mary's there and you're no use to anyone mid-air."

Stephen tuned his ear in to the phone conversation in the office and when he heard his father sobbing, even as Mary was listening to Dimitry sobbing in unison on the other side of the world, his body started to shake. He buried his head lower onto Margarita's bosom and let her hold him together.

Later, as Pappous cradled Toffee-*gata* watching his coffee going cold, and Stephen sat in the office refreshing the display on his mobile phone each time it faded out, Margarita laid her hand on his forearm. "Do you want me to make the calls?" she offered.

"It's my job," Stephen squared up his shoulders with a deep breath, picked up the phone and carefully punched in the long sequence of numbers for Claire's U.S. mobile.

~

What can I tell her, my daughter, of this moment, of this pain, of all this love, and of why things must end? How can I fold my arms around her to shield her from a moment not of my making, not within my power or any power, just a moment that is because it is? A moment that, along with everything else we did and others did and she did, will contribute to everything she becomes from this point. A moment that builds her and reveals her in her strengths and weaknesses for the very fine human I know her to be. I would save her, if only it were possible, but instead I must let her endure and grow. I can but watch and hope that my love, and the vestige of it in her self, holds her true, now and forever.

The brick is lodged in her chest as soon as she hears Stephen's solemn voice on the phone. It breaks outwards and through her, in heavy shards as she listens to the detail of the thing she already knew just because the call has been made. She is thinking "Not again" and is stunned by the cruelty even though she does not logically believe in any hand that serves out her fate. She swings to the possibility of a miracle even though her uncle counsels her against it, the urgency steels her with a course of action – it will be later, and only when it is unavoidable, that she fully explores her loss. Just now she explores her responsibilities, and in the end, not without self-doubt, she lets Stephen make the initial call to David. She will book her flight; she will call David when her plan is set, when he has had some time to think for himself.

And my son, more like his father than me, with thoughts I can't run through in quite the same way, feelings he doesn't bring to his own attention which means that I can only guess at them. He protects himself, with this lack of self-awareness, but also slows his own growth and maybe, like his father, he will only look at himself much later in his life. Maybe he too will regret that he followed an easy path that he thought was given to him, instead of carving out his own, truly fulfilling way of life. For some time, after this day, he will think about life being short, he will muse about seizing the day and he will read books about the importance of 'Now', and 'Living in the Moment'. But for the long run, he will return to his unquestioning life, and be happy there. And why not? I cannot find a reason, any more, as to why he should not.

I would shield my son from the pain that I know is traumatizing him, but indeed he shields himself effectively. He remains numb throughout Stephen's phone call, and then through Claire's. He accepts their suggestions. Claire will go. He and Uncle Stephen will stay and wait for her advice. He sits at his desk to the end of his working day, making none of the phone calls he would otherwise have made, failing to attend the lunchtime game of pool in the canteen, doing work he has to do again when he revisits it next week. He doesn't tell his wife-to-be until he gets home, and then he sits down to watch his favourite sit-com. The normality of it keeps him steady while he waits.

XXII

Wednesday 16th April 2008

Theo was thankful that the flight from Milos arrived on time. Nevertheless, he was fretting as he waited for Mary to arrive at the domestic terminal door. He had left Tayla at the check in queue in the international terminal, and he had less than thirty minutes to get back to her with the luggage Mary was bringing.

When Mary swanned through the door and withheld the bag in her hand because it was her own, not Tayla's, Theo launched a furious diatribe against her in Greek.

Mary waved his anger aside and condescendingly explained that she could not possibly travel without her own cabin bag and the airline would not allow more than one. The airline would not check Lynne and Tayla's luggage through to London, so they would have had to wait for it to arrive in the luggage hall, and check it in again. The 45-minute connection to the morning flight to London would have been simply impossible.

Theo was not satisfied, and berated Mary for not bringing at least Tayla and Lynne's personal belongings and documents in a carry-on. Mary patted him down, arranging his T-shirt smoothly on his broad chest, and then took his left hand in her right one and squeezed it. She was accustomed to men misunderstanding her logic.

"Theo, Theo, Theo – silly boy. You want to see Tayla again don't you? It's easy -you're going to personally take the bags to her in London."

Enlightenment swept the anger from Theo's face, but the idea had ambushed him and he started to protest in surprise.

"It will be no problem Theo – consider it done. Now go and tell your girl you will see her in a few days." Mary pulled a neoprene satchel out of her bag. "Here are the important things – the passports are in there with the laptop. Go now, hurry ... and come back for me, I'll be waiting in the café."

~

Tayla anxiously watched the queue of passengers steadily streaming through the check-in counters; her eyes searched the terminal impatiently when she saw the blinking green text on the departures board flick to an orange "Last Call" for her flight. When she eventually saw Theo running through the departures hall, dodging travellers and luggage carts, she interrupted the girl at the counter she had been guarding to say, "He's coming, he's coming." The check in attendant politely excused herself from her current client and summonsed a short, whiskered man whose airline uniform was badly in need of a size upgrade. The passports Theo was holding passed quickly through Tayla's hands to the attendant, who promptly handed one of them to her colleague who then trotted away, talking into a radio that was strapped to his shoulder.

Tayla accepted the laptop, and did not ask for an explanation for Theo's otherwise empty hands. Indeed, she was thankful she did not have to spend time checking in luggage. On return of her passport she took Theo's hand and ran with him to the departure gate. With a quick hug and brush of lips, she left him and was already out of his sight, measuring the number of people between herself and the x-ray scanner when she registered that he had called after her "I will see you in London – soon!" Putting her questions on hold, she ducked the straps that ordered the queue and forced her way towards the front until an indignant official blocked her path. He seemed to understand none of her words, but her urgency was clear, and after looking at her ticket he parted the line at a scanner and inserted her, arranging two plastic trays on the rack that was trundling towards the black curtain and motioning to her laptop and pockets. On the far side of the body scanner she was stopped while a woman laboriously patted down her clothes and then she had to wait for a wand scanner searching for traces of explosive powders. The official had been standing by, and it was only after his radio crackled with a short, indecipherable rush of words that he made an OK sign with his thumb and forefinger and the security staff waved her on.

The staff at the boarding gate were standing idly at the counter, chatting. The seats in the hall had all been vacated, the ramp towards the plane was empty and the departures board said 'Closed'. Tayla fronted up to the desk, breathless and ready to fight, but she met no resistance. One of the attendants simply took her arm and guided her towards the ramp, which caused Tayla to dig in her heels and stop.

"Is my mother on board?" she challenged.

"*Né.*" The attendant turned Tayla towards the window beside the entrance to the ramp where she could see an ambulance standing with its back doors open. A reassuringly empty stretcher was alongside and as Tayla watched two blue-uniformed paramedics were folding it in order to load it back into the ambulance.

"Can I see my mother?" Tayla demanded at the door of the plane, as the attendant handed her over to a hostess.

"Please take your seat, your mother is comfortable, and you can see her after we have taken off. I will come and get you when the seat belt sign goes off." Tayla luxuriated in the crisp,

Greek accented English of the young airline hostess. There had not been a single thing that she could fault in the way everyone in Milos and Athens had looked after her mother. They had cooperated with the insurance company to organise a quick medical transfer, and they had been very generous in the help they had given her, but still, Tayla had felt bewildered by the language gap, traumatised by her own lack of understanding of what was happening. Thank God for Theo, she thought as she settled into her seat, and thank God she was now back in English-speaking territory where she could at least imagine she had some control over what was going on.

Theo had said he was coming to London. Once she was seated Tayla replayed their hasty parting with regret. She reached for her phone as the aircraft was pushed back from the dock and was pleased to see three bars of reception. She furtively looked around the cabin and started texting.

~

The squawk of the text jumped from Theo's jeans pocket as he returned to the café after booking Lynne and Tayla's luggage into the airport's storage facility. Mary watched his smile and his quick one-handed thumbing of an acronymic reply.

"Missing you already?"

"Asking what I meant about coming to London."

The text alert rang again. Theo busied himself copying and pasting details from an SMS he had already received from the agent at the airport's ticket counter. Twice more the text bell rang, then silence. Theo darted over to a window and watched the airfield for at least five minutes before giving up.

"*Efharisto Theía, efharisto parapoli,*" Theo's eyes were glistening when he turned back to Mary.

"You're very sweet," Mary replied, standing up to receive Theo's warm hug. "And you're very welcome. Now Romeo, be a darling, carry my bag out to the taxi stand and you do all the talking so that the driver charges us the proper local fare. I want to see my brother."

~

Mary was unusually silent for her first few minutes in the hospital ward. Her eyes took in the purpled swelling of her brother's face; the endotracheal tube stretching between his mouth and a large ventilator on a trolley beside the bed; the chest tube inserted to the underside of his ribs; the electrodes taped across his bare chest and up his arms connecting him to a large cathode ray monitor she suspected of being an antique; the drip inserted in his wrist, its clear fluid running from a plastic bag hanging limply from a metal stand. Theo hovered, waiting for her to speak, wondering if she were about to faint.

Mary's inspection stopped at a tube that was plugged into the right hand side of George's head. With one hand she covered her mouth and with the fingers of the other she reached towards the tube, but did not touch.

"I want to know what all this is. Theo - get someone who will tell me what's happening to him," she said imperatively.

Theo darted away, and in his absence Mary dropped to her knees on the hard-vinyl of the hospital floor, took George's hand and pressed it to her face, closed her eyes and began to pray.

"Hail Mary, mother of mercy, our life, our sweetness and our hope. To thee do we cry. To thee do we send up our sighs, mourning and weeping in this valley of tears. Turn then, please Mary, thine eyes of mercy toward us, and show unto us the blessed fruit of thy womb, Jesus.

Remember, Oh most gracious Virgin Mary, that never was it known that any one who fled to thy protection, implored thy help or sought thy intercession, was left unaided. Inspired by this, I fly unto thee, Oh Virgin of virgins my Mother; to thee do I come, before thee

I stand, sinful and sorrowful; Oh Mother of the Word Incarnate, despise not my petitions, but in thy mercy hear and answer me, in thy mercy save my brother Giorgos.

Oh clement, Oh loving, Oh sweet Virgin Mary! Pray for us, Oh holy Mother of God, that we may be made worthy of the promises of Christ. Amen."

When she saw a white-coated arm offering her assistance, Mary drew a final sob, and leant heavily on both the arm and the side of the bed to raise herself to the doctor's eye level. He quietly offered her a tissue and she studied him, evaluating his competence, as she dabbed her eyes and blew her nose. It benefited her appraisal that he reminded her of Stephen, bald with smooth skin and dark watchful eyes. His nametag said 'Doctor Kapriokakis'.

"*Efharistó* doctor, *me synchoreíte,*" Mary fluttered her hand to rest against her heart, describing her distress.

"*Parakalo*, you are the next of kin?" The doctor's English was clear and competent.

"His sister."

"Please write your name down here," he handed her a clipboard and pointed to a text box on a form written in Greek, with occasional English sub-titles.

"Please explain his condition to me, explain what you are doing." Mary held the clipboard hostage against her chest, unsigned, ensuring that the doctor could not escape without satisfying her.

Doctor Kapriokakis walked around to the other side of the bed where Mary could see him better, and began his explanation with the clip that was attached to George's left forefinger.

"Monitoring the oxygen level in his blood. Would be very low, because one lung has collapsed, the other almost - but the respirator, this is breathing for him. Without it, he cannot live. This tube drains the chest, there is much build up there."

"And this, in his head?"

"He has much intracranial pressure. Very high. It is hematoma – the brain is swelling. We help by draining some fluid, but cannot help much. It was a long time before he got to the hospital. There is already brain damage. I'm sorry."

"How much?" Mary drew a shuddering breath, watching George's face. "How serious is the brain damage?"

"We think he cannot recover from this, I'm sorry," the doctor repeated.

"You can keep him alive though – the respirator is keeping him alive?"

"Yes, the brain is not re-inflating the lungs, but the respirator is keeping him alive since six hours."

"We must keep him alive. His daughter is coming. She will be here soon – very soon. We will keep him alive." Mary was nodding to herself in affirmation.

Doctor Kapriokakis eased the clipboard from her arms, flipped the pages and closed the cover. Her signature was no longer required.

"Is there anything else we can do for you? There is a waiting room down the corridor. You go there to use your mobile phone, you cannot use it here please." The doctor switched to Greek, telling Theo he wanted to see George's daughter as soon as she arrived, and asking for her name.

Mary bristled and answered him in Greek. The doctor bowed his head to her and left the room, pulling a blue curtain across behind him.

Mary collapsed weakly into the waiting chair that was revealed by the unfolding curtain. Before Theo had found any words to say to comfort her she rebounded.

"Where is this waiting room? I have to ring your uncle Stephen."

Grateful for something to do, Theo led her out of the ICU department.

Thalassa

~

Five members of the New South Wales branch of the Kostis family were assembled in the living room at Brooklyn to listen on the speakerphone to Mary's tearful account of George's condition. Margarita sat on the sofa, holding Toffee-*gata* to her chest to keep him out from under Stephen's heavy pacing feet as much as for her own comfort. Pappous listened quietly, his body limp, withering into the sofa beside her. Melinda and Michael were emptying the biscuit jar at the kitchen bench.

"The doctor says he won't recover, but how do they know?" Mary's voice was shrill, punctuated by static and echo across the speakerphone. "They don't know. He could just wake up and be okay. Our prayers can save him."

"*Theléma*," Pappous spoke the word softly.

"Papa? Papa, did you say something?"

"He means it's God's will, it's in God's hands," Stephen explained.

"Yes – we must pray and God will help us," Mary confirmed.

Stephen, who had prayed awkwardly yesterday for the first time since Michael was born, felt uncomfortable with this option.

"What do you think of the hospital; the doctors. Should we bring him home?"

"They say he can't be moved. They say he will die as soon as he is disconnected from the life support. There are all sorts of things connected to him – it looks like they know what they are doing. Theo says it is a good hospital."

Pappous muttered something.

"Papa?"

"He said that the Greeks were the first doctors and have always been the best," Stephen interpreted.

When Pappous continued his muttering, Stephen's face reddened with anger. He stalked over to the sofa and towered over his father, fists clenched.

"I cannot go - the flights are full because of Pascha! I can't get a flight this week, not even at the first class price!"

Stephen's threatening pose had no effect on Pappous, he kept muttering in words meant for Stephen alone.

"That's fucking bullshit, and I'm not listening to any more of it!" Stephen stormed out of the house.

Margarita quickly dumped Toffee-*gata* on the sofa and leant forward to pick up the phone. Pappous was carrying on, and his volume was increasing.

"Hi Mary, I've switched off the speaker. I think we need to wait for Claire to get there." Margarita got up and walked further away from Pappous to stand at the windows and look over the river. "We'll talk again with Claire and David. Michael says he can set up a session on Skype so that we can all talk together. When Claire is ready, get her to call and then we'll set up the Skype session from here." Margarita paused while Mary agreed, then she continued. "Stephen has tried to get a flight but they're booked out for Easter. He can't get a flight before Tuesday week. He's been trying to call Sam, but no answer yet. We'll get off the phone now – ok? … Ok, bye."

Margarita came back across the living room and stood in front of Pappous, shaking a finger at him. "Now that's enough, Papa. You are being *very* unfair, you are *in the wrong*, and you're to stop *right now*!"

In the kitchen Michael elbowed Melinda lightly in the ribs. "Never thought I'd hear her say *that* to Pappous," he whispered.

Margarita raised an eyebrow at them as she passed on her way to the back door to follow Stephen. "*Put* the biscuits *away*," she demanded over her shoulder.

~

Later on a seat looking along the jetty to the calm evening water of The Gut, Margarita sat with Stephen, soothing him.

"Yes, it's bullshit. He is an old, superstitious man and he's wrong. There's a part of you that believes him, and you must not. You are too ready to think that you're the centre of the universe, you know. Always too ready to think it's all your responsibility, and it's all your fault, and it's all because of you. It *isn't*. Even your father doesn't think that, he thinks it's all because of *him*. He knows he can't do anything about it now, so he transfers the responsibility and the blame *he* feels to you. You don't have to take it on."

"I know, I know," Stephen rubbed the corners of his eyes and sniffed. "I just feel so useless. There's nothing I can do. Nothing I can do. I can't even pray properly any more."

"God knows what is in your heart. Mary and I pray, and God knows about you. Don't worry about that."

The phone that was resting on the seat beside Stephen suddenly vibrated, starting to turn itself in a circle before letting off a ring tone Margarita had never heard it produce before. She saw the letters NSB on the screen before Stephen snatched the handset up.

"What the fuck took you so long?" Stephen answered with a level of aggression that startled Margarita. "Where are you?" Margarita could hear a man's voice on the other end and she realised it must be Sam. She heard him decline to answer the question before Stephen launched into a description of what had happened to George, and finished with what she assumed was a completely unreasonable demand that Sam get to the hospital in Athens right away.

Instead of the argument she expected, Stephen resumed with the address of the hospital and the name of George's doctor.

"One more thing," Stephen added, "did you take Amphitrite's arm from the church?"

Sam's answer was too long to be either 'yes' or 'no'.

"Don't give me any bullshit. Did you take the arm from the church?"

Again, Sam's answer was qualified, which Stephen took to be affirmation.

"You fucking put it back. You're a fucking idiot." Stephen raised his voice to a sobbing howl, "PUT IT BACK!" He ended the call and stuffed the phone deep in the inside pocket of his jacket, while Margarita looked at him with astonishment.

"I don't understand any of that," she said softly.

Stephen was breathing slowly through his teeth, tapping the toes of his boots on the jetty slats. She waited for his anger management to take effect.

"Later," Stephen said eventually. "When I've heard back from him. There's got to be a reason I'll get out of him. Meanwhile – he'll be at the hospital in a few hours."

"Is he in Athens then?"

"He didn't say. Must be close."

"He has a new phone number?"

"Emergencies only, forget you saw it."

"Still playing war games," Margarita snuggled into Stephen's chest, causing him to automatically wrap an arm around her.

"Not my game, his. I don't have a fucking clue what he's up to most of the time. I've no idea why he's not using his normal phone or why he took the relic. Pisses me off. Why can't he be *normal*? Why can't he live round the corner from me, meet me at the pub, go sailing on Saturdays. Why didn't he fucking marry my sister and stay home so we could all be happy?"

"You married me and stayed home, and *we're* happy darling. You have given me a wonderful family, and I'm very happy," Margarita stretched up to give him a kiss and settled her head back on his chest.

Stephen stared across the silver rippled water for a moment; then kissed the top of her abundant black hair. "You're a miracle worker, that's what's done it. Mama should have found Sam a woman like you."

"She couldn't, I'm unique."

"True enough."

Thalassa

~

I sit with Claire on the plane, holding her thoughts, dissolved by the tears that come and are fought back. If only she could know. How this hurts to watch and is yet such a joy for me, to be with her, to know her thoughts and to be so proud of her. Her humanity runs way beyond her, she loves from an infinite source and she is brave with her feelings, instead of hiding.

I don't know how it is that I have had this privilege of waiting; I don't know if this will continue or change; I don't know if it was intended or by accident; I think maybe it was an experience I was open to, and maybe others will experience what they are open to; maybe they will see their God, while I feel my people. George and Claire can feel me in return, because they are open to feeling me. Sadly, David cannot, but after this, when she goes back to Australia, Claire will get over her uncertainty, and she will tell him; she will tell him I have been with them both, for so much longer than he understood. He will believe her because he wants to.

I think of my mother, when multiple sclerosis had driven her into bed but before she lost the ability to talk. She spoke of her enormous frustration. She said she still felt young; she still felt the same even though her body had given up on her, and she had given up on it. The matriarchs, Iliana, Aretha and Jean, who grew old in time loving the people who have come together in this tragedy, have all said the same thing, and this is how it is for me too. I still feel the same, but time and space don't challenge me any more. It is my children I worry for, which is why Iliana showed me how to look and that looking has been much kinder to me than it was to her. I don't know what happens to me after this, but I do know I have been very privileged, to have this wait with the past, present and future of the people I love.

~

Claire is experiencing first class for the only time in her life. She has a seat twice her width; she has downed a glass of champagne and eaten the best food she has ever eaten on an aeroplane. She can lie comfortably flat and, having left Boston at 9.45pm, she is only too ready to sleep – but still, sleep won't come. She wants sleep to come; she wants the flight to be over sooner; she doesn't want to lie here imagining that she will be too late. She brings Leah to mind; so light at only 5'1 that Claire can pick her up, bundle her over a shoulder and spin her around, her brown wavy hair falling freely down Claire's lower back while she slaps Claire on the thighs in excited protest. Claire imagines Leah at Rose and Mark's place, explaining with brightly obvious tears in her soft brown eyes why Claire had cancelled out of dinner. Leah is an evocative storyteller; she has that American gift of the gab – an apple-of-her-parent's-eye confidence that lets her breeze through anything she wants to say without fear of her own emotions or another's criticism. She will make them marvel at the drama, laugh at her comic view, and still empathetically grasp the tragedy. Claire loves listening to Leah tell stories; in time her telling of this story will help Claire manage its reality. She will tell them what she only knows by phone and text, as if she were right at the scene. How Swiss Air promised Claire the first available seat if she came immediately to the airport. How the hostess at the boarding gate told Claire she was lucky enough to be the last emergency arrival they could accommodate, so would first class be acceptable? She would tell them, Claire thinks, that she is late to dinner because she jumped in a taxi herself, with a spare bra, underpants and a tooth brush in her pocket, but the airline staff told her that 'daughter's girlfriend' was not a category that allowed them to bump passengers off the flight. She would tell them, like she had told Claire, that it's the last straw. She wants to be 'wife'. Leah had stood with her nose pressed against the window and her ear pressed to the phone, reciting her love like a mantra until Claire had laughed and shut her phone as the hostess performed a final check of the cabin. Claire has still not told her dad about Leah, and now she desperately hopes she will still get the chance; she wishes George and Leah had met.

As the cabin lights fade-in, and the smell of omelette provokes her nose five hours into the flight, Claire sees me. She cannot see anyone else in the cabin, just empty chairs, and me, standing by the curtain that screens her compartment. "Oh Mum," she says, over and over. I tell her she will endure; that this will pass; that our love is always with her and that I am proud of who she is, and what she is about to do. "Mum, stay," she entreats, and I do stay, but she doesn't know that, because the hostess pulls back the curtain and her full consciousness intrudes.

~

Claire stood out in the midst of the pack of people pushing trolleys stacked with luggage along the arrivals hall at Athens airport. Her smooth white skin and long blonde hair were enough to distinguish her, but she was also tall enough to look over the heads of everyone else in the slowly moving queue. Instead of a trolley she had, hanging casually from her tall shoulder, a single purple tote bag bearing the logos of several different sports brands. She was slim, her body taut and evidently at a peak of fitness. She carried herself with a lanky, easy grace.

Theo was certain she was his Australian cousin as soon as she walked through the doors, and he moved towards the front of the crowd holding the sign with her name on it above his head where she would see it easily. She came towards him with a beautiful smile that reminded him of Aunt Mary's in the generous parting of her lips but unlike Aunt Mary she was wearing no make up, her brown eyes were bloodshot and reticent, wary of what news he might have for her.

"Theo," Claire held out her hand.

"Nice to meet you Claire. Your taxi is here – no luggage?"

Claire shrugged her shoulder bag. "Hopefully I put my toothbrush in here, otherwise I will have to shop."

"I have Euros for you, and the taxi - he has been paid for the return trip."

"You aren't coming back to the hospital?"

"I go to London, two hours. *Theía* Maria has arranged. I have time to get Tayla's luggage and check in. You must hurry. They wait for you." Theo held a fifty Euro note and a piece of notepaper towards Claire as he led her past the queue at the taxi stand to a white cab standing separately in the pick-up zone. Claire tried to refuse the money, but Theo insisted. "This from Maria. She say you must have money in your pocket – you fix with her later."

The taxi driver pushed himself off the bonnet of his car. Seeing that Claire carried no luggage he walked around the front of the car to get into the drivers seat. Theo opened the door to the rear seat. "This taxi, he knows where to go and he is paid by Maria already. The note it is for the hospital – they show you where to go."

Claire could understand only two digits, everything else on the note was written in the Greek script that was completely foreign to her. She felt half her genes mocking her. She knew so little about Greece, or the Kostis family. The first time she had heard Theo's name was when Mary rang her just before she boarded the plane.

"Thank-you Theo – I wish I had more time to get to know you," Claire extended her hand again formally, and Theo took it, pulled her forward and gave her a firm hug.

"At a better time. We are cousins, I hope we meet again too." Theo looked briefly at his sandaled feet, then directly into Claire's eyes. "I am so sorry. Your Papa, I like him very much. This month with him, it has been a very good time."

Claire nodded, blinked her eyes away from his gaze, and thanked him again, though her words, if they escaped her head at all, were inaudible amidst the clamour of the concourse.

When her legs were clear of the taxi door, Theo closed it and tapped the roof sharply. He watched the taxi drive away, and then turned back to the airport doors with a lighter step, his mind now facing London.

~

There was a large red sign with white lettering secured to the wide metal door of the ICU department at Tzaneio hospital in Pireaus. Claire was initially drawn into a hopeless attempt to understand the Greek letters, before she gave up and read the English translation below. Visitors had to be checked in and out by a member of staff. Admission was allowed for family only. Use of mobile phones and other electronic devices was prohibited. The nurse tapped her finger against the mobile phone ruling as she pushed the door open and showed Claire inside. Claire held down the button on the top of her phone until the phone bleeped and blacked out.

The nurse led her past the central care station to a compartment in the far corner of the ward and drew back the curtain, revealing first Mary, uncomfortably asleep in a plastic chair, and then the hospital bed. The nurse said something that included the word 'Doctor', and closed the curtain behind her as she departed. Claire tiptoed to the far side of the bed, grateful that Mary was asleep.

She found the scene very much as she had rehearsed it. Her father looked bruised but peaceful, as much as a body could with so many tentacles leading away from it towards such a variety of appliances. The ventilator was quite loud, like someone slowly sweeping a corridor, a sweep ended by a metallic thud, a pause, then another sweep. Its twin LED screens were showing steady peaks that followed the rise and fall of George's chest. On the other side of the bed the large cathode ray monitor was tracing out George's vital signs in five coloured lines. There was an encouragingly steady blip on the green Heart Rate line at the top of the screen and the temperature display at 37.1 degrees seemed normal. Claire could guess that the white SpO2 line was monitoring oxygen saturation, and even that, at 99% was surely good? Daunted by the unfamiliar technology, she picked up the clipboard that was hanging on the end of the bed; then quickly put it back with a shake of her head. Indecipherable.

Claire lifted her father's right hand and squeezed it, watching his face closely but seeing no response at all. She weighed her wish to speak to him against the probability that Mary would wake. She leant down towards his ear.

"Dad, it's Claire, I'm here. I hope you can hear me, I'm here."

Claire had spoken softly, but Mary was startled awake, issuing a loud cry of "Oh!" and slapping the arm of the chair. "Oh!" she repeated more gently, fussing with her necklace against her throat, and then composing herself by arranging her shawl. "Claire, it's you." After a glance at George's chest movement she continued, "You made it, thank God."

"Hello Mary. Thank-you for sending Theo to meet me."

Mary pushed herself out of the chair and smoothed her blouse and her skirt with one stroke before stepping forward to meet Claire at the end of the bed with an enveloping hug. "Oh Claire baby," she wailed, "I am so sorry, so sorry for you and Davy."

Claire cringed in Mary's hug. There was an emotional overload that Mary added to any event that had always put Claire on the back foot. This time, unlike normal family visits, Claire was not going to be able to make an excuse and escape. She reminded herself of Mary's thoughtfulness, she disciplined herself to be kind, instead of reactive. She extricated herself gently and moved back to George's side.

"What's been happening Mary?" Claire marvelled at the cool rationality of her own voice. Somehow it was the Mary effect: Mary had claimed for herself all the emotion in the room.

"Oh, you sound so like your mother, every year you grow more like her. So slim and beautiful and intelligent. What about your Masters darling? You must be nearly finished? Are you missing exams or assignments to come here?"

"I'll claim compassionate evaluation, it will be alright. But Mary, please, tell me what happened."

"I was at Dimitry's darling. We were waiting for George to get home for dinner when Theo rang and told Anton there had been an accident. It was the water truck, it hit Anton's car–George was driving–and it dragged it off the cliff. Theo didn't see it, Tayla saw it."

"Who is Tayla?"

"Theo's girlfriend, English girl. Anyway, Anton and Petros rushed off ..."

"Who are Anton and Petros?"

Mary looked disapproving as she settled back into the chair. "Our cousins. Anton is Theo's father. Petros is Anton's brother. Uncle Dimitry's family. Anyway, it was dark, they took a long time to find your father – he was not in the car. They say he must have tried to get out and the car rolled on him. The driver of the water truck was still in the truck – he died. It was a terrible accident, the road there is very dangerous. Anton says it was the water truck. He says the water truck was very old, he says they all knew the brakes were going to fail one day. Everyone knows it was not your father's fault." Mary sought earnestly to reassure Claire, and Claire realised that the thought of blame had never crossed her mind.

"And once they found him?"

"Well, Milos doesn't have a hospital. They sent a plane and transferred him here in the middle of last night. Tayla and Theo came with him last night, I came this morning."

"Why did Tayla come?"

"Oh ... her mother was injured too, and they flew her here as well ... but she was flown back to England this morning."

"Hang on, was this English woman in the car with Dad?"

"No, no ... another car was behind your dad. The truck hit two cars. It pushed the car with Lynne and Tayla into the cliff."

"Is she alright then, the English woman?"

"Yes, I believe so. A lot of broken bones and they're worried about her neck, but Theo says she'll be ok."

"And Theo's girlfriend?"

"Unhurt. Not even a scratch. Awful ... *awful* ... for her though, to watch it."

Claire regretted that Tayla had already gone. She felt she needed to know exactly what Tayla had witnessed first hand. "So what injuries does Dad have?"

Mary drew a deep breath and Claire saw her hesitate. "Tell me everything, exactly," she ordered.

"Well, I might not know everything exactly ... I don't know if they have told me everything. They say they know the car rolled on him because he has broken ribs and ... " Mary struggled with the words, and Claire waited in silence. "His back is broken. One of his lungs collapsed at the scene, and by the grace of God the other held on until they got him here."

"He has a head injury, they're draining fluid from his head," Claire pointed at the tube, prompting her aunt to continue.

"Yes, yes. They need to relieve the pressure."

Claire had two critical questions she desperately wanted to ask, but decided not to further upset Mary. After all, it was the doctor's opinion she wanted, not Mary's.

"Has he been conscious at all?"

Mary drew a sobbing breath. "No, not at all. Not at all." Mary continued to sob, noisily, while Claire stood tall and stiff, focussing on the steady rise and fall of her father's chest. She had counted past ten when Mary pulled a tissue from a box on the table beside her chair and blew into it.

"I'll go to the ladies room and get myself together, sweetheart. It's down the hall past the waiting room if you want it." Mary gathered herself and her handbag and left the compartment.

With a promptness that made Claire wonder if he had been waiting for this opportunity, Dr Kapriokakis slipped past the curtain as soon as Mary had gone. He introduced himself and checked the information relayed to him by the nurse.

"You understand you are his next of kin," Dr Kapriokakis sat the words heavily on Claire's shoulders. She nodded. "We must go to my office and talk, but first – your questions."

"His back is broken?"

The doctor nodded. "In two places."

"Will he be paralysed?"

"Paraplegia is likely, in other circumstances with rehabilitation he might be able to recover."

"Other circumstances," Claire repeated with no question mark in her voice. "His head injury is severe? He has brain damage?"

"Yes."

"Can he recover?"

"I'm sorry, but no."

Claire gripped the rail at the side of the bed and concentrated on her breathing until she felt able to speak. "How do you know?"

"He is on the ventilator because his brain cannot regulate the work of the lungs. If we turn this off, he will die, he cannot take his own breath." Dr Kapriokakis moved around her to the top of the bed. "I will give you reading, but now you look." He took a small penlight from his pocket and opened George's right eye wide. "You look closely at his eye please."

Claire shuddered, but leaned in to look directly into her father's evidently un-seeing eye as the doctor shone the penlight into it. She didn't know what she was looking for; it occurred to her that the doctor was suggesting she would see through the eye to where her father had gone.

"The pupil it does not react at all," the doctor explained, and she realised that it was true.

"Does that mean he is … he is brain dead?"

"Not quite, the EEG shows traces still. I show you in my office. You will come with me now please."

Claire followed Dr Kapriokakis unsteadily, feeling the hot-cold differential between her skin and underlying muscle that implied she was in danger of fainting. She concentrated hard on her breathing and her steps, and nodded when the Doctor offered her a drink from the water cooler. In his office she sat gratefully in a less than comfortable plastic chair, the cup of water in hand, as he settled on the opposite side of his desk, leafing through papers in a manila folder until he found the one he wanted to give her. The paper was wrinkled and grubby as though it had passed through many hands over years, and it was titled 'Indications of Brain Death'.

> *The indications of brain death include:*
> *The pupils don't respond to light.*
> *There is no reaction to pain.*
> *The eyes do not blink when the surface of the cornea is touched.*
> *The eyes don't move when the head is moved.*
> *The eyes don't move when ice water is poured into the ear.*
> *The person does not gag when a spatula touches the back of the throat.*
> *The person does not breathe when the ventilator is switched off.*
> *An EEG test shows no brain activity at all.*

Claire read through the bullet points, feeling glad that the doctor had not chosen to demonstrate the truth of each point to her. When she had finished he had the EEG stretched out before her.

"There is some activity, here and here and here," the doctor pointed his pen towards parts of the graph which showed small spikes. "But this is very little."

"What could be causing that?"

"We cannot say. Some muscle reflex, some response to messages from his organs as they work. His organs, except his lungs, they are all good. His heart, his kidneys, his liver, as long as they get oxygen they work still. His skin is still warm, his look is normal, but he cannot wake. The coma is irreversible. I'm sorry."

"How often do you take an EEG?" Claire asked.

"This one since two hours. We take another in four hours." Dr Kapriokakis pushed his clipboard across the desk to her, papers folded back to the page of his choice. He indicated a box with his pen. "As the next of kin, we need you to sign here to take responsibility."

Claire looked at the form with suspicion. "I need to see an English version."

"This is English version," the doctor tried to sound patient; he pointed to some parts of the form where the text boxes were sub-titled in English. As she looked carefully at the small print Claire could see other parts of the text in English as well, but the words were broadly un-explanatory and there seemed to be not nearly as many of them as their Greek counterparts. "What it says is that you accept responsibility for deciding the care of the patient, and you accept responsibility for the bills in the event there is no reciprocal arrangement with your country, and no insurance. He has insurance?"

Claire shook her head, still trying to make sense of the form, turning back the pages. "I don't know if he had any insurance. I don't know about reciprocal agreements."

"Australia does not have, no."

"I'm – I'm very tired from the flight," Claire gave up her effort to understand the form and appealed to the doctor. "I need time to read this, and think about it. I need – I need to ask my brother in Australia if he knows about the insurance."

"Né." Dr Kapriokakis took charge of the clipboard again and reorganised its pages before showing it to her again. "There are two other boxes you must decide, you cross which box, and you initial. Here – that we resuscitate or not resuscitate, and here – that you agree to organ donation."

"If I check not to resuscitate do you turn off the life support?" Claire asked in alarm.

"No, no … there is another form for that. This box is for emergency. If his heart stops. But this won't happen now, the ventilator keeps him."

"Do you have a counsellor who speaks English … to help me?" Claire struggled to get the words out.

"Would you like to see our priest?"

Claire stared at him in alarm. "No, thank-you, but no."

"Then you have just my advice. I am sorry, but we think he cannot recover from this. You take this and read, and you see me again in one hour. We must have this signature." Dr Kapriokakis removed some papers from the clipboard and then gave the clipboard to her, with his pen. He got up from his chair and walked out of the office to speak to a nurse, then returned as Claire was wondering if she had been meant to follow him or not.

"Your father, he is being changed. Your aunt, she is in the waiting room. You go to the waiting room now. You talk with her. You call your brother there." The doctor shepherded her out of his office to the wide, foreboding door of the unit, and let her out into the corridor.

Claire paused as the door closed behind her, looking down the wide, brightly fluorescent, antiseptic corridor, recalling the location of the waiting room pointed out earlier by the nurse from reception. Yes, she could talk to Mary, and she could ring David, but Claire had never felt more alone in her life.

~

Mary could speak Greek much better than she could read it, but her understanding of the letters was sufficient to determine that the Greek text of the pages of the hospital admission form was broadly in line with the English translation. Given the privacy in which to read the admission form she and Claire agreed that it was appropriate that Claire should sign it. But when they reached the check box labelled DNR, followed by the check box for Organ Donation, they found themselves in stark disagreement.

"Absolutely not," Mary proclaimed. "We will not turn off the respirator. God needs time to do His work. We will give God time to do His work."

Deciding to defer that argument, Claire explained patiently. "This box is not about switching off life support, Mary. This is to say that if he has a heart attack, for example, they should not use a defibrillator ... "

"Well they should. Whatever it takes. They will do everything in their power to save his life. Once they do everything they can, it is up to God to decide the rest. This box is the one you cross." Mary tapped the 'Yes' box on the Resuscitation Order.

Claire distracted Mary by moving straight on to the organ donation question without marking the paper.

"That has to be with his permission. Do you have his permission? Is he on the donor register? If it will bring benefit to others, if they guarantee they will not mutilate his body *and* if he had given his permission then you can say yes to that," Mary said authoritatively.

"Mum donated her organs," Claire said softly. "Dad said she wanted it – they'd have been the same. He would want the same thing." Claire crossed the box and Mary took exception to being pre-empted.

"Your father did *not* just blindly agree with everything your mother said and did. Your father is Catholic; he is *not* an atheist. He might not have argued with her in front of you, but I know he believed in God, I know at heart he is a good Catholic and he will be redeemed. What will your Pappous think if the body comes back home to him with holes in it?! Oh!" Mary picked up the clipboard and Claire's first thought was that she was going to tear up the forms, but instead she employed the clipboard as a fan. "This is terrible talk, terrible talk, I won't continue it ... *if* it happens you must make sure they don't mutilate his body. This is *your* responsibility."

When she had cooled herself sufficiently, Mary turned to the last sheet of paper in the clipboard.

"*What* is this? *This* is authority to switch off life support. *No. This* you do not do!"

Before Claire could move or speak Mary had torn away the lower part of the form. The top half remained stubbornly stuck under the clip. Mary crushed the offending paper into a tight ball in her hand. Claire eased the remaining scrap of paper from the clipboard and similarly crushed it, dropping it into Mary's lap.

"You are right, Mary," she said tersely. "This is *my* responsibility. David and I will make this decision."

Suddenly, Mary's face contorted, she cried "Oh!" and leapt to her feet, knocking Claire aside in her rush to throw herself at Sam.

~

I've come to know Sam in such small pieces. A layer of the onion at a time. He is not so much revealed as unravelled, he does not want to be known. Each peeling is accidental, when circumstances contrive against his privacy. Each revelation is to just one person, and in fragmenting the things people know of him he feels his whole truth is safe from harm. Even Mary, who has known more than anyone, does not know very much. Neither do I, because Sam has not been amongst my primary concerns, until now, when he comes to my daughter's rescue.

Mary thinks she has monopolised him, but his eyes are holding Claire's, and he manages to step, with Mary still fastened to his chest, towards Claire and reach, with that surprisingly long arm to touch her cheek with three fingers. Her lips make his name silently; she leans her cheek along his fingers, undone by the sincerity of his simple gesture and slips onto the lounge chair where she lies, her head along her arm, and cries quietly in exhaustion and relief.

~

"You're mascara has smudged," Sam stroked Mary's cheek, spreading a little black a long way. "I hate to tell you, love, but you're looking terrible."

Mary looked around the waiting room, failing to find a mirror, daunted by the presence of two other people in the farthest corner from them, who were trying to pay no attention. She pulled a tissue from her pocket and wiped her cheeks, the blackened tissue proving Sam's point. "I'll go and fix myself up. You'll stay here?"

"Of course," Sam said smoothly.

With Mary gone, Sam settled himself in the chair opposite Claire, propping his body forward, long arms on long thighs and querying her with just one word. "Summary?"

When Claire finished Sam simply nodded with a sigh. "Stephen and I will deal with Mary. This is for you and David to decide."

Sam picked up the clipboard and glanced through the admission form, then placed it before her, alongside the pen. "Stephen and George would both want you to check the DNR box. You don't have to decide about the life support now. He has to be kept under observation for longer before they can switch it off anyway, don't let the doctor push you into anything right now – tell him you need to sleep, your family needs time to think about it, and you'll give him a decision in the morning." Sam checked his watch. "It's 3 am in Sydney. Take this form to the doctor now before Mary comes back, stay away ... give me thirty minutes."

Claire took up the pen, crossed the DNR box, and placed her initials and signature where required. She arranged the sheets of paper under the clip, closed the clipboard, and stood. She had intended to thank Sam, maybe with a hug, but he was leaning back in his chair, hands behind his neck, staring at an empty spot on the wall and she felt too disturbed by his expression to intrude.

Mary found Sam's position unchanged a few minutes later, but she wasn't worried by it. When he did not get up to greet her she knelt down beside him and pulled on his left arm until his fingers unlocked. She brought his hand to her mouth and kissed it lightly, searching his eyes.

"I am *so* glad you came. Sam, it's been awful, just awful. Thank-you so much for being here." When Sam stared back at her, unblinking and unyielding, she continued. "You're here to help me because Stephen can't get here, I understand. We won't even talk about your letter, or about us – unless you want to. I do get it. I don't agree, but I do get what you are saying. You are here to support me, in this terrible time, thank you." Mary rested her head on Sam's chest and smiled to herself when she felt his fingers automatically thread into her hair to stroke her head.

"I support Claire, and I am only going to support you if you support Claire."

Mary stared at him with narrowed eyes and when she had divined his meaning she spoke slowly and with all the authority she could muster. "You don't understand the Faith, you never have. And Claire is just a child, completely swayed by her mother, what does she know? Life is sacred. We won't agree to turning off the ventilator."

"You're on your own Mary. Who do you think 'We' is?"

"Stephen won't agree with you. This is his brother's life. It's not an abortion."

"Given what the doctor is saying, Stephen will *absolutely* want the ventilator turned off."

"You're a smug bastard. What if you don't know him as well as you think?"

"We had a pact."

"Forty years ago, he's not that boy now."

Sam pulled his hand away from Mary and pulled his mobile phone out of his shirt pocket.

"You need to settle an argument," he said by way of 'hello' to the sleepy voice that eventually answered his call, then handed the phone to Mary and leant back into the cushions listening to her alternately sob, cajole and argue.

"Say goodbye now," Sam held out his hand and tucked his fingers towards his palm, beckoning the phone back when he heard Mary's protests subside.

"Do I need to be there?" Sam could hear the angst in Stephen's voice.

"Not for us, not for George. I can't answer for you. Do you know if he has insurance?"

"No idea."

"I hate to be mercenary, but waiting for you to get here could be very expensive."

Stephen was quiet for a moment, and Sam let him think. "You make sure they've got it right buddy," he eventually whispered.

"I will." Sam fixed Mary's gaze as he put his phone down, but she had no more fight in her, and quickly looked away. She reached into her bra for a new tissue, an action he had always found provocative and now steeled himself against.

"I've organised a hotel room nearby," Mary sniffed and then blew her nose.

"Good, Claire needs to sleep."

"Sometimes I hate you," Mary spoke softly, but vehemently.

"Likewise," Sam smiled back.

~

David was watching cartoons. Bugs Bunny was on his way to the grocery store while Daffy Duck, who had given him a long shopping list of scribble and drawings, was watching TV. David was sprawled in an armchair, mirroring Daffy Duck, but in his hand there was a phone, instead of a remote control. He jerked and dropped it, as it rang loudly for the first time in the long hours he had sat there. He lunged for it, and answered in the way I hate, "Yo!" As Claire talked to him he searched the armchair for the remote and eventually found it in order to mute Bugs and Daffy's helium voices. Claire didn't have to wait to ring him, he said, he had been more or less awake all night.

Claire relayed her disagreement with Mary. They talked about what they did and didn't know about their father's wishes. They wondered why they weren't better informed. They filled the gap in their knowledge with precise recollections of me, and my feelings. They debated whether George felt the same, or not. David remembered over-hearing the argument we had, when he was twelve. He had asked if he could join the local Baptist Church youth group because they would let him play his guitar on stage. He was happy because Dad had won that argument, and he'd been allowed to go. But it hadn't lasted long, the band wasn't much good, and he had felt uncomfortable amongst the youth group, with their passionate hand waving and praying. He had asked Dad about it-their one and only religious discussion–and Dad had said yes, he did believe in God, but that he couldn't call himself a Catholic, and he did not want to go to church himself. Religious belief was a very precious, very comforting thing to millions of people, George had told him, and all people should be free to choose which way they wanted to relate to God. George had offered to take him to a Catholic Church with Yia Yia next time they were together, but David's enthusiasm for the church band died before that happened, and the subject never came up again.

David and Claire agreed, even if they didn't know the specifics of his belief, that their father would not want to be

Thalassa

kept alive in this condition and that neither he, nor they could have any faith that God would intervene to save him.

David remembered Sam, but was surprised to hear of him after so many years. Lucky he happened to be in Athens; good that he had sorted Mary out. David didn't know anything about insurance. He wouldn't be surprised if Dad didn't have any – Mum always did that sort of thing. They wondered together how they could find out, and David promised to go to George's place after work to search through his filing cabinet. Claire questioned his intention to go to work today and David took pause. Maybe he wouldn't, maybe he would go to Dad's this morning. Claire thought that would be better, and in this way David's plan for the day was set. They agreed on a time, several hours away, for another call.

When the call ended, David listened to the house; he watched the silently silly contortions of Bugs Bunny and Daffy Duck and Mrs Porkbunny without any desire to turn the sound back on. All was quiet. He reached for the photo album on the top of the pile in front of him on the coffee table. He had already looked through them all, but he started again with the nearest book. '1998', my handwriting says, and the photos start in January at the Sailing club. George on deck, one hand on the front stay and one hand raised in mock salute to me. David, hanging on to his dad's pocket and dragging one side of the stubby shorts perilously lower with each rock of the boat. Claire is not in the picture.

I remember. She was on her new Christmas roller blades, showing off on the concrete path along the side of the loading ramp. I put a close-up of her bloody knee on the next page.

~

Sam held his open palm towards Claire, showing her two small orange pills branded with an 'S'. In his other hand he offered her a glass of water.

"Normison," he explained. "You'll get four hours sleep – with a bit of luck you'll stay asleep for the night."

Claire reached for reasons she shouldn't, but found none. She knew she was at the end of her tether. She trustingly picked the pills off his hand and swallowed them with the water and a slight toss of her head.

"Why do you have these Sam?" Claire asks.

"I spend a lot of time in airplanes."

"How come you're in Athens?"

"I'm covering a story here. A week ago I was in Iraq. Before that England, before that Macedonia, before that Belgium, before that England – all since Christmas in Australia."

"Do you get sick of it?"

"Yes … these days … yes."

"Why don't you stop?"

"I will, soon. After this, I hope."

"And you'll come back to Australia?"

"No, London's my home now."

"I might stay in America."

"Why is that?"

"I've met someone - Leah. In America we can get married, but it's not legal in Australia."

"That's terrific, I hope she's a great girl."

"She is," Claire looks at her phone, "but she must be in class, or she'd have rung me back."

"Go to bed. Leave your phone here."

"No … I'll take it with me, I know she'll call." Claire kept her phone firmly in hand, and took it with her to the bathroom, before retiring to bed.

Forty minutes later Sam opened the bedroom door lightly and checked that she was asleep. He reached forward, quietly stole the phone from the bedside table and retreated. He switched the phone to silent, and placed it face down on a soft cushion on the coffee table. Then he laid himself down across a sofa, his legs overhanging the armrest at one end, his head

Thalassa

on a cushion at the other. When Mary returned from prayers at the St Nikolaos Church in Pireaus, she found him like this and despite the movement and noise she created around him, he would not wake up. She soon gave up, added her phone to the cushion and crept into the bedroom to take up the king single bed alongside Claire's.

XXIII

Thursday 17th April 2008

It was not yet 4am and Claire reached for her phone before she was fully conscious. Not finding it woke her up quickly. Within a few minutes of tiptoed search she discovered it and crept out of the hotel room to the empty lobby where she could get Wi-Fi reception. Two missed calls from Leah, and a text saying Leah assumed she was asleep and would wait for her call. Several other texts that showed her news was spreading quickly amongst her friends, and there were even more messages on Facebook. Email was very slow to load, but eventually it coughed up a missive, with attachments, that David had sent less than an hour ago.

No insurance policy, per se, David had written, but he had looked up the credit card statements in Dad's banking file. Dad had paid his airfare with his premium card, which provided travel insurance cover. He had rung the insurance company and had notified them; he had attached the details of the claim and the insurer's instructions, including a phone number to ring if she needed any help. He was relieved about the insurance and glad, he said, that he had been able to do something useful.

Claire opened up a Skype session and was rewarded with an immediate notification that Leah was online and waiting for her call.

When Sam arrived in the lobby, looking for her two hours later, she told Leah it was time to sign off.

"I should be there with you sweetheart, I wish just sometimes I didn't do what you tell me to. I wish I was there with you." Leah rushed her words out before Claire hit the End button. "The phone is taped to my head and the volume's up loud – you ring me. Just ring me soon as you need. I love you."

"I love you too."

"I love you more."

"Leah, go away," Claire smiled and pressed *End*.

"Feel like you can face the day?" Sam looked down on her kindly.

"Yes, much better for the sleep and the support, thank-you," Claire stood and took his offered arm. "Don't steal my phone again," she said mildly.

"No ma'am."

~

Mary had stayed at the hotel for three reasons. She knew that watching the tests the doctors were to perform on George that morning would be too distressing for her; she preferred to be absent than have no role in the decision-making; and she couldn't stand being near Sam when he was so well-guarded against her. George's hospital compartment was relatively calm without her, the ventilator swept, the monitor alarms occasionally chirped, and George lay unchanging as Dr Kapriokakis, two nurses, Claire and Sam gathered at the appointed time.

Dr Kapriokakis had been looking critically at the EEG the nurse took at four am. To Claire it looked just like the one he had showed her yesterday. He offered it to her and she shook her head, so he handed it to Sam who spent only a moment looking at it before folding it, and returning it to the nurse.

The doctor took out his penlight and motioned to Claire to step forward with him like she had the day before. Sam took up a similar position on the other side of the bed and as he did so, he took George's right hand in a firm handshake grip.

The pupil of George's left eye stayed fixed, without dilation under the glare of the penlight. When the doctor rolled George's head first left, then right, up and then down, his eye keep staring from the centre instead of rolling with the movement. When the doctor produced a cotton bud and directly brushed George's cornea with it, Claire felt her stomach lurch, but George gave no reaction, not even a blink. One of the nurses stepped up with a small, needle-less syringe, and as they all watched George's motionless eye, she squirted ice water into his ear canal. Finally the doctor took a spatula from his pocket, and opened George's jaw wide enough to insert the spatula alongside the endotracheal tube, far inside George's mouth to tickle the back of his throat. Claire felt her own throat gag, but there was no response from her father.

"Now the other side," Dr Kapriokakis walked slowly around the end of the bed while Sam and Claire stayed in their positions. On the way he paused beside the second nurse's shoulder and read the form she was holding to confirm she had been correctly checking the boxes. Both nurses looked very young, and Claire assumed they were interns. The tests on George's right eye had the same results; he was completely unresponsive.

"Now the Apnoea test," the doctor told them, as he gave a nod to the first nurse. "Here we give him saturated oxygen, we turn the ventilator off, and we see if he will breathe on his own."

Dr Kapriokakis switched to Greek and started giving instructions and explanations to his two students. The first nurse brought a catheter to the bedside and inserted it into the endotracheal tube in the spot the doctor indicated. The doctor instructed her on the pressure settings on the oxygen monitor and watched her manipulate the buttons on the soft-touch pad.

"We must wait ten minutes now," Dr Kapriokakis explained. "I will come back." The doctor and the nurse with the clipboard left the room, while the other nurse remained, diligently watching the oxygen monitor.

"The Apnoea test is difficult," Sam spoke softly into the quiet of the room. "It provides conclusive proof of brain death, if it can be completed properly. If it is conclusive, then it does not have to be your decision to turn off the ventilator. If it is not conclusive, then you must decide. The neurology tests, and the EEG, show he is in a persistent vegetative state. He has irreversible brain damage."

"Why might the test not be completed properly?"

"If his blood pressure falls below a certain point, or if he starts to go into cardiac arrest, they have to stop. It's not necessarily that the hospital doesn't do the test properly, it's that his body can't take it. They can't let it be the test that kills him."

"How do you know these things? Have you done this before?"

"I'm a journalist," Sam gave his customarily evasive reply, but something made him soften. "Yes, three times, though the procedure has changed over the years. I've had friends in dangerous places, and three times I've been the one to witness this for their families. Once I've been the person on the bed."

"What happened that time?"

"Mary wouldn't let them turn the ventilator off."

"Oh," Claire gasped.

"It was different, Claire. I was in a coma, not a vegetative state. I passed the brain stem tests you've just seen the doctor do. They didn't even perform the Apnoea test on me. What they didn't know was whether I would wake up eventually. Mary insisted that I would. She stayed with me day and night, she talked me into it, she says. I don't remember. I just woke up one day and she was there."

"When did that happen?"

"1995, I was caught in a bomb blast in Sarajevo."

Claire frowned, working on some mental maths. "That's after Jacinta and Rachel were born, not when the two of you were living together."

"That's right. Ian was very generous to let her stay with me."

"I can't imagine she gave him any choice in the matter," Claire smiled.

"You're probably right."

"She still loved you very much then?"

"Mary's not the kind to stop loving. She doesn't give up. She loves George and won't give up on him either."

"What if she's right?"

"Mary doesn't try to understand the facts, she just believes one hundred per cent in what she wants to believe and she puts all her energy into that. Sometimes what she believes is right, and sometimes–*this time*–it isn't."

They fell silent for a while, watching George and the monitors and thinking their own separate thoughts about Mary, until Claire drew her thoughts to a conclusion.

"Thanks for letting me know that Sam. It helps me understand where she's coming from."

A few minutes later, Dr Kapriokakis returned to the room and started checking each monitor in turn, stating the readings in Greek while the nurse with the clipboard noted them down on her form.

"We can turn off the ventilator now."

Completing one last sweep, the ventilator shut down and the room was suddenly terribly silent. Claire held her breath.

"We wait again, for ten minutes." This time, however, Dr Kapriokakis did not leave the room. He sat on the edge of the bed, placed his stethoscope on George's chest above the heart, listened and watched. The nurse who had been at the oxygen monitor was now watching the readings on the large CRT.

After five minutes of eerie silence the nurse at the monitor made an announcement. The doctor looked quickly at the CRT and pursed his lips. Claire saw that the $PaCO_2$ line on the monitor was gradually climbing, currently at 50mm Hg, while George's systolic blood pressure was falling and the nurse seemed to be counting the numbers down. Ninety-two, ninety-one, ninety.

Dr Kapriokakis tore the stethoscope away from his ears and gave a terse instruction to the nurse.

"We cannot complete," he said to Sam, as the ventilator sprang back into life. He stood watching the CRT with his hands thrust deep in his white coat pockets. Eighty-nine, eighty-eight, eighty-seven, eighty-eight, eighty-nine, ninety. The nurse stopped her counting. George's chest rose and fell with the sweep of the machine. Claire felt faint and quickly sat down in the waiting chair, her face white.

"His chest injury makes impossible, I think," Dr Kapriokakis continued. "He has hypotension and some arrhythmia too. His heart will arrest if we continue."

The doctor gave the nurse at the ventilator further instructions, and she moved to withdraw the oxygen catheter from the endotracheal tube. He leant over the nurse who was recording the test and tapped the clipboard with his forefinger as he gave instructions on how she was to complete the form. When she had followed his instructions he took the clipboard from her and used it to wave Sam and Claire towards his office.

As Claire stood, her giddiness returned suddenly. She reached out quickly but the arm of the chair was too far below, and it was Sam's arm that caught and steadied her.

"Thanks," she murmured.

"From the colour of your face, it was obvious that was going to happen," Sam said sympathetically. "Keep hold of my arm, can you walk?" Claire nodded and they made their way to the doctor's office.

The doctor seemed to be impatient, standing at the door, waiting for them to catch up, but he kept his thoughts to himself. He closed the door behind them as they took the two seats on front of his desk, and he quickly took up his own seat and arranged his paperwork on the desk.

"The tests, they are not conclusive for the certification of brain death," Dr Kapriokakis began, focussing his attention on Claire. "His injuries, they stop us from certainty. Because of the heart we cannot certify the Apnoea test. Because of the break high in his spine we cannot certify all the reflexes. But all tests we are able to do are consistent with brain death. The tests are same since twenty-four hours. His brain damage, it does not reverse. Maybe his heart can get strong, and we can do Apnoea test again in two weeks. Maybe in months his spinal chord can repair and we see some activity on the EEG from there, but this is very unlikely when he cannot rehabilitate. His brain damage, it will never reverse. We call this the 'persistent vegetative state'. So now, this is up to you. The Apnoea test may never work, we may never get certain. But do you want to wait two weeks, or do you want to stop the ventilator now?"

Claire stared blankly at the paperwork for a moment. Eventually she asked Dr Kapriokakis the question he had all too often been asked before. "What would you do Doctor, if this was your father, or your brother?" She wondered if it was an unfair question, half-expecting him to refuse to answer, but he responded without any equivocation.

"I would stop the ventilator now."

Claire nodded rationally, she thought, but with her next breath a deep sob escaped and she pressed her hand over her mouth to contain her despair.

"You will speak with your family on this," the doctor continued, "but there is one more thing to say with them. You have checked the organ donation box?" Claire nodded. "Then what we do is this. We first operate and remove the organs, and then we turn off the ventilator."

"Which organs?" Claire whispered.

"His heart and his lungs, they are damaged in the accident. But these organs – kidneys; liver; pancreas - we can use. They will do much good. There may be patients matching transplant right now, or we can store."

"Do you close up ... after surgery?"

"Everything like a normal operation."

"Do we get to be present when the ventilator is switched off?"

"If that is your wish. We bring him back here. Exactly the same."

"How long?"

Dr Kapriokakis checked his watch. "Make this one o'clock if you bring this back with signature by nine."

"I have to speak to my brother," Claire gathered up the form and the pen the doctor had pushed across to her.

"Of course," Dr Kapriokakis pushed himself to his feet and showed them out of his office.

~

David was making time pass by playing Crash Bandicoot PS3 when his phone vibrated on the coffee table. The Bandicoot missed the next platform and exploded on screen as David grabbed the phone and answered with his customary "Yo!" As David listened in silence his girlfriend Madeleine came into the living room, kitchen towel drying her hands, and sat beside him on the sofa, putting the towel aside and taking up his spare hand in both of hers.

"David?" He was so quiet, when Claire's account was finished, that Claire wondered if the connection had been lost.

"I agree," David took a shuddering breath, "with the doctor. Dad would want us to switch off the ventilator. We know that."

Claire sobbed on the other side of the world. She had the pen in her hand, and the clipboard on her lap. "My hand is shaking, Davy, I can't sign it. This is so fucking hard."

"I'm signing it with you, sis." David startled Madeleine by turning his right hand in hers so that he was covering her hand as if writing with it. When she realised what he was doing, tears welled up in her eyes and overflowed silently. "I've got your hand in mine, and we're ready to sign this, okay?"

Claire took up her breath in a long shudder and David waited to hear her breathe evenly. "Ready? Steady? GO," David signed his name on the coffee table, through Madeleine's unresisting hand, as Claire placed her signature on the authorisation to remove life support. "Okay," David said, "Can we read that?"

"It's pretty wonky," Claire sniffed.

"Well, what do you expect when two people sign at the same time? Will it do?"

"I guess so."

"Okay then. You call me afterwards, when you're ready. Doesn't matter how late it gets."

"I love you Davy."

"I love you too."

David fumbled quickly for the *End* button; then gasped as if he had been underwater to the limit of his endurance. Madeleine caught each side of his head in her open palms, and drew him to her, smothering his wrenching sobs in her chest and wetting his hair with the free-flow of her own tears.

~

"I need to tell you about Leah, Dad." Claire tugged George's hand, the child in her, drawing his attention. She spoke quietly, leaning close to his ear, her hair falling across the endotracheal tube onto his white-gowned chest.

"I was going to tell you at Christmas but I thought I could get you to come to Boston for Easter, and when you said you were going to Greece I thought I'd ask you to come after the spring examinations. I wanted to tell you in person, I didn't want to say it in an email, or even on Skype. I wanted you to meet her, so you'd understand.

"Leah's fun. She's smart, she's so full of life, she's optimistic and she makes me feel ... like it's all possible, you know? Like life's waiting for us to enjoy it, today, tomorrow ... with Leah I feel like I can leave the past behind and head off into a new, exciting future. It feels right; it feels normal. It feels like I belong with her; like she makes me whole; like she's the one I've been waiting for.

"I guess Mum didn't say anything to you when I broke up with Jarrod. She said I was young, I was trying to work out my identity and it was natural for me to have close friendships with girls. She said I shouldn't be thinking I was gay just because it hadn't worked out with Jarrod. I shouldn't be in such a hurry to 'pre-form' my identity. I know she thought I would find a man I could love if I kept on looking for one. But I know that's not how it is for me, Dad. And I'm so lucky I've found Leah.

"Mum said you would be surprised, but you wouldn't be upset or disappointed in me. She said you both just wanted me to be happy. She just thought I shouldn't decide yet, what my gender identity was, and so I didn't say anything about it to you.

"But now I've decided, Dad, and I'm really happy. I've felt so confused about it, but now, with Leah, it feels so right and I hope you're glad for me. And ... I didn't know how to tell you I'd be staying in America, not until you could see us together, until you could see why. We can get married in Massachusetts. We can have children by IVF or adoption. It's legal. It's not even an issue, like it is in Australia. We walk down the street holding hands, Leah introduces me to everyone as her girlfriend, and it's all just ... so normal, and that feels so good."

Claire was struggling to find words to fill the non-interactive conversation. She was quiet for a while, listening to the sweep of the ventilator ask her father's questions before she responded.

"We met on campus, in October, only a few weeks after I got to Boston. I was going back to my room from basketball training and there was a poetry reading going on in one of the lecture halls. There was a billboard outside and ... I don't know why ... I decided to step in and listen. I was just standing at the back of the hall. And up the front of the hall was this tiny-petite-girl with a beautiful voice performing a poem she had written. It was about her mother and how her mother had first explained death to her, when she was a small child and her guinea pig had died. It was a long poem ... not just about the death of pets, but also about her mother's reaction when Leah's uncle had been killed in the Vietnam war and her mother talking about the death of Leah's grandmother, before Leah was born. Leah made it very real, very sad but also uplifting somehow, like death had the most important role in making us appreciate life. It made me cry, but I couldn't stop listening and by the time she finished the poem I felt ... she'd done more for me than the psychotherapist ever did. I waited for her to leave the hall and I told her how much I liked her performance; how much it had resonated with me ... and then I went back to my room, not expecting to see her again. I hadn't even told her my name.

"But a week later, at training, she was there, watching from the stand. She came down when we finished and asked me to have coffee with her. She said she thought I had something I'd like to talk to her about. We talked all night – not just about Mum. About anything and everything. She ... unraveled me. I'd never felt so understood. I'd never had so much to say, or so much I wanted to hear from any one. It's been six months and we still haven't run out of things to say to each other.

"I wish you had met her. I wish she knew you, I wish she would be able to remember you. She wanted to come here to be with me, but I wouldn't let her. She's performing one of her poems in a slam at the Nuyorican Poets Café in New York tomorrow night, and it's such an honour to be invited to do that. I'm going to miss it, but one of our friends will record it for me. I hope she can focus on it, I hope what's going on with me isn't going to put her off. She has so much talent, Dad. I just can't believe she's chosen me."

Claire's thoughts about Leah and their life together fall into silence, and George looks to me to knit his understanding together. All he wants to know is that it is right for her, and I assure him it is.

~

The hours drag for the Kostis family, but those hours don't impose themselves on me. I am with George on the cliff face at night, I am with Claire on the plane and in the hospital, I am with David as he waits to play his part, I am with Claire as the HR signal on the monitor splutters and flat lines, I am with George, now and always.

It's as if I see them all at the same time, and yet I am not overwhelmed. Three-dimensional words fail me, they cannot be assembled without a sense of time, but I must use them to reach you. Think of seeing all of a table, and being able to view the different surfaces - to look at the legs, or the table top, or the underside – by orientating your body. Now go one dimension further. By orienting my consciousness, I can see the table being made, I can see the families who eat at it over the years, and I can see it burn to ash. Here – or now - I take that extra dimension for granted, but I can no more imagine what is beyond that dimension than I could have imagined, when I was limited by my body, what it was to have all of time open to my consciousness like this.

I have learnt though, that not being able to imagine something, not being able to find adequate words, is insufficient evidence that it doesn't exist.

~

They are gathered at the bedside, and even though he has just saved two people from the ongoing trauma of kidney dialysis, one from cirrhosis of the liver and one from pancreatic cancer, George looks exactly as he did before. Mary is on her knees at the bedside, crying and praying, as a black robed priest says the benediction. Claire stands at the curtain and watches the busyness of the ward, until the priest helps Mary up from the floor and into a chair. Then Claire moves to the bedside and takes up her father's still warm right hand. It is easier to be near him, she realises. There are fewer tubes; the drip stands and their monitors have been moved away. The persistent alarms have been turned off.

Dr Kapriokakis relays Claire's nod to the nurse, and the ventilator sweeps and clanks and stops, leaving that same eerie silence behind. The doctor steps forward, peels the plaster from George's face and removes the endotracheal tube. A nurse uses a suction device to dry any saliva in his mouth. With her thumb Claire rubs the traces of plaster from George's cheeks. It is nice to have him back, she thinks, without all the equipment getting in the way. He looks peaceful, and she hopes that the respiratory sounds and reflexive movements that the doctor has warned her about are not going to disturb that peace. She has been told that there is no possibility that he will 'wake up'.

I'm there, holding her, but there is too much going on in her consciousness for her to feel me. She is thinking of me though, remembering what she heard me say to her on the plane.

Over the minutes in the room, nothing changes but the occasional rise and slow fall of Mary's weeping, and the gradual decline of the blood pressure reading on the CRT screen. Sam is almost unnoticeable, standing to attention in the corner made by the cubicle curtains. Dr Kapriokakis and one of the nurses have left. The remaining nurse waits respectfully silent, clipboard and pen in hand, watching the monitors. It is when the nurse raises the clipboard and readies her pen that Claire looks towards the monitor to see what has happened. She sees a Mr Squiggle line that has interrupted the spO2 pattern, a tower block instead of a spike on the HR, and 0/0 BPR. A straight yellow line erases the squiggle from left to right across the screen. A green line flattens the tower block. The nurse checks her watch and writes the time on the form. She pauses for a discrete moment, then switches the monitor off and quietly leaves the compartment, pulling the curtain across behind her.

A few minutes later Claire leans over to kiss her father's cheek. She stands, shows Sam her phone by way of silent explanation, and leaves the room.

Epilogue

May 2008: London

Sam turned right through the open doors titled 'Ward 20 Surgery' and sub-titled 'Visiting hours 2-4pm and 6-8pm'. The Queen Elizabeth Hospital at Greenwich was quiet, reassuringly orderly in comparison with the apparent chaos of the Intensive Care Unit at Tzaneio in Athens. The corridors were wide and clear; the air carried a surprisingly pleasant whiff of antiseptic mixed with air freshener. The staff he passed were smartly uniformed, unflustered and had, at least, been efficient in giving him directions to Lynne's room.

He was glad to find Lynne on her own, sitting in a recliner chair beside the rain-streaked window, her left leg in plaster, her left elbow resting on a pillow on her stomach while she raised a squeeze ball from her knee to her shoulder – with considerable difficulty, judging by the grimace on her face. Sam interrupted her by tapping lightly on the door. Her look of surprise, he noted, held a strong tint of displeasure and it emptied him of the cheerful "Hello" he had been planning to say.

"I didn't think I'd be seeing you again," Lynne's flat voice ironed him out further.

"Then maybe I shouldn't have come." Sam resisted the impulse to turn smartly and leave.

"Then maybe you shouldn't be here."

"They said you had surgery on your shoulder yesterday."

"Your sources are correct. What else do you know?"

"Stellate fracture to the patella which was operated on ten days ago. Tension wires in your knee, plaster cast for at least two weeks then a knee brace while you do 6 to 8 weeks of physiotherapy. Your clavicle was not setting properly; it would have been deformed so they've operated to put in an intramedullary fixation pin which is why you're here now instead of being at home."

"Martin is still a fount of information for you, I see."

"He also told me you hate me."

"Right," she should have left it there, but she couldn't. "Martin tends to hyperbole."

"I hoped that's what it was."

Lynne's head reeled with a surge of Endone dizziness unfairly accompanied by pain from her shoulder. She put down the squeeze ball and fumbled with her sling, trying unsuccessfully to fit it back onto her arm. Sam took her forearm with an improbable gentleness and adjusted the sling to support the weight of her arm. He unnecessarily undid and re-tied the knot on her good shoulder. Then he knelt beside her, his left hand on her shoulder, his right hand on her right knee and a sympathetic expression on his face. She closed her eyes to shut him out.

"Are you alright?"

"No, you should go."

Sam made no move to leave, and after a moment, feeling less dizzy, Lynne opened her eyes to look at him.

"You owe me an explanation," she said weakly.

"Yes, I'm here to give you that."

"Not now ... I can't take it in now. I'll let you know when I'm ready."

"But I have to tell you now," Sam said earnestly, "because it will be in the papers tomorrow morning."

Lynne stared at him wearily, intrigued in spite of herself.

He stroked her right clavicle through her blouse, from the join of her arm to her neck, watching his fingers as they moved and speaking softly as if they were making love.

"Did you know the left arm of the Venus De Milo statue was joined to the torso with a metal pin? Not so unlike what you've just had put in your shoulder?"

"Please go on," she whispered.

It had been easy. The metal detector found the arm and its pin exactly where Sam had expected it to be – in pride of place behind the altar. The four small blocks that had been used to wall-in the cavity were easy to cut out with a chisel, and easy to put back in place. Knowing that the plasterers would be at work the next day, and not expecting that anyone else would come looking for the arm, Sam had not even bothered to replaster the wall. While George and the Kostis were eating dinner the night before Lynne had arrived in Milos, Sam sat on the floor of the church, behind the altar and wrapped the marble arm in many rounds of bubble wrap, placed it carefully in his duffle bag and carried it out to his car.

Lynne was on fire with questions. What had he done with the arm, had it been authenticated, why had he not told her right away? He put his finger against her lips and told her to let him tell the story.

"You need to understand," he entreated her, "that I had to use the arm for something very important, something that had to be kept a secret, and I knew you wouldn't allow it."

"You 'used' the arm of the Venus De Milo?? For what?!" Lynne had a handcuff grip on his wrist.

"A lure. A bait for a criminal I've been pursuing for a long time."

"A bait! Where is the arm now?!"

Sam smiled, he stood up, flexing his knees and turned away from her.

"DON'T you go!" her shout faded into a whimper of pain as her shoulder reacted to her effort.

"I'm not going anywhere," Sam reached for the guest chair and swung it to her side, settling into it. She did not resist when he took her hand in his and threaded his fingers between hers. He had her hooked, and he had no intention of jumping to the end of his story so soon.

~

Sam's Story

August 1995: Sarajevo, Bosnia and Herzegovina

It had been Meliha's idea to go to the Markale market that morning. She wanted to cook a celebratory dinner for the news team. In the early hours of the morning the Bosnian Serbs had tentatively agreed to the Peace Plan proposed by Richard Holbrooke, the US Assistant Secretary of State to Europe. Sam accompanied her because he wanted to get the Adriatic Coast's response to the news from his favourite fishmonger from Split. Jusuf joined them, because he was in love with Meliha and was always looking for a dramatic moment when Allah would give him the chance to tell her. Heavily laden with the two cameras that were his permanent appendages, Jusuf still had enough hands to carry Meliha's shopping bags home. Meliha, after only 4 weeks in her internship, was fast becoming the most popular member of the news team. Everyone had a job for her … food shopping, mailing runs, arranging transport and accommodation, interpreting whenever the Arabic was too challenging, advising on Bosnian etiquette … sometimes she even got the chance to write a story for the Arabic press. Sam had surprised everyone in the office by agreeing to mentor her; his workmates gossiped discreetly to each other about his penchant for petite, dark-eyed girls who were half his age. Sam responded by mentoring Jusuf in his romantic ambitions. ("Don't be too keen Jusuf, take time to get to know her, look for your opportunity.")

At 11 am the trio were walking towards the markets along Mula Mustafe Bašeskije. Meliha and Jusuf were agreeing on which market stalls were the best for fresh produce while Sam's ever-wary attention was on the street, pedestrians, vehicles, movements in windows above the road, laneways opening left and right. He saw the wall of the market bulge a fraction before the sound of the explosion. He saw black smoke spewing through the main entrance door before the concussion of the blast shook the pavement from under his feet. He was slow to get up, sheltering his head under his arms and watching for debris. Jusuf had managed to stay on his feet, protecting his cameras, and he was immediately off at the run towards the market, with Meliha close behind.

"DON'T!" Sam screamed after them, but the two story-hungry youths paid him no heed. "Meliha, Jusuf – STOP!" The eerie post-blast silence had already ended, and the marketplace had erupted with the sound of screams, shouts and hysterical wailing. Sam got to his feet and hesitated, knowing it was stupid to run towards a blast site, but compelled by his urgent need to pull his foolish team members out of the marketplace.

The second mortar hit as he reached the doorway. A trestle table top flew through the door inside a black billow of smoke and knocked him off his feet, back out into the street.

Five mortar shells hit the market area. Forty-three people died, including Meliha and Jusuf. Seventy-five were wounded, including Sam.

Sam woke up four months later, in Sydney, with no memory at all of the bombing. In January 1996 he returned to duty in Sarajevo, and his first visit to the marketplace restored his memory, at least in as much as he was now able to tell Lynne. By that time NATO's operation *Deliberate Force* against the Bosnian Serbs was over, and the Dayton Accords had been signed. Responsibility for the attack on the market had been attributed to the Bosnian Serbs, under the command of Dragomir Milošević. The Serbs denied the

Thalassa

accusation, asserting that Bosnians had attacked the marketplace themselves, trying to turn public opinion against the Serbs.

At first, Sam just wanted to find the truth of the matter. He had experienced enough of this hateful war to know that both sides were regularly committing atrocities. The country was littered with corpses; ruled by mass murderers; populated by shattered people who needed justice they would never receive. But this massacre was personal to him; his young team members had been murdered, *on his watch*. This time he would make sure the people responsible were brought to justice. As the years passed his quest became an obsession.

In 1999 the United Nations, assisted by testimony and evidence Sam, amongst others, had compiled, issued a determination that the Bosnian Serbs had been responsible for both Markale Massacres, February 1994 and August 1995. At the end of that year Stanislav Galić was arrested, charged with Crimes Against Humanity for his leadership during the Siege of Sarajevo and the first of the Markale Massacres. Sam was thrilled by the arrest and followed the proceedings of Galić's trial closely, through to his conviction in 2003 and extension on appeal to a life sentence in 2006. But it was not enough. Galić had not been in command during the 1995 massacre. Sam wanted to see Dragomir Milošević convicted as well, and worked hard to gather the evidence that helped the International Criminal Tribunal for the Former Yugoslavia convict Milošević in December 2007.

When it came, the judgment was hollow for Sam. Milošević was not enough, indeed Sam had learnt enough about the atrocities in Bosnia to want desperately to bring Radovan Karadžić to the court as well. Karadžić, however, had proven very elusive.

Sam's pursuit of Galić and Milošević had unearthed a common funding link, which he had not revealed to the Tribunal. During the war the Serbian army had ransacked museums and had stolen valuable artworks and sculptures from many collectors. Their booty had merged into the worldwide art trafficking network that had initially blossomed with works stolen by the Nazis during the holocaust. Proceeds from sale of the art had supported many of the fugitive leaders of the Serbian Army, but the golden years of art trafficking were coming to an end. Now, in 2008, it was very difficult to cash in any of the art works that remained outstanding. The dealer funding Karadžić's cronies was in need of fresh booty, preferably ancient artefacts with rock-solid provenance. Sam's information had it that the dealer's life depended on it.

Sam had traced the movement of a number of sculptures and archaeological artefacts, from Bosnia, Kosovo, Macedonia and Greece through the dealer to a variety of museums and collectors. Some pieces had been genuine finds. For some, the dealer had faked provenance and had sold them on to museums and collectors who did not ask enough questions. Word had it that faking the history of the pieces was becoming increasingly risky. When he had heard from Martin about the arm of the Venus De Milo, it struck Sam that he might be able to offer the dealer an ideal, genuine find.

In Athens, straight off the flight from Milos, Sam took a taxi to Piraeus where he asked the taxi to wait while he booked a ferry ticket. In the ticket office, instead of a ferry pass, he received from his contact at MI6 a GPS tracker the size of a small screw.

The taxi then took him on to an engineering workshop where the arm was x-rayed before the metal pin was delicately removed at the cost of just a tiny bit of marble. The GPS tracker was inserted, pushed down by the metal pin, which had been smeared with glue to make it resist a second withdrawal.

That evening, Sam spent two hours briefing an Athens based plasterer on his supposed trip to Milos to repair the Church of St Nikolaos, and the find he had made behind the altar of the church. The next morning the plasterer took the arm to the address Sam had given him and asked for an opinion about whether the arm was worth anything. By the afternoon an answer had come back ... "It is not a significant piece, but we'll pay you one thousand Euros for it." The plasterer re-visited the address, signed papers, was given a receipt and happily folded the money into his wallet, pleased with his easy day's work.

MI6 tracked the arm from Athens to Belgrade. When the Serbian police raided the dealer's house they found not only the arm of the Venus De Milo, complete with a certification of authenticity and supporting documents relaying the story of the plasterer's find; they also found the names, addresses and bank details of the dealer's clients. Given the cooperation the dealer had promised in exchange for leniency ... finding other stolen artworks, and arresting Radovan Karadžić would be just a matter of time.

~

May 2008: London

"So where is the arm now?" Despite the painkillers in her system, Lynne had been alert and glued to Sam's every word.

"It's in a police station in Belgrade. I believe The Louvre is sending an armoured van tonight."

"What's it like? Is it alright?"

"I thought you might want to see it," Sam drew his phone from his pocket and pushed buttons for what seemed to Lynne to be an eternity before he turned the photo towards her.

"Oh my God! Oh my God!"

"The Louvre still has to do their due diligence. Don't get too excited," Sam smiled. "And even if it is part of the Venus De Milo, it belongs to the Kostis and to Milos. Papa isn't going to let The Louvre keep it, they'll have to take a cast of it."

"But ... it has to be in The Louvre ... how could the Kostis keep it?" Lynne was absorbed in the photo, dismissing Sam's words as ridiculous. "It's all in one piece-just the way Stavros drew it-it's wonderful! Oh Sam! How could you risk this?"

"There was very little risk. Believe me. If you ask for *The Guardian* in the morning, I think you'll see that photo on the front page if there's no more exciting news. The news report is speculating that the arm has been found and is on offer to The Louvre. It's the next step in the sting. There is no mention of Milos or Firopotamos or the Kostis family. If the rest of our plan works we'll have Karadžić in custody within a fortnight. I'm trusting you not to go and blab to any Serbian war criminals."

"It's not my discretion you need to worry about, it's Martin."

"Then I trust you to keep him under control. At the moment he doesn't know, but I need you to convince him before he sees the paper."

Lynne had flicked backwards and forward through all the photos of the arm that he had on his phone. She stopped on a photo of him, clearly not a 'selfie', standing by the gangway to the Thalassitra on the harbour front at Adamas. She showed him the photo and offered him the phone. "I don't think I want to look any further," she said in a voice that had lost its enthusiasm.

"Are you satisfied with my explanation? You understand that I couldn't tell you. If you had not come to Milos I would have come back to you in April, as I promised, with all this a fait accompli."

"If I had not gone to Milos, George would not be dead," Lynne said bluntly, looking down at her plastered leg.

"We all have 'If only' arguments to persecute ourselves with. It's called self-pity. I suggest you give it up."

Lynne was stung by his words, even though his tone had been gentle. "You're hard."

"I'm experienced. Indulging in the 'If only' thinking can do absolutely no good, and it can do a lot of harm. You have to get on with your life ... best foot forward." He patted her right thigh and she scowled at him with glistening eyes. "My 'source' tells me Tayla's been helping you."

"She's been a rock. She's taken care of everything: getting me home from Athens, organising the first operations, dealing with the insurance claim. She's been my chauffeur, nursemaid, rehab boot camp sergeant and psychotherapist. She's even been cooking the Sunday roast that Martin's life depends on."

"I thought Marcus was the cook in your house?"

"On Sunday mornings he's at soccer, and the roast has to be served to Martin at 1pm–he can't cope if we get the time wrong–so Tayla has to stand in. She has proved she can cook after all. It's been good for her. Marcus cooks most of the other meals – he's been great too."

"Are you going to invite me to a meal so I can meet Tayla and Marcus?"

Lynne looked at him in surprise. "Maybe not," she replied uncertainly.

After a moments silence he asked, "Did you love George?"

"Do you love Mary?" she returned instantly.

"I will take your answer as 'no'. My answer is 'yes'. I have loved her for forty years. We have a very long story that I'll tell you, some other day if you really want to know it. I can't change that history and not love her. *But*. There have always been insurmountable 'buts'. Mary lives in Australia with a husband and five children. She has a way of life she will never leave, and I can't be part of that life. I live here in London and I won't be going to Australia ... maybe I'll never go back. I told Mary that last December. I told her we were finished. She wasn't supposed to turn up in Milos any more that you were."

"And where is Mary now?"

"She flew back to Sydney with George's body. They had the funeral last Tuesday."

"Did you go?"

"No. Lynne ..." he paused, and she was moved to see the dejection that crossed his face while he searched for words. "I love my Kostis family, they were good to me after mum died, but I'm not one of them. I never have been, I'm the 'Foster boy' - just a pretender. I wasn't invited to George's funeral, and I didn't expect to be. I wasn't invited to Mama's funeral two years ago, and that really hurt. That really showed me. I don't belong. I've been thrown out – I threw myself out because of my relationship with Mary – too many times. Mary is fifty-two going on nineteen. It excites her to meet me in secret, she fancies herself, having a lover. She always has a scheme, and I can't promise she won't show up here – I simply can't control what she does. But I'm over it. Believe me, I am so over it."

Lynne thought for a moment. "So, where next for you. Flying out to Iraq tomorrow?" There were still traces of bitterness in her voice.

"No, I have a lot of work to do right here. Hopefully I'll be coming and going from The Hague when they have Karadžić on trial ... but the wheels move so slowly, it will take years before we have a conviction. Meanwhile, I'm on the Tribunal's payroll, compiling evidence for their prosecutors. That's been my second job for years already. It's not a glamorous salary, but it keeps me from going hungry. Maybe I'll go to Belgrade to do some interviews. He has spent quite a few years in Vienna, so I'll probably go there. Day trips in Europe, basically ... stretching out for years ahead."

Sam stroked his fingers gently through her hair and she leant into his hand, weariness overtaking her.

"I'd like to pick up where we left off that night," he said softly.

"I'll need some time ..."

He kissed her lightly and she pulled him closer to kiss him back.

October 2008: Brooklyn, New South Wales

"Here's the honeymoon suite!" Dimitry pushed the cabin door open and stood back so that the diminutive Leah could look into the small, inverted 'Y' of the forward cabin. Claire leant over the top of Leah to view the cabin as well.

"Ooooh!" Leah crooned. "Rock and roll!" Then to Claire "You won't fit – you're too long. I need someone shorter."

Claire pushed past and dived onto the foam pad that was the double bed, proving that her feet fitted just inside the door. Leah pounced on top of her.

"I see," Dimitry said drily. "I guess *your* boat tour is over already. Come topside and get your bags when it starts to get too stuffy for you." He closed the door on them, turned and opened the doors on each side of the narrow passage.

"Alright Theo ... you two can fight over who gets which side. I can assure you ... it is pretty cramped when you're in the same cabin." Dimitry moved out of the small corridor and motioned Theo and Tayla into the space he had vacated.

Tayla looked briefly into her cubbyhole before she thumped the door of the forward cabin. "Quit kicking the fucking door Claire or we'll throw you overboard." To Dimitry she said "I hear you have great beaches we can pull into each night?"

"If you want sand up your crack, no problem," Dimitry laughed.

"Which side is the sun going to come up on?" Tayla asked.

"You'll get the best sunrise on the starboard side."

"Which side is that?"

"The right hand side, East," Dimitry made his explanation even clearer by pointing to the door.

"Right, I'll take this one," Tayla dropped her shoulder bag onto the bed inside the opposing door.

Theo shrugged at Dimitry, "She is not the morning person!" he said happily.

"Mate – come and look at the chart while the girls settle in." Dimitry punched Theo lightly on the shoulder and ushered him through the galley and up the steps to the rear cockpit where there was a small table. He pulled a roll of laminated paper from a pocket in the side of the boat and flattened it out on the table.

"Here we are," he pointed to Brooklyn, and then described, with his index finger and words, how they would motor out to Brooklyn Bay, sail past Lion Island and out to sea, heading North to Newcastle for their first night.

Theo was keen to identify the Barrier Reef. He stabbed at some narrow lines on the chart, "here is the reef."

"No mate, you're not there yet. They're the Solitary Islands, we stop in at Coffs Harbour on night 3.

"Then here is the reef." Theo tried again.

"Not yet, that's Fraser Island – night 6. Biggest sand island in the world. Musgrave Island is where the reef starts, just here by Lady Elliott. We spend three nights going through the Whitsunday Islands and on day 10 we should get to Cairns, which is pretty much the middle of the reef. We have 3 days there exploring the reef and then Claire, Leah and I fly back to Sydney and leave you to it. Sweet as. Your first customer wants to spend two weeks going North from Cairns right up to Cape York. Your second customer is coming back in the reverse direction."

Theo followed Dimitry's finger along the contour lines to the top of the map. "All this?" he marvelled.

"*All* that," Dimitry agreed. "Two thousand three hundred kilometres. Longest reef in the world. Best reef in the world. You'll see," he boasted.

Theo gave a low whistle through his teeth.

"You know that Dad will dock your pay for every little scratch, every thing that breaks on this boat don't you?"

Theo nodded seriously, his enthusiasm undented.

"And don't trust your passengers till you get to know them. Some people aren't honest you know. You'd be amazed what people knock off. Check everything before you let them off the boat at the end of the trip – right? It won't do any good telling Dad someone stole something. He'll still hit you for what it cost. He's the toughest bastard in the world ... you won't get off because he's your uncle."

"I know this," Theo assured.

"This girl of yours," Dimitry lowered his voice, "has she ever been at sea before?"

"Oh yes," Theo said happily.

"You're joshing me Theo, I can tell she's never been on a boat like this. Does she know she's got to face downwind when she pukes?"

Theo shrugged. "What is 'puke'?"

"A chunder. A starboard quiche. A technicolour yawn. Vomit."

"Oh," Theo added the terms to his rapidly expanding lexicon.

"You tell her buddy, she better have got used to it by the time we leave you in Cairns, or she'll have to come back with us. Dad won't put up with complaints from his customers about the staff. I'm not kidding. She's gotta work, she's not a guest."

"She knows this," Theo nodded.

"You're one of the most optimistic minions I've ever met buddy, still ... she's hot, eh?"

"She is better than you see, cousin, you will learn. She will prove it to you like she did to me. Have no doubts. What is 'minion'?"

"A slave, a servant – I figure she's got you at her beck and call."

"What is 'beck'?"

Dimitry clapped Theo on the back and made him look up from the chart to see the three girls negotiating the small hallway into the galley. "I can tell we're going to have great conversations while you learn Australian buddy."

"So, are we ready to cast off?" Tayla announced her arrival cheerfully.

"Just waiting for my father to get here," Dimitry replied.

"He's already here," Claire chipped in, "he's tying a fender on the port side."

Dimitry looked surprised. He turned quickly and scurried up the galley stairs, bouncing off Stephen as their paths intersected on the deck.

"You only had one fender on port. You should have had three," Stephen told him gruffly.

"Well where … ?"

"They're in the shop, you just get what you need and write it in the book. Any re-provisioning comes off the profit for the voyage. What else didn't you have?"

"I think I've got everything."

"Reef anchor." Stephen pointed to an anchor, chain and rope coiled on the pier. "You need that as well as the sand anchor. Put it in the for'ard hatch."

"OK Dad, thanks."

"You need to think harder Dimitry. Plan it out, get it right."

"Yes Dad."

"Your mother's coming before you go."

"Yes Dad."

"Theo?"

"Yes, Sir?"

"You've got ten days to show Dimitry you can do it. If you're not good enough he stays and you come back. I'm not going to be soft about that. This is not a paddle pool like the Mediterranean."

"I know that Sir. I'll get it right, don't worry."

"Claire – you're a customer. Make them work, don't do it for them."

"I sure will Stephen."

"Everything alright Leah?"

"It's terrific Stephen, I'm so excited! Thanks so much for this opportunity."

Margarita arrived, carrying four fully laden supermarket bags. Claire stepped forward to lift the bags into the boat.

"Just a few last minute things for you," Margarita said. "This one's heavy - a jar full of *kourabiethes* - try to make them last a week."

Claire started to take the bags down into the galley, but paused under Stephen's critical glare and handed them over to Tayla.

"Have a wonderful trip," Margarita gave Claire a warm hug, and turned to offer the same to Leah. "We'll have a bit more time together when you get back."

"Get your engine running." Stephen liked short farewells. He cuffed Dimitry on the shoulder, stepped out of the boat and went to the bow to untie the for'ard mooring line. Claire untied the stern line and held it loosely around the cleat while Dimitry instructed Theo on starting the engine.

"Watch that mooring line. Don't snarl the propeller!" Stephen gave his last instruction to Dimitry as he pushed the boat away from the pier with his foot.

Only Margarita and I hear the soft but firm instruction Stephen gives to the sea that foams in their wake: *"Thalassa na eísai evgenikós."* Thalassa be kind.

~

July 2009: Milos

It is like the days past in Firopotamos. There is feasting and dancing to celebrate the return of the arm of Amphitrite that some call Venus De Milo. There is even more feasting and dancing to celebrate the long awaited homecoming of Dimitry's brother. Like the best parties, there are many men and women sleeping on the beach, still wearing the clothes they wore to the church in the morning to watch the unveiling of the arm, which is put in the wall behind a glass that can never be broken and will now earn money to keep the church. My Dimitry and Stavros are still awake; they have outlasted my grandsons, Anton and the youngest Stavros who has come from Australia for the first time. The youngest Stavros has no modesty. He has opened his white shirt and has pulled off his black pants because he is too hot. He has rolled the pants up under his head because he did not find his suit coat. He is sleeping in the shorts they make for jockeys, showing that he is hairy everywhere on his body except his head. There is an empty bottle of Ouzo balanced on his chest by Anton to show in a photo that the Australian Stavros fell asleep first.

My Dimitry and Stavros are still passing a bottle back and forth between them beside the sleeping boys. At their age they know to sip and pass the bottle all night. They are not wanting to waste any of this time together by sleeping. They will sleep enough, they say to each other, when Saint Nick remembers to come back for them. It will be soon, they both say. Stavros wants to toast Aretha's beautiful eyes. Dimitry say his own Maria's eyes were more beautiful. They agree to toast their Mama Iliana's beautiful eyes. They wish their Mama's eyes could see them now. They toast each of their six beautiful children and the bounty of grand children they cannot count due the Ouzo. They cry together for Giorgos and toast to the happiness such a good boy must be having in Heaven. Dimitry toasts the youngest Stavros for helping his Papa come back home to receive the arm and put it back in its place in the church. Stavros IV brags about his son Stavros V in many words his son never hears him say. They toast Sam's friend, the tough lady lawyer who promised the Art Museum that if it did not return the arm, Milos would sue for the entire statue. They promise each other that whoever catches Sam first will use the knife for filleting the fish to cut off his balls and will send them to the other side of the world in an Ouzo bottle. They rock into each other, laughing at the thoughts they have.

And same as in life, I tell Lizabeta as a mother to a mother, it is the seeing of your children laughing with each other in a happy moment like this that helps you think that the storms you-and they-have endured were worthwhile.

Thalassa kisses the moonlit beach with a gentle, forgiving wave that stretches out to lick Stephen's bare toes and sneaks quietly away.

Acknowledgements

Milos lies at the southwest end of the Cyclades group in the Aegean Sea, north of the Sea of Crete. With a population near to 5000 people, it struggles through each uneconomic year on tourist receipts that are minimal in comparison with better-known islands such as Santorini and Mykonos. Its coastal scenery is stunningly beautiful, its small villages are largely unspoiled and its people are friendly to strangers like myself who land serendipitously on the island due to a ferry schedule mishap.

The Church of Saint Nikolaos is a real church, located on rocks at the edge of Firopotamos. The story I have written about its past and its people is entirely fictional. Throughout the novel resemblance to any person, living or dead, is unintentional.

Brooklyn is a village on the edge of the Hawkesbury River in New South Wales, and Dangar Island is a 15-minute ferry ride from the Brooklyn public wharf.

I am indebted to Sophie-Jan who made her fisherman's cottage on The Gangway at Cromer available to me for 6 weeks of peaceful, dedicated writing time.

My thanks also go to Stephanie and Leonie for their encouragement, critical comment and suggestions.